# PRAISE FOR SUSAN LEWIS AND HER BOOKS

"A compelling, timely mystery."

—Lisa Ballantyne, Edgar Award–nominated author
of *The Guilty One*, on *My Lies, Your Lies*

"Full of drama and intrigue, and with so many twists and turns,
I promise you'll be surprised and captivated right to the end."

—Carmel Harrington, *Irish Times* bestselling author of
*A Thousand Roads Home*, on *My Lies, Your Lies*

"Rich, seamless, and masterful storytelling with so many 'oh my
god' twisty moments. . . . Absolute genius. I was total gripped."

—Rebecca Thornton, author of *The Fallout*, on *My Lies, Your Lies*

"Susan Lewis writes with the most brilliant sense of place that I
was there imagining each location vividly."

—Fionnuala Kearney, author of *The Book
of Love*, on *My Lies, Your Lies*

"Heartbreaking but ultimately hopeful, with a protagonist you
can't help but relate to."   —*Woman's Own* (UK) on *Home Truths*

"This hard-hitting story lays bare the problems of drug-taking,
internet grooming, and homelessness but is saved from bleak-
ness by the strength and warmth of the characters."

—*My Weekly* (UK) on *Home Truths*

# FORGIVE ME

## Also by Susan Lewis

FICTION

*A Class Apart*
*Dance While You Can*
*Stolen Beginnings*
*Darkest Longings*
*Obsession*
*Vengeance*
*Summer Madness*
*Last Resort*
*Wildfire*
*Cruel Venus*
*Strange Allure*
*The Mill House*
*A French Affair*
*Missing*
*Out of the Shadows*
*Lost Innocence*
*The Choice*
*Forgotten*
*Stolen*
*No Turning Back*
*Losing You*
*The Truth About You*
*Never Say Goodbye*
*Too Close to Home*
*No Place to Hide*
*One Minute Later*
*Home Truths*
*My Lies, Your Lies*

BOOKS THAT RUN IN SEQUENCE

*Chasing Dreams*
*Taking Chances*

*No Child of Mine*
*Don't Let Me Go*
*You Said Forever*

FEATURING DETECTIVE ANDEE
LAWRENCE

*Behind Closed Doors*
*The Girl Who Came Back*
*The Moment She Left*
*Hiding in Plain Sight*
*Believe in Me*
*The Secret Keeper*

FEATURING LAURIE FORBES
AND ELLIOTT RUSSELL

*Silent Truths*
*Wicked Beauty*
*Intimate Strangers*
*The Hornbeam Tree*

MEMOIRS

*Just One More Day*
*One Day at a Time*

# FORGIVE ME

A NOVEL

# SUSAN LEWIS

ᴡᴍ

WILLIAM MORROW

*An Imprint of* HarperCollins*Publishers*

P.S.™ is a trademark of HarperCollins Publishers.

FORGIVE ME. Copyright © 2021 by Susan Lewis. Excerpt from ONE MINUTE LATER © 2019 by Susan Lewis. All rights reserved. Printed in the United States of America. No part of this book may be used or reproduced in any manner whatsoever without written permission except in the case of brief quotations embodied in critical articles and reviews. For information, address HarperCollins Publishers, 195 Broadway, New York, NY 10007.

HarperCollins books may be purchased for educational, business, or sales promotional use. For information, please email the Special Markets Department at SPsales@harpercollins.com.

Originally published in the United Kingdom in 2020 by HarperCollins UK.

FIRST U.S. EDITION

Designed by Diahann Sturge

Smiley face emoji on page 346 © popicon / Shutterstock, Inc.

Library of Congress Cataloging-in-Publication Data has been applied for.

ISBN 978-0-06-290662-5

21 22 23 24 25  LSC  10 9 8 7 6 5 4 3 2 1

# FORGIVE ME

You know how it goes, some people you like and some you just don't. I can tell you this much, you're not going to like me. No one does. I don't even like myself, especially not after what I did. Not even before it, really.

My name is Archie (you might already know that), I'm nineteen, and before all this I lived with my weirdo mother in the kind of house someone like you wouldn't want to put a foot inside of. She's not into housework, see, or decorating, or stuff to make the place smell and look good. She doesn't really get any of that. Everyone laughs at her like she's mental and doesn't understand what's going on. OK, she's different, but it don't mean she's not a good person inside, despite all the stuff that goes on with her. I know she is, and that makes me feel even worse about being ashamed of her sometimes. Trouble is, it's not easy having a mum like her, and I hate myself for minding—really, really hate myself. I want her to be normal like everyone else so she won't get poked fun at and have stuff thrown at her when she walks down the street. Kids do that to make her chase them and she nearly always does.

When BJ came to take me away to work for him he

beat her up to make her let me go, and I didn't stop him because I wanted to go.

BJ's another story, don't let's get into him here.

We haven't ever met, you and me. I don't know if we ever will, but I'm laying all this out for you because Dan talked me into it. I know you know him, although he doesn't talk about you much, but we both know you're the reason he comes to see me. I find him to be a regular bloke who looks a lot like Superman's alter ego, Clark Kent, with his black-framed glasses and chiseled features. OK, he's got Prince Harry hair, but catch one of his smiles and they light him up like a proper movie star, don't you reckon? He's a decent type, you can tell by looking at him, with the right sort of manners and a way of listening that makes you talk even when you don't want to.

He does that to me a lot. If he didn't, I don't suppose I'd be writing this, it would never have occurred to me. I guess Dan's superpowers are of a particular sort.

No one would feel worried about letting him into their front room, the way they would me; and I have to be honest, I'm getting to like the time we spend together. I don't know anything about him personally, like if he's married or has kids or anything; I've never asked and I don't think he'd tell me if I did.

He's probably afraid I might send someone to find his family and hurt them.

I wouldn't, but I don't blame him for thinking I would.

The first time I met him I didn't bother speaking to him. To me he was just another tosser wanting to get inside my head. I'm only doing this now because over time I've found it's easier to go along with him than to fight him. He's got something about him that makes you want to shut him up, not in a rough way—I've never felt like smacking him—but in a way that if you do what he's asking you're both happy. I could say he has some serious personable shit going on that everyone warms to, even someone like me.

I can hear him in my head telling me to stop writing about him and get back to the point of why I'm doing this.

I can't see the point myself, because it's not going to get me anywhere, but now I'm visualizing one of his looks that usually ends up with me thinking he knows more than I do—and frankly that wouldn't be hard. He's a smart bloke. Do I wish I was like him? Sure, I'd have to be crazy not to when he seems to have everything going for him. I wonder how rich he is; he gives off the scent of it and I should know, I've sniffed enough of it.

So, what can I tell you about me that you'd be interested to know?

I'm not as tall as Dan—he's about six foot and I'm five ten—and he's probably twice my age.

What a crack if he turned out to be my long-lost dad.

If he was, I wouldn't have done what I did to you. That's a fact.

I asked him before I started this letter if I had to spell out what I did.

"We already know what you did," he reminded me.

He's right, and it was a dumbass question. I guess you want to know why I did it?

Well, that's not something I can tell you without bringing

a whole heap of trouble down on us all, and I think you've already had enough of that, thanks to me.

So, where do we go from here?

Dan's advice was to keep writing anything that comes into my head, and he'll look it over the next time he's here. He has to do this because of all the swearing and street slang that comes out of me. He says you won't want to read all that and I can see he's probably right.

It's weird, me sitting here thinking about you and how our paths crossed. It shouldn't have happened, but it's no good saying that now because it did, and in our different ways we're both paying the price. It's a high one for me, I'm coming to terms with that, but for you . . . I don't know how you're going to live with what happened to you.

# CHAPTER ONE

Marcus Huxley-Browne looked up from the warning call he'd just received on his mobile phone. His handsome face was taut, pale, showing none of its usual boredom or arrogance—or the self-satisfaction that came from having so much. He'd been born into an established family; he had all the right contacts and was as famed for his City successes as he was for the celebrations he threw when deals came off.

"They're coming for me," he muttered, the paleness of his skin turning to gray. He wasn't looking at his wife, maybe he wasn't even speaking to her.

"Who?" she asked, unnerved by the fear in his deep gray eyes.

He stared at her, seeing her past the commotion in his head. "You know *nothing*," he instructed her tightly. "You've seen nothing. You've heard nothing. Have you got that?" His fists clenched, and she wondered if he was going to hit her, blame her, or something worse.

*Who was coming?*

She knew better than to ask a second time and stepped aside as he headed out of the room, across the hall, and into his study.

"Come here!" he shouted.

Obediently she hastened after him and stopped on the threshold of the room she was rarely invited into. He was standing behind his desk, a Huxley-Browne heirloom, one of many that cluttered the house with stately gloom. He looked haunted now, agitated—*hunted*—as if not knowing where to turn or what to do. Had things been different, she might have felt sorry for him.

"You don't speak to anyone," he told her gruffly.

She nodded. She'd had this instruction before, but usually he didn't take any chances; he'd whisk her upstairs and lock her in one of the top-floor rooms.

She used to fight it, but she'd learned not to.

She often heard things from up there, but she never saw the comings and goings outside—cars pulling up, people entering or leaving the house—the windows were too high. However, voices carried even if she couldn't make out who they belonged to, or what was being said.

She knew what kind of people came. They were his set: the all-male network that he and others of his ilk had created at university, in the City, in private clubs, in various capitals, to trade information, or to start rumors, or to import and export insider knowledge. Girls came too, for the after-parties, lots of them, paid well she imagined—and the dealers in mood- and sexual-performance enhancers came too. Shady, sinister characters from an underworld she could barely imagine.

On the nights Marcus didn't come home she guessed someone else was hosting proceedings at their luxury apartment or town house. She never asked, and he never told her, but she'd come to recognize a descent from the drug-fueled highs when it was in front of her.

There were other nights—lots of them—when he behaved like a regular family man, sober, a little tired, but happy and feeling generous at the end of a long, productive day. She could easily mistake him then for the man who'd comforted and befriended her after the tragedy of her first husband's death. She still felt strangely attached to that man and the way he'd spoken so softly to her during that terrible time, and had smiled into her eyes as if he couldn't believe how fortunate he was to have found her. He'd never been frightening then, just loving, attentive, interested. She'd married him believing he loved her, and feeling certain it was the right thing to do for her—and for her eleven-year-old daughter who'd been devastated by the loss of her father.

Now here they were, or here she was, watching him frantically snatching files from his desk and stuffing them into an old-fashioned attaché case. She hadn't seen it before.

"For Christ's sake, don't just stand there," he raged, "get that cabinet away from the wall."

Quickly she moved to do as she was told, but the cabinet was too heavy.

He shoved her aside and did it himself, grunting, sweating, swearing . . . Was he crying? Or were those beads of sweat? How much did she care? How afraid was she?

She wasn't surprised to see the safe behind the cabinet. She'd known it was there, but this was the first time he'd opened it in front of her, pressing the numbers in slowly, deliberately, not wanting to waste time on mistakes.

She couldn't calculate how much cash was stacked on the five shelves inside, but it surely ran into hundreds of thousands of pounds, all the bills neatly bundled until they were chaotically rammed into the case along with the files. Too much to fit in, but he was going to make it happen . . .

Someone knocked at the front door. Three heavy raps.

"Shit!" He turned to the window. Beyond was the back garden, and she wondered if he was about to throw himself out onto the lawn and make a run for it.

With lightning speed he rammed the case into the safe, spun the combination lock and heaved the cabinet back into place.

Their visitor—or visitors—tried the bell.

Police? Drug dealers? Who else would he be so afraid of?

She gasped as he grabbed her by the neck with one hand and pressed her against the wall. "Remember, you know nothing," he hissed into her face, "you've seen nothing, and you've heard nothing."

She nodded, gasping for breath, clawing at his hand.

He let her go and pointed along the hall to the door. "Answer it, but if you even think about betraying me . . ." His eyes bored into hers; he didn't have to tell her that it wouldn't end well, she already knew.

She started to move, hardly knowing who or what to expect when she opened the door.

"Stop!" he seethed under his breath.

She turned around. "I don't know where this is going to end," he growled, "but just in case you get any ideas about leaving me, you'll be watched; you won't get away and if you try, I'll find you and by then you'll wish I hadn't."

She didn't doubt him; she never had. She knew what he was capable of, and as he turned to the door she found herself hoping with all her heart and soul that he was about to be taken out, not merely taken away.

# CHAPTER TWO

$A$re you sure you're OK to drive?"

Claudia Winters glanced at her sixteen-year-old daughter, the one who was sounding like the parent right now, and tightened her grip on the steering wheel. "Sure," she confirmed, and fixing her eyes on the road ahead, she pressed down on the accelerator to pull away from the curb. It was a jerky start, but it was a new car—bought with cash from a South London dealer who'd asked no questions—and at least she didn't stall the engine.

"Don't look back," she advised Jasmine.

"Would it make a difference if I did?"

"Do you want to?"

"No! Let's just go."

The place they were leaving was a smart redbrick town house in the heart of Kensington, where they'd lived for the past five years. Their departure—escape, to give it the correct term—had been carefully planned during the last few months. They'd removed their most precious belongings in bags and suitcases as if they were just off for long weekends, or perhaps to make generous donations to a charity shop. Where they'd actually been taking their cargo was to Claudia's mother's house in Somerset, in order to store it in a weatherproof garage. Yesterday, under her mother's supervision, everything had been transported from the garage to the place Claudia and Jasmine were traveling to now.

Nauseous with nerves, Claudia drove along the leafy street,

careful to avoid the parked cars on either side of her, aware of a hundred or more windows bearing witness to their departure.

Was anyone actually watching? He'd said someone would be, but they'd never spotted anyone, nor had the private investigator they'd hired to check for them.

There were the neighbors, of course, but it surely wouldn't occur to any of them that the mother and daughter from number forty-six were about to disappear without trace.

Claudia hoped it would be that way, but a lot could happen between now and the day they finally felt safe. The past could reach for them in any number of ways; traps they hadn't yet been able to imagine might already have been set by their own oversights and unwitting mistakes, or even by fate.

Pushing the dread of it all aside, she drove on past the homes that backed onto the school her daughter had attended since they'd moved here. It was private, expensive, and should have been where she'd complete sixth form before going to uni. Now she was set to continue her education at a school close to their new home, using the name she'd chosen for herself—Jasmine—and sporting a totally new look.

Once as dark-haired as her beloved father, Jasmine was now blond, with a cute pixie cut that had been executed by her mother's inexpert hand only last night. Jasmine loved it, thank goodness. Up to the age of eleven, she'd been a bright girl with a warm personality, and her dad's sparkling enthusiasm for life. However, these past years in her stepfather's home, subjected to his erratic moods and overbearing personality, she'd lost the buoyancy of her spirit and had even withdrawn from friendships and activities that should have been normal for a girl her age. So she was as ready to escape and start again as her mother was—as relieved to be making this journey as she'd ever been about anything in her young life.

At the end of the road Claudia indicated to turn left and headed toward the Hammersmith overpass. As they passed the shop that used to be hers, Dream Interiors (secretly sold as a going concern over a month ago and soon to be renamed All About Home by the new owners), she caught a glimpse of her reflection in the empty window and it made her feel oddly light-headed. Until yesterday her hair had been fair, shoulder-length, and wavy—now it was a rich chestnut color styled in a messy sort of bob that she actually quite liked. It gave her features more definition, she thought, and seemed to warm her pale complexion. She was nothing like the woman who'd started the shop fifteen years ago, although her eyes were still sky blue, and the delicate bone structure that Jasmine's father, Joel, had captured in so many paintings and sketches remained the same. She'd been tall and curvaceous back then; confident, ambitious, and quick to make friends. She was still tall, of course, but so slender now, even gaunt, that it was like watching the ghost of herself passing from the windows of her old life on her way to the new.

She was going to miss her business, and her workers and the clients, but when the time was right she'd start creating the same all over again.

As they circled under the overpass and joined the A4 she was still regularly checking the rearview mirror, not so much for moving traffic as for anyone who might be following. It wasn't possible to tell, nor was it possible, surely, for Marcus to have set someone on their tail so soon.

She glanced anxiously at Jasmine, and felt a momentary relief when she received an ironic smile in return.

"Will you please stop stressing?" Jasmine scolded with teenage exasperation. "You have to let it go, Mum. We're on our way to a new life and that's all we should think about. We're actually pulling it off."

Claudia followed the traffic and contemplated the truth of those words—we're pulling it off—although they were hardly ten minutes from what used to be their home, so such optimism was perhaps a little premature. However, everything was going to plan so far. The BMW they were in had been delivered on time late last night; they'd picked up their new phones from a "dealer" a week ago; and, most crucially of all, the money from the sale of her business had been successfully transferred from an escrow account into the one she'd opened just after her new passport had come through. Dealing with the bank had been the trickiest part of the operation—did she really look like a money launderer?—but it was done now, thank God, and she'd already managed to draw cash using one of her new cards.

"So," she said, as they finally approached the M4, "shall I call you Jas or Jasmine from now on?"

A tilt of a platinum-blond head, followed by "mm," preceded "Either's fine. It's a cool name, don't you think?"

They'd had this conversation before, several times, so Claudia dutifully said, "I do, and it suits you. I wish I'd thought of it when you were born."

Jasmine glanced over at her mother, her big blue eyes sparkling with mischief. *God, she was like her father.* "Are you OK with Claud?" she asked cheekily.

Claudia wrinkled her nose. "Mum's better, coming from you."

Jasmine laughed and pointed to the red light they were approaching too fast.

As they came to a stop, Claudia's breath caught on another rush of nerves as the reality of their flight descended over her again. To those traveling in the cars around them they must look so ordinary, so unremarkable in their blue station wagon with nothing on its roof, or sides, or anywhere else to alert anyone to what this two-year-old 3 Series was actually involved in.

"How come you're so relaxed?" she asked as Jasmine continued downloading apps to her new phone.

Jasmine frowned as she considered the question. "Well, I thought one of us ought to be, and as you're the responsible adult in the car I decided to leave all the negative stuff to you."

"So kind."

They both started as someone blasted a horn behind, urging them on, and at the same instant Jasmine's new phone rang. Only one person had the number and to their relief they saw it was her.

"Hey, Nana," Jasmine sang out as she clicked on, "we're on our way. Hang on, I'm going to put you on speaker so Mum can hear."

"Have you left London yet?" Marcy, her grandmother, asked.

"We're just about to join the M4. How's everything on your end?"

"So far, so good. I'm at the flat and it's even lovelier than the first time we saw it, probably because the sun's shining and the shutters are open. Actually, we had some mail delivered this morning. A letter from the energy company confirming our new account, and another from the local authority about the council tax."

"I'm guessing both were in your name?" Claudia asked.

"They were."

Her mother didn't have a new identity as such, she'd simply reverted to her maiden name—Kavanagh—which had been a straightforward enough process to arrange, enabling her to rent the flat with references provided by a nonexistent ex-employer. Luckily the new landlord hadn't checked—why would he, when Marcy presented as the world's most trustworthy individual—so all had gone through quite smoothly.

"Is our stuff there yet?" Jasmine wanted to know.

"It is, and the new furniture is due in about an hour, so the delivery chaps should have been and gone by the time you arrive. I don't know how we're going to put it all together, I'm sure, but I suppose we'll work it out somehow. Oh, and before you ask, yes, I remembered to bring a tool kit."

"Super-nan," Jasmine cheered.

Surprised again by her daughter's high spirits, and relieved, Claudia said to her mother, "Shall we pick up some groceries on the way?"

"Don't worry, I'll do it, and if I run out of time we can always get pizza delivered."

And here was another concern, how matter-of-fact her mother was sounding when there was absolutely nothing matter-of-fact about what they were doing.

Was she the only one who was scared out of her mind?

She needed to do as Jasmine said and stop stressing.

"Have you checked if you're being followed?" her mother asked, setting Claudia's nerves off again.

"She's doing it every thirty seconds," Jasmine chimed in, "but I scoped the whole neighborhood before we left and I promise you no one was there, so no one watched us leave."

"Good girl," her grandmother praised. "What have you done with your old phones?"

"We left them at the house," Claudia replied, "along with our laptops, tablets, and keys. Obviously we made sure there was nothing left on them to give anything away. Do you think it was the right thing to do? Should we have brought them with us?"

"We discussed it," her mother reminded her, "and we decided they needed to stay there."

This was true, but now Claudia wasn't so sure it had been such a good idea. Great escape planners they were, but since they'd never done anything remotely like it before they'd had no experience to draw on, only Internet advice, which didn't seem to have let them down yet.

"I have the replacement iPads and computers here," her mother was saying, "so we can set them up later."

"Did you abandon your old stuff too?" Jasmine asked.

"Of course. Actually, I tossed them in the lake—and very freeing it was too."

Claudia didn't know whether to be shocked or impressed. The image of her respectable mother, owner of a contacts book to rival a royal's, driving up to the lake near her home—or rather, old home since she'd left it yesterday—and ending her previous life with a random fling of Apple devices into a wildlife reservoir was hard to get her head around.

Suddenly it was making her laugh. It was hysteria, of course, for there was nothing funny about it, but now that she'd started she was finding it difficult to stop.

"OK, she's losing it," Jasmine declared. "I'll calm her down and we'll call when we're about an hour away."

As the connection ended so did Claudia's mirth, although the outburst did seem to have soothed her slightly.

"Are you all right?" Jasmine asked.

"I'm fine."

"Are you sure?"

"I'm sure."

"No one behind?"

Claudia's heart clenched.

"Sorry, bad joke. No, don't check."

"I'm driving, I have to."

Accepting that, Jasmine opened her phone again, and as she began setting up her new social media accounts, Claudia said, "No photos."

"I know that, but I can look at other people's, right?"

"You mean your old friends?"

Jasmine shrugged. "I didn't have so many, and I'm not much interested in what they're doing. I'm trying to find some students who're at my new school."

Since the information about that had been on her old laptop before they'd deleted it, Claudia wondered how much she minded searching for it all over again. Their Internet escape planner had warned against forwarding anything: if they did it wouldn't take long to trace it to their replacement devices, and in no time at all their new lives would be over.

They should have done the same as her mother and thrown everything into a lake, but it was too late now.

Had her mother remembered to turn off the tracking feature?

She was bound to have done so. They'd discussed it enough times, and Marcy was anything but stupid. In fact, she was the joint mastermind of this operation, had even come up with the original plan, having no idea at that time how complicated it would be to pull off. But step by step they were getting through it and now, here they were, five months on with some of the most difficult challenges already behind them.

At a service station Jasmine ran in for coffee while Claudia locked herself in the car and checked her own new phone to make sure there were no messages. Fortunately, there were none—and why would there be when she hadn't set up any accounts yet? No one apart from Vodafone, Jasmine, and her mother had the number. Using Bluetooth, she connected to the car's hands-free system so that she and Jasmine could listen to one of the audiobooks or podcasts they'd downloaded in preparation for this journey. Chances were, they'd be unable to focus, but the option was there if they wanted it, and setting it up was giving her something to do as she waited.

She didn't look around to check if she was being watched, she simply told herself that she had no chilling sense of it, which could mean either that she was in denial or that her instincts were working.

No one knocked on the window or parked too close.

At last Jasmine returned with two skinny lattes and a granola bar to share. As soon as the passenger door was closed Claudia hit the locks again and after taking a sip of her coffee she started back to the motorway.

It was shortly before eleven o'clock, when they were passing the turnoff for Cirencester and Chippenham, that Jasmine said, "Should we try the radio now?"

Experiencing yet another sickening jolt of nerves, Claudia simply nodded.

As they listened to the headlines she was aware of how tightly she was gripping the wheel. Not that she was expecting to hear anything about their disappearance—it was still far too early for that—or about her failure to appear in court this morning—that might not have been noticed either. It was *his* name she was listening for, and when it came with the information that a verdict was expected at any minute, she felt the blood pounding too fast in her heart.

Jasmine turned the radio off and said, "We'll try again at midday."

They were both subdued now—simply hearing his name was enough to do that to them. Jasmine seemed to revert to the withdrawn and anxious teenager she'd been before her mother and grandmother had plotted the escape. Claudia was internalizing her fears, doing all sorts of bargains with God and the universe if they would just make sure the jury did the right thing.

Maybe she shouldn't have brought the attaché case.

"AND SO WE reach the end of the line," Jasmine murmured, coming awake as Claudia finally brought the car to a stop outside the freshly whitewashed Victorian villa that was to be their home for the next few months—possibly longer. It was at the end of a seafront terrace on the busy Promenade, and the apartment they'd leased comprised the entire first floor with three good-sized bedrooms, two bathrooms, and a spacious sitting-cum-dining area with an open-plan kitchen. Its tall sash windows at the front overlooked the windy bay of Kesterly-on-Sea, where a mile-long stretch of sandy beach was hugged by two grassy headlands, and the restless waves provided a playground for surfers, sailors, and skiers.

Jasmine was right about it being the end of the line, for the train could go no farther than the station at the far end of the Promenade—and access from the motorway was as arduous in parts as it was spectacular in others, as it passed through ever-changing countryside. They'd chosen to come here quite randomly, for their Internet search had thrown up many remote towns and hidden villages that could have provided equally good cover, if not better. However, when Marcy had mentioned that she'd come here on holiday a few times as a child, Claudia had allowed that to be the decider. It was the only link they had to the place, which was no link at all really, but Claudia had seen right away how pleased her mother was to agree.

Since their first visit just over six weeks ago, when the three of them had come to check it out, they'd found that it really did have everything they were looking for. They'd wasted no time in contacting an estate agent and by the following day they'd not only managed to secure this flat, they'd also registered with the local authority, and even enrolled Jasmine in the local school to sit her GCSE exams. No references from her previous school had been asked for yet, but Claudia already had a plan for how to handle that when it came up. (Honesty was usually the best policy—and the story she'd concocted was a fair version of it.)

It was as they'd driven back to her mother's house in the Chew Valley, south of Bristol, that they'd received a call informing them that a completion date for the sale of Claudia's childhood home had now been set. As requested, it would happen during the week of their planned departure.

Claudia felt more guilt over the loss of that house than she did over anything else, for it was the first and only home her parents had lived in until her father died.

"If he were here," her mother had argued when Claudia had protested at the suggestion the house should be sold, "he'd be doing the exact same thing as I am. *You* were what mattered to him, and your daughter, and if he knew that selling this place would make you safe he'd have it on the market quicker than you could choose an estate agent."

Now most of Marcy's eclectic assortment of furniture, along with much else that had been collected over the years, had been sold with the house, and like Claudia and Jasmine she'd brought only her most precious possessions to Kesterly. However, she had almost three million pounds in her new bank account after cashing in all her other investments, so she could consider herself a wealthy woman by anyone's standards. And if her small fortune was combined with the profits from the sale of Claudia's business and the cash in the attaché case in the back of the car—presuming it wasn't counterfeit—it was fair to say that right now money was the least of their problems.

As Claudia climbed out of the BMW and stretched her too-thin limbs after the long drive, her eyes closed as she found herself assailed by the warm, pungent scent of salty sea air mixing with the sweetness of cotton candy and the metallic taste of traffic fumes. She could hear the hum of the tide surging along with the sound of engines, a musical merry-go-round somewhere close by, and the laughter of holidaymakers enjoying the beach. It reminded her of how calming and welcoming she'd found this place the last time they were here—and it was working its magic again.

It was her mother's voice that broke the spell and, turning to see her coming down the front steps of the villa, Claudia's heart swelled with love and relief. When had she ever needed her mother more? And when had her mother ever let her down?

"Nana," Jasmine cried and ran straight into her grandmother's outstretched arms. Marcy was a picture of sixty-four-year-old elegance with short fair hair, warm brown eyes, and a smile that was so like Claudia's there could never be any doubting their relationship. And dressed as she was now in blue-striped Capri pants and a baggy white T-shirt, she looked almost as young and sprightly as her teenage self must have been.

"Are you OK?" she asked, coming to embrace Claudia. "You look tired."

"A bit," Claudia admitted, hugging her hard.

"It's stressful," Jasmine put in, "when you're afraid you've got someone after you."

Through a smile Marcy reminded her to keep her voice down, and following Claudia to the boot of the car, she reached for the brown leather attaché case. "I presume this is it?" she said quietly.

Claudia nodded. *She should have left it behind.*

"OK, I'll take it in," Marcy said, and winced as she discovered how heavy it was. "You two bring the rest of your things."

"Did my new music stand arrive yet?" Jasmine asked, shouldering a holdall and picking up another.

"DHL tried to deliver while I was at the supermarket, but we can pick it up tomorrow." Marcy's eyes sparkled again as she said, "Come and see the furniture. Some of it's already assembled, thanks to Rog, the very handyman the delivery chaps put me in touch with. He's coming back to finish off in the morning."

As she started to turn away Claudia asked, because she had to, "How did you feel leaving the house yesterday?"

"It was OK," her mother assured her, although the light in her eyes dimmed, "but we can talk about it later."

Claudia's mouth was dry. If that wasn't bad enough, she knew what else she needed to ask, so forcing herself, she said, "Have you seen the news?"

Marcy's expression turned to dismay. "You didn't listen to the radio?"

Claudia hadn't heard the latest bulletin because Jasmine had been sleeping—and because she was hiding behind a wall of dread.

"We can get it on my laptop," Marcy told her, and led the way inside.


ONCE PAST THE large blue front door with its sculpted boxtrees on either side and bold brass numbers, they had only one flight of stairs to climb to their flat, where the hall was an obstacle course of un-opened boxes, and the sitting room, equally chaotic, was flooded with sunlight. A gentle sea breeze was wafting about the place, add-ing its scent to the earthiness of cardboard and newness of three mint-green sofas that were half in and half out of their protective covers. A wooden dining table with six upholstered chairs was already assembled and positioned in front of the kitchen, where a kettle looked, for the moment, to be the only appliance on duty.

Marcy carried the attaché case through to the far en suite bedroom that they'd already agreed would be hers, and after sliding it inside a closet she returned to the sitting room to turn on her laptop. When she'd found the news item she was looking for, she hit pause and rested the computer on the boxes stacked against one wall before hitting play.

As she listened and watched, Claudia was aware of bile rising in her throat and Jasmine's hand searching for hers. She linked their fingers and held on tightly.

*Guilty.*

She wanted to sob with relief, leap for joy, bury herself away so he could never find her again.

"He hasn't been sentenced yet," her mother told her, "but they're keeping him in custody; he's still deemed a flight risk."

Oh yes, he was certainly that. With all those contacts, all that missing money, give him half a chance and he'd never be seen again.

The screen changed and a reporter began talking to the camera.

"So, as widely predicted, financier Marcus Huxley-Browne, son of the former trade minister Sir Robert Huxley-Browne, has been found guilty on multiple counts of fraud and insider trading. Sir Robert, who's believed to be suffering with dementia, was not in court to hear the verdict, but we're expecting a statement from the family lawyer in the next few minutes."

As the reporter continued to speak, a still shot of Marcus filled the screen, and Claudia felt so sickened and afraid that it was almost as if he was right there in the room with them. He was a strikingly handsome man, she'd never deny that, with his unruly fair hair, flirtatious smile, and smooth features, but even in this shot where he was supposed to appear nothing but friendly she could see the arrogance, the underlying cruelty that governed him.

". . . although other arrests have been expected since Huxley-Browne was first taken from his home in West London," the reporter was saying, as they cut back to him, "none have so far materialized. However, a spokesperson for the Serious Fraud Office has made it clear that their investigation does not end here. As we know, all sorts of rumors have dogged Huxley-Browne and many of his colleagues in the City for several years, but perhaps the most sinister are those concerning gangland connections. If—I stress *if*—any of these are true, it's not likely Huxley-Browne will be helping police with their inquiries anytime soon."

"They're true," Claudia muttered.

"Was his wife in court today?" a voice from the studio asked.

Claudia's heart turned over and she'd have stopped the video there if she hadn't felt masochistically compelled to know what was said.

"No, she wasn't," the reporter replied. "She hasn't been seen since the start of the trial, and all attempts to reach her today have so far failed."

Up came a shot of the Kensington house surrounded by media, and Claudia could only feel thankful that she and Jasmine had managed to get out when they had. *Please don't let them mention anything else about me*, she prayed inwardly. *Please, please.*

To her relief they didn't, so for this report at least there were no shots of her.

A rangy, stooped man with sharp features and thinning gray hair was now ready to give a statement: the family lawyer.

"Today has shown us what a travesty of justice looks like," he declared, raising his lawyerly voice to be heard. It was hard to tell how many cameras and microphones were trained on him, but his piercing eyes found Sky News as though he somehow knew it was the channel she'd be watching. "We will not rest," he said, looking straight at her, "until this verdict is overturned and my client is once again free to resume his family life."

The threat was thinly veiled and sent a shiver through Claudia that felt as sharp and cold as ice. She'd never met this man, but she knew instinctively that he was as untrustworthy and dangerous as Marcus. He had probably even benefited from the crimes his client had committed. However, he surely wouldn't have known when making his statement that the house in West London had already been abandoned, or that the shop on Kensington High Street had been sold. But he'd find out soon enough, perhaps as early as today, and then there was every chance that the hunt for his client's wife and stepdaughter would begin.

# CHAPTER THREE

Dan! How are you? Come in, come in."

Andee Lawrence stood aside for her very welcome visitor to enter the stylish Georgian house she shared with her partner Graeme Ogilvy at the heart of Kesterly's exclusive Garden District. She was a tall, dark-haired woman in her mid-forties, with such arresting aquamarine eyes that some, when meeting her for the first time, became momentarily dazzled.

This didn't happen to Dan Collier as he embraced her warmly, for several months had passed since he'd first been introduced to her, when he had actually momentarily lost his words. His old uni friend Graeme had clearly been as amused by the double take as Dan had been embarrassed, while Andee had politely pretended not to notice. Now Dan paid little more attention to her looks than he did to his own, which he considered far less remarkable than his late wife, Ellen, had. Although she'd been biased because, as she'd put it, she'd been clever enough to see in him what others hadn't.

"I never thought I'd end up with a ginger," she used to tease, "but that's because I didn't know they came with sleepy eyes trying to hide behind sexy specs, and serious muscles."

"They also come with broken noses, oafish hands, and loads of brains," he'd inform her, and while saucily admiring the first two she'd usually scoff at the third.

He wished Andee had met Ellen, for he knew they'd have gotten along like the proverbial house on fire, but two years before he'd moved his legal practice to Kesterly Ellen had been killed in a car crash. Sadness was his companion now, and although he never gave it a public airing, when he was at home he spent much of his time grieving her loss and wishing they'd had children. At least then she would continue to exist in other human beings whom he'd love perhaps even more than he'd loved her, although that was hard to imagine.

"Graeme's cooking," Andee informed him, pointing him across the hall toward the kitchen, "and don't worry, we haven't fixed you up with a blind date."

"Thank God for that," he responded with feeling. "I'm too much of a gentleman to tell you about some of the potentials that have been thrust my way since I got here. Just suffice it to say I wasn't so much put off by their charms as scared to death of them."

Andee had to laugh. "Well, hopefully Graeme has told you that we're not into matchmaking unless it's specifically requested."

"That was her decision," Graeme informed him as Dan entered the large kitchen, where his host was concocting something that smelled so delicious it made Dan's stomach growl with unseemly impatience.

"Don't worry, we have canapés to be going on with," Andee chuckled. "I've set them up outside in the garden, but let me get you a drink first. Wine? Gin? Vodka?"

"A white wine would be great," Dan responded, dropping his battered leather briefcase on one of the sofas that flanked a magnificent fireplace before going to shake hands with Graeme. "You're looking good," he told his old friend, who indeed always did, and always had, although there was plenty of silver in the thick dark hair these days, and the increasing intensity of his expression might have intimidated those who didn't know him. It only took a smile to transform his features completely; the trick was getting the smile.

It wasn't slow in coming among friends. "You're not looking too bad yourself," Graeme responded, "and we're one short for the cricket team this summer, so I've signed you up."

"Another attempt to get me to go out more?" Dan replied, pleased to be asked.

"Unless you've lost that unerring eye for the boundary," Graeme replied, "we need you," and reaching for the TV remote he was about to turn off the news when Andee said, "Hang on. Let's just listen to this."

The large screen over the fireplace was showing a five-story house on a well-heeled London street that had featured in several bulletins over the past week, so it was generally known to be the home of the recently convicted financier Marcus Huxley-Browne. However, during the past few days the focus had switched from the man himself to his wife, Rebecca, and stepdaughter Cara, who apparently hadn't been seen since the end of the trial.

At that moment a smartly dressed detective captioned as DI Carl Phillips was ending a statement to the press.

". . . I'm afraid there's no more we can tell you at this stage, but if anyone has information regarding Mrs. Huxley-Browne's whereabouts, or that of her daughter, we'd ask them to please get in touch."

"Do you suspect foul play?" a female voice called out.

The detective didn't answer; he was already merging into a small group of officers standing in front of the house.

"Have you asked Huxley-Browne where they are?" someone shouted after him. "Is it true their personal devices have been found inside the house?"

The police team walked away and a dark-haired young man appeared on the screen, fiddling with his earpiece as he said, "So, the mystery of Mrs. Huxley-Browne and her daughter's disappearance continues to grow. As you know, Paula, it was thought at first that they'd probably gone to stay with friends or relatives to escape the press. Then came suggestions that Mrs. Huxley-Browne had cooperated with investigators to secure her husband's conviction, so was that the reason for going into hiding? Now that the police are asking for information on their whereabouts, we can more or less rule out the possibility that she's been working with them."

"What about the rumors concerning further arrests?" he was asked. "Can you tell us anything about them?"

"Not at this stage, I'm afraid. The police are playing this very close to the chest. So, a lot of questions, and as yet no answers. Back to you in the studio."

"Thanks, Damon, and if anyone does have any information regarding Mrs. Huxley-Browne and her daughter you can call the number at the bottom of the screen."

As a shot of the missing pair flashed up, Andee said, reflectively, "That picture is so blurred the police have to know they won't get much of a response to it. I wonder if they chose it deliberately, or is it all they could find?"

To Dan, Graeme remarked dryly, "It doesn't take much to get the ex-detective mind up and running. Me, I'm guessing the missing pair have taken off to deposit a tidy sum into an offshore bank somewhere. A nice little nest egg for when he comes out?"

"I could go for that," Dan agreed. "They're in it together and he's decided a stretch at Her Majesty's pleasure is a price worth paying for the millions they've managed to stash in some tax haven."

Andee wrinkled her nose. "Maybe," she conceded. "I suppose we'll find out at some point—or not. But what I do know, my darling, is that smoke is billowing out of the oven behind you."

Graeme swung around quickly, before remembering gazpacho

didn't even go in the oven, much less burn. Andee laughed and led Dan out of the wide-open French doors to the small, lavishly planted walled garden where a table had already been set for dinner.

"I'm embarrassed," Dan confessed as she offered him a plate of freshly made canapés. "When I said I wanted to pop round for a chat I wasn't expecting anything like this. I'd have at least brought some wine if I'd known."

"We have plenty," she assured him, "and Graeme loves to show off his culinary skills."

"I heard that," he shouted from inside.

"And you know it's true. Anyway," she said to Dan, "we don't see enough of you, so I was glad when you called. I've been wondering how the new junior partner's working out."

"Maxim? He's great. Sleep deprived—his girlfriend's just given birth to their first—but he knows his stuff and he's keen. Actually, I'm pretty impressed with all five of my staff."

"So, taking over Henry Matthews's practice is turning out to be a good move?"

"Given how much existing business it came with, I'd have to be a pretty poor sort not to say yes."

His smile showed a dimple in one cheek that she always found endearing. "I'm reliably informed," he added, helping himself to another canapé, "that you haven't exactly broken with the law yourself."

Her eyes showed surprise, but he could see that she'd picked up the segue and was intrigued by it. "Why? Do you need help with something?" she asked carefully.

"Not in the sense you're meaning it," he replied, and pulling out a chair, he sat down at the table. "I've been thinking about something you told me the last time I was here, and it prompted me to go and have a chat with an old friend, ex-colleague, of yours."

Regarding him knowingly, she said, "Are we talking about Detective Chief Inspector Terence Gould, by any chance?"

"We are. I met with him last week to discuss something I'd like to set up here in Kesterly, and I wasn't surprised when he suggested I should talk to you."

"This is sounding interesting," Graeme commented, coming to set a tureen of perfectly chilled gazpacho on the table.

"Isn't it?" Andee commented dryly. "No disrespect, Dan, but Gould usually sends people to me when he wants to get them out of his office."

Dan laughed. "He told me you'd say something like that, but yours wasn't the only name he mentioned—we'll come on to the others, most of whom you'll know. For now, Gould confirmed my own thoughts that there are few better placed than you to help get the project launched."

Andee's eyes widened. "Okaaay," she responded, glancing at Graeme and clocking his clear amusement. "Are you in on this?" she asked suspiciously.

He held up his hands. "I'm as in the dark as you are," he assured her.

She turned back to Dan.

Coming to the point, he said, "You know about restorative justice, right?"

She nodded slowly. "Weren't you running a team in your previous life?"

Graeme said, "You might have to enlighten me."

Dan explained, "Restorative justice is basically about putting victims of crimes together with offenders to try and come to a resolution that will help both parties to move on."

Graeme arched an eyebrow. "So, someone vandalizes my car, is charged with the crime, then I get to meet him so he can say he's sorry? Do I get to thump him?"

Dan laughed. "Yes, apart from the thumping bit, but it can be about much more serious offenses."

Graeme waved for everyone to help themselves to soup, and began refreshing the wine.

Turning back to Andee, Dan warmed to his theme as he said, "I'm sure you'd agree that this community is crying out for an RJ service, but in order to get funding we have to impress the Ministry of Justice with a cracking business plan and a board of experts. These need to be police and probation officers, local authority officials, magistrates, councillors . . . we can draw up a list of who we think would be interested and influential, and as you're so well connected in the area I'm hoping you'll come on board to approach them with me."

Andee was so taken aback that she wasn't sure what to say.

"You'd also make a brilliant practitioner," Dan continued, "someone who deals with victims—or offenders—on a personal level."

Andee blinked.

"You'd be perfect for it," Graeme chipped in. "Whatever the qualifications are for practitioners, people skills have to come into it and I don't know anyone who's better at people than you."

"Exactly," Dan agreed. "Empathy is what's needed for the task, patience as well, obviously, in fact a whole slew of good qualities, but empathy is the most important. You have that; you also have a good knowledge of the community and unless you tell me differently you have a stronger belief in rehabilitation than you do in punishment."

Andee couldn't deny it, although she did say, "Some crimes have to be punished. Murder, rape, assault . . ."

Dan's hand went up. "No one will argue with that, although there are cases where even murderers and rapists have met their victims or the victim's family and, believe it or not, there have been some positive results."

Graeme regarded him skeptically. "Why the heck would anyone want to meet their rapist?"

"Or their son's or daughter's killer?" Dan added. "Most certainly don't—and don't have to. But there are some victims who find themselves wanting to ask why. Why me? Why my mother, son, grandfather? If it's a burglary, they ask, What did you do with the photos or the jewelry? Are you coming back to take more of what's mine? And sometimes it helps to have answers."

"But the perpetrators still go to prison?" Graeme prompted.

"If someone is found guilty of a serious crime, then yes, they do, and often the restorative process can begin during the sentence. In fact, I'd say more than seventy percent of the cases I've worked on have happened in the run-up to parole, when victims are approached to find out how they feel about an offender returning to society. The RJ program can work well at that time, if we can get them together. Or it can happen while someone is awaiting trial. It basically depends on when they're referred to us."

Graeme's eyes returned to Andee as she began to ladle gazpacho into her bowl.

"In principle," she said as she set the ladle down again, "of course I'm interested, but before we start drawing up a list of potential board members—I've got about half a dozen names already in mind—I'd like to read some case histories, if you have any."

Clearly delighted, Dan said, "No problem. I've a mountain of stuff you can look at, so I'll email you the links and passwords as soon as I get home. Oh, and I don't want you to worry about your interior design business, I know you're busy with it. This is something that can be made to work around it."

"Unless there are prison visits involved?"

"Yes, we'd have no say on timings there, but I'm happy to take on those cases as we get started—and further down the line I hope we'll have a number of practitioners to call on."

"And who'll be running your legal practice while you're doing all this?" Graeme wanted to know.

"I will, for the most part, but having Maxim on board will free up some time for me to start pulling together an impressive board, appointing a chief exec, applying for Ministry of Justice accreditation and funding . . ."

"Wouldn't you be the chief exec?" Graeme asked.

"Probably, unless we felt someone else might be more suitable."

"Unlikely," Andee retorted, "given we have no experience of the service in this area. I'm assuming case referrals will come from the police, lawyers, prison staff, victim support groups . . . ?"

"All of the above, and of course we'll need to be out there talking to them too, making sure they fully understand the program by the time we're ready to launch it."

When he stopped, Andee felt herself drawn to the warmth in his eyes, the depth of the passion he clearly felt for the project. As its leader, he would be inspirational.

"It's good to hear you're interested," he told her, "but you don't have to give me a final answer now. Especially as you'd likely find yourself back dealing with some of society's least desirables, who you gave up some time ago . . ."

"Aren't we supposed to believe that redemption is possible even for them?" she countered wryly.

"Of course." He smiled, and lifting his glass, he clinked it to hers, while Graeme looked on with undisguised amusement.

# CHAPTER FOUR

Dan's been on my case again to tell you something real about my background so you'll get an insight into who I am and where I come from but do you know what? I can't really be arsed. I mean, why would you care? It's not the kind of story you're used to, not someone like you. There's nothing here to make you feel good or happy like you were reading some romance book. All you're going to feel is sick that my words have even reached you, sicker still that I ever came into your life.

But I guess I can give you the bare facts about my family.

My dad's never been around—getting it on with my ma was the only part he played in my life before effing off to God knows where. I've never tried to track him down and can't imagine I ever will. I'd have to find out his name for a start, and who can be bothered with that when you're talking about someone who clearly has no interest in you? My granddad, Brookie, used to live with us before he died. I've had a couple of foster brothers and sisters over the years, my mum took them in to get more benefits—when you need the money you do what you have to—but then she was deemed unfit, so the kids stopped coming, along with the extras.

You'd have thought they'd have taken me into care, given all the parental neglect and stuff. I suppose if I'd stopped going to school they might have, but school was somewhere I could get warm and fed, provided we had some cash for meals. So, I learned to read and write, and I was always on the football team right from an early age. Being a good goal scorer saved me from getting picked on, although going after me would have been a waste of some sad-ass bully's time because even when I was a kid I could take care of myself — not that I went out looking for trouble. I mostly wanted to get on with my own shit, but if provoked I can get the blood flowing pretty quick, and that seems to scare most kids, so that's what I did. Oh, I wasn't bad at drawing, my teachers used to say, and I have a bit of a head for maths. Stephen Hawking me!

I was really into music as well. Still am, I guess. I was always plugged in to stuff you'd never imagine someone like me listening to. I don't care what it is; it just has this way of transporting me out of whatever bad situation I'm in. I can sing too. I mean it, I really can. All I have to do is listen to a number a couple of times and I've got the lyrics down. It was my party piece. Bought me lots of cred, it did, and it was always a good crack watching people's faces like they couldn't believe what they're hearing. I've been in quite a few bands, mostly house or garage, but once I started with BJ on a more permanent basis, I was always getting kicked out for not showing up.

So that's my sob story. Tbh, I don't even know if you can read after what I did to you, maybe someone has to read to you. Am I sorry about that? 'Course I am, I'm not a total assw***. I seriously wish it hadn't happened, but I can't do anything about it now and I don't see how hearing from me will make anything better for you.

So, Dan—I know you'll be the first to read this—nice try, but that's it. I'm not up for any more. And yeah, OK, I'm probably depressed, that's what you'll say, isn't it? But hey, if you can come up with something for me to feel good about, I'll take it. 'Cept it's too late for that now, and it's not me who needs to feel good, really, is it? Not after what I did.

# CHAPTER FIVE

Marcy was sitting at the dining table in their sunny seafront apartment, staring down at the mobile phone in her hand. She wasn't actually seeing it; she was focused instead on the call she'd just ended and how she was going to explain it to Rebecca—*Claudia*.

Almost a month had passed since they'd left their old lives, but it was going to take a lot longer than that to get used to calling her thirty-six-year-old daughter by another name. It was likely to take even longer to stop missing her old friends, she was coming to realize, not to mention her beloved home.

Best not to dwell on it, it wouldn't make anything feel better, only worse, and that wasn't going to help any of them.

Curiously, she wasn't having a problem with her granddaughter's name, for Jasmine seemed to suit her better than Cara. Just like the flower, she was sweet and pretty and appeared far more delicate than she actually was. She'd always had plenty of spirit, had known her own mind, and had been filled with optimism until the horrors at home had effectively crushed her. Since they'd arrived here it had taken almost no time for her to come back to life, to blossom into the lively teenager who'd been subdued for so long. It was like giving water to a parched plant. She was settling in well at school, had just almost finished her exams, and had made several friends already. Moreover, only yesterday she'd passed an audition to play with the school orchestra in the new school year. This was the first time for several years that she'd put herself forward to be part of a musical

ensemble; her violin performances, private lessons, and even practice had stopped when she'd realized what her talent, her limelight,
was costing her mother.

*Marcus Huxley-Browne, that brutal, conniving egotist who'd tricked*
*them all at the start into believing he was a decent and caring human*
*being. How far from the truth that had turned out to be.*

Taking an unsteady breath, Marcy looked around the room full
of sunlight and soft, natural colors. She took in the mint-green sofas
with pale blue cushions, the coral-colored rugs covering pale oak
floorboards, the coffee table that was a refashioned door, the artfully
distressed vintage sideboard, and all the small touches Claudia had
added to reflect a nautical theme. Her daughter's design skills were
exceptional, and turning this place into a home with all her sewing and sanding, painting and crafting had done much to help her
through this difficult time.

Glancing down at her phone again, Marcy felt her heartbeat
quicken with concern. What had she done?

She escaped the question by tuning in to the sounds of the waves
sweeping gently through the open windows. Diaphanous drapes fluttered in the breeze and in a fanciful part of her mind she could hear
Jasmine's bow gliding over the strings of her precious violin, haunt-
ing and ephemeral, proud and sweet. She loved to listen to her granddaughter play, to marvel at the gift she'd been blessed with that was
all her own. No one in the family that Marcy knew of had passed on
this artistic gene, but as soon as they'd recognized it they'd nurtured
it. Her father, Joel, had bought Jasmine her first instrument when she
was only three, and for her ninth birthday he'd presented her with a
copy of an Il Cessol Stradivarius. He'd known by then that he wasn't
going to make it to her tenth birthday, and so had given her the magnificent piece for her to play when she was older, maybe for her first

professional engagement. It had always been her most prized possession, nothing else had ever come close, but for the past few years Marcy had looked after it at her home where it was safe.

Now it was here, carefully stored beneath Jasmine's bed, as exquisite and treasured as ever, and it wouldn't be long, Marcy felt, before Jasmine was ready to play it in public.

Getting up from her chair, Marcy went to put on the kettle. She wasn't sure she wanted tea, but it was giving her something to do as she tried to decide how to tell Claudia what she'd done. Her daughter and granddaughter had always come first for her, they still did, otherwise she wouldn't be here—and she truly didn't regret coming, in spite of the hankering for her old routines. She'd find new ones, immerse herself in charity work, maybe even find a part-time job. However, none of it could happen if the news reports about them didn't abate.

The search for Marcus Huxley-Browne's missing wife and stepdaughter, and now his mother-in-law, had begun to stir up so many lurid and outlandish theories that Marcy was losing sleep over them. She'd known for a while that something had to be done, but Claudia wouldn't discuss it. For her, immersed in her world of decorative pillows and hand-painted shell accessories, it was as though it wasn't happening. Marcy had no such distraction, and the latest report that the police were preparing to dig up the back garden of the house in Kensington meant that she'd had to act.

"Hey, Nana," Jasmine trilled cheerfully as she came in the door, making Marcy jump.

"Hello, darling," Marcy responded, turning to watch her granddaughter dump a heavy schoolbag and battered violin case on the table. "You're early. I wasn't expecting you until six."

"I've just popped in to change out of my uniform," Jasmine

explained, giving her a hug. "Are you OK? You looked miles away when I came in."

Marcy forced a smile. "I was, but I'm fine. Do you want anything to eat?"

"No, I'm cool, thanks. Where's Mum?"

"She went to buy some wiring for a lamp she's making, but she texted just now to say she was popping into the post office to pick up a form for your provisional driver's license."

Jasmine's eyes lit up. "Awesomazing," she cheered joyfully. "Not only about the license, but that she's actually gone somewhere apart from the beach." Sobering slightly, she added, "Poor Mum. It's all been so hard for her, hasn't it, and not even knowing he's gone to prison for two years seems to have cheered her up."

"Because he could be out in as little as eighteen months," Marcy reminded her. "But don't let's talk about him. Have you booked your first driving lesson yet? You know I'm paying for a course of six as your birthday present."

"You are the best, and I will, but my birthday's not for weeks, so what's the hurry? Oh, I know, you guys want me to be the chauffeur so you can have a drink when you go out."

"Guilty," Marcy replied wryly. In truth they were so close to everything that they could walk, unless they were after a major supermarket shop or a browse around the factory outlets over in Somerset. "The instructors get pretty booked up," she cautioned, "so you should look into it soon. Did you ask your friends for some recommendations?"

"Actually, I did, and apparently there's a woman who lives out in one of the villages who gets everyone through first time, so I'll give her a try. Now I need to get changed fast. I don't want to be late for my lesson."

Remembering she was seeing Anton, her violin coach, today, Marcy watched her bound off to her room and all over again she felt glad, happy to see how well she was settling into this comparatively parochial world. That alone made the change, the sacrifice, worthwhile.

A few minutes later Jasmine was gone, violin case in one hand, mobile phone in the other as she chatted to her new BFF, Abby. Her contacts list must be growing by the day, Marcy reflected, and it was certainly about time she was able to live a normal life, if this was indeed what they were living. It didn't always feel that way, but of course it would take time, and she had to admit that her own contacts list had accumulated a few numbers too. Dentist, doctor, estate agent, landlord, and a few new friends she'd made at the community center. There was even quite an interesting man among them, Henry Matthews. He was a recently retired solicitor, about her age, whose cheery and somewhat dry demeanor seemed to incite goodwill in everyone. She hadn't mentioned anything about him to Claudia; why would she when there was nothing to tell? He was just someone Marcy had got talking to the last time she was at the center.

Hearing the front door open and close, she experienced a sharp pang of nerves. She would have to explain what she'd done now, and she had no idea how her daughter was going to react.

As Claudia came in from the hall, looking too thin, but now tanned and almost as lovely as she used to be, she put down a shopping bag, a few brochures from an estate agent, and the driving license application form.

"Everything OK?" Marcy asked breezily.

Claudia turned to gaze at her, her eyes soft with affection, and yet shadowed by the fear that continued to haunt her. "You don't have to look like that," she said, "I already know."

Marcy frowned. She couldn't know. It wouldn't be possible. "Know what?" she countered, feigning surprise.

Claudia smiled wryly. "That you've spoken to the police in London to tell them we're alive and well."

Marcy's heart skipped a beat. "How . . . But . . ."

"I called too," Claudia interrupted. "I spoke to a Detective Inspector Phillips and he told me he'd already heard from you." Uneasy amusement showed in her eyes. "God knows what he must think of us, and I've no idea yet if we're going to face charges for wasting police time, but apparently he's coming to talk to us to verify that we are who we say we are."

Moving past her astonishment, Marcy said dryly, "Well, good luck with that."

Claudia had to smile. "So, what exactly did you tell him?" she asked, pulling out a chair to sit down.

Knowing there was no point trying to pretend she'd held anything back, Marcy sat down too and said, "I explained what a monster Marcus turned into after your marriage; about the abuse that's been going on, and how much worse it became once the investigation into his business affairs started."

Claudia nodded slowly, trying to imagine what the detective must have thought as he'd listened to the tale of domestic terror that would have been so much easier to describe than it had been to endure. The belittling, the intimidation, the insane jealousy of her dead husband, Joel. It had reached a point where Marcus couldn't even bear to hear Joel's name; just thank God he'd never turned his rage on Jasmine—only threatened to. However, Jasmine had somehow found out that he punished her mother for her musical talents, as if she was encouraging them just to spite him.

So Jasmine—Cara as she'd been then—had stopped playing the

violin and had gradually broken with her friends to avoid having to invite anyone home.

Why had she, Claudia, allowed it to go on as long as it had? Why hadn't she found the courage to leave sooner? People only asked those questions when they'd never been in such a situation themselves, trapped, smothered by a bully, bereft of confidence and terrified he'd carry out his threats to harm her daughter if she ever tried to leave.

"All I need to know," he'd said the last time she'd visited him in prison—yes, she'd visited him while he was on remand, she'd had to or he'd have sent someone to the house to check on them—"is that you'll stand by me if this doesn't end well. Tell me you'll still be there when I come out."

She hadn't answered, had been unable to find any words.

"Swear to me that you will," he growled urgently. "If I know I can trust you no one will come after you."

*No one will come after you.*

Her silence made him draw back suddenly, gray eyes darkening with fury. "Jesus Christ," he hissed. "Tell me what I'm thinking is wrong."

"I don't know what you're thinking," she replied helplessly.

"You fucking helped them, didn't you?" he spat. "That's what I'm seeing . . . Bitch! You've been working with the police . . ."

She shook her head desperately.

"If I find out you have, you'll pay, I hope you know that."

She'd wondered who would make her pay, the foreign investors—launderers—he was protecting, no doubt because he knew his life wouldn't be a long one if he didn't stay silent? Or, more likely, one of his even more dubious connections.

He'd never mentioned the case he'd stuffed into the safe the day the police had come for him, so she hadn't either, and no one had pulled aside the filing cabinet during a search of the house. For a long time she'd expected someone—his lawyer, maybe his sister (a raging sociopath if ever there was one)—to come for it, but no one had. It had remained where it was until the night before Claudia had left, when she'd used the code she'd watched him tap in the day of his arrest and discovered she'd memorized it correctly. She'd thought then that it might prove a kind of insurance policy, a way of protecting herself and Jasmine if anyone found them; she wasn't sure what she thought now. In fact, for the most part, she tried to forget they had it.

"When you made your call to the inspector," Marcy said carefully, "did you ask if it was possible to keep our whereabouts a secret?"

Claudia swallowed dryly as she shook her head. Neither of them knew for certain what would happen if Marcus found out where they were, but there was no doubt in either of their minds that he wouldn't be in prison for nearly long enough and when he got out he'd feel the need to punish Claudia for trying to escape him.

IT WAS JUST after eleven the next morning when Claudia showed DI Phillips and another detective into the flat. Both men wore somber expressions, though they were polite and even friendly in the way they greeted and thanked her for seeing them. Phillips was just above average height with thick gray hair and shrewd brown eyes, while his colleague, clearly a decade or more younger, was a fiery redhead with a face full of freckles.

It felt odd, she reflected as she followed them along the hall, to have men in this space that she'd made so essentially feminine, but for the moment at least they didn't feel threatening.

Her mother was in the kitchen making coffee to accompany the pastries she'd picked up from the bakery earlier. Jasmine had an exam today, so she'd gone to school. She knew that the police were coming to talk to her mother and grandmother; they'd decided at the start of this that they must never hold anything back from each other. She'd been nervous when she left, even afraid that she'd come home to find they'd been arrested and taken away, but Claudia had assured her that wouldn't happen.

She hoped she was right.

"This is my mother, Marcy Kavanagh," Claudia announced as they entered the living area.

Phillips stepped forward to shake Marcy's hand and introduce himself.

Claudia could sense her mother's anxiety, but Marcy's expression remained confident as she said, "It's good of you to come all this way to see us."

Without commenting on that, Phillips identified the younger man as Detective Constable Leo Johnson from the local CID, and after Johnson had also shaken hands, they both accepted the offer of coffee.

Claudia directed them to the table and as she set down the croissants and pain au raisins her mother carried through a tray of mugs and a cafetière.

Phillips was the first to speak, in a tone that was gruff but not aggressive, and Claudia thought she detected tiredness in his eyes. "Following on from the conversation I had with your mother yesterday," he said to her, "I must ask why, if you felt you needed protection, you didn't contact the police?"

Having expected the question, Claudia watched Marcy pouring the coffee as she said, "I needed to get away from my husband completely, to make sure my daughter was safe and do everything I could to stop him from finding us again. All you would have offered me was protection during the trial—or maybe a few weeks after— but that wouldn't have been enough."

Marcy added, "As I explained on the phone, he's violent and un- predictable. And it's not only what he did to my daughter, he also made threats against my granddaughter. We have reason to believe that while he's in prison others have been instructed to 'keep an eye on us.' He's very controlling, you see, frighteningly so."

Phillips's expression revealed little as he took his coffee and de- clined a pastry, while Johnson tucked hungrily into a croissant.

For the next few minutes, to the accompanying sounds of sea gulls, traffic, and tourists drifting in from outside, Phillips outlined the offenses they had committed and how wasting police time could be punishable by a custodial sentence.

Claudia felt her insides clench. "You don't understand," she told him, her voice thick with emotion. "We weren't thinking about the trial. We just had to get away." She took a gulp of coffee to calm herself, before adding, earnestly, "I really didn't mean for our dis- appearance to cause so much . . . concern. I am very sorry for the trouble we've caused."

How naïve did that sound? Unbearably, she realized, but at least he wasn't looking scornful, or angry.

Marcy said, "Why did you start looking for us? We hadn't done anything wrong; it's not a crime to change your name, or to move house, or to erase your profiles from social media."

Phillips said, "You could have done all that and still let us know you were doing it. No one would have stopped you. But to answer your question, you were reported missing, so we were obliged to follow it up."

Claudia's eyes met her mother's. She said quietly, "I'm guessing my sister-in-law, Eugena, contacted you?"

Phillips neither confirmed nor denied it, only regarded her in a way that caused color to rise in her cheeks. "Why did you leave your phones and laptops in the house?" he asked curiously. "Wouldn't it have made more sense to dispose of them?"

Claudia accepted that it would have, but it was too late now. "I suppose it was my way of telling my husband, and his sister," she said, "that we'd gone for good and there was no point looking for us because we'd left our old lives behind." She didn't mention anything about the Internet advice on disappearing; it was a site that might work well for some and so needed to remain in place.

Phillips arched a single eyebrow as he said, "Didn't it occur to you that your disappearance could be interpreted another way?"

"Not until I saw it on the news," she replied, managing to hold his gaze in spite of the intimidation she was starting to feel. *He's not Marcus*, she reminded herself forcefully. *He doesn't mean you any harm, at least not in the same way.*

"And you didn't come forward then because?" he prompted.

Marcy said, "Because we didn't want to be found. I think that's already been established."

Phillips inhaled and glanced at Leo Johnson as he leaned back in his chair. "What I think," he said, addressing Claudia, "is that you assumed if your husband and sister-in-law came under investigation regarding your disappearance, which they did, it would delay them from trying to find you. In other words, you made your disappearance seem suspicious in order to buy yourselves some time."

"That's not true," Claudia responded quickly, and heard the faint rasp in her voice that weakened her words. She never used to be so apprehensive or afraid to assert herself, but it would change, she determined, just not in time for this. "I had no idea Eugena would report us missing. If anything, I expected her to try and find us herself, or employ someone to do it for her." Her eyes went briefly to her mother and she could see that their thoughts were the same—contacting the police to help find her brother's missing wife had clearly backfired on Eugena in a way she should have foreseen, but apparently hadn't. So perhaps she wasn't quite so clever after all.

Marcy said, "My daughter has already apologized for the trouble we've caused, and I'd like to apologize, too. I should have contacted you sooner, I realize that, but the problem was—and remains—if the press finds out where we are, our attempts to start afresh will have been pointless."

Phillips regarded her carefully, apparently measuring his words before responding. "It's going to be necessary to explain why the search has been called off, have you thought of that?"

Marcy nodded bleakly.

"Do you have any answers?"

She said, "You wouldn't have to give any details of where we are."

After a moment he surprised her by saying, "No, we wouldn't."

Claudia wasn't sure if she was understanding correctly. Was he really agreeing to keep their whereabouts a secret? Marcy was very still as she waited for him to continue.

Phillips stared at his empty mug and spoke almost as if he was only working this out now. "The press will bombard us with questions," he said, "but the only answer we need to give is that you're alive and well and that we won't be pursuing matters any further."

Claudia and Marcy stared at him.

Johnson cleared his throat as Phillips went on, "Of course there's nothing the police can do to stop a member of the press from launching a search of their own."

Claudia's eyes moved to him. "Do you think they will?" she asked, certain they would. The press loved nothing more than exposés and exclusives. And then there was Eugena: on behalf of Marcus, she would certainly initiate a search, if she hadn't already.

"They won't learn anything from us," Phillips assured them. "I haven't shared anything with my team yet, and there's no reason for anyone, either press or public, to be in touch with Leo here concerning yourselves. As long as you are able to keep your identities quiet, I see no reason why it can't stay a secret."

Claudia couldn't think what to say. It was everything they'd hoped for, but there was more to it, she could sense it as solidly as if another presence had stolen into the room.

His head went down again, and he pressed his fingers to his eye sockets, digging in hard; the gesture of a fatigued and troubled man. "My daughter was the victim of a violent marriage," he confessed in a tone that belied the torment beneath it. "We—*I*—should have done more to protect her. There was a restraining order, but he got to her and . . . She was an only child and our lives have never been the same since we lost her."

Tears instantly stung Claudia's eyes to see how broken he was inside. A father who'd lost the most precious person in the world to him, and because of who he was, what he did for a living, he was unable to forgive himself. "I'm so sorry," she said hoarsely.

He nodded briefly and his tone became crisp as he replied, "We don't want the same happening to you." He stood and looked Claudia in the eye. "You have my number," he said, "but Leo is here, on the ground. Don't be afraid to contact him if you feel the need to."

Leo put his card on the table as he stood too. "Anything," he told them. "If you feel it needs checking out just call."

Marcy thanked him, and Claudia could see that she was as dazed as her daughter was by the unexpected turn this had taken.

"There's just one other thing," Phillips said, before leaving.

"According to your sister-in-law something is missing from the house. Can you throw any light on that?"

Heat spread all the way through Claudia as she pictured the attaché case, now hidden beneath her mother's bed. "I don't know what she means," she said, trying for confusion and hitting a note that was slightly too shrill. "Did she say what it was?"

He shook his head. "No, but she seemed keen to get it back."

AFTER THE DETECTIVES had gone Claudia returned to the sitting room to find her mother gazing down at the street below, watching the two men getting into a car.

"Do you think he believed me?" Claudia asked, twisting her fingers anxiously.

Marcy turned back into the room. "About the attaché case? I don't think it matters. He's clearly not interested in pursuing it."

Claudia stared at the empty mugs and cafetière on the table. "If we could work out a way of getting it to her do you think she'd stop trying to find us?"

Her mother replied without hesitation. "No, I don't, and as far as I'm concerned the money at least *belongs* to you."

Claudia didn't argue with that, since she was only too aware that Marcus had taken the profit she'd made from the sale of her and Joel's house to invest and she'd never seen as much as a single penny in return. Whether the cash in the briefcase covered the amount, she had no idea. She hadn't counted it, but it was certainly a sizable sum. "What about the documents?" she said, certain they were of as much, if not more interest to Marcus and his sister.

Marcy shrugged. "Let's hang on to them," she replied. "At least for now."

# CHAPTER SIX

S orry I'm late," Andee apologized, sinking into a booth at the Seafront Café where one of her closest friends was waiting. "It's been a crazy morning in the world of interior design. How are you? You look wonderful, as usual."

Leanne Delaney twinkled happily. She was a striking woman in her mid-forties with a Pre-Raphaelite look about her that was at once romantic, earthy, and fiery. "Right back at you." She smiled. "And don't worry about being late, I've only just got here myself. I've ordered you a glass of white, tell me I did wrong."

"You did not. I need it after the showdown I've just had with a contractor."

Curiously, Leanne asked, "Are we talking about the new builds up on Westleigh Heights?"

"The very same. I'm supposed to be dressing the show home this week, but they're so behind that the decorators can't even start to wallpaper and half the furniture is about to be delivered."

"Mm, awkward. Anything I can do?"

"If you know how to make curtains I'd worship at your feet forever. The woman I normally use has just let me down, and everyone else on my list is up to their eyes."

Leanne grimaced. "Not a part of my skill set, I'm afraid, but I'll definitely give it some thought and let you know if I come up with anyone. Aha, here's Fliss, the goddess of grapes."

They greeted the café's owner affectionately, and for several minutes the three of them discussed how their various businesses were doing. The Seafront was always busy no matter the time of year, given its status as the town's go-to breakfast and lunch venue, while Leanne's vintage emporium further along the Promenade had done exceptionally well over the summer. Andee, as always, was involved in so many projects besides her design business that there was too much to go into, so she mostly let the others talk.

"So, who's joining you?" Fliss asked, nodding at the table's third setting.

"Dan Collier," Andee replied. "Don't be surprised if he gets on both your cases to become practitioners in our restorative justice program."

"Oh, yes, how's that going?" Fliss asked, waving goodbye to someone who was leaving. "I hear you've already got an executive board in place. Are you just waiting for funding to come through?"

"Not anymore," Andee responded warmly. "Thanks to a very generous donation from a local businessman, we're already taking in referrals."

Intrigued, Leanne said, "You mean actual cases? No more rehearsals?"

"We have two genuine cases running at the moment," Andee told her. "One is a burglary and the other's a hate crime, but there are others under consideration, so we need to start recruiting. I thought your mother would be a good candidate," she suggested to Leanne, "and I wondered about Klaudia," she added, referring to Leanne's partner in the vintage shop she owned. "Speaking Polish will make her a tremendous asset."

Leanne blinked. "Mum will definitely want to be involved," she assured her. "I'll talk to Klaudia and let you know, but I'm sure she'll say yes."

"If you need more men," Fliss said, glancing over her shoulder at the sound of a crash in the kitchen followed by angry voices, "I'll put my thinking cap on. Now I'd better go and find out what's up in the paradise of my workplace."

Left to their wine and menus, Andee said, "OK. I'm opting for the spicy lentil soup. It seems right for this miserable weather."

With a sigh Leanne replied, "Will it ever stop raining? But at least we had a lovely August and the forecast isn't bad for the coming weekend, thank God. We've promised Abby a barbecue for her seventeenth birthday party, although at the moment she's only invited her latest best friend, Jasmine. So not too much work there, but watch this space. Actually, there's a thought: I'm sure Jasmine mentioned something about her mother being into soft furnishings. Maybe she's someone you could talk to about curtains?"

Ready to grasp at any straw, Andee said, "Do you have a name or number for her?"

"I know her name's Claudia, but I'll have to ask Abby or Jasmine for her details. I'll text Abby now, if you like. She might get back to us by the end of lunch."

After the message was sent, she put aside her phone and leaned in to Andee conspiratorially. "OK, to the real reason for this lunch— but you must promise not to breathe a word for now."

Andee drew a cross over her heart.

"Tom's asked me to marry him and I've accepted."

Andee's eyes widened. "You accepted?" she cried in mock horror. "I felt sure you'd turn him down when he finally got around to it."

Leanne shot her a meaningful look and as they both laughed, Andee started to get up to hug her.

"No, don't make a fuss," Leanne cautioned, waving her back down. "I don't want anyone to know yet, although the chances of my mother being able to hold it in are about as good as mine of fitting into the size ten wedding dress we have in the shop."

Andee laughed. "So, when are you planning to do it?"

"We're still discussing that, but it'll definitely be just close friends and family, so obviously that includes you, Graeme, and your mother."

"On behalf of us all, I accept. Will it be at the Tramonto?" She was referring to the exquisite Italianate villa on Kesterly Heights that Tom had inherited a couple of years back from an aunt and which Graeme and Andee, with their joint skills as developer and designer, had helped turn into an exclusive twelve-suite hotel.

"Probably," Leanne replied. "It'll depend on bookings, but . . ." She broke off as a furious-looking waif of a woman stomped out of the kitchen, banged against tables as she crossed the café, and slammed noisily out of the door.

Andee said, "Wasn't that Maria Colbrook?" She watched the diminutive woman's awkward gait as she marched off through the rain, trying to remember the last time she'd seen her, and decided it must have been years rather than months ago.

"No idea," Leanne replied. "I've never seen her before, but it's looking like she's just lost her job." She checked her phone as a text arrived. "Great, it's from Abby with Jasmine's mother's number. I'll forward it to you." After doing so, she said, "They're a sweet family, grandmother, mother, and daughter, much like we were at Ash Morley before Tom changed our dynamic. To fill you in a bit, they haven't been in the area for long, only a few months, and according to Jasmine her mother hasn't made many friends yet."

Picking up on that, Andee said, "So we need to come to the rescue?"

"Maybe, if she wants it. Although she almost never comes in when she drops Jasmine at ours, so it could be she'd rather keep herself to herself."

"What about the grandmother?"

"A different story. My mother's got to know her a little through the community center, and apparently she's just become a trustee of the theater. And wait for this, she's offered to sponsor a concert next spring."

Andee was impressed. "That's very generous of her."

"Isn't it, but I suspect she's doing it mainly so Jasmine can show off what a brilliant violinist she is. She's incredibly talented, can play just about anything you throw at her, and not just classical. Abby, who has no such skills, is planning to be her manager or producer, maybe agent, I forget which." With a maternal sigh, she added, "Actually, it's wonderful to see the two of them together. Abby was quite lost after her best friend Tanya moved away, but she and Jasmine have been inseparable over the school holidays."

Andee said, "Aha, here comes our soup. I don't remember ordering it, do you?"

"You didn't," Fliss informed her. "This is just to keep you going while we sort things out in the kitchen. It's on the house."

As she set the bowls down, Andee said, "Was that Maria Colbrook who stormed out just now?"

With a sigh Fliss said, "It was. Honestly, you can't help someone for trying. This is the third time I've given her a job and she either burns the food, clouts one of the other staff, or offends the customers. Today she threw a cast-iron pot at Kevin, the cook. Missed, thank God, but I had to fire her or Kevin would have walked. I'll put money on her being on the doorstep again before long begging for more work. If she doesn't get hiked off to prison again first. Anyway, I'd better get back to it, the orders are piling up and I'm trying to do the till as well."

"I'll finish this and come and take over the front of house," Leanne promised. "It'll leave you free to chat with Dan when he comes," she said to Andee. "But first, I've been thinking, should we try to find a partner for him? He's highly eligible, and he must be very lonely rattling around that lovely duplex over his office."

"I think he prefers it that way," Andee told her. "He's been incredibly busy with the RJ project lately as well as his law firm, but don't worry, Graeme and I are keeping an eye on him."

By the time Dan arrived, Andee and Leanne had finished their lunch. After a warm greeting, Andee hopped up from the table, saying, "I'm going to make a call. I'll be right back."

In the café's cloakroom, which was full of wet coats and umbrellas, she moved farther along to the rose-scented area outside the bathrooms and connected to the number Leanne had given her for Claudia. Disappointingly she was bumped through to voicemail, so she left a message. "Hi, my name's Andee Lawrence. Leanne Delaney gave me your number. I was hoping to talk to you about some drapes that I need made in a hurry. It's quite a big order, for a show home. If you're interested and would like to talk more you can get me on this number. I'm really hoping to hear from you. Thanks."

# CHAPTER SEVEN

Claudia watched her mother's face as she replayed the message from Andee Lawrence, knowing very well what Marcy was thinking. It was probably much the same as she'd thought herself when she'd first heard it, although her mother would have far more optimism going on than she'd had.

*At last something that might persuade Claudia to emerge from her shell.*

"Are you going to call her back?" Marcy asked, returning the phone and carrying on brushing her hair in the mirror. She was clearly trying not to make a big deal of it, continuing to get ready for a meeting at the community center, and given how carefully she'd applied her makeup Claudia wondered, not for the first time lately, if there was someone special on her mother's horizon.

"I think if I don't call back you'll leave me," Claudia quipped.

Marcy smiled, her blue eyes softening in a way that made her seem younger and happier than she'd looked in a while. "It's a great opportunity to start building your business again," she said, "and to meet someone new."

Claudia wasn't going to deny that, for it was what she'd thought herself, and turning to look at the dining table laden with dishes of colored beads and charms, special threads and wire, her pliers, glue, and needles, she gave a small sigh. She'd made jewelry several years ago and sold it online, and now she was in the process of doing more, rebranding her designs as Simply Baubles. It wasn't going to make her a fortune, but it wasn't a fortune that she needed.

It was a life.

"You shouldn't waste any time," Marcy urged. "If you don't get back to her right away, she'll find someone else. You can *do* this."

In spite of the anxiety tightening her heart, Claudia said, "OK, I'll call her now," and tapping Andee Lawrence's number on the phone screen, she looked at her mother again as she waited for the connection.

Marcy's face was full of hope, eyes bright with encouragement, and Claudia knew she was doing this as much for her as she was for herself.

"Hi, Andee Lawrence speaking."

Claudia's eyes drifted to the rain on the windows. "It's Claudia Winters," she said, feeling oddly as though she was stepping into another world, with no knowledge of where she might land. "I got your message. It's possible I could help you, but I need to know more about . . ."

"Oh, thank goodness," Andee replied in a rush. "Maybe we could meet at the property so you can see exactly what's required—and I'll have to pray you won't go screaming off into the night when you see what I'm asking for."

With a smile, Claudia said, "We only arrived in the area a few months ago and I haven't really set myself up yet, so I don't have any workers or suppliers, at least not locally." Could she contact the team she'd used before? No, of course not. Was she out of her mind? "If you're in a hurry . . ."

"Don't worry, we can work it out together," Andee assured her. "I have plenty of contacts, and if you need help sourcing fabrics I can make several suggestions, although I'm sure you're much better connected in that field than I am."

Since she wouldn't have to use her old name when placing orders, Claudia said more confidently, "OK. If you text me the address and a time I'll be there. I have no other commitments so I can fit in with you."

"Music to my ears. I'll do it right away."

Clicking off the line, Claudia wondered where her mother had gone but didn't go to look. Instead she walked to the window and rearranged the folds of a gauzy drape. She really didn't think Andee Lawrence's call was a trick, something set up by her sister-in-law, but she could no more stop the thought than she could the traffic outside. She scanned the Promenade for familiar faces, but saw only raincoated tourists braving the late September weather and locals going about their business.

"No one's out there," Marcy said gently as she came back into the room. "You don't need to be scared."

Claudia turned around. "I know," she replied, and drew a hand down her slender neck as though to relieve the tension, "and one of these days I might stop thinking there is." She smiled. "It's not happening as often now."

It was true, the sense of being followed or watched was no longer as consuming, and she'd even stopped seeing Eugena in the supermarket, coming out of the station, in the café, walking toward her on the beach . . . Women who actually looked nothing like Eugena could morph into her for brief, horrifying moments, but thankfully Claudia was getting this under better control.

It wasn't quite the same with Marcus, for she still had nightmares about him and his cruelty; awful, terrible scenes of violence and anger that stayed with her after she woke up, that even revisited her during the day. Eugena had known what he was like, and some sadistic part of the woman had actually seemed to enjoy all the terror and misery her brother inflicted. "That'll be the address," Marcy said, as a text arrived on Claudia's phone.

Claudia read the message twice and turned shining eyes to her mother. "She wants to meet later this afternoon," she declared, surprised by a pleasing rush of eagerness. "She says to bring wellies, an umbrella, and a portfolio of my work."

With a cry of joy Marcy came to embrace her. "This is going to be your first commission as Claudia," she stated determinedly. "We should celebrate when you get back. Jasmine's going to be over the moon."

Knowing how true that was, Claudia felt another burst of happiness, while thinking of the interior magazines she'd had to leave behind that contained lavish color spreads of her designs. It wasn't possible to use them, for they connected her to the past. However, she had an impressive PowerPoint presentation on her iPad that didn't identify her at all. "I should text Leanne Delaney to thank her for suggesting me," she said, starting to clear the table. "Even if I don't get the job, it was lovely of her to do that."

"We could always," Marcy suggested carefully, "invite her to celebrate with us, if she's free, and if it happens."

Claudia tried to picture it, someone else here in the flat, raising a glass with them as if they were friends. It was an exhilarating thought, and she'd certainly warmed to Leanne on the few occasions their paths had crossed.

*I can do this, I really can*, she told herself as she began collecting everything she was going to need. And by the time she'd lugged it all down to the car her imagination was so busy conjuring a dynamic and fruitful meeting that she didn't even think to check if anyone was watching her.

# CHAPTER EIGHT

Dan's been here today and, surprise, surprise, he's "very disappointed" by the last letter I wrote. "Archie," he said, "you and I both know you can do better than this, so come on, lad. Step up to it."

What he doesn't seem to understand is that I never really care too much about disappointing people; I've been doing it for so long I might even be better at it than memorizing songs.

Anyway, he said he wouldn't come back if I didn't start playing the game (he didn't use that phrase, because none of it's a game to him), what he actually said was, "You've seen the last of me if this is how you're going to behave."

I said, "Bye, mate. Nice knowing you."

He looked at me with those laser eyes of his and kept on looking at me until I chucked up my hands and said, "What's going on, man? What do you want from me?"

"You know what I want."

I did. He thinks you have a right to know about the person who hurt you, and he reckons that deep down I want to tell you.

I don't know what kind of planet he lives on—can't remember where Superman comes from now—but hey, like I've said before, he's not an easy bloke to argue with, so in the end I gave it up. I don't want him to stop coming (wouldn't tell him that) and he could be right that I do want to tell you, though it beats me why I would. Or why you'd want to hear it.

Let me warn you right off that mine is not a good story, and I've got no skill as a writer, but I guess you've got that picture already.

So here goes: I already told you my mother's a nutjob and that we lived with my grandparents until one croaked and the other got carted off to the whacky shack. Before that happened it was their job to keep me out of the hands of social services when my ma was away. Everyone knew Ma would go mental if she came back and found I was gone, and I promise you really don't want my ma going mental. Where did she go when she was gone? Depends. Sometimes she was in the nick for not paying her council tax, or shoplifting, disturbing the peace, that sort of thing. Other times she was taken away to places I didn't know anything about until I was older. BJ would turn up when he felt like it, give her a beating, then stuff her in his car and drive off. Sometimes we didn't see her for weeks and when she came back she'd be in a right state, shaking and crying and needing a fix so bad we had to give it to her. (Shit is never difficult to get hold of on our estate.)

When she wasn't in the nick or off doing stuff for BJ — what I really mean is when she was sober and not feeling shit-scared of the world or mouthing off at it the way she sometimes did (complex woman, my ma) — she'd have a go at taking care of me. She'd buy me clothes, cook my food (terrible cook), and tell me to get on with my homework like she even knew what it was. My mates all thought she was weird, but they kind of respected her because she never got in my face about stuff and would let them treat our house like it was theirs.

I never told any of them about the clearing up me and my gran had to do after one of her bad days. Gross it was, and I didn't talk about the low-grade smack I used to get for her from Leroy two doors down to stop her tearing herself to bits. No one needed to know about any of that, although they probably did anyway, just never mentioned it. Most of the kids had one parent or both who got rolling stoned every day—and there was none of the good stuff in our neck of the woods, I can tell you that.

Did I ever try it myself?

'Course I did. I've done it all, collie weed (that's some dank-ass marijuana, that is; you can get really toked on that, know what I mean), crack, meth, black tar, all the trippy shit, you name it. First time I had some I was about six, I guess, and I remember how much it made the grown-ups laugh. I expect it was a hilarious sight watching a kid get high, although I think mostly it sent me to sleep.

My big connection to the recreationals started when I was about ten and BJ decided it was time to get me initiated into the real world, meaning his world. So next time he turned up at our place, instead of taking my ma after he'd roughed her up and helped himself to what dough she had, he took me instead.

Was I scared? You bet, but he made me feel kind of grown up, so I soon got over it, especially when he explained what I had to do.

"It's simple," he said. "I get the gear from the dudes I

know—you don't ever want to upset them, Archie, not if you got an urge to stay alive—and then I drive you around to make the deliveries. A kind of newspaper round, if you like, but these days we've moved on a bit."

"What are we delivering?" I asked him (talk about green, but remember I was only ten).

"Stuff. You don't need to know what it is, but it's serious quality and it's our job to get it to the PCs who pay top dollar for it."

"PCs?"

"Posh C***s. They buy big, I mean seriously big, for their carousels—orgies, pimp fests—but you don't need to know about that, cos you're too young for it all, and it don't involve you. You just have to make the delivery while I wait on double yellows, then I take you to the next drop-off, and same thing happens. Never, _never_ hand anything over to the client until you've got the cash in your hot little hand. Understood? Whatever excuse they give for not having any on them, we're not NatWest with the telephone banking, so you _do not_ part with the goods until they've paid. If they start kicking off, you just leg it back to me, bringing the stuff, and I'll sort it out. Got it?"

"Got it."

"You'll be expected to keep your mouth shut about this, so don't go bragging to your f***wit mates and playing the big man when you get home. If you do I'll know and I won't be happy. And you know what happens if I'm not happy. Your old lady gets it, that's what'll happen, and you don't want that now, do you?"

I began earning some decent cash almost from the get-go, and you should have seen some of the places we delivered to. These PCs lived in some serious houses all over the West End, down by the river, around the City . . . I never knew where we were half the time, or what the areas were called, I only got to know that later when I was older and able to get the Tube on my own if BJ wasn't available. I understood by then that the dudes he worked for were based in North London—sorry, no names or exact places, info classified—and that what I was delivering was mostly chem-sex drugs, which can be crystal meth, GHB, miaow miaow, that sort of thing. Sometimes though it was cash or phones—that was more intergang stuff—and later, when I got myself a reputation as someone reliable, it was shivvies and even toolies (that's knives and guns to you).

Yeah, I moved weapons around the country, sometimes going as far north as Manchester or even Glasgow. I slipped between the cracks like a shadow, they said, meaning no one ever really noticed me. It seemed I had a knack for keeping my head down, or looking harmless, or just plain dumb. The other kids didn't have it so easy and a few got caught. If that happened and the PCs heard about it, all hell would break loose with the dudes because business would have to shut down for a while. But everyone knew to keep their mouths shut; if they didn't, someone close to them would pay and they'd never snitch again.

Anyways, when I wasn't working, believe it or not I was at school, turning up randomly after being away for a week or two, and the teachers would say, "Where you been, Archie?" "Did you bring a note from your mother?" Once or twice the head called me in for a chat, but it never really came to anything. You see, I never acted up or caused trouble like some of the others; I wasn't violent, or disruptive, or a threat to their points system. When I was there I just kept my shit together and did the work. Otherwise I think they'd have excluded me for all my absences, but that only happened a couple of times and they always took me back.

I'm going to stop this letter now because I have to be somewhere, but I'll give it to Dan the next time he comes so he can "clean it up," as he puts it.

Before he leaves I'll ask him how you are, and I expect he'll tell me, and then I'll wish I hadn't brought it up. It always goes like that, but I can't just say nothing, can I, not when I'm doing this for you even if it never ends up getting to you.

# CHAPTER NINE

As Claudia drove up to Westleigh Heights, following the directions Andee had texted her, she was doing her best to spot any "For Sale" signs outside the properties she passed. This was one of the areas where she, her mother, and Jasmine had agreed they'd like to settle, on the edge of town, close to the moor, and overlooking the bay. However, homes here didn't come up often and there didn't seem to be anything new to the market today.

Finally reaching the billboard she'd been told to look out for announcing an exclusive development of eight detached residences each with half an acre of land, she indicated to turn in. Fifty meters or so along a wide dirt track pitted with puddles and potholes she arrived at what she presumed to be the unfinished show home. Its style was mock Tudor, not exactly to her taste, but it was certainly striking and would probably turn out to be quite impressive on completion.

As she parked alongside a sleek black Mercedes, a tall, dark-haired woman in a padded raincoat and welly boots appeared from around the side of the house and waved a greeting.

Waving back, Claudia ran to the boot of her car, gathered up her heavy fabric-sample books and the holdall containing the tools of her trade, and ran through the wind and drizzle to where the woman was now waiting at the unvarnished front door.

"Hi, you must be Claudia." She smiled warmly. "I'm Andee. Lovely to meet you."

Immediately arrested by the unusual blue eyes, Claudia felt a swell of gratitude toward the woman as she shook her hand. "I hope you haven't been waiting long." She grimaced. "I got caught up on the coast road, I'm afraid."

"Roadworks, I know, but don't worry, I have plenty to do here to keep me occupied. Let's go in out of this gale. It's still pretty much a shell, as you'll see, but at least the main structure is complete and the windows are in. Kitchen not finished, I'm afraid, so I can't offer you tea or coffee, and plumbing not connected either, so if you need to spend a penny you'll have to go behind a hedge or along the lane to the Portaloos."

"Where are the builders?" Claudia asked, taking in the spacious entrance hall with black and white checkered floor tiles, ungrouted, freshly plastered walls, and large oak staircase. "Everywhere seems so quiet, and didn't I read on the sign that completion is due by Christmas?"

Andee groaned as she went through an open set of double doors into a substantial room with a granite fireplace at its center, built-in bookshelves, two large smeary windows at one end and double French doors at the other. "They've just been fired," she explained. "They only got the job because the firm the developer normally uses was tied up elsewhere. Fortunately, the builder of choice has unexpectedly come free, so he and his team are starting tomorrow, which gives us a fighting chance of completing by early spring." She held up two fingers, firmly crossed. "Late, but not as bad as it might have been."

Claudia smiled and stooped to set down her bag and books. "Are they all sold?" she asked, not sure whether she was interested, but there was no harm in finding out.

"I know that six have deposits on them," Andee replied, "but there are two left on the south side, closest to the moor, and frankly they're going to be dark."

Claudia wrinkled her nose. They certainly didn't want a dark house.

"Are you looking?" Andee asked. "Because if you are there's a gorgeous old Georgian coach house that's just come on the market. It belongs to the original Haylesbury estate. We're on the Haylesbury estate here, by the way. It's in serious need of renovation, but the structure seems pretty sound. Would that sort of thing interest you?"

Claudia's heart had already tripped with excitement. "Absolutely," she confirmed. "It's a dream of mine, bringing an old Georgian property back to life."

"Then I think you're going to love this one. It's mostly single-story, for the carriages to drive in and out of once upon a time, with a clock tower at the center and beautiful arched windows along the front of each wing. We can take a look at it after, if you like. It's not accessible from this plot; we'll have to go back to the main road and in through the old estate gates about a hundred yards farther on. The manor burned down about ten years ago and was never rebuilt, so there are just open fields behind it that lead onto the moor." Picking up a laptop from the small trestle table she was using as a desk, Andee said, "I've got some photographs of it here somewhere, but before we get to it we probably ought to focus on this place. I can show you the sort of thing I have in mind because the developer wants it to be similar to another show home we did together last year. Which isn't to say I'm not open to new ideas, if you have any."

"Is the developer someone you work with often?" Claudia asked, taking out her iPad ready to present her own portfolio.

"And also live with." Andee's smile was so infectious it made Claudia break into one of her own.

As they swapped devices Claudia said chattily, "Are you from this area?"

"Indeed I am. Graeme, my partner, isn't, but he's been here so long he might as well be. And you?"

Claudia felt herself flush. Although she'd expected to be asked about her life before Kesterly-on-Sea, she already didn't want to deceive this woman. "Oh, I—I'm from London," she said awkwardly, and opening up Andee's show-home file on the laptop she began to scrutinize what had been done before.

Minutes later she was feeling almost childishly proud as Andee swiped through the shots of her work on the iPad, murmuring words like, "Wow," "Amazing," "Stunning," and "So original."

Realizing she might be appearing too interested in her own designs, Claudia continued scrolling through Andee's photographs, but she hadn't gotten far before Andee said, "Put that down. What you have here is so much more . . . sophisticated, different, but please don't ever tell Cassie I said that. She's who usually does the drapes and soft furnishings for me. She's gone to take care of her invalided father, by the way, and isn't expecting to be back anytime soon. Did you do all the cushions and throws in these shots?"

Claudia nodded.

"And the bedspreads?"

Claudia nodded again. "Making things is my passion," she said, trying to sound modest, but not sure she'd succeeded.

Andee swiped through the presentation again. "You have an incredible eye for color and detail," she commented admiringly, "and presumably a thriving business—unless all these pictures were taken in your own home."

Claudia laughed as a flutter of nerves went through her. "No, they're from clients' homes," she replied, "or past clients." She couldn't think what to add to that apart from, "I'm glad you like what you've seen."

"I love it, and if you're interested in the commission we need to start talking dates, styles, fabrics, pricing . . . You mentioned on the phone that you haven't built up a team of workers yet, but there's a good chance you can take over Cassie's. Do you have someone to do the installations?"

"I don't," Claudia admitted, "but if . . ."

"Not to worry, I can help with that. Now, if you take a look at the show home on my laptop you'll see the furniture that we'll be bringing here. The colors have come out reasonably well, but it's probably best if we visit it in storage so you can be certain of shade. Before that though, we should discuss style. So, over to you. Can you talk me through how you see these windows and French doors being dressed?"

In her element now, Claudia began to describe her ideas, illustrating them with examples of drapes she'd made before, suggesting modifications here and there, varying lengths and swags, pleats, tucks, linings, and waterfalls, always careful to gauge Andee's responses before continuing.

Two hours later, having been into every one of the six downstairs rooms and all five upstairs, with Claudia taking photographs, making sketches, and explaining her vision, they were back in the hall and laughing at how fast the time had flown.

"I think we're going to work very well together," Andee announced, clearly as pleased with their new partnership as Claudia was, "especially if you can pull most of it off inside a month. Obviously you'll need plenty of backup for that, so I'll make some calls from the car on my way home to pave the way for you."

Claudia said, "Thank you, and I'll try to email over estimates of cost by tomorrow. If I think I'm going to have any problems sourcing the fabrics we've discussed I'll let you know right away."

"Excellent. And thanks so much for coming today. I finally feel as though everything's going to be possible again."

Thrilled, Claudia tucked away her measuring tapes and camera and heard herself saying rashly, "I'd really like to see the coach house before we go?"

"Of course, I'm glad you reminded me. If I'd known I'd have brought the keys with me, but you'll get a pretty good idea of it from the exterior and if you don't fall in love with it on sight I'll have to review my already high opinion of you."

It took all of three minutes to drive back down the lane and along the road to where a set of dilapidated gates was wide open and partially unhinged. Claudia drove in behind Andee and followed the Mercedes along a short track with one simple curve, and although the rain was coming down heavily now nothing, absolutely nothing could detract from the charm of the house they saw before them as they pulled up. It was just as Andee had described it, with a central clock tower, and two single-story wings on either side of it, each with three huge arched windows that had clearly once been carriage doors. Apart from its perfect symmetry and the exquisite limestone facade (badly stained and cracked, but repairable), its character seemed so alive and welcoming that Claudia was ready to believe it was waking up just for her.

Her passenger door opened and Andee jumped in, quickly closing it behind her. "What do you think?" she asked eagerly.

Claudia couldn't tear her eyes away. "I already love it," she murmured, gazing at the weather-beaten front door with a broken transom above it and crumbling pillars holding up a storm-damaged porch. "I'm going to take a closer look, if that's OK?"

"Be my guest. In fact, I'll come with you."

Pulling up their hoods they picked a path through what must have once been a carriage turning space, now cracked and weed-strewn, and went to peer in through the arched windows to the left of the front door. Claudia's heart instantly swelled at the sight of a huge, old-fashioned kitchen swathed in grime and cobwebs, with a boarded-up window on the far side above a grimy butler's sink, and barred French doors leading to the backyard. It had so much potential that she simply couldn't stop her imagination from flying.

"Something else, isn't it?" Andee commented.

"It certainly is," Claudia agreed.

Through the arched windows to the right of the main door was a large rectangular room with a high corniced ceiling, an eyesore of a tiled fireplace, an upturned chair and rags on the dusty floorboards, and a staircase in one corner.

Not caring about getting wet anymore, Claudia stood back to look up at the tower. "Are there rooms up there?" she asked.

"Two quite big ones," Andee replied. "And there are more either side of these main wings—you see the smaller windows? I'm guessing the old coach master lived at one end and probably other staff were housed at the opposite end. More recently they've been converted into bedrooms, but they can be anything you want them to be."

Rain was running down Claudia's face as she shook her head in wonder, taking in the sheer elegance of the place in its secluded setting of old trees and ragged bushes. "I don't have to go inside or around the back to know that this is perfect for us," she declared.

Andee quickly took out her phone. "I should have done this before," she muttered. "I need to check with Graeme that it's still available."

Claudia stiffened with horror. It hadn't occurred to her that it might not be, but moments later Andee was smiling again as she gave the thumbs-up and Claudia unraveled with relief.

"I expect you'd like to know the price?" Andee suggested as she rang off.

Claudia was ready to pay anything.

"They want five hundred and fifty thousand, but I reckon you could probably get it for five. And being realistic, you'll probably need about the same to fix it up."

"It's not a problem," Claudia assured her. "We can make an offer right away, although I probably ought to let my mother and daughter see it first."

Clearly delighted, Andee said, "Let me know when they can make it and we'll come again with the keys."

As they returned to their cars Claudia said, rashly, "We're thinking of having a little celebration later, to mark my first commission since arriving here—I mean, if I get it . . ."

"You've got it . . ."

". . . So I was wondering if you might like to join us?"

Andee's eyes lit up. "I'd love to," she said warmly. "Just tell me where and when."

Surprised and thrilled, Claudia said, "Does seven work for you? We're in an apartment at the station end of the Promenade. I'll text the address. I thought I'd ask Leanne if she can make it too. After all, it's thanks to her that this has come about."

"I'm sure she'd love to come if she's free."

After thanking Andee again, Claudia got into her car, but didn't immediately drive away. She wanted to look at the house a while longer and continue to feel the sense of connection that had come over her the minute she'd laid eyes on it. She couldn't remember the last time anything had felt so right in her life, and because the draw was so powerful she wanted to hold on to it for as long as she could.

In the end, after feeling certain that Joel had been watching it with her, she said a silent au revoir and turned the car around to begin the drive home. She needed to call her mother to let her know that their little celebration was on, and she should text Leanne to invite her to join them. Already she was imagining champagne glasses sparkling, corks popping, friends toasting one another, and realizing how widely she was smiling, she broke into a happy laugh.

# CHAPTER TEN

thought we were going to the cinema," Graeme protested when Andee informed him of the evening's change of plan.

"We can go tomorrow," she promised, planting a kiss on his cheek as she passed him to get to the fridge with the groceries she'd brought in. "She's a godsend, she really is. So talented and *available* and definitely very keen to buy the coach house. She's interesting too, because I Googled her after I left the Heights and the only Claudia Winters that came up were definitely not her."

He raised his eyebrows. "Why on earth did you Google her?"

She shrugged. "It's the kind of thing I do, you know that."

Of course he did. "And what are you deducing from your lack of findings?" he inquired with mock seriousness, taking the avocados she was passing and putting them in the fruit bowl.

Rolling her eyes at him, she said, "She's definitely a professional. I saw her sketching and the way she articulated her ideas could only be done by an expert. So, what I'm *deducing* is that for some reason she's changed her name—maybe to break with her old life." She turned to face him and wasn't surprised to find him regarding her with the expression he usually adopted when attempting to keep up with the way her mind worked.

"So now you're thinking what?" he asked, amused. "That she's in witness protection or something?"

With a smile she pulled a box of muesli from the bag to put aside for the pantry. "No, of course not," she replied, before adding—not able to help herself—"When the Protected Persons Service—that's its official title, by the way—sets someone up with a new identity they provide social media profiles, pages on search engines leading to past history, all sorts of stuff to give them cover. And Claudia doesn't have any of that." Her eyes narrowed thoughtfully as a few scenarios played out in her mind, but they were cut short by her mobile jingling the arrival of a text. It was from Leanne.

*See you at Claudia's. So glad she's able to help. Xx*

Replying with *I owe you*, Andee put the phone down and turned back to Graeme. He was checking his own phone now, scrolling through emails, deleting as he went or thumbing off quick replies, and as she watched him, she found herself feeling sorry there was so little time before she had to go out.

Looking up as she removed the mobile from his grasp and slipped her arms around his neck, Graeme drew her in close and murmured, "To what do I owe this pleasure?"

"It's just for being you," she replied, gazing suggestively into his eyes.

"So, I'm getting something right?"

"You always do, or almost always. Did you see Tom today, by any chance?"

"I didn't."

"Then he hasn't told you that he's asked Leanne to marry him?"

His eyebrows rose. "No, but I think we saw that coming, didn't we?"

She nodded and after a moment said, "Can you do me a huge favor and *not* ask me? Just in case you were thinking of it, which you probably weren't, but we're OK as we are, aren't we?"

His eyes moved curiously between hers. "If you say so," he replied carefully.

She frowned. "Not quite the answer I was expecting."

He smiled and kissed her. "You know," he said, taking back his phone, "I think I'll give Dan a call to see if he's free for a bite, seeing as you're now otherwise engaged."

# CHAPTER ELEVEN

OK, so I need to give you a heads-up on everyone who's coming tonight," Jasmine declared as she slotted her neatly cased surfboard into a hall cupboard—this being one of her several new hobbies she'd taken up during the five months since settling here. "You know that Abby's mum, Leanne, has a partner called Tom who owns the Tramonto Hotel on Kesterly Heights. Abby's grandma is called Wilkie and she's a blast, completely eccentric, and you'll love her on sight, if she comes. Abby's dad died, which is something else us two have in common besides all the other stuff, and the local theater is named after him, the Delaney. Oh, and she has a half sister who lives in the States called Kate." She frowned irritably. "Is anyone listening to me?"

"Of course," Claudia and Marcy answered in unison. They were in the kitchen laying out the canapés Marcy had picked up from M&S on her way back from the community center, while Claudia had rushed home to make sure there was champagne in the fridge and the flat was presentable.

"Good, so who's Leanne's partner?" Jasmine tested.

"Tom," Claudia replied. "Now tell us what you know about Andee Lawrence."

"Absolutely nothing." Jasmine smiled sweetly, and taking the pile of hand-embroidered napkins she was being offered she began to fold them into the shapes her mother preferred.

"Actually, I can tell you something," Marcy offered. "I mean besides the fact that she's an interior designer. Apparently, she used to be a detective and is who everyone goes to if they're in any kind of trouble."

Slightly thrown by that, Claudia turned to look at her. "A detective?" she echoed.

"That's right," Marcy replied distractedly. "Henry said she gave it up a few years ago and—"

"Who's Henry?" Claudia interrupted.

"Oh, just someone I know at the community center."

Jasmine said, "Have you still not told her about him, Nana? I thought you had."

As Claudia's eyes widened Marcy became defensive. "There's nothing to tell," she retorted. "He's just a friend."

"But you've got a thing for him. You told me that yourself."

"I didn't say a *thing*, I said he's an interesting man, that's all."

As she listened to them squabble and tease Claudia realized that her suspicions earlier were correct: this was why her mother always made such an effort when she went out. "Well," she commented loudly, "I thought if any one of us was going to come home with a boyfriend it would have been Jasmine . . ."

"He's not a *boyfriend*," Marcy interrupted. "In fact, I've never been alone with him, apart from for a few minutes here and there. However, it seems that now might be as good a time as any to tell you that in the event he does get around to asking me out, I will probably say yes."

Claudia watched Jasmine bounce into her grandmother's arms, as thrilled as if she had a potential date lined up herself.

Marcy regarded her daughter curiously. "Would you rather I didn't go?" she asked over Jasmine's shoulder.

Jasmine spun around. "Don't you dare say no," she warned her mother.

"I wasn't going to," Claudia protested. "It's not up to me, and actually I think it's . . . wonderful. I'm just asking myself. . . . I mean, are you going to be interested in this new house if you've got other plans?"

"For heaven's sake," Marcy exclaimed. "Talk about getting things out of perspective. I want to see the house *and* if it's right for us, I want to live in it."

"Excuse me, what house?" Jasmine demanded. "No one's mentioned anything to me about a house."

"I saw it today," Claudia explained. "It's on Westleigh Heights: as far as I'm concerned it's a dream home—or it will be—and I can hardly wait for you to see it." She turned back to her mother, determined to hide how crushed she'd feel if Marcy answered her next question with a no. "Are you sure you want to live with us? You're used to your independence . . ."

"And you're going to rob me of it? Don't be silly. Of course I want us to be together. It's what we planned and it's what we'll do. Now, how many glasses are we going to need, and someone should fill up the ice bucket because our guests will be here any minute."

Andee and Leanne arrived promptly at seven, bringing Abby with them, and in what seemed no time at all Claudia was opening a second bottle of Moët while the guests ate canapés and lounged on the sofas as if this was somewhere they came all the time. There was an easy flow of conversation right from the start and virtually no awkward moments, apart from Claudia's embarrassment when Andee and Leanne lavished praise on her various handicrafts.

"She makes everything," Jasmine stated proudly, "candles, diffusers, lamps, soap, photo frames. She even did some of the paintings . . ."

"OK," Claudia said softly, "I think that's enough."

*Look how pathetic you are, lapping it up as if the junk you make is something special. Get a grip, you're embarrassing yourself.*

Claudia shook Marcus's vicious words off with a shiver and forced herself to reconnect with the real conversation.

"You've transformed this place," Andee was commenting admiringly. "I came to view it for Dan, a friend of Graeme's, about a year ago and it was nothing like this then. He decided it was too big for him, but it seems just right for you."

"It's a great spot," Leanne agreed, "but isn't the noise a problem?"

With a sigh, Marcy said, "It was worse during the summer when the windows were open, so many parties and concerts on the beach . . ."

"Which were totally cool," Jasmine put in quickly, "you even came to some of them."

"It was a Beatles night," Marcy explained, "so we all went. And actually, it wasn't the music that bothered us so much as all the shouting and swearing when the bars turned out. It still happens, but at least the windows are closed now."

"Do you get people parking in your space in front of the building?" Andee asked sympathetically.

"All the time," Claudia groaned, "which is another reason we'll be glad to move."

"Are you thinking of it?" Leanne asked, helping herself to another canapé.

"You should come and live nearer us," Abby informed Jasmine.

"Actually, we might," Claudia told her, and aware of Abby's and Leanne's interest piquing, she felt a little thrill of excitement as she said to Andee, "We'd like to view the coach house as soon as possible."

"What coach house?" Abby demanded, looking from her to Jasmine and back again.

"It's on Westleigh Heights," Jasmine replied, "so if we do move there we'll be about ten minutes from you and I'm definitely going to need a car."

"Then you'd better work on passing your test," Marcy reminded her.

"Give me a chance, I've only had three lessons."

Accepting a top-up of champagne from Claudia, Andee said, "Let me know when the three of you are available and provided the others feel the same way you do, we'll set everything in motion."

"Thank you," Claudia said warmly. "And don't worry, I'll be putting in orders for fabrics first thing tomorrow before I go to meet Cassie's team. So, your commission remains my priority."

"I'm not worried," Andee assured her, and looking into Claudia's eyes she added, "and you shouldn't be either."

It wasn't until everyone had left that Claudia was able to say to her mother, "I think Andee knows something about us, or at least suspects it."

Marcy frowned. "Like what?"

"I don't know, I'm not sure."

"You're just paranoid," Jasmine told her, carrying dishes through to the kitchen. "If you ask me, I think our little party went really well."

"I'd agree with that," Marcy responded, "although it seemed a bit odd that no one asked where we're from, or what we were doing before we came here."

"They know what Mum was doing," Jasmine pointed out.

Marcy nodded pensively. "What do you tell Abby about your past?" she asked.

Jasmine shrugged. "Just that I was at school in London, and that my dad died when I was nine. Oh, and that Mum had a design shop.

Other than that, it never really comes up. We're kind of into other things, like studying, surfing, hanging out with friends, and in my case violin lessons, practice, and rehearsals."

"So busy," Claudia commented dryly.

"Tell me about it, and now you're going to be as well. This is just the best thing for you, Mum, a new commission, a new house by the looks of it, so please don't start getting all suspicious about things. Andee seems really nice, so whatever she said, I'm sure she didn't mean anything bad by it."

Finding herself able to believe that, Claudia smiled as she let go of some tension. "I guess I'm out of practice when it comes to making friends," she sighed, and banishing the dark memories of Marcus that inevitably came to her mind, she added, "Time I learned to start trusting again."

Outside on the Promenade Leanne and Andee were following Abby to the taxi rank, slowing their pace so as not to be overheard. "OK," Leanne said, keeping her voice down, "are you going to tell me now why you didn't want me to ask about their lives before they came here?"

Judging Abby to be sufficiently engrossed in her phone, Andee said, "I'm pretty sure they're not who they're saying they are."

Leanne came to a standstill, eyes wide with surprise. "What on earth makes you say that?"

"You saw for yourself how talented Claudia is, and she wasn't a bit fazed by the size of the order I've just put her way. This means she must have been in business before, and yet she doesn't have an Internet presence or history, and nor does her mother."

Leanne took a moment to process this. "So, who are they?" she asked, trying to get her head around it all.

Though Andee had a theory she decided to keep it to herself for now, and said, "I'm still working on it, but rest assured I don't think it's anything to worry about."

"Well, that's good, because Abby's pretty tight with Jasmine, and I found myself warming to Claudia tonight. And her mother's a delight."

"Isn't she?"

"Actually," Leanne said as they started to walk on, "I'm thinking of inviting them to the little engagement party we're throwing the Saturday after next. I take it you and Graeme are free?"

"We'll make sure of it, and yes, do invite them. I think it would mean a lot to them, especially Claudia. Who else is on the list?"

"Family mostly, but I was wondering about asking Dan. Do you think he'll come? He gets on very well with Tom."

"I'm sure he will. I'm seeing him tomorrow for one of our RJ meetings. Would you like me to ask him?"

"No, I'll do it myself, but perhaps you could assure him that we're not trying to pair him off with Claudia, because that's exactly what he'll think when we introduce them."

Andee frowned. "Aren't we?" she countered dryly.

Leanne laughed. "I could say yes, but do we really want him to get involved with someone who might not be who she says she is, and who, for all we know, could take off again at any minute?"

"No," Andee replied seriously, "we definitely don't want to do that. And please, please don't let her take off before the show home is done."

# CHAPTER TWELVE

So, here's a conversation I had today with Dan:

"How are you doing, Archie?"

"How do you think?"

"Tell me."

"I'm crap. How else would you expect me to be?"

"I was hoping you might feel ready for more honesty about your mother."

"I haven't told any lies about her."

"You haven't told the entire truth either."

It frigging gets me, the way he manages to know stuff he shouldn't. "Why do you want to know more about her? She's got nothing to do with any of this."

"She thinks she has."

"You've talked to her?"

"Of course."

"I could get really mad about that, Dan."

"Why?"

"Because I told you, she's got nothing to do with this. No one has. It's just me. I'm the one who did it, right? That's why I'm in here."

He doesn't say anything after that, and it really starts getting to me, like he knows I want to speak, but I don't. Or not about my ma, anyway, so I end up suggesting we change the subject, and he predictably says, "To what?"

"Anything you like. I know, let's talk about you. What

makes you do this stuff with people like me? I suppose you think you're some sort of Samaritan or something."

He laughs at that and I laugh too, though God knows why because it wasn't funny. "Do you have a mother?" I ask him.

"No. She died a few years ago."

"What about your father?"

"I lost him when I was sixteen."

"Mm, tough. Did you like him?"

"Very much. Do you like yours?"

"Give me a break. I don't even know who he is."

"Then who's BJ?"

Some of his questions set my teeth on edge and make my fists clench. "He was my handler, you know that, and he's definitely not my old man."

"How did your mother come to know him?"

I go silent, and he's the first to break it.

"You know you could end up in prison for a very long time. Is that what you want?"

"Makes no difference to me."

"Why do you say that when we both know it isn't true?"

I just shrug.

"What are you hiding, Archie? I know there's something, so why don't you tell me what it is?"

"I'm protecting my ma, right?" I nearly shout at him. "If I tell you anything they'll go after her and it won't be pretty. Is that what you want?"

He doesn't say anything, but we both know it's not what he wants. "Who are we talking about, Archie?"

I don't answer, but I don't think he expects me to.

"Wouldn't it be better for your mother if you told the truth?" he asks.

"I already have," I remind him. "I wouldn't be here if I hadn't."

"I mean the whole truth."

"You've got it."

He shakes his head and I can see how disappointed he is in me. Join the club, Dan. Membership's free.

In my head I'm thinking about you and what difference it would make to you if I said any more—and the answer is, it's too late, it wouldn't change anything, so what's the point?

I committed the crime, so I do the time.

He left just after that and I was so mad and scared and all kinds of other shit that I decided to sit down and write you what happened, like as if you're ever going to see this, or even care.

Don't worry, I'm not seeing you as some kind of friend I can run off my mouth to, or anything like that. I get how sick it would make you feel if I did. I guess it's just easier to write down how afraid I am that he won't come back than it is to tell him.

# CHAPTER THIRTEEN

The past two weeks had been so hectic—and challenging—that there were times when Claudia had seriously questioned her sanity for taking on such an order without her tried-and-trusted team around her. However, Cassie's workers were proving to be every bit as skillful and committed as any Claudia had worked with— and were probably already friends for life since learning they were going to be paid almost double their usual rate if they managed to bring things in on time. Why not? She didn't need the money, what she needed was the distraction and adrenaline rush, the sense of reconnecting with who she really was, and a new place to belong, which was already starting to happen.

Virtually overnight the living space of the flat had turned into one big workroom with sewing machines at each end of the dining table, two computers in the middle, bolts of fabric cluttering the sofas, and curtain poles turning the floor into an obstacle course. Since the original discussions with Andee many changes had been made to the order regarding length, style, even color, all with Andee's approval, largely due to delivery times—or because Claudia had come up with what she hoped might be an even better design.

During this coordinated chaos Graeme, Andee's partner, had taken her, her mother, and Jasmine to view the coach house, and to her relief they'd also fallen in love with it on sight. By the end of that day Graeme had accepted their offer, and since no mortgage was involved there was a good chance it would be theirs by the end of the month. In excited anticipation of this, Marcy was already driving about the countryside visiting antique markets and reclamation yards in search of original Georgian features such as cornicing, shutters, even pilasters. After photographing them she'd relay the shots to Claudia for a decision on whether or not to buy.

It was a whirlwind of activity on every level, and with the show home scheduled for completion in less than two weeks Claudia could feel the pressure building.

However, this evening, in spite of needing to catch up on some sleep, she'd happily set everything aside for a few hours so that she, her mother, and Jasmine could go to a party at Leanne's. They'd been thrilled to receive the invitation, especially when they'd discovered that it was to celebrate Tom and Leanne's engagement.

"We must get a card and take a gift," she'd informed her mother as soon as they'd agreed they would go.

"But we hardly know them, what on earth would we get?" Marcy cried.

"That's easy," Jasmine piped up. "We can wrap a selection of Mum's special scented bags. You know, the ones that go in drawers and cupboards. Everyone always likes them."

With that agreed they only had to decide what to wear, which was something Claudia didn't give much thought to until she got out of the shower on the evening of the party and stood, wrapped in a towel, staring into her closet.

"Well, you can't go like that," Jasmine informed her as she passed the open door. "Are you in need of some help?"

Claudia was, and more than Jasmine realized, because wrenching her mind from the anxiety she used to feel before nights out with Marcus was making it hard to move.

*Do your best to look glamorous. I know it's hard, but don't let me down.*

Seeming to sense what was happening, Jasmine rapidly sprang into action, and less than twenty minutes later Claudia was standing in front of her cheval mirror amazed by the transformation her daughter had achieved. She was now wearing a knee-length black lace dress with long gauzy sleeves and discreet V back, suede pumps with three-inch heels, and the diamond earrings Joel had given her as a wedding present. She'd been in jeans and baggy tops for so many months now that it was like looking at a stranger, especially with the way Jasmine had styled her hair. She'd caught it up in an artful French roll at the back, held in place by a million grips and a single crystal-studded chopstick, while at the front several loose strands fell to each side of her face, creating an effect that was both casual and classy.

"You look sensational," Jasmine declared, admiring her own handiwork in the mirror. "You know your neck is one of your best features, and with your hair like this it shows off how lovely and slender it is."

Claudia smiled. "Dad always liked my neck," she said, thinking of the way Joel would run his fingers over it and kiss it and tell her how beautiful she was.

Jasmine smiled, but then saw her mother's expression suddenly change. "What is it?" she asked.

Claudia was trapped in another awful moment and couldn't seem to escape it. Marcus's thick hands circling her neck and squeezing . . .

"You're thinking about him," Jasmine stated, her eyes darkening with worry. "I can tell."

Claudia shook herself quickly. "It's OK, it's gone," she assured her, pushing the memory back into the shadows.

Jasmine was still concerned, so Claudia smiled. "Really it has," she promised, "and you've completely transformed me from a dull old mumsie sewing bee into a . . ." She couldn't think how to describe herself without sounding immodest.

"Into a sophisticated and alluring businesswoman who's totally going to be the belle of the ball," Jasmine finished for her.

As they laughed and hugged Marcy came into the room, and both Claudia's and Jasmine's eyes rounded with surprise and approval.

"Wow, Nana," Jasmine murmured. "You look amazing too. I don't think I've seen that before."

"You haven't," Marcy admitted, and twirled to show off her new navy silk jersey jumpsuit with frivolous bell cuffs and slightly risqué V-neck. "And you, Claudia, look so lovely I could look at you all night, but I think we should be going or we'll be late."

"Excuse me," Jasmine protested as they started for the door, "isn't anyone going to say that I look amazing too?"

Laughing, Claudia said, "You look *so* lovely that I'd like a photo of you before we go."

Obligingly, Jasmine struck a pose in the cluttered sitting room, one hand on her hip, the other reaching above her to offer the best view of her slinky, cold-shoulder sweater, ripped-knee leggings, and block-heel ankle boots.

Half an hour later they were driving over the cattle grid that marked the entrance to Ash Morley Farm, where the ramble of old buildings had been converted into dwellings. Leanne, Tom, and Abby lived in the converted barn, Wilkie, Leanne's mother, was in the old farmhouse, and Klaudia, the pretty Polish lady who worked at the shop with Leanne, occupied the stables with her two young children. The place was a rural idyll, so characterful and welcoming that Claudia could only wonder now why she'd always been in such a hurry to drop Jasmine off and leave.

*"Please excuse us for being late. You wouldn't believe how long it's*

*taken my wife to get ready this evening. Or looking at her, maybe you would.*" A typical put-down from Marcus, humorous, teasing, even affectionately delivered, but the cruelty was always there.

Bringing the car to a stop next to Andee's Mercedes, Claudia took a brief moment to steel herself against any more unwelcome voices, and unfastened her seat belt.

As they approached the barn Abby came bursting out to greet them, looking almost Goth-like in the moonlight with her recently dyed black hair and kohl-rimmed eyes. "Everyone's here already," she told them, "but don't worry, Grandma can't find her glasses and nothing can happen until she has them."

"Claudia, Marcy," Leanne cried warmly as they entered a large, rustic kitchen that turned out to be the first third of an enormous vaulted living space. Bifold doors were spaced all along one wall and an impressive fireplace was at the far end with lively flames at its heart. "I'm so glad you came. Here, let Abby take your coats and I'll introduce you to Tom."

A tall, striking man of around fifty was already coming toward them, holding out a hand to shake first with Marcy, then with Claudia. "You must be Marcy and Claudia. I'm Tom, Leanne's partner— I've heard a lot about you," he told them. "All good, of course."

Remembering what she'd heard about him, that he'd once been a spy, Claudia returned the friendliness of his smile as she said, "It's so kind of you to invite us this evening. We feel very honored to be part of such a special celebration."

*You're only here because they feel sorry for you. Don't initiate a conversation unless someone else does. You're boring, so just listen.*

"We're honored you could make it, especially given how hard I hear Andee is working you at the moment," Tom commented wryly.

"Sounds like Andee," a young man in his mid-twenties piped

up as he stepped forward to be introduced. "I'm Richie, Tom's son. Good to meet you both."

"He's running the local paper," Tom informed them, "so if you're interested in advertising your business, Claudia, I'm sure he'll give you a good rate."

"Which I would have offered myself," Richie stated, casting a meaningful look at his father, "but hey, I've spent a lifetime with him stealing my thunder, so why would it be any different now?"

Tom grinned. "Come on," he said, taking Claudia's and Marcy's arms, "let's introduce you to some more important people."

"You'll pay for that," Richie warned as they walked away.

As they merged into the room full of other guests, an older man with neat silver hair and small glasses came forward to draw Marcy into an affectionate embrace. "You look a treat," he told her softly, although loud enough for Claudia to hear.

"You don't look so bad yourself," Marcy replied flirtatiously. "Very dapper, in fact."

Apparently thrilled with the compliment, he turned his merry eyes to Claudia.

"This is my daughter, Claudia," Marcy came in quickly, "and my granddaughter . . . Jasmine? Where's Jasmine?" she asked, looking around.

"Gone with Abby to hang the coats," Claudia informed her as Tom was called back to the kitchen. Her eyes returned to the man who was reaching for one of her hands with both of his.

"Henry Matthews," he said, with such an amiable smile it was impossible not to respond with one of her own. "I'm very glad to meet you, Claudia. I'm not sure if it's appropriate to comment on how you look too, but if it is, may I say stunning?"

With a quick look at her mother, Claudia said, "I think I can live with that. It's lovely to meet you, Henry. Mum's told us about you, and I . . ."

"I haven't told them much," Marcy interrupted hastily. "Henry and I are just friends," she informed Claudia, making herself blush and Henry twinkle with amusement. "We belong to a few of the same groups at the community center."

"And I've been promised the great pleasure of teaching your mother to play golf once the weather improves," Henry added.

Golf? Her mother hated golf.

Stifling a laugh, Claudia moved on to where Andee and Graeme were in animated conversation with another couple, but just before she reached them a voice in her head said, *Don't you know better than to interrupt people?*

She hesitated, but Andee had already spotted her and came to greet her. "You look lovely," she said softly. "Quite a change to this afternoon."

Claudia laughed at the tease. "Same goes for you," she countered.

Clearly enjoying the banter, Andee drew her into the small group, saying, "Graeme you already know, and this is Klaudia—same name, different pronunciation."

"We've met before," the slight, pretty woman with silky blond hair and almost childlike blue eyes reminded her, while taking her hand. "In Glory Days, the vintage shop in town?"

"Indeed." Claudia smiled, recognizing her. "It's lovely to see you again."

"And this is Dan Collier," Andee continued, "who's also a newcomer in town, relatively speaking. How long have you been here now, Dan?"

"Ten months," he replied, and as his eyes met hers Claudia quickly looked away, though she wasn't sure why. He didn't seem threatening in any way, or resemble anyone she knew, but there was something about him . . .

"Dan took over Henry's law practice when Henry retired," Andee explained, "and I expect you've heard me mention him once or twice, because of our Restorative Justice program."

"Only once or twice?" Dan objected. "I thought I might warrant a full onslaught of gushing given how marvelously we're doing."

Laughing, Andee gave him a playful nudge and turned around as Graeme said, "Wilkie's found her glasses."

"Thank God," Andee murmured. "I'm dying for a drink."

"Hello, everyone," a diminutive, hippyish-looking woman of around seventy called out from the chair she was standing on. She glanced behind her, spotted Tom close by, and said, "Oh good, you're there."

"She gets overexcited sometimes," Andee whispered to Claudia, "so he's ready to catch her in case she flings herself off."

Claudia laughed with everyone else as Wilkie took the glass of champagne Abby was passing her and waited until everyone else was holding one before crying out joyfully, "It gives me the greatest happiness to toast Tom and Leanne. May all your blessings be small and problems big . . ."

"Grandma!" Abby shouted.

Wilkie looked startled.

"Big blessings, small problems?" Abby said through her teeth.

Wilkie blinked. "Did I get it wrong? Oh goodness, well, you know what I meant, absolutely big blessings . . ."

Laughing, Tom stepped forward and circling an arm around Wilkie's waist he turned to Leanne and said, "To my beautiful fiancée, thank you for agreeing to be my wife."

As the room chorused, "To Tom and Leanne," Claudia noticed

her mother clinking glasses with Henry and laughing at something he murmured in her ear.

"So how long have you been in Kesterly?" she heard someone ask.

She turned to find Dan Collier beside her and looking, she thought, as relaxed as he sounded. Why, then, was she feeling so tense?

As she answered, "Almost six months," she turned to watch more champagne being passed around—anything to avoid his unsettling eyes, made bigger and somehow more knowing by the lenses of his glasses.

"And are you liking it?" he pressed.

"It's taken a little getting used to, but yes, on the whole. What about you?"

"It's OK. I still haven't found a proper place to live, but the flat over the office works pretty well. Where are you?"

"We're renting an apartment on the Promenade."

"Ah, yes, I believe Andee told me, and you're buying the old coach house on Westleigh Heights?"

She didn't want him to know that, but it was too late now—and why didn't she want him to know? She didn't seem to be handling herself well; she had to do better. "Have you seen it?" she asked, deliberately ignoring Jasmine's expressive eyebrows as she came to refill their glasses.

"I confess I have not, but I hear it's a gem. Thank you," he said as Jasmine poured. "I don't think we've been introduced, I'm Dan."

"I'm Jasmine," she replied with a winning smile. "Claudia's daughter."

"And my best friend," Abby called out from where she was topping up a small group of other guests.

As Dan was drawn into another conversation, Claudia looked around for her mother and spotted her still with Henry and apparently enjoying herself immensely. For almost as long as her father had been dead Claudia had hoped her mother would meet someone just as wonderful, kind, and humorous. Now, she just felt terrible for hoping that it wasn't happening.

"You're looking worried," Andee declared, coming to join her again. "Is everything OK?"

"Yes, it's fine," Claudia replied with a smile, "just thinking about what I have to do tomorrow—sorry, no work tonight."

"Exactly. Now, let me introduce you to everyone else."

The next hour passed swiftly and easily enough for Claudia finally to find herself starting to relax. The voices in her head and cruel memories had stopped, there were only these friendly people from all sorts of professions, trades, and callings and most of them around her age. In fact, probably thanks to the champagne, she was enjoying talking to Dan Collier again. She was no longer as unnerved by the way his eyes held hers as she spoke, never searching the room for someone more interesting to talk to. However, she knew he'd soon start asking about her past, so to prevent it she clumsily steered the conversation to the restorative justice program Andee had told her about.

"Ah, no, you're just being polite," he protested. "Unless Andee's been on your case about becoming a practitioner? Has she?"

"No, she hasn't, and I'm not sure I'd be right for it. I mean, the idea of it seems a good one, and if it works . . . Does it work?"

"In a lot of cases, yes."

"But not in all?"

"I guess it depends on what you term to be a success. If it helps a victim to overcome the trauma of what's happened to them, you'd have to agree that's a good thing. Does it erase what happened? No. So really it's about finding a way to unlock someone from a place of fear, or anger, injustice, revenge, so they can move on."

Absorbing that, she said, "But it's also about the person who committed the crime?"

"Absolutely. Understanding the impact of your actions, regretting them, and wanting to show remorse can put a perpetrator in a whole different place in his or her own mind, as well as in the mind of the person they've harmed."

Unable to imagine herself ever wanting to come face-to-face with Marcus again, much less wanting to hear the excuses for his cruelty, she asked, "How did you get into it?"

His eyes flickered away for a moment as he said, "My wife was a practitioner and she persuaded me to become one too." With a grim sort of smile he added, "That was back in a previous life, before I moved here."

Wondering where his wife was now, Claudia started to speak, but as though reading her mind he said, "She died, three years ago."

Sensing the devastation behind his words, Claudia's heart melted as she thought of Joel. "I'm so sorry. I really am. Was it unexpected?" she asked gently.

"A car accident. Ice on the road, an oncoming lorry . . . It wasn't anyone's fault . . ."

Realizing he was still grieving, she said, "So you moved here. To try and start again?"

He nodded. "I met Graeme at a reunion party, we got talking, and when he called a few months later to tell me there was a law practice coming up for sale here, I decided a change of scene might help."

"And has it?"

"In a way, yes. Now tell me more about you. Am I allowed to ask if you're married?"

Feeling her mouth turning dry, she said, "Jasmine's father died when she was ten."

"Gosh, I'm sorry to hear that. A really tough age to lose a parent."

"Yes, it was, not helped by the fact that my father died around the same time. So now we're just the three of us, me, Jasmine, and my mother."

He was about to say more when Jasmine weaved a happy path to her mother's side. "Hope I'm not interrupting," she hiccupped, "but I just wanted to say that Nana's bloke is totally cool. You need to meet him, Mum."

Claudia said smoothly, "I already have—does Nana know you're referring to him as her bloke?" She glanced at Dan and was relieved to see his amusement.

"Probably not," Jasmine admitted. "His name's Henry and apparently he used to own the law firm that you now run," she informed Dan.

"Isn't it a small world?" he said dryly.

"Tell me about it," and catching hold of her mother's arm she gave it a bruising squeeze. "I'm so glad we came tonight," she said. "Everyone's amazing and it's starting to feel like we've been here forever."

Fearing for how far she might go in her enthusiasm for the evening, Claudia said, "Could we have a quick word?"

"Of course," Jasmine cried ecstatically. To Dan she said, "She's about to tell me off for being drunk, so if you'll excuse us . . ."

"Good luck." He smiled, and saluting her with his glass, he turned to talk to someone else as Claudia took her daughter to the edge of the room.

"Please watch what you say," she whispered. "I know it's fun and you're having a good time, but . . ."

"It's all right, you can stop worrying. I won't have any more and I promise, I'm being very careful about what I say. So now tell me, do you fancy him? He's pretty ripped, and those glasses are kind of cute."

Claudia's heart contracted as she drew back in protest. "I was just chatting with him, nothing more, and actually I think it's probably time we made a move. We don't want to outstay our welcome."

"Like as if. Anyway, Abby's invited me to sleep over and I think I will."

"Not while you're like this. Please come home with me and Nana."

Jasmine's expression turned mutinous and Claudia experienced a bolt of unease.

"In case you've forgotten," Jasmine drawled, "I'm seventeen years old, so I can do what I like . . ."

"Don't let's argue about it . . ."

"I'm not, I'm just saying, we can't go on hiding ourselves away . . ."

"We're not hiding, but we do have . . ."

"I'm not listening to any more of this. We've done everything your way, to make *you* feel safe, well you're OK now so it's time we lived our lives like normal people."

A wave of panic was rising through Claudia, cutting off her breath, and her words. She tried to speak, but her throat was constricted and sweat was starting to bead on her skin.

Suddenly realizing what was happening, Jasmine grabbed her hands. "It's OK, you're fine," she murmured urgently. "I'm sorry, I didn't mean . . . Just breathe, in, out. That's it. And again. I'm coming home with you so you don't need to worry. Everything's fine."

Blowing out some air, Claudia shook her head. "It's passing," she said, certain it was. "Is anyone watching?"

"No. Shall I get you some water?"

"No. I just need to go home. You stay. You're right, I have to stop . . ."

"I'm coming with you. I can always sleep over another time. Best smile now, someone's coming our way."

It turned out to be a couple they'd met earlier wanting to say goodnight, and soon others started to drift away too.

"I'll get our coats," Jasmine said. "You go and round up Nana."

Claudia found her mother near the kitchen with Henry and two others whose names she'd forgotten. Seeing her coming, Marcy put down her empty glass and said, "There you are. Is everything all right?"

"Of course," Claudia assured her, "I just thought it was time we were going."

"OK, if you say so, but you seemed to be getting along so well with Dan the last time I looked . . . Where is he?" As she turned to search for him Claudia said quietly, "Mum, don't," and putting on a bright smile she thrust out a hand to shake Henry's. "It was lovely to meet you," she told him in her friendliest tone.

"My pleasure," he assured her, but she could see from the way he regarded her that he'd picked up on her misgivings. She didn't want to make him feel awkward, or worried, or in any way reluctant to be friends with her mother, but at the same time she didn't want him in their lives.

"So, what happened?" Marcy asked as they started the drive home. "And don't say nothing, because I can tell that it did."

"She freaked out," Jasmine said from the back seat. "Or she was on the brink of it, anyway."

Marcy glanced at Claudia in the darkness. "What brought it on?" she asked gently.

"I don't know. I just . . . It doesn't matter, it's over now." She didn't want to admit to hearing Marcus in her head, or to how badly Jasmine's small rebellion had thrown her. The last thing she wanted was her daughter feeling afraid to speak her mind. "Shall we change the subject and talk about what a lovely evening we had?" she suggested.

"Totally awesomazing," Jasmine yawned, "but seems I'm the only one in this car who's going home without a potential date in the next few days."

Marcy's eyebrows rose. "Are you going to see Dan again?" she asked Claudia.

"No!" Claudia replied snappishly. "Just because I was chatting to him doesn't mean we're starting something. What about you and Henry? When are you seeing him?"

"Probably on Tuesday at the community center."

"You live such wild lives, you two," Jasmine commented with another yawn.

They drove on in silence after that, with Claudia fighting back all the cutting things she wanted to say about Henry, and denials about Dan, and annoyance with Jasmine until she finally blurted, "If you're having a problem meeting boys because of what happened to me, Jasmine, we need to—"

Marcy cut her off. "You're tired, Claudia, so don't let's have this conversation now."

"But if she is—"

"Just stop," Marcy cried despairingly. "We've all had too much to drink, including you, which means you really shouldn't be driving, so if you want something to sober you up consider what you'll tell the police if they pull us over."

# CHAPTER FOURTEEN

Claudia was at the top of a stepladder in the show home marking up for curtain poles, while Andee stood on the bottom rung holding it steady. Outside it was trying to be sunny, although it was bitterly cold and this unheated house wasn't doing much to warm them, especially since they'd had to take their boots off before coming in.

"Everything's checking out," Claudia informed Andee, and reeling in her tape measure she tucked the pencil behind one ear before making her descent. "We should be able to start hanging the drapes in here on Monday."

"Excellent," Andee replied, glancing at her phone as it rang. "Ah, I should take this," and leaving Claudia to fold up the steps, she wandered into the hall.

As Claudia began packing her bag on the dusty floor she checked her own phone for messages and found several from her machinists, although thankfully no one was in need of urgent attention. This meant she might have time when she'd finished here to pop over to the coach house to check on progress there.

Since the sale had completed the builders had moved in, and because no room dimensions were changing, the kitchen was already being constructed, by hand, in a workshop on the edge of town. There was a lot to do, even more than she'd expected, but when it was finished she knew in her heart that it was going to be the most beautiful home she'd ever owned, and as special as if it were another member of the family.

"You know," Andee said, as she came back into the room, "I'd be very happy to start recommending you, if you'd like me to."

Claudia's eyebrows rose. "But you haven't actually seen anything yet," she reminded her.

"I've seen enough to know how good you are, and how highly Cassie's team regard you. So, if you're OK about me sharing your details . . . Actually, what prospective clients will really want to see is a website with a gallery of your work if you have one."

Claudia swallowed and looked down to zip up her bag. "Not yet," she replied. "I mean, I used to, but it wasn't very good, so I need to find someone to help with a new one. Maybe you could suggest a designer?"

"Of course. You should have a chat with Eddie over in Paradise Cove who did mine. He's very good, not too expensive, and is in your kind of league when it comes to speed. Actually, he set up the restorative justice site for us too, so there's another example of his work you could take a look at, although that's a very different sort of business. It shows his versatility."

Since the mention of restorative justice brought Dan to her mind Claudia kept her eyes lowered as she said, "I'll make it my first task once this order is ready."

Andee smiled, and hefting her bag onto her shoulder, she led the way across the newly laid hardwood floor into the freshly painted hall. As she opened the front door, she said, "I guess now is as good a time as any to bring this up—Dan's been in touch with me to ask if he can have your number."

Claudia's heart gave a jolt. She'd been trying not to think about him since the party, and not always successfully—actually not very successfully at all.

"I told him I'd have to ask you first," Andee continued, digging her feet into the boots she'd left on the doorstep, "so would you be happy for him to call you?"

Stuck for an answer that wouldn't sound cold or rude, Claudia said, "Actually, I'm quite busy at the moment, so maybe it's not a good idea."

Andee nodded and started down the path. "I think he'll be disappointed," she commented, not quite ready to let it go yet. "This is the first time, as far as I know, that he's shown any interest in a woman since his wife died. In fact, he's always warning us not to try pairing him off."

Though Claudia felt flattered by Dan's interest, it made no difference; she knew she couldn't see him.

"He's a really great guy," Andee persisted, "and you seemed to be getting along well at Tom and Leanne's . . ."

"You're right, he's very nice," Claudia interrupted, "but I don't think . . . I wouldn't want to give the impression that I'm interested in being in a relationship, because I'm really not."

"OK, I'll tell him, but if you change your mind . . ."

"I won't, but thanks."

As Claudia drove back toward town, a quick visit to the coach house forgotten, a surge of frustration was building up inside her. She hated and resented the fact that Marcus continued to impact her life, and in so many ways, from the voices in her head to the fear of someone finding her and now this. For the truth was, she'd like to see Dan again—she'd even imagined where they might go and what they might talk about, but she was afraid to chance it. One single date was all it would take for him to realize that she wasn't who she was pretending to be—or that she was hiding something—or that she was quite simply dishonest. He didn't deserve that.

No, it was best they didn't meet again. That way no misunderstandings could occur, and no damage would be done.

"I'M REALLY SORRY," Andee said when she caught up with Dan later at his law firm. The staff had all gone home, but Graeme was there, signing a property contract that Dan had drawn up for him.

"She doesn't want me to call," Dan said, resignation masking his disappointment as he passed her a gin and tonic. "I just hope it didn't create any awkwardness for you."

"I wouldn't say that," she assured him, and sitting on one of his blue leather sofas, she raised her glass to him and said, "Actually, if you want my opinion, I think she's been badly hurt in the past and she just isn't ready to take the risk again."

With a certain wryness he replied, "Well, I think we can all understand that."

Graeme put down his pen and sat back comfortably in Dan's chair. "Andee, I think you should tell him what you've found out," he said quietly.

Dan regarded Andee with interest.

Slanting Graeme a look, Andee said, "OK, but if I do, it must go no further than this room."

Dan put a hand to his lips as a seal and watched her as she sipped from her glass, clearly taking time to choose her words.

"Do you remember the case of three missing women several months ago?" she asked. "Grandmother, mother, and daughter?"

He frowned. "I think so, vaguely. I remember you were interested in it. Weren't they found?" His eyes widened incredulously as he connected with what she was saying.

"It's them," she confirmed.

"How do you know?"

"Because when I realized things weren't quite . . . as they should be with Claudia, I was reminded of the missing family, so I decided to pull up some police and press shots from the time of the search. Claudia and Jasmine have changed their hair color, but it's definitely them."

Dan sat quite still. He wasn't sure what to say, or even what to think.

"It turns out," Andee continued, "that Claudia's husband is Marcus Huxley-Browne, the financier who went down for insider trading."

Recalling the case, Dan said, "I didn't read much about it, but. . . . Are you saying Claudia was involved in some way?"

Andee got up to put more ice in her glass. "I did wonder it at first," she confessed, "but after a little more digging around I discovered something else about Huxley-Browne. He has a history as an abuser."

Dan's distaste showed. "So it could be she's trying to escape him?" he prompted. "Isn't he in prison?"

"Yes, but there's no knowing what sort of reach he has. If he's as controlling as most abusers there's a good chance he already has someone looking for her. Hence the change of name and flight to the other side of the country."

Graeme said, "The police must know where she is because they called off the search, but how much protection that gives her . . ." He shrugged, obviously having no idea.

Having none either, Dan said to Andee, "I'm guessing you haven't mentioned anything to Claudia about this?"

She shook her head. "I'm taking the view that if she wants me to know she'll tell me."

He nodded in agreement and took a sip of his drink. "And meantime, we do what?" he asked.

Andee sighed. "There's nothing we can do apart from carry on being her friend—and respecting the decisions she's made to protect herself and her family."

# CHAPTER FIFTEEN

Dan wasn't himself when he came today. He's been off before, but I could tell this time that something was eating him up, and I don't think it had anything to do with me. Don't worry, I get that I'm not the center of his world.

It's a shame really, because I was all fired up to tell him the stuff I'd been thinking about since we last had a visit, you know, about my ma, and maybe even a bit about BJ, but when I saw he wasn't with me I backed off.

After he'd gone, I wrote my shit down so he can see it the next time he comes, if he's interested. Maybe he's sick of me, thinks I'm not worth his time anymore. Screw him, if he does, he won't be the first to bail on me and he won't be the last.

He's kind of stuck in my head though, and I can't stop myself wondering what was menacing him today. It bothers me to think he's not in a good place. Not that I can do anything about it, I'm just saying, is all.

It could be some woman is giving him issues. (I like that he's going to read this before you and find out I've been sussing him this way.) I bet he does have a woman, someone hot and sassy who knows how to treat a bloke.

I've noticed he wears a wedding ring so it could be that wifey's cheating on him. Or he's cheating on her. Either way doesn't make for a good situation and I can't help feeling for the guy. I know what it's like to have troubles with the girls. I might only be nineteen, but I'm no girvin (that's an anagram so I expect you can work it out). I lost mine when I was fourteen to one of the chicks who hangs out under the railway bridge. Got no idea where she is now, might even be dead, although I'd probably have heard if she was.

I don't go in for actual girlfriends, you know, the type you date on a regular basis. Too much hassle, especially in my line of work when I have to be away a lot of the time. Tbh I get more of it when I'm making deliveries than I ever do at home. Some of the PCs' wives are more than keen to show their gratitude, know what I'm saying? (Bet Dan takes that bit out.) But it's true, they are. You just don't want the other half catching you, is all. He'll contact the top dudes, you know, the bosses who run us mules, and let me tell you there's no good outcome there. Luckily it's never happened to me. A mate of mine walks with a permanent limp after he got caught and the injury isn't in either of his legs.

OK, I get that you don't want to hear about any of that. It was rude of me to go there. Let's back up and pretend I never said it.

It's in my mind to ask how you are. I'd really like to know, but it kind of scares me too.

You might not realize it but I think about you a lot, and what happened. In my head I see myself going through it again, doing what I did, and you being there . . . Why the fuck _were_ you there? Sorry about swearing, but why the eff were you?

I'm going to ask Dan that the next time he comes. I hope he comes. See that, Dan? I said I hope you come, and once you're done getting on my case about my language maybe you'll answer the question.

Why was she there?

# CHAPTER SIXTEEN

The last thing Marcy had expected when she'd moved to Kesterly was to find herself becoming involved with a man, especially one who was, if not in looks then in character, so like her husband of over thirty years. However, it was happening, and there was no resisting it, for Henry Matthews was as charming as the stars and as kind and entertaining as any man she'd ever known. She was even prepared to admit, but only to herself, that when she wasn't enjoying his company she spent a good deal of the time looking forward to seeing him again.

They worked well together at the community center, organizing all sorts of activities from special outings for deprived children, right through to tea dances and old movie nights for those of their own age and over. They'd joined the same poetry group—neither of them could write it, but they enjoyed listening and having it explained—and the dreaded golf lessons were actually going quite well. She'd even managed to get him onto the selection committee for the spring concert she was sponsoring mostly as a showcase for Jasmine, but also to help promote local musicians.

And now here they were meeting for dinner at the Crustacean, one of the town's fanciest restaurants, before Henry left for Hereford in the morning to spend Christmas with his son and daughter-in-law. The place was aglow with seasonal lights and carols were playing softly on the music system, creating such an infectious sense of goodwill that as Marcy looked into Henry's humorous brown eyes, she was finding it hard to stop smiling. She liked this man, she really did, and why wouldn't she? His easygoing nature, effortless integrity, and sixty-five-year-old laughter lines were an irresistible combination.

"Thank you for coming," he said, his words imbued with their habitual hint of irony.

"Did you think I wouldn't?" she countered.

"Let's just say I would have been disappointed if you hadn't, but do you realize this is the first time we've actually been out on a date, just the two of us?"

She feigned shock. "This is a date?" she whispered, pressing a hand to her heart as she glanced around to see if anyone was listening.

Staging his own pretense, he said, "Are we supposed to call it something else? An audition for the concert?"

With a laugh she said, "Just as well neither of us is trying out for that. I don't know which one of us is more embarrassing with our nonexistent knowledge of current sounds."

"Thank goodness we have your granddaughter and her musically gifted friends to mask our shame." He signaled the waiter to top up their glasses. "Speaking of whom, how are rehearsals going for her school Christmas concert tomorrow?"

Marcy rolled her eyes and sighed. "Let's just say that she's so wound up about it that we're afraid to talk to her, although she can't talk about anything else."

"Does she always get like that during the run-up to a performance?"

With a shake of her head, Marcy said, "She never used to, but she was younger then and this is the first time since we've been here that she's committed to playing a solo." Jasmine used to love nothing more than performing in front of an audience before Marcus had stopped it, she was thinking; now, not surprisingly, it was taking time for her to get her confidence back. "I think she's just nervous about being up there in front of so many of her friends," she continued airily. "You know the way teens are—much more self-conscious than during their earlier years." She smiled fondly. "She'll be fine once she's underway and lost in the music."

"I'm sure she will," he agreed, "and I'm very sorry to be missing it. I've heard from her coach that she's an outstanding student. One of the best he's had."

"You know Anton," she said in surprise. "Oh no, don't tell me, he was once one of your clients?"

"He was, but he's also a good friend going back over many years, and he taught my son the violin before it became evident we were wasting our money. Now tell me what your plans are for Christmas, so I can imagine where you are and what you're doing."

Pleased by his interest, she sipped her wine as she said, "Well, tomorrow night, Christmas Eve, we have the concert, of course. Then we're planning to get up early in the morning to open presents before going to the shelter to serve hot meals for the homeless. Leanne and her mother organized it, so there are several of us going. After, we were expecting to return home for a roast turkey, just the three of us, but Andee and Graeme have invited us to join them and we've accepted."

His eyes lit up. "Marvelous!" he declared approvingly. "Two of my favorite people. And will any of their children be there?"

"Apparently Andee's daughter has already flown to South Africa to be with her brother."

He nodded. "And Graeme's sons?"

"I'm told they alternate between their mother and father and this year they're with their mother, but coming to Kesterly on Boxing Day. When are you back, by the way?"

"On the twenty-eighth, so I'm hoping I can claim you for the New Year?"

Loving the idea, she said teasingly, "That might depend on what you have in mind."

With playfully narrowed eyes he said, "You'll find out when you open the Christmas gift I have for you," and to her surprise he reached into his pocket and pulled out an envelope.

Taking it, she glanced at him curiously, and realizing he was hoping she'd open it now, she did so. When she saw what was inside her eyes lit up with amazement. "Tickets to see *Les Misérables*," she declared joyfully. "How did you know that I've never seen it?"

"I heard you telling someone a while ago," he replied, "so I hoped it would be a welcome surprise."

"It is," she assured him with feeling. "This is such a lovely gift. So thoughtful and . . . generous."

He was watching her intently, seeming to wait for her to notice something else. In the end he cautioned, "It's not a matinée."

She located the start time and her heart tripped as she processed what it could mean. "It probably won't finish until ten or even eleven o'clock," she said, looking at him.

He nodded agreement.

"Too late for a last train?"

"Not quite, but do we really want to see the New Year in a Great Western carriage?"

Enjoying this a lot, but managing to sound serious, Marcy said, "No, I don't think we do. So, should we stay over?"

"Wow! That sounds like a good idea."

Daring to go further, she said, "Hotels are very expensive in the West End, so perhaps we should . . . share a room?"

He looked amazed, as if the thought had never occurred to him, and as she laughed, he sat back to allow their seafood starters to be served.

Though she couldn't have been more thrilled with her Christmas present, she soon began worrying about how Claudia was going to react when she found out. They hadn't talked about Henry much; she'd sensed that Claudia didn't want to, so Marcy hadn't pushed it. However, she obviously couldn't just take off for New Year's without saying where she was going and who with, nor could she feel happy about leaving her daughter to spend the time alone. Jasmine would almost certainly be seeing friends, although if she thought her mother was going to be lonely she might well cancel. So, if she, Marcy, accepted Henry's wonderful gift she could be spoiling the New Year for her family.

"You're looking troubled," he told her as the waiters left the table.

With a sigh, she picked up a fork and said, "I am. I promise, it's not that I don't want to come with you . . ."

". . . you just don't want to leave Claudia."

Her expression showed how right he was and how wretched she felt. "I know you're going to say that she's old enough to take care of herself, and of course you're right, she is, but . . . She's been through a lot, a heck of a lot . . . It's why we came here, so that she and Jasmine could start again, put it all behind them. I could say I felt it was my duty to come too, but it wasn't a duty. They're my family and they need me, so of course I want to be with them."

"And you don't think Claudia's ready yet to stand on her own two feet?"

She realized how preposterous it must seem when Claudia was doing so well with her business—since finishing the show house she'd received several more commissions, and she was doing wonderful things with the coach house. Apparently, it could be ready as early as February or March, and Marcy suspected that if it wasn't, they'd move in anyway. "When she's working," she said softly, "she is a much stronger and more capable person, but inside she's still damaged by what happened to her."

He looked concerned and curious as he waited for her to continue.

With a regretful sigh she said, "There are things I really can't tell you. Not because I don't trust you, but because Claudia wouldn't want me to."

"It's OK, I understand, and I'm not trying to make you. I'm simply going to say that I don't think she'd want to stop you having a life of your own."

Marcy's eyes went down as she considered that. "No, I don't suppose she would," she murmured, certain that on some level it was true, "but what I'd really like to see is her having one too." After a moment she added, "I know I've mentioned this before, how she won't see Dan unless others are around . . . He's asked her several times now to meet him for lunch, or coffee, but she won't. I *know* that in her heart she wants to, but she still hasn't regained enough confidence to take what she sees as a risk."

He nodded slowly. "I guess I'm not allowed to ask who made her like this?"

She wanted to tell him, she really did, but she simply couldn't when she knew that Claudia would never forgive her. "I'm sorry," she said, meeting his gentle eyes, "it's not my story to tell, so I can't. Do you mind?"

Holding her gaze, he allowed his own to twinkle as he said, "Of course not, as long as there are no dead bodies buried anywhere."

She started to laugh, but as she glanced across the restaurant her face suddenly froze.

"What is it?" Henry asked, looking over his shoulder.

Marcy watched the woman who'd just come in and was now hand-ing her coat to the maître d'. Her back was turned, but the glimpse Marcy had gotten of her face, her stocky stature, the shoulder-length brown hair . . .

"Who is it?" Henry asked, following the direction of her eyes.

The woman turned around and Marcy almost gasped as she found herself breathing again. It wasn't Eugena. Thank God, *thank God*. "I'm sorry," she murmured, her heart still pounding. "I thought . . . The woman who just came in reminded me of someone, but it's not her." She looked at him and seeing his confusion she made herself smile. "It's OK," she assured him. "It just gave me a bit of a start. Ghosts from the past, strange timing, and all that. Now, what were we saying?"

His eyebrows arched as he said dryly, "Well, I was asking about dead bodies, and you suddenly looked as though there might be some."

She managed a laugh. "I know, we were talking about Claudia and New Year's Eve and how much I'd love to come with you."

Apparently pleased with this, he said, "Talk to her. Tell her you want to see the show and spend a little time with me, and perhaps she'll find someone else to celebrate with."

"WELL, OF COURSE you have to go," Claudia insisted as she and her mother had breakfast together the next morning. "It'll be a lovely way to see in the New Year."

"But what will you do?" Marcy asked, reaching for the toast.

Claudia shrugged. "I don't know. Does it matter?"

"I just don't want to think of you being here on your own."

Claudia looked around as Jasmine came through from her bedroom like a whirlwind, snatched up bag, violin, toast, and a vacuum mug of coffee and declared, "I have to go," as if they hadn't already gathered that. "I don't want to be late. I'll see you at school tonight, OK?"

"OK," Claudia promised.

"Are you coming, Nana?"

"Of course. You surely can't think I'd miss it."

"No, I didn't. I just . . . I don't know what I thought. How was your date by the way?"

Marcy smiled. "Lovely, thank you."

"Henry's invited her to spend New Year's with him in London," Claudia told her.

Jasmine's eyes rounded. "Cool. *Wicked*."

As Marcy laughed, Jasmine planted a kiss on her forehead, followed by another on her mother's cheek, and ran for the door.

"You really don't mind if I go?" Marcy asked, as Claudia began clearing the table.

"What concerns me more is what you'll do if he proposes, or suggests you move in with him . . ."

"You're way ahead of the game here," Marcy scolded. "We're just friends . . . OK, some benefits are going to be involved quite soon—I know I'm your mother but you don't have to look quite so grossed out. The point is, *nothing* is going to change my plans to move into the coach house with you and Jasmine."

"Great, then there's nothing to worry about," Claudia said sweetly, and taking a loaded tray to the kitchen, she began filling the dishwasher.

After watching her for a while and listening to her humming "God Rest Ye Merry Gentlemen," Marcy asked, "Am I missing something?"

Surprised, Claudia glanced over her shoulder. "Why do you say that?"

Marcy shrugged. "I guess because you seem much more relaxed about things than I'd expected you to be."

Claudia threw out her hands. "I'm in a good mood, if that's allowed. It's Christmas and there's a lot to look forward to. Jasmine's giving her first public performance this evening, we're going to spend tomorrow with friends who we've really come to like, and when I think of where I was this time last year . . . Actually, I try not to think of it. Will you pass your mug if you've finished?"

Taking it to the kitchen, Marcy folded her arms and leaned against a countertop. "Do you know that Dan is going to be at Andee and Graeme's tomorrow?" she asked carefully.

Claudia paused, but only slightly. "Yes, I do, and why do you mention it?"

"I just wondered if that's what's putting you in a good mood?"

Turning around, Claudia said, "You know your trouble, you think everything's about sex."

"Isn't it?"

Claudia laughed. "I need to run," she said, checking the time. "There are a few more presents to wrap in my bedroom, would you mind?"

"If I can be trusted."

"I'll do the finishing touches when I get back."

"Where are you going?"

"To deliver gifts to my fabulous team, then I've got a meeting with a new client in Uley village. And when I've finished there, I'm hoping to see the electricians at the coach house before they clock off for the holiday."

"So busy," Marcy sighed, although she was thrilled to see Claudia so upbeat. And when she heard the front door bang closed a few minutes later she was glad of her decision not to say anything about the shock she'd had last night, when she'd thought it was Eugena Huxley-Browne coming into the restaurant. Just the mention of the name would have thrown Claudia back into the paranoia of a few months ago; it might even have proved difficult for Marcy to convince her that it really hadn't been Marcus's sister.

It hadn't, Marcy was certain about that, and now that she was over the shock of it she realized how foolish she'd been to think Eugena would come looking herself. She'd have people to do it for her, which was so far from being a comforting thought that she pushed it straight out of her mind. Much better to focus on Henry and how much she was already looking forward to New Year's Eve.

As CLAUDIA RAN down the steps at the front of the villa, where she and Jasmine had strung bright star lights a week ago, she came to a sudden stop as a man she thought she recognized walked into the front area. He wore a heavy dark raincoat and a charcoal-gray scarf. Her heart gave an uneasy beat as she tried to place him.

"Mrs. Winters. Leo Johnson," he reminded her, and though she didn't relax exactly, she no longer felt poised to run. It was the young detective who'd come to visit with DI Phillips all those months ago. Why was he here? What had happened? So many awful scenarios flashed through her mind, all involving Marcus, that she barely heard herself say, "Are you here to see me?"

He reached inside his coat and drew out a handful of envelopes, some white, probably Christmas cards, others brown and official-looking. "These arrived for you from London," he explained, holding them out to her.

Alarmed, Claudia backed away. "I don't want them," she protested. "Who sent them?"

"They came to me via DI Phillips," he explained.

"He should have just thrown them away."

Johnson glanced at them himself. "There could be something here that you want," he said, apparently believing this sounded reasonable. To him it probably did.

"There isn't," she assured him. She didn't want anything from her old life.

He continued to stand there looking faintly perplexed, but not yet ready to leave. "The thing is," he said, "it would be an offense for us to throw your post away when it's addressed to you."

"I'm not that person anymore," she reminded him shrilly.

He looked pained, but before he could speak a familiar voice claimed their attention.

"Claudia, great, I caught you. Would you mind taking . . ." Andee stopped as she clocked Johnson. "Leo, I didn't realize it was you." She smiled affectionately. "What on earth are you doing here?"

Claudia frantically tried to think of an explanation, something that would sound remotely plausible, and it was apparent that Leo was trying too, but all that happened was a clumsy sort of stammering that amounted to nothing more than confusion.

Moving smoothly past it, Andee said, "Well, it's lovely to see you, as always. I've just stopped by to ask you, Claudia, if you'd mind taking a few things over to Cassie for me? You are still going there this morning?"

"I'm just on my way," Claudia replied, and reached for the bag Andee was holding out. To Leo she said, "My mother's inside if you'd like to talk to her."

"Uh, yes, that would be great," he replied. "Lovely to see you too," he said to Andee. "Merry Christmas to you and yours."

"Same to you and yours," she responded, and with a friendly little wave she walked back to her car.

"I really have to go," Claudia said, as Johnson tried again to give her the post, and brushing past him she opened her boot to drop everything inside.

As she drove away she quickly connected to her mother to let her know what had just happened, but Marcy's line was busy and she knew that by the time she got hold of her she'd probably already have let Leo Johnson into the flat.

It didn't matter. Her mother would find a way of dealing with it, which would probably be simply to take the mail to the nearest shredder as soon as Johnson had gone. She should have done that herself, and would have if she'd had more time to think, but he'd thrown her, turning up out of the blue like that.

He must have understood her reaction, but heaven only knew what Andee was thinking now. She didn't even want to imagine it. She could only think about the glimpse of what might have been a prison letter. Pulling over, she sent a quick text to her mother and willed her to reply quickly. Thankfully, she did.

*Don't worry, I'll destroy them all.*

As ANDEE DROVE up to the new builds on Westleigh Heights she was mulling over the scene between Claudia and Leo Johnson, wondering what it had really been about, although the handful of mail had been a clue. Had Leo brought it from Claudia's previous address? If he had, it would confirm that the police here in town knew who Claudia really was, presumably because someone at the Met had tipped them off.

She considered calling her old boss DCI Gould to find out what he was prepared to tell her, but then asked herself why she would do that. She already knew who Claudia was hiding from, and had a fair idea of why, so what was the point of trying to get it confirmed when it was actually none of her business? Claudia had done nothing to harm anyone, quite the reverse in fact, and as long as she wasn't in any difficulty or danger, which she didn't seem to be, it was no one's place to go around asking questions about her just for the sake of it.

So no, she wasn't going to call Gould, nor was she going to tell Graeme or Dan what she'd witnessed just now. She wouldn't even mention it to Claudia when she saw her at the concert later, for the last thing she wanted was to make her feel as though she had to explain herself.

# CHAPTER SEVENTEEN

I s everyone ready?" Marcy called out from the sitting room. "We're going to be late and I don't know about you two but I'm *hungry*."

First thing this morning they'd all piled into Claudia's bed to open presents from each other—Marcy couldn't actually remember what they all were now but was certain it would come back to her—before pulling on tracksuits and trainers to jog over to the shelter to serve turkey specials to the homeless. Andee's ex-husband, Martin, and his partner, Angie, had been there (everyone seeming to be the best of friends), and thanks to them Claudia now had an invitation for New Year's Eve. Whether she'd actually go to the black-tie charity ball at the Royal Hotel had yet to be seen, however Marcy was determined to stay hopeful, especially now that she knew that Dan had also been invited.

As Claudia came through from her bedroom wearing a red sequined dress that she'd bought at Glory Days especially for today, smiley Santas in her ears and a garland of silver tinsel around her neck, Marcy exclaimed, with joyous approval, "My God, you're going as a Christmas tree!" Being so fancily dressed was a truly big step forward for Claudia, for she and Joel had always embraced the season with the most outrageous costumes. Nothing like it had happened after she'd married Marcus, and this time last year she'd been so afraid of upsetting him in some way that she simply hadn't known what to do with the house, or herself, or even for Jasmine. Marcy still didn't know the full details of how Claudia had apparently ended up getting it wrong, but she would never forget the phone call she'd received from her granddaughter begging her to come and get them.

Well, she didn't have to go anywhere to get them today. They were right here under her watch, and since the triumph of last night's concert they'd all been in such frivolous, festive moods that it had been difficult to sleep. Jasmine's violin solo had received so much praise that she'd glowed brighter than Rudolph's nose all the way home. And Claudia had surprised herself by actually giving Dan a quick embrace before they'd left.

"Oh, wow, Mum, you look amazing," Jasmine declared, coming out of her room in a cream flared mini dress, thick black tights, and bright red lipstick. "I told you as soon as we saw it that it was made for you. And look at *you*, Nana the banana."

Marcy winced. "Really not how I wanted to be described," she protested.

"Then you shouldn't wear yellow, but you give jumpsuits a good rep, I'm telling you that. I bet Henry's wild about them."

"He's never said."

"Wait till he has to get you out of one . . ."

"OK, time to go!" Claudia declared, picking up the bag of gifts they'd prepared for the Secret Santa at Andee's.

"Before we leave," Jasmine cried, holding up her hands, "I have an announcement to make."

Intrigued, her mother and grandmother turned back.

"I've decided," she told them, eyes bright with excitement, "that for the opening night of the spring concert I'm going to play Dad's violin."

As Claudia's heart melted, she pulled her daughter into a loving embrace. "That's wonderful, wonderful," she murmured, holding her close. "Oh God, after last night . . . I thought, I hoped you might feel ready . . ."

"I think I am." Jasmine smiled as Marcy joined the hug. "I'll take it to Anton after Christmas so he can make sure it's properly tuned and we can start using it during rehearsals."

"It's going to be very special." Marcy's voice shook a little, knowing already that many tears would be shed that night and a lot of them hers.

"This is the best Christmas present I've ever had," Claudia said softly, cupping Jasmine's face in her hands.

"You've made us very happy," Marcy added. "We're both so proud of you. I know I've already told you this, but the way you played last night will stay with me forever. Everyone was so moved, and opening the spring concert on your dad's special gift to you . . . That's going to be even more memorable."

Laughing, Jasmine said, "I hope you'll be one of those out there dancing, because it's not going to be a wholly classical performance. Plenty of pop and jazz."

"You can count on it," Marcy assured her.

"And now we really should go," Claudia told them. "Are you sure you're happy to drive?" she asked Jasmine.

"Totally," Jasmine insisted, and held up the key to the bright blue Mini with a painted daisy on top that her mother and grandmother had bought for her two weeks ago when she'd passed her driving test. An early Christmas present, they'd told her. She went everywhere in it now, and it had already been decided that she would leave them to get a taxi home later while she went to spend the evening with Abby at Ash Morley.

By the time they arrived at Andee and Graeme's, Andee's mother Maureen was already there and welcomed them at the door. She and

Marcy were like old friends these days, given all the time they spent together at the community center, but this morning at the shelter was the first time Claudia and Jasmine had met her. She was as gracious and good-natured as her daughter, and eager to break out the champagne, they discovered, as they entered the kitchen. The smell of roasting turkey, potatoes, and stuffing was so delicious that they could almost feast on the air.

Graeme immediately popped a cork, and as the glasses were filled and everyone joined in a toast Claudia didn't like to ask where Dan was; no doubt he'd turn up any minute. However, as the smoked salmon canapés and Brie and cranberry twists were passed around, and crackers were pulled for silly gifts and paper hats, he still didn't show.

Maybe he was going somewhere else for lunch and coming later. Or he could be unwell and had called to say he couldn't make it.

"Oh my, look at this," she heard her mother gasp, and turning she saw that Graeme had opened the set of double doors into the dining room, where the table was laid for a banquet and a giant Christmas tree glittered silver and gold in front of a tall sash window. The candles, ornaments, and place settings were silver and gold too, and seeing there were seven people expected to sit down, Claudia found herself relaxing without having realized she was tense. Right now they were only six, so it seemed Dan was coming, and she really had to stop fixating on it, because even if he did, what was she going to do? Tell him she'd changed her mind and would like to meet him for a coffee or lunch? She wouldn't do it, she knew that already, so why was she giving herself such a hard time over where he was?

As everyone took a seat, sitting where they liked, Graeme seemed aware of her thoughts, as he said, "By the way, Dan is definitely joining us, but he's been held up so he's insisting we carry on until he gets here."

"What's happened?" Maureen asked, pulling up next to Marcy. "Is he all right?"

"He's fine. He had a call from his in-laws after the concert last night, apparently one of them had had a fall, so he drove to Dorchester to check that they're OK."

"And are they?" Marcy asked.

"I believe so. Their son and daughter-in-law have arrived from Manchester now, so when Dan rang earlier he was just setting off to come back to Kesterly. My guess is he'll arrive in about half an hour."

Leaning in to her mother, Jasmine murmured, "You thought he wasn't coming, didn't you?"

Claudia kept her head turned away as though she hadn't heard, while under the table she gave Jasmine a pinch.

He turned up just as the sizzling, bacon-strapped turkey was being carved, and as he was ushered into place at the table opposite Claudia—and given wine, a cracker, and a napkin—she was aware of how pleased everyone was to see him. He, too, was evidently thrilled to see them. The party seemed complete now, slightly more balanced even, given that Graeme was no longer the only man.

Much of the talk over the meal was of Christmases past, hilarious anecdotes of disasters and surprises, long-forgotten memories retrieved and retold with shameless exaggeration. Marcy joined in unabashedly, describing incidents from both Jasmine's and Claudia's childhoods as though Christmas with them had always been a joyous and close-family affair. Claudia said little, but found herself laughing along with everyone else, and loved the way that Jasmine did too. Today, with such good friends as these, was no time to remember the terrible recent years with Marcus.

When the table was finally cleared, they moved over to the drawing room, where Graeme had already rekindled the fire and lit up another Christmas tree. After relaxing in front of the Queen's speech and some dozing during *It's a Wonderful Life*, coffee and liqueurs were served, along with a flaming Christmas pudding and brandy-flavored cream.

It was almost six by the time Jasmine left to drive to Ash Morley, far more flushed by the boisterous rounds of Taboo they'd played than by alcohol, as she'd had none since the glass of champagne on arrival.

As the door closed behind her daughter Claudia felt a strange mix of pride and loss, as if this was the best and worst part of the day. It was wonderful to see her claiming her independence, as she would more and more now that she had a car, but Claudia was already missing her little girl. She wondered fleetingly where they all might be this time next year, and experienced a wave of emotion as she realized that a year ago she'd never have imagined herself to be somewhere like this today. It would have been beyond her wildest dreams.

Feeling Dan's eyes on her, she smiled as she looked at him, and gave a laugh at the comical way he arched his eyebrows.

"So, Claudia," Maureen said from the comfort of a cream leather fireside chair, "can I ask how the renovations are going at the coach house? I've been hearing great things about it. Is it true it'll soon be ready for you to move into?"

Thrilled to be asked, Claudia said, "We're hoping it'll be sometime in the next couple of months. The builders are doing an amazing job of bringing the place back to life."

"The builders are?" Andee cried in protest. "You mean *you* are. You should see some of the things she's done! All the original features have been restored or replaced, cornices, fireplaces, windows and doors, even the kitchen has a centuries-old feel about it in spite of it being brand-new—and I can't wait to see it when the refectory table is in. The whole place is already feeling so much like a home that I could hardly tear myself away when I went in the day before yesterday. Don't you love it?" She turned to Marcy.

"Completely," Marcy assured her. "To borrow one of Jasmine's words, it's awesomazing. I don't suppose anyone but my daughter would have thought to have purple walls with blue and yellow globe lamps hanging from stainless-steel rods over the kitchen table, but amazingly, I can see it working."

"Andee would have thought of it," Claudia put in with a laugh, "because it was her idea."

"We came up with it together," Andee insisted, "but the saffron drapes are all yours and they're a stroke of genius, in the way they're going to be there, but not there, so they take nothing away from the windows. Frankly, it's going to give a whole new meaning to Georgian chic. We're still searching for art, but Claudia has some wonderful ideas for the spaces she wants to fill."

Claudia grimaced. "It'll be a matter of finding the right shapes and sizes, colors, styles . . . Some art nouveau, others more classical. It's going to be a big job, that's for sure."

"I might know someone who can help with that," Dan informed her. "An artist who's making a name for herself by creating bespoke works for clients."

"You're talking about Julie Forrest," Andee came in excitedly. "Why on earth didn't I think of her? She lives out in Mulgrove village? Yes, you guys should definitely meet," she told Claudia. "She has the kind of vision that sets your head spinning, but in a good way. I didn't realize you knew her, Dan."

"We only met a couple of months ago," he said. "She needed some help with a studio she's buying, so the firm's acting for her." To Claudia, he said, "You'll meet her at the ball on New Year's Eve, if you're going to be there. I'll be happy to introduce you."

Claudia's smile didn't falter in spite of the way her heart did. "That would be lovely. I'll look forward to it," she said, feeling the heat of her mother's eyes on her.

They were both thinking the same thing, that it sounded as though Dan already had a partner for New Year's Eve.

# CHAPTER EIGHTEEN

The days between Christmas and New Year passed quickly for Claudia. Although she joined a long hike over the moor on Boxing Day with Leanne and her family, she was so engrossed in the needs of the coach house now that she spent most of her time there. She sanded, stained, painted, plastered, polished, and always visualized: the Decorum sideboard could go here, the vintage chaise longue there, the sitting room would be a perfect home for the coffee table she'd created out of a door, the refectory table was going to need at least ten chairs.

Each time she let herself into the place she was filled with happiness, for the main front door opened straight into the heart of the house. Everything was open plan, with the kitchen and its arched windows to the left, the sitting room and its matching spectacular windows to the right, and doors leading from each end to the east and west wings. Her craft room, bedroom, and bathroom were on the far side of the kitchen, her mother's study and en suite bedroom was off the sitting room, and Jasmine's domain was in the tower.

The densely brambled chaos that stretched between the house and the moor was going to become her mother's project, and Marcy was already talking to a landscaper about which trees, shrubs, and beds could be saved and restored.

What Claudia loved most of all about being there, however, was how welcome and safe the house made her feel. It wasn't only the solidity of the centuries-old walls, or the shelter of the roof, it was the quiet and soulful character of the place, the intangible yet present sense of it taking care of her, the way she was taking care of it.

It already felt like an old and trusted friend, she told Marcy. "Do you feel it too?" she'd asked that morning when they'd brought more paint samples and cleaning equipment. At the time they'd been standing side by side just inside the front door gazing into the half-finished sitting room and partly installed kitchen and out through the set of double French windows at the rear to a dilapidated terrace and wilderness beyond.

"Yes, I do," Marcy replied earnestly. "I never imagined I'd feel like this about anywhere again, but it's very special, and what you're doing with it seems to honor it in ways I'd never have dreamt of myself."

Loving the answer, Claudia rested her head on her mother's shoulder.

"We've met some wonderful people here," Marcy commented softly, "and now you're creating this beautiful home. I can see us doing quite a bit of entertaining, can't you?"

Yes, Claudia could, in fact she was already planning a house-warming and a special dinner to say thank you to Andee for all she'd done to make this happen. She wouldn't admit it to Andee, but more than anything else this house, and her growing business, had helped her to stop obsessing about Marcus, imagining him in his prison cell, furious, vengeful, plotting how to find her. It was always there, lurking beneath the reality of her new existence, his voice finding her in moments of insecurity, his threats combining with the dread of his sister, or someone else, suddenly turning up on her doorstep. However, she was finding it easier to move past the fear now, to clear her thoughts of the darkness that emanated from all memories of him.

Noticing the time, she said, "You should go, Mum, or you won't be there when Henry comes to pick you up."

Glancing at her watch Marcy agreed, "You're right, but don't stay long, will you? You'll need to get ready for the ball."

"Don't worry about me." Claudia hugged her. "You have a great time, and happy New Year."

"To you too," Marcy said warmly. "Love you and see you tomorrow."

It had long been dark outside by the time Claudia finally locked up the coach house and returned to her car. It shouldn't take much more than twenty minutes to drive back into town, but she was in no hurry, for she'd decided several days ago that she wouldn't be going to the ball. She hadn't told anyone; if she had it might have stopped her mother going to London, or Jasmine celebrating with her friends at a party in the Old Town. Plus, Andee and Leanne would probably have done their best to persuade her to change her mind, and Dan . . . Well, it was unlikely to make a difference to him whether or not she was there. He could always introduce her to Julie Forrest another time; it didn't have to be tonight.

Checking the time as she drove away, she imagined her mother arriving at the theater with Henry around about now, looking glamorous and excited in a sequined black dress and mock-fur cape. It pleased her so much to think of Marcy and Jasmine being happy that she didn't really mind about herself; after all, in her way she was happy too. Moreover, the sudden bouts of anxiety she'd suffered when they'd first gotten here only ever seemed to happen now when she left her car outside the flat and ran up the steps to go inside. She couldn't prevent herself from thinking someone was going to appear from the shadows to stop her, and she never felt totally safe until the front door was closed and locked behind her.

This evening her mind was so full of what still needed to be done at the coach house that she made it into the villa and was kicking off her boots behind the locked door of the flat before it occurred to her to feel worried. Clocking it up as another small milestone achieved, she went through to the living area, where the chaos of a teenager getting ready to go out was strewn like a still life across the table. She regarded it thoughtfully, although her mind wasn't on it. She was thinking more about how quiet the place seemed and what she might have worn if she had gone out.

Since it was hardly relevant now, she put on some music and poured herself a drink before starting to tidy up. Later she'd make herself something to eat, take a shower, and since it would be pointless trying to sleep any time before midnight, she'd go to sit in the window to watch the revelries on the Promenade. She might even open a bottle of champagne. It would be good to toast in the New Year with so much to look forward to, even if she was on her own.

What she didn't plan to do, but had known in the back of her mind that she might, was go through to her mother's room to find out if Marcy really had shredded the mail that DC Leo Johnson had brought. She'd said she had, but would she actually have destroyed the prison letter before finding out what it contained? Yes, Claudia had noticed it in the pile, and though she'd pushed it out of her mind since, she felt compelled to know if her mother had kept it.

She found it, opened, in Marcy's shoe cupboard, and as she stared down at the familiar and detested writing she felt bile rising in her throat. She was certain it contained something terrible, couldn't imagine anything else coming from him.

My darling wife,

I am heartbroken by your desertion. Your failure to write to me, or come and see me is making the time here almost impossible to bear. Some days I feel I simply cannot go on, for without you in my life there seems no point to it.

Please, wherever you are, reconsider your decision to leave me. I know I have not always been a perfect husband, but I love you, my angel, and I have always done my best to give you everything you ever wanted.

Eugena tells me that you have taken some keepsakes from the house, and I felt so happy when I thought you wanted to hold on to something of mine to remind you of me. But then you didn't get in touch, and we don't know where you are, so please contact Eugena, or write to me, my darling, to let me know that you are safe.

Your safety means everything to me, you know that.

I will never give up on you, my precious. Not ever.

Your beloved
Marcus

Claudia shivered with fear and revulsion. The sugarcoated words, the declarations of love that were so artificial and insidious they were sick, were all for the censors, of course. Those cold and disinterested eyes wouldn't see the threats between the lines, nor would they pick up on the intimidation the way she had, the way he had meant her to.

She understood him completely and she wasn't surprised by this letter, only afraid and already trying to plan what to do.

"WHY DID YOU keep it?" Claudia demanded, almost as soon as Marcy returned the next day. "Make me understand, Mum, because we didn't need him back in our lives, and now by opening this and reading it you've let him in."

Marcy looked pale and tired, and only mildly upset that Claudia had gone through her room. "I don't know why I kept it," she admitted. "And as for opening it . . . I suppose I couldn't bring myself to throw it away without knowing what it said. I'm sorry, I realize it wasn't a good decision, but he still doesn't know where we are. Isn't that what really matters?"

"What matters," Claudia argued, "is that he's not going to give up until he finds us. He's made that perfectly clear. Eugena is bound to be doing all she can to track us down and I'm afraid, as I've always been, that it's only a matter of time before she succeeds. And *this*," she added, hitting the letter, "reminds us that we need to be afraid."

"So what are you saying?" Jasmine asked quietly. "That we should live in denial until someone catches up with us?"

Claudia's heart clenched as her eyes closed.

"Or maybe," Jasmine continued, "we should give the attaché case back."

Marcy shook her head. "Even if we do that, there won't be an end to it," she said. "The names on those documents might not mean anything to us, but they obviously do to someone and the fact that we've seen them . . ." She let the sentence hang, not knowing how to finish it.

Jasmine said, "The money's yours, Mum. We're all agreed on that."

"He stole a lot more from you than we've taken from him," Marcy stated.

Claudia didn't argue with that, for it was true, but she wanted him out of their lives, and if that meant giving everything back she would do it.

"I understand how you feel," Marcy said, when Claudia voiced her thoughts, "but it's not as simple as that. We have to think about how vengeful he is, and we agreed before you emptied the safe that having the money and the documents that incriminate others would be our protection. Our insurance. If anyone came after us we could threaten to go to the police . . ."

"But we didn't know what we were doing," Claudia cried in frustration. "Looking back, I can hardly believe how crazy we were to think we could get away with it, that we could just disappear and turn ourselves into other people who couldn't be traced . . ."

"Crazy, maybe," Jasmine put in quickly, "but we've done it."

"Except the police know where we are," Claudia reminded her, "so we haven't been that successful."

"They wouldn't know if you and Nana hadn't called them," Jasmine reminded her. "Anyway, it's not really about how we have or haven't managed to pull off a disappearance, it's about that briefcase. So what I propose is that we give Eugena the documents and keep the cash."

Claudia covered her face with her hands. "I want to agree," she replied wretchedly, "I really do, but now I'm afraid that whatever we do we'll end up making things worse for ourselves."

"Then what do you suggest?" Jasmine pressed.

"I don't know. I just wish we'd never taken it, but even if we hadn't he'd still have come after us, and by now he must be going out of his mind trying to find a way to punish me for escaping him."

Aware of how true that was, Marcy got up from the table to go and put on the kettle. Her weekend bag was still on the floor where she'd left it when she'd come in to find Claudia sitting at the table waiting for her. Jasmine had been holding the letter so Marcy had known right away what it was about, she just hadn't been ready at the time to deal with the fallout.

"There is something we could consider," she said, turning back to face them. "I've been going over it in my mind for a while, but it's a decision we need to make together."

Claudia and Jasmine regarded her with anxious and hopeful eyes.

"We could talk to Andee about it and ask her advice. We know she's someone we can trust and . . . what? Why are you shaking your head?" she asked Claudia.

"We're not her responsibility," Claudia cried, "and she's already been so good to us. I can't burden her with this."

Marcy looked at Jasmine, hoping for some support, but Jasmine merely shrugged.

Marcy continued to make the tea. She was too tired to deal with this now, or at least to deal with it well, so it was best to let it go until she could think more clearly.

Going to embrace her mother, Claudia said softly, "We don't have to do anything right away, after all it's just a letter, sent over four months ago, and he still hasn't found out where we are. So why don't we just carry on as we are for now, and as soon as any of us wants to discuss it again we will. Does that sound OK?"

Marcy nodded and attempted a smile. "That sounds fine," she agreed, and put aside her other suggestion, which had been to tell Henry, since that wasn't likely to be met with any more enthusiasm than telling Andee.

"It sounds fine to me too," Jasmine told them. Her eyes were fixed on Claudia. "I just don't want you to start obsessing about it, Mum, and making yourself ill."

"I promise I won't," Claudia told her, and because the tension needed diffusing, she said, "Now I think we should change the subject and ask Nana how she got on in London with Henry."

With a weak laugh Marcy said, "It was wonderful, thank you, but I think we drank a little too much champagne last night. I'm awfully hungover. What about you? How was the ball?"

"She didn't go," Jasmine declared hotly.

Claudia turned to her in surprise. "How do you know?" she asked.

"Leanne told me when she and Tom came home. They were trying to call you to find out where you were, but you weren't answering your phone. It's only because you'd texted Happy New Year to me that I didn't flip out and come looking for you."

"Why didn't you go?" Marcy wanted to know.

"Because I didn't want to risk being a third wheel?" Claudia countered, trying to make it sound amusing.

Marcy's eyes closed in dismay. "I was afraid that might happen," she groaned, "but you've got no idea if this artist person was Dan's partner for the evening—and you told me before I left for London that you were going."

"I had to, or you wouldn't have gone—and I was fine. It didn't matter, honestly."

Exasperated, Marcy said, "So you shut yourself up here and went through my room to find a letter from the very person you should be eliminating from your life, a letter I shouldn't have kept, but did, and now we've got ourselves all unsettled . . ." She raised her hands, stopping herself from ranting any further. "This is my fault," she stated, "so how about I try to make amends and take us to the Italian for an early dinner?"

"Deffo up for that," Jasmine cheered eagerly. "I'm starving."

Claudia said, "It's not your fault, but we'll let it go now, and I'll call to make sure the restaurant's open . . ."

"It is," Jasmine assured her.

"OK, so do you think Henry would like to join us?"

Marcy's eyes rounded with surprise. "Are you sure?" she asked carefully.

"Of course, I wouldn't have said it otherwise."

"Then I'll give him a call," Marcy responded, still looking doubtful, but starting to smile. "And while I'm at it, why don't you get in touch with Dan to see if he'd like to come too?"

Claudia regarded her incredulously. Had she already forgotten the letter they'd just been discussing? Surely she realized what a mistake it would be for Claudia to allow anyone to come too close again, and not only because of how wrong she'd gotten it the last time. What bothered her just as much was the mere thought of inflicting the specter, much less the potential reality, of Marcus on anyone as decent as Dan. "That really isn't going to happen," she said shortly, and before anyone could argue she went through to her room and closed the door.

# CHAPTER NINETEEN

Dan's gone and tried blackmailing me in a way that I could easily make backfire on him, but I've decided not to. Although I had a bit of fun at first when he said that if I didn't tell you the truth about my ma he'd wash his hands of me and I told him there was a lot of shit to get off so he ought to start scrubbing.

He didn't laugh and I don't blame him because it wasn't all that funny; I just wanted him to look a bit less bleak than he did when he came in. I get the feeling something's eating him. Well, I suppose I know what it is; coming here to see me has got to remind him of what he's really dealing with, and that can't be a good place for him to be. Not much of a good place for me either, but hey, I'm the psycho bastard who did this, so no sympathy for me.

Anyways, to keep him happy, and because he's right about owing you the truth, I'll tell you the real deal about my ma. Her name's Maria and she's all the stuff I said before, a bit of a junkie, a hooker (because sometimes it's the only way she can pay the rent), an ex-con for stiffing the council tax and a spot of dealing, and a nutjob. She also happens to be the person I love most in the world.

Did that surprise you? I guess not, given the way I've gone on about protecting her, but it's something I've always tried to keep hidden. Dan didn't seem surprised the first time I told him, but then he always thinks people like me are hiding their best sides, and that's where he's wrong, because some just don't have one.

So yep, I care about my ma and I'll do anything to keep her safe, and believe me that's not always easy. See, she's vulnerable, weak, not all that clever, she gets hit around a lot by men, especially BJ, and she's not strong enough to fight back. I never used to be able to do anything to stop them, I was too small and half the time if I got in the way they'd deck me too, or worse. But then I got bigger and learned how to take care of myself, and her, a bit better, so the f***wits started to be more careful around me, especially when they got to know I was working for the London gangs.

I was earning by then as well, although not as much as I should have been, because BJ is a robbing b******. Still, I usually had something to give my ma when I got home, I just had to try and make sure she spent it the right way. She's a basket case, sad and mouthy, bewildered and opinionated, but afraid of her own shadow most of the time. She shouts at someone in the street, then runs inside to hide and sends me out to deal with it. Generally I tell whoever it is to fuck off, and because everyone knows I carry (that means I always have a weapon on me), they usually do.

I was fourteen the first time I pulled a blade on someone, and guess who it was. That's right, BJ. I came in from school one day to find him smacking around my ma and my granny (this was before she was carted off to the care home) and I made sure he never did it again. See, the big difference between me and him is that he's a coward, and I'm not. He saw the blade, backed off, and from then on he treated me with a bit more respect. He even told people what I'd done, like he was boasting about it, and that was fine by me.

Anyways, I've kind of got into the habit of acting like my ma don't mean much to me, because it's part of what helps keep her safe. If certain people knew I cared they'd use her as leverage to make me do stuff that would end me up in the nick, or dead. It's how they work, and the ones who run me and BJ are some of the worst. If they went after my old lady they'd really have me, so I had to make out like she meant f***all. They put it to the test a couple of times, which got her a few beatings, but she understood why it had to happen. I kept a note of those who harmed her and promised that one day they'd pay.

Twisted, yeah? Well, you didn't think anything in my world was going to be straight, did you?

I reckon you might be asking where she is now, today, so I'll tell you. She's still in the same house, on that shitty estate, struggling to hold down a job and pay the rent and feed herself. She knows where I am and she comes as often as she can, which probably isn't a good idea, but it's hard to stop her. So, Dan, when you read this, back off her, please. Leave her alone and let her get on with her life, miserable as it is. You can't fix her, it's beyond even you, but nice of you to want to try.

Actually, that's about all I have to say about her. She means as much to me as yours does—or did—to you (don't know if she's still with us). It's just we're different sorts of people and there are a lot out there who think that those like me and my ma don't have the same sort of feelings. Or consciences, or morals, or understanding of anything outside the warped and dangerous world we live in. We are the dregs and you are the cream and what's happening to you now is proof of what we already know, that society cares about your sort a lot more than it does about mine. That's not me getting defensive, or feeling sorry for myself, that's just me telling it as it is.

# CHAPTER TWENTY

E xcited?"

Claudia was many things at that moment and, yes, excited was definitely one of them. She glanced over at her mother in the driver's seat and felt such a rush of happiness that she broke into a laugh. "Of course. Are you?" she asked.

Marcy's eyes were shining. "We have a lot to feel excited about," she replied. "We're on our way to spend the first night in our new home; Jasmine's rehearsals for the upcoming concert are wowing everyone the closer it gets; and you have finally agreed to go on a date with Dan."

Claudia spluttered a protest. "It's not a date!" she cried. "I just invited him to join us for our little moving-in party later. It would have been unforgivable not to when everyone else is coming, and anyway, we want him to be there."

"Of course we do, but it's been quite a while since you found out the artist Julie Forrest is married to one of the big landowners around here, *who was also at the New Year's Eve ball*, so you could have cut poor Dan some slack before now."

Turning away, Claudia said, "You know I felt nervous after reading that letter from Marcus. It's taken me a while to get over it." She still feared they were about to be found, although in a less panicked way now, and the feeling she sometimes had that they were being watched she usually managed to put down to paranoia. She had to, or she'd never have been able to live her life. "Anyway," she continued, "we've hardly seen Dan since the New Year, we've all been so busy. And Andee tells me they've taken on so many restorative justice cases now that they're starting to become desperate for more practitioners."

"Which is why it'll be a lovely break for everyone to come and celebrate with us tonight," Marcy responded. "What time do we have to pick up the food from M&S?"

"Jasmine and Abby are collecting it, and I think Richie, Tom's son, is giving them a hand. We just have to dig through all the packing boxes to find glasses, crockery, cutlery, kitchen roll or napkins."

"Well, let's feel thankful the snow came to nothing, or we'd all have had difficulty getting there. What on earth is this lorry doing in front? Is he going to turn? Yes, thank goodness he is," and once the road ahead was clear Marcy put her foot down to speed up over the hill onto Westleigh Heights. Most of the grand homes they passed were securely hidden behind high walls or tall iron gates, those to the right enjoying uninterrupted vistas of the estuary and those to the left backing onto the undulating drama of the moor.

By now Claudia was in such a state of anticipation that she had to pinch herself to make sure she drank in every moment of their arrival, as they finally turned in through the old gates that still lolled drunkenly into the bushes. Progress along the short drive was bumpy and lit only by their headlights, although that would change once the outside power had been connected.

Then there it was, their exquisite coach house, looking as inviting and pleased with itself as if it had never been neglected for a day. It was a jewel of Georgian architecture, and Claudia knew they were more than lucky to be able to call it home.

As they let themselves in through one side of the double black front door with its smart transom window above they were instantly embraced by warmth, proving that the heating was working. The sitting room was crammed with boxes, suitcases, and unpacked furniture that a removals company had picked up from various locations throughout the day and delivered. The kitchen was flooded with light from overhead spots that Claudia quickly dimmed before hitting another switch to turn on the lamps suspended over the refectory table. There were dozens of boxes piled up in here too, masking the quartzite worktops and many of the pale gray cabinets.

Taking off their coats they quickly set to work, freeing furniture, tearing open boxes, and laughing at how unprepared they were for a party while eager to make it happen. What did it matter that they might have to drink champagne out of mugs or eat canapés off kitchen roll? No one was going to mind, in fact they were expecting it; some were even bringing picnic chairs in case those destined for the refectory table hadn't yet arrived. They hadn't, so it was just as well backups were on the way.

By seven the guests were all gathered in the kitchen, admiring everything about it from the double Belfast sink and pale flagstone floor, to the handmade cabinetry and large center island. Just as Graeme opened the first bottle of champagne, Jasmine found a box of glass tumblers. Everyone cheered, and cheered again when Henry proposed a toast to the beautiful new home and its even more beautiful new residents.

Although most had already seen the place while the work was being done, Wilkie, Leanne's mother, had not been among them so Leanne appointed herself guide and took both her and Tom on a grand tour. As they went into the sitting room for the first stop Richie plugged in his phone to play some music, and Jasmine and Abby began passing around plastic trays of canapés.

Noticing Dan beside the Aga leafing through the album she'd put together of "before" photos, Claudia made herself go and join him.

"You've done a remarkable job with this place," he commented glancing up to see it was her.

"I had a lot of help from Andee," she said modestly.

"Just so you know," Andee called out, "all the whacky ideas are hers—and if you're into draperies you'll be swooning by the time you've seen them all."

"I reckon we should call *Interiors* magazine to get them to photograph the place," Abby suggested. "I mean when it's properly finished."

"Oh, please, no publicity," Jasmine cried, making her genuine protest sound like mock horror.

"Carpets!" Wilkie declared excitedly when she came back into the kitchen with Leanne and Tom. "You have carpets in the bedrooms *and* the bathrooms. It makes everything so cozy, so ready to be lived in."

"The free-standing tubs blew her away too," Leanne announced, "especially the one in your bathroom that's next to a fireplace."

"I was very tempted to get in," Wilkie admitted. "I'm sure I would have if the fire had been lit. It's all so beautiful, my dear, and such a long time since this house was properly loved, but there's no doubt it will be now. Champagne, someone, let's drink another toast to the ladies of Haylesbury Coach House."

As everyone echoed the lively rhythm of the words, Henry decided to swing Marcy into a dance and Richie did the same with Wilkie. There was soon so much laughter and joie de vivre in the room that Claudia felt as intoxicated as if she'd drunk an entire bottle herself. She was hoping to talk some more with Dan, but then Leanne came to join them, and when she began asking his advice about a legal case she was involved in, Claudia discreetly moved away.

She wasn't sure who asked Jasmine to play the violin, she only knew it was going to happen when it began. Everyone stopped to listen, eyes shining with pleasure as they were lulled into the sweetness and drama of Brahms's Sonata No. 3. Then they were laughing as she broke into a joyous Irish jig, and marveling as she followed up with a medley of famous pop songs before finishing with Gershwin's "Summertime."

She radiated so much delight as she took the applause that Claudia had to swallow a lump in her throat. Joel would have been so proud of his girl, and the fact that she'd just played his violin for the first time in front of an audience was something that only she and Marcy knew. Claudia wanted to tell everyone, but understood why Jasmine hadn't; it might have brought a somber note to this wonderful evening of celebration.

"Wow, am I glad that I have my ticket for the opening night of the concert," Dan declared, coming to stand with Claudia again. "She isn't just talented, she's gifted." He frowned. "Is one better than the other?"

Claudia laughed. "I don't know, but I understand your meaning, and on her behalf, thank you." Then without giving herself the chance to back down, she added, "Would you like to sit with us for the opening night? It'll be me, Mum, and Henry in our box, but there's room for one more."

His eyes widened with surprise and pleasure. "I'd love to, thank you," he replied. He seemed about to say more, but stopped himself.

"Go on," she prompted.

He laughed. "I was going to overdo things by asking if you'd like to meet for dinner some time before that, but I realize . . ."

"I would," she told him. "Thank you. Do you have my number?"

He pulled a comical face, and she blushed as she remembered asking Andee not to give it to him.

"I'll call you," he promised after storing the number in his phone, "but I'm afraid I have to go now, an early start tomorrow. Thanks for the invite tonight, it was good to be here for this special occasion."

"Thank you for coming. I'll walk you to the door."

"No, don't leave your guests. Just let me know if you need help with anything as you're settling in. You never know, I might be useful."

HE CALLED THE very next day, just as Claudia was about to tear out her hair with frustration. How could she not have realized these antiquated dining chairs, bought at auction, had such uneven legs, and how was she going to balance them? When her phone rang with a number she didn't know she was tempted to ignore it, but just in case it was a delivery driver needing directions she clicked on with a tired "Hello?"

"OK, I'm going to either provide a welcome break, or get my head bitten off for calling at the wrong time."

When she recognized the voice immediately, her irritation fled. "Hi," she said, abandoning her impossible task and sitting up against an unpacked box.

"Is this too soon?" he asked dryly.

She gave a laugh. "No, it's fine."

"So how are things going? Great party, by the way."

"Thank you, and I'm glad you rang now because I was about to stab something with a chair leg."

"Ouch! Anything I can do?"

"It's OK, I'll work it out. So how are you?"

"I'm good, thanks, apart from feeling as though the RJ program is taking over my life. It's why I'm calling, because it's going to have me pretty tied up most evenings for the foreseeable and I didn't want you to think I was backing out of our dinner. So I thought if I rang now and we put a date in the diary, I'd make sure to work around it."

"That sounds a good idea," she responded, hoping she hadn't sounded as eager as she felt—or as apprehensive, but she wasn't going to allow herself to dwell on that. "I'm free most of the time, or at least I can be flexible, so I'm happy to fit in with you. Oh, apart from Mondays and Thursdays; that's when I go to watch Jasmine rehearsing with her violin teacher."

"Four weeks to the opening night," he responded. "Does she suffer with nerves?"

"Some days are worse than others, but I think she'll be pretty wound up by the time it comes around." She glanced up as her mother passed her a cup of tea and mouthed a thank-you.

"Is that him?" Marcy whispered.

Claudia raised her eyebrows—all the answer her mother needed.

"So, how about next Friday?" he suggested. "I have a meeting at six, but I should be through by seven so I could pick you up at eight? Is that too late?"

Disappointed it wasn't going to be sooner, she said, "No, but to save you driving all the way here, why don't I meet you somewhere in town? Or how about the Mermaid in Hope Cove? That would be an equal distance for us both?"

"Perfect. One of my favorites. I'll book it right away for seven forty-five. You should have my number now, so you can call if something comes up and you need to change."

"I'm sure it'll be fine. I'll look forward to it."

"Me too."

As the line went dead Claudia clicked off her end and continued to sit where she was, going over everything that had been said. Perhaps the best part of the call, she realized, was the fact that he didn't appear to be trying to sweep her off her feet the way Marcus had when she'd first known him. He hadn't been able to wait to see her, and had made it happen virtually every day until eventually he'd charmed her right into marriage.

Sickened by the thought of it, she picked up her phone as it bleeped with a text. *Mermaid booked for 7.45 next Friday. Dan.* No kisses, no smiley faces or other emoticons to make her laugh or feel anxious or pressured, unintentional as that would be, just "Dan."

"So," Andee said with a smile as she joined Dan in his conference room where they often held their RJ meetings. This evening they were due to meet with a couple whose beloved dog had been abducted when a car thief had made off with their Volvo while they were loading groceries into the boot. Andee had spent many hours with the owners over the last few weeks, discussing the effects it had had on their mental health, mainly because of what might have happened to the dog—he was safe—and the fear that something awful like it might happen again.

At the same time, Dan had been talking to the perpetrator who'd been released on bail after his arrest.

Looking up from the file in front of him Dan regarded her curiously, apparently sensing she wasn't about to discuss the case.

"Did you call her?" Andee asked, taking off her coat and hanging it on the stand beside the door.

"I did," he replied, making a show of continuing his annotations. "Two days ago, and we're meeting at the Mermaid next Friday."

Andee's smile widened. "Just what I wanted to hear," and sitting down at the table, she began to unpack her files. "Are you going to ask her anything about . . . ?"

"Who she really is? Of course not, unless she brings it up, but I don't think she will."

Andee didn't think she would either, and letting the subject drop for the moment she opened her laptop to the notes she'd made during her most recent session with the dog owners. They, and the person who'd harmed them (to use RJ speak), were due to arrive ten minutes from now, so there was plenty of time for her and Dan to acquaint each other with how far they'd come with other cases these past few weeks.

The meeting went well, and by the time it was over the pet owners were much closer to believing that the "abductor" had not targeted them personally. He'd had no idea that there was a dog in the car when he'd taken it, and he had zero intention of ever doing anything to harm them again. So both sides left satisfied with the encounter, and thankful that they'd engaged in the process.

It had been one of their easier cases.

"How are you getting along with the girl who was stabbed?" Dan asked as he and Andee packed up their notebooks and laptops.

"Pauline Mansfield. She's still not sure about meeting her attacker, but her counselor's advising it so we're meeting again next week."

"OK, just keep me updated."

"Of course. So now, would you like to come home with me for something to eat?"

Checking his watch, he said, "It's late, so I'll take a rain check if you don't mind. I've got a lot of day stuff to catch up on."

"No problem. Email me some of the RJ referrals if you like, let me help to assess and assign."

As they left the room to enter his office, he said, "Going back to

Claudia. I've been debating with myself whether or not to do some research on Marcus Huxley-Browne."

Andee's eyebrows rose. "With a view to mediating between them?" she asked skeptically.

He let out a laugh. "God no, I'd have to be insane to consider that when she's gone to such lengths to escape him. I wouldn't even want to admit I know his name."

"So why do you want to find out more about him?"

"Natural curiosity, I guess, and maybe it'll give me an insight into what sort of life she had before coming here." He was looking and sounding doubtful about his own proposal. "I guess it's a bad idea, too interfering, too . . . disloyal somehow. Forget I said anything, but thanks for listening. It helped me come to a decision."

THE FOLLOWING FRIDAY came around so quickly that Claudia felt slightly bemused by how slowly the time had seemed to pass until right this minute. Each day, crammed as it was with client meetings, location visits, unpacking her own home, and buoying Jasmine through her bouts of nerves, had seemed to drag endlessly. And yet here she was now, wondering where the time had gone, and what to wear, what to talk about, should she be a little late so he got there first, or slightly early so she was waiting for him?

The problem of what to wear was solved by her mother and Jasmine, who were unanimous in approval of black jeans, pale pink blouse, and wedge ankle boots. Not flashy or seductive, perfect for the pub and a first date.

"Get him to talk about himself," her mother advised when Claudia sought advice on this much trickier matter. "Men love talking about themselves."

"That's true," Jasmine agreed, as if she had all the experience in the world. "But if you run out of stuff you can always talk about me, because what could be more fascinating than how I'm going off my head trying to study, sit mocks, and rehearse for the concert all at the same time?"

"You're doing brilliantly at it all," Marcy told her. "Your talents know no bounds, and apparently I'm doing pretty well too, according to Leanne. Working at Glory Days two afternoons a week is suiting me down to the ground."

Smiling and hugging her mother, Claudia said, "She's lucky to have you."

With an overly modest sigh, Marcy said, "Maybe, but she misses Klaudia since she left for Ireland, that's for sure, and those are shoes I cannot fill unless I want to commit to three full days a week, which I don't. Anyway, time to get yourself off. Are you sure you wouldn't like one of us to drive you there and pick you up again later?"

"I'll be fine," Claudia assured her. "This way I'll be less likely to drink and end up saying something I might regret."

By the time she got to the pub it was crowded, not unusual, but Dan had already texted to say that he was at a table in the library snug, just off the main bar, so she found him with no trouble. As he got up to greet her she felt so nervous and pleased to see him that she choked on a laugh and bumped his glasses as he embraced her.

"I'm sorry," she wailed as he straightened them.

"Don't be. They're always in the way. You look lovely—if I'm allowed to say so."

"Thank you." She smiled. "So do you."

He laughed and gestured for her to sit in the chair opposite his, which was beside a window seat where she could put her bag and, had there been moonlight, they'd have been able to watch the waves lapping the grainy shore.

"What will you have to drink?" he asked, handing her a cocktail menu. "Some of them have quite raunchy names, so a warning here, I might blush if you suggest a comfortable screw against the wall, or sex on the beach." Even as he said it, he was reddening, and how could she not warm to him for that?

"Maybe wine is safer," she suggested.

"You could be right. They serve a great white Rioja here. Would you like to try it? If you haven't already had it."

"I haven't and I would," she confirmed, "provided you're having some too."

"Oh, I'm definitely up for it," and signaling to a young girl whom he called by name, he placed their order and added a bottle of sparkling water.

"You know her?" Claudia asked as the waitress took off to the bar.

Leaning in conspiratorially he said, "She's going through the RJ process at the moment as a person responsible for harm, as we term it."

"You mean she committed a crime?"

"She did, but she's very sorry and promises she'll never whack a queue jumper again, not even one who calls her the n word."

Claudia grimaced. "And the person she whacked?"

"Is sorry too, but to be honest, I think the racism runs deep in her veins, so I'm not convinced that word won't blast out of her again at some time in the future. Still, we'll have to deal with that then; right now we have much more important things on the agenda, such as what we're going to eat."

As they chose their food and the wine was poured, more of Dan's clients—from RJ cases and his law firm—dropped by to say hello, much to Claudia's amusement and his frustration.

"I promise, I had no idea just about everyone I know would be here this evening," he told her, after a thickset tattooed man had insisted on shaking his hand and telling Claudia how, thanks to "this bloke here," he'd become good mates with the lowlife who'd broken into his house and robbed him.

In a quiet voice Claudia said, "I know this is unforgivable stereotyping, but if you'd asked me to guess I'd have said he was the person responsible, rather than the one who was harmed."

Dan laughed. "And another time you wouldn't have been wrong, because he's been on the other side of the table before now. It worked for him then, which is why he's prepared to give it a go now."

Nodding her understanding, she asked him more about his role as a practitioner, genuinely interested to know, and he seemed quite relaxed to talk about it. It was a good way to keep the subject away from her, although it wasn't long before he was asking how everything was going at the house. She was glad to entertain him with the frustrations and disasters of the last ten days, and to admit to how much she already wanted to change.

They talked about Jasmine and the other acts who'd been booked for the concert; about Marcy and her new job at Glory Days; and about Leanne's offer to let him rent the house at Ash Morley that Klaudia had left.

"I was tempted," he admitted, "but I need to get back on the property ladder with a place of my own."

"Are you looking?"

"I would if I had more time, but I'm in no hurry. The flat suits me well for now, although living over the shop does mean I keep forgetting to take time off. I imagine it's a bit the same for you, working from home."

"It is," she admitted, "but I love my new craft room so I'm happy to spend as much time in it as I can. Unfortunately, it's not as much as I'd like because I've been very lucky with all the orders that have come my way since I did the show home, so I'm often out measuring or fitting, or picking up and delivering to the machinists. I haven't made much for the coach house yet, apart from the drapes of course, and a few other things here and there."

"So, what else would you like to add?" he asked.

Not sure if he was really interested, she decided to go with it and said, "More lamps. Those I've made since coming to Kesterly are mostly of driftwood and pebbles, so they're more suited to a place near the beach. For where we are now, I'd like to let myself loose on so many things I hardly know where to start."

Appearing impressed he said, "You've clearly got an eye for this sort of thing."

She smiled. "I enjoy taking unusual items of furniture, whether they're footstools, chairs, old chests, drums, tin baths, and repurposing or reviving them. At some point I'd like to get a kiln and learn how to make pots." She felt sure she was talking too much, but seemed unable to stop. "There's an old shed in the garden that could be turned into a small studio," she continued, "although I think Jasmine has her eye on that for a music room."

"Ah, but she'll be off to university before too much longer," he pointed out, "so maybe you'll get your studio." He took a sip of wine and spoke curiously as he went on, "I hope you don't mind me saying, but you remind me of my wife with your passion for creating things. She was much the same, although she couldn't quite get along with a sewing machine, she was more into jewelry and greeting cards."

"Did she do it for a living?" Claudia asked, liking the way he sounded when he talked about his wife.

"No, she was a PE teacher at a primary school, so the other things were more of a hobby. She had a market stall now and again near where we lived, and her creations used to sell pretty well. Do you ever do markets, or sell through shops?"

Feeling his words pushing her into the more recent past, she avoided his eyes and struggled to block Marcus's mocking voice in her head. "I had a shop myself before I came here," she said, "but I haven't ever braved a market stall. I think I'd like to, at Christmas. It could be fun."

At that moment their food arrived and they continued to talk as easily as if there were no secrets between them, discussing how he'd got into law, what had prompted him to come to Kesterly, their favorite movies, music, and books, the holidays they'd enjoyed the most and other places in the world they'd like to visit.

It wasn't until Misty, the landlady, delivered the bill with an interested smile that they realized how late it had become. Dan paid, because he insisted, but he agreed that Claudia could treat him the next time.

"I'm sorry," she said, reddening, "I'm presuming you want there to be a next time."

"I do," he assured her, "and I'm hoping that you do too."

She nodded, and looked down at her empty glass. "It's been lovely," she said softly.

"For me too," and reaching across the table he covered her hand with his. It was the kind of gesture Marcus had often made before they were married, a touch of her hand, gentle words, a fake but convincing interest in everything she did—and because of that she stiffened.

"Come on, I'll walk you to your car," he said, getting up from the table. "And maybe you'd like to take the rest of the wine home to share with Marcy?"

Retrieving their coats from the rail inside the door, they wrapped up warmly and went out into the night. The scent of sea air was so pungent that it felt tangible, and the roar of the waves as they crashed up against the nearby cliffs was almost deafening.

"Are you missing being by the sea?" he asked as they walked around to the car park.

"A little," she admitted, "but it's always there. I can visit anytime I like."

They came to a stop beside her BMW, and as she unlocked it he handed her the wine. "Not so bad?" he asked teasingly.

She frowned.

"Going for dinner with me?"

She had to laugh in spite of her awkwardness. "Definitely not so bad," she assured him. "I enjoyed it, a lot."

"Me too. I'll call soon to arrange when we can do it again."

"That would be lovely, but don't forget we're seeing you on the concert opening night."

"Don't worry, I'm looking forward to it," and taking a step back he waved her into the driver's seat, as though sensing that anything more would be too much.

She appreciated the gesture, in spite of feeling that she might not have minded if he'd squeezed her hand, or even given her a peck on the cheek.

# CHAPTER TWENTY-ONE

Andee's smile was one of amusement and fondness as Tom's son, Richie, embraced her warmly enough to melt the icy raindrops on his jacket. It was bitterly cold outside, and so cozy in the Seafront Café that the windows were steamed up and the posters Fliss had put up to promote the upcoming concert were starting to wilt.

"How are you?" she asked, signaling to a server to come and take their order as Richie sat into the booth opposite her.

"Yeah, great, thanks, and thanks for meeting me."

"No problem. It was lovely to get your call. Is everything working out at the *Gazette*?"

He rolled his eyes comically. "If the owners understood that we're now in the twenty-first century it would be a start," he replied, "but I'm kind of getting there. Actually, I've been told that if I don't succeed it'll fold, so no pressure."

Andee grimaced with sympathy and after they'd ordered their coffees she said, "I'm sorry I don't have much time, but it sounded urgent when you rang."

"Actually, I'm not sure if it is," he confessed, "but Dad and Leanne agreed that I should tell you what happened."

Andee was intrigued.

"OK, it was a couple of days ago. I was coming out of my office in the Old Town when this guy, fortyish, brown hair, and smart parka, approaches me out of nowhere and asks if he can have a word.

I was on my way to a meeting so I asked him to walk with me, you know, in case he had a good lead on a story. However, right off the bat, without introducing himself he starts asking me if I know someone called Rebecca—surname's escaping me for the moment. I said I didn't, so he pulls out his phone and shows me a photo. Now, I can't be certain about this because the hair color was different, but if Claudia was fair I'd swear it was her."

Andee regarded him closely as her mind went into overdrive. "What did you say?" she asked carefully.

He shrugged. "I told him I'd never seen her before. That was a kind of instinct kicking in, not sure why, but with him coming out of the blue like that . . . And once I took a proper look at him, I felt kind of glad I'd held back. I wouldn't say he was sleazy, or anything, but there was this air about him that seemed a bit . . . off. I asked why he was looking for the woman and he said something about her coming into money, so I decided he must work for one of those inheritance agencies. I offered to put the picture on the paper's website, but he didn't want that. He said he'd carry on asking around and gave me his card so I could be in touch if I saw her or heard anything about her." His eyes narrowed curiously. "You're looking worried. It was Claudia, wasn't it?"

"Do you know who else he was talking to in town?" Andee countered.

"I didn't think to ask. I was already late so I just wished him good luck and went into my meeting. To be honest I forgot about it until Claudia popped into Dad and Leanne's yesterday while I was there. I didn't want to tell her in case it wasn't her in the photo—or in case it was, I guess. I waited until after she'd gone and told them, which is when they said I should call you. So, what's going on?"

Picking up her coffee, she sipped as she thought. In the end she avoided his question again and said, "I know you're scenting a story, but please hold back for now, at least until I've had time to talk this over with someone who probably needs to know."

"Meaning Claudia?"

"No, not her."

His eyes twinkled. "Enter the infamous DCI Gould?"

She didn't deny it.

"OK. And if this guy contacts me again? Do you want me to put him on to you?"

"No, don't do anything to suggest you might be engaging with him at all, but let me know if he does. And if you still have his card I'll take it from you."

Reaching into his pocket he handed it over. "You realize a scoop for the *Gazette* is something I really need right now."

"I do, and as soon as I can send one your way, I promise I will."

DCI GOULD WAS a large man in his early fifties with a lot of presence and not much tolerance when it came to someone holding him up as he was leaving for an important meeting. However, as it was his favorite ex-DS doing the holding, he sat back down at his desk and waited as she closed his office door.

He listened carefully to what she was telling him, his blue eyes sharp and narrowed, and said nothing for a while after she'd finished.

"OK," she said in the end, "I get that you probably can't tell me if I'm right about Claudia and her family being the ones . . ."

"You're right," he assured her, "it's them. I'm just trying to think of the best way to handle this. Have you tried getting in touch with this . . . What's the name of the guy who approached Richie?"

Reading from the card, Andee said, "Miles Montgomery. I'm guessing he's some sort of private investigator. Probably he's working for Claudia's husband or someone close to him."

Gould's eyebrows arched. "Have you called the number?"

"I thought I'd speak to you first."

"Good. The less contact he has from anyone in this area the better. We don't want him thinking that he's stirring something up, or he'll be straight back here. If he's even gone away, and I don't suppose we know if he has."

"I've tried several hotels, but there's no one staying at any of them with that name, which doesn't mean much because he could be using Airbnb, or one of the hundreds of guesthouses. I talked to Fliss at the café, and a few other business owners. No one's approached them, but again I'm not sure that means anything."

Gould nodded slowly. "And no one's spoken to Claudia about this?"

"Not yet. They're crazy busy getting ready for Jasmine's big night tomorrow so I've hardly seen her lately. Are you going, by the way?"

"I am, and I'm sure you and Graeme are. Maybe we can have a drink together beforehand?"

"Great, let's do that. I'll get Dan to join us as well. Claudia and Marcy will be too busy backstage. Anyway, how urgent do we think this is?"

He shrugged. "We have no way of knowing, but I think I should be in touch with Carl Phillips, in London. He was the investigating officer when they were thought to be missing. I'd like to get his take on what we should do."

"And in the meantime? Do I say anything to Claudia?"

He threw out his hands. "You know her better than I do. Is it going to freak her out if she thinks she's been found?"

"Possibly, probably. I'll wait until you've spoken to Phillips."

# CHAPTER TWENTY-TWO

I've been trying to think of how to get around to this bit of my story, as Dan calls it. <u>Story!</u> Makes it sound like some kind of fairy tale, but as we know it's a long way from that.

I've been dreading it, knowing it was coming, but I get that it has to be done. I mean, I could always say fuck it and move on, the way I usually do, but that's not making me feel too good. I guess it's talking to Dan that's got me seeing things differently. He says I'm starting to see myself differently, but I'm not sure he's right about that.

Anyway, here goes with the first part of how our paths came to cross. I just want you to know that I'm not in the business of naming names. That's not going to happen. I have to think about my ma and what might be done to her if I put someone in the frame over this. Hope you understand.

So, it kicked off when BJ turns up one day and says he's got a job for me. It's not him who wants it done (it never is), it's his bosses, obvs. One of the PCs has solicited their assistance with a certain situation and they've called in their man, BJ, who passes it to me because it's in my neck of the woods.

It turns out to be a spot of breaking and entering and they're paying well. The PC and his reps want a briefcase thought to be in a house on Westleigh Heights. I'm no expert when it comes to that sort of job, but it turns out to be easy enough. I scoped the place for a couple of nights, getting an idea of who was in when, and times it was most likely to be empty, and on the third night I went in through a back window.

I poked around for over an hour, keeping alert for anyone returning. No one did, but the longer I was there the greater the risk so I left—minus a briefcase.

I went in again the next night but still couldn't find it, and I spent even longer looking, always careful to put stuff back where it belonged and even waiting till I got outside to pee.

I presumed the bosses—or the PC—would accept it just wasn't there, because that was my conclusion, but I turned out to be wrong. The job had changed now and as soon as I found out how I told BJ I wasn't his man. He doesn't make with the threats or anything, which is what I'm expecting, he goes on more about how much we're going to make and all the kudos we're going to earn with those who matter if I pull it off. Earning kudos with the bosses means a lot to him, and I have to admit I'd rather be on the right side of them than not.

Anyways, I still wasn't keen, having never done anything like it before, but then BJ starts going on and on about the money and what a difference it was going to make for my ma if she had some cash behind her. She wanted to fix up the house as best she could, get some glass put in the boarded-up windows, replace old carpets, and put in a washing machine. It might even make it possible for me to do a proper apprenticeship as a car mechanic, or a builder, or something to help me turn respectable. I got that was probably never going to happen, not when I knew they'd come back for me anytime they felt like it.

So, I ended up telling him that before I did anything I had to talk to someone with experience of that sort to get some wisdom. The only person I knew was doing a stretch, so I got a train to Durham and by the time I came home again I was ready to roll.

I got everything together, borrowed a van, and drove up to the Heights. I'd seen you and your family a few times when I was scoping the place for break-in, but I know you'd never seen me. I was very careful about that as I watched you come and go. With it being dark and having so much wilderness to hide out in, it wasn't hard.

# CHAPTER TWENTY-THREE

'm going to turn the car around," Jasmine shouted from the front door.

"OK, we'll be right there," Claudia called back. "Are you sure you should come?" she said to her mother, wincing as Marcy broke into another fit of sneezing. "That cold's getting worse and you don't want it ending up on your chest."

"I'll be fine," Marcy protested, catching her breath and reaching for another tissue. "I don't want to miss tonight."

"It's a dress rehearsal. If you go to bed now and spend the day there tomorrow you'll have a fighting chance of being OK for the main event."

"I know, I know, but I sound worse than I am. Let's just go or we'll make her late."

With an exasperated sigh Claudia left her mother to wrap up warm while she dashed through to her craft room to fetch her bag. Finding it beneath the worktable, she checked her phone was inside and was about to leave when she came to a stop. She looked around, not sure why, for she hadn't heard anything and everything seemed to be in its place. This wasn't the first time, however, that she'd got the feeling recently that someone had been in here. Someone other than her mother or Jasmine. She hadn't mentioned anything to either of them, she didn't want to worry them, and she certainly didn't want them thinking she was becoming paranoid again.

Her gaze quickly scanned the organized chaos, from bolts of

fabric propped up in one corner, to trestle tables laden with projects in progress, along the walls full of pegboards, design sheets, and Post-it reminders, to the sewing-machine cases stacked into a floor-to-ceiling niche. It looked as it always did, the domain of someone who had more work than she could cope with.

Her phone buzzed with a text, and grabbing it from her bag she turned out the lights as she left the room.

*Fingers crossed for the dress rehearsal. If you're free after would love to take you all for a bite. D.*

Smiling happily, she tapped a message back. *That would be lovely if not too late. Will call when it's over. C.*

Since their evening at the Mermaid, a couple of weeks ago, they'd been texting each other regularly with last-minute suggestions for coffee, or a quick lunch, or maybe a drink at the end of the day. It was the most either of them could manage, given how busy they were, but she was happy to take things at this pace—and really looking forward to him sharing their box for the concert tomorrow night.

To her astonishment, as she dug her arms into her coat, she spotted Jasmine's beloved Stradivarius on the refectory table. Grabbing it, she ran out to the car. "Forgotten something?" she asked, holding it up.

Lowering her window Jasmine said, "Anton tuned it today, so I'm using my old one tonight."

"OK," and dashing back inside she tucked it out of sight inside the coat cupboard and set about locking up.

Minutes later she was in the front seat of the Mini, but they'd got no farther than the end of the drive before Marcy said, "I'm really sorry, but I think I'll have to sit this one out after all."

"No problem," Jasmine assured her. "It's more important that you're well for tomorrow," and putting the car into reverse she was about to return to the house when Marcy said, "Drop me here. I can walk back."

"Do you have your keys?" Claudia asked, getting out to tip her seat forward.

"No, I don't think so . . ."

"Take mine. We'll use Jasmine's when we come home. Straight to bed now, OK?"

"Promise." Marcy smiled, giving her a hug.

"Dan's invited us for a bite to eat after, so we might be a bit late."

"Don't rush. I'll probably be fast asleep."

# CHAPTER TWENTY-FOUR

So, I'm standing outside your house, hidden from view in the bushes. It's like a jungle, brambles, cobwebs, you name it, but I can see everything you're doing. At last, the front door's locked, you all get in the car and drive off. After you've gone, I sneak round to the old shed at the back to collect the gear I brought with me. I wait there for a while; I'm not sure why. I could have been losing my nerve, or I just didn't want to do it. Whatever, I end up carrying my stuff back to the front and I settle down in the bushes again.

There are the same lights on inside the house as there were when you left, nothing's changed. There's no one about, just a couple of cars passing on the road now and again, so I can take my time, make sure it's done right.

I was told not to bother about trying to hide it was arson, I wouldn't be able to anyway, but that was my instruction. I thought, someone, somewhere wants you to know it was deliberate. What did you do to them?

I start by smashing one of the big arched windows. I brought a proper sledgehammer for that so it's done in a couple of hits. Next I empty a petrol can through the hole, sloshing it about for good cover. Then I do the same on the other side, smash the window, slosh the petrol, make sure to soak as much as I can.

Everything stays quiet apart from the rustle of whatever is in the undergrowth. I don't even hear myself pouring petrol through the letter box I'm so quiet. I finish up by tossing the canisters through the broken windows. Then I light a fueled-up rag, post it fast, and back off even faster.

To be honest, at first, I didn't think it had taken. Nothing seemed to happen, but I wasn't going to go and check and have the whole thing blow up in my face. I stayed where I was, masked by the bushes, close to the road, watching and waiting. I remember the moon reflecting in the windows I hadn't smashed and a bird scaring me as it fluttered out of a tree.

Then everything started to take off, flames shooting up like crazy, smoke billowing out through the broken panes. I'd been told oxygen would fuel the fire and it was happening, because suddenly the whole of one side was ablaze. I watched kind of mesmerized, waiting for the heat to reach me. I don't think it did, I don't remember it anyway, I just remember someone shouting and running up the drive and someone else coming after them yelling that they were calling 999. I read later it was a couple of gay neighbors walking their dog.

You might think it weird that I didn't run. I know I do. But it was like I couldn't make myself move. I watched the whole thing unfold, more people rushing in, someone grabbing a hose, flames lashing out of the windows curling up to the roof . . . In my head now I've lost a sense of time, but I remember sirens wailing up the main road and two fire trucks thundering into the drive. I was still there while the firemen got to work and a crowd gathered on the street, their faces brightened and strobed by emergency lights.

Then a car screeched to a stop behind a fire truck and two people jumped out. I saw who it was right away, recognized the car, but I couldn't understand it. Why had they come back? What was happening? The girl was screaming, "Nana!" and that was when I realized someone—you—were inside.

I swear I thought the place was empty. I'd watched the three of you go out, ffs, but somehow YOU WERE IN THERE.

# CHAPTER TWENTY-FIVE

Claudia started forward, desperate to get through the smoke and crowd as her mother was carried out of the smoldering front door. She was hauled back; the paramedics needed space, focus, no family emotions.

Noxious clouds swirled around them. Someone shouted that the fire was out. Jasmine clung to her, and Claudia choked on a sob of terror. How badly was her mother injured? Were they going to save her?

Through the mayhem, everything seeming surreal in the strange, smoky light, she caught glimpses of Marcy being lifted on to a spinal board, a respirator and IV tubes already attached . . . She must still be alive.

"I need to go with her," Claudia cried, as the stretcher was hoisted into the back of a paramedic vehicle to be sped to the helicopter that had just landed at the edge of the moor.

A fireman grabbed her. "You can't," he yelled over the noise. "She's in good hands . . ."

"Where are they taking her?" Claudia shouted back, so traumatized she hardly knew what she was asking.

"Swansea. It's . . ."

"Why Swansea?" she almost screamed.

The fireman moved off; someone had called from inside the house, and she was suddenly being wrapped in blankets and led away from the heart of the melee. Pulling Jasmine close, she clung to her in stunned despair. "We have to do something," she muttered, but seemed unable to make her brain or her body work beyond holding that truth.

Suddenly, in the near distance, an air ambulance rose into the night, monstrous and flashing and swooping away from them.

"I have to go with her," Claudia sobbed wretchedly. "She can't go on her own."

"I'll drive," Jasmine croaked. Her throat was parched by floating ash.

Aware of hands grasping her shoulders, Claudia spun around. Andee and Graeme were there, their faces ghostly and strobed by the emergency lights turning night into horrific day.

A fireman approached, ungainly in his protective gear, face smudged, helmet open, and introduced himself as Rajid Khatri, crew manager. He asked Claudia if she was the owner of the property.

Claudia looked at her beloved home and seeing its ruined facade cruelly exposed in the overbright lights, she let out a cry of grief. Charred embers and smoke continued to pour from the smashed windows and clung to the scorched exterior. The roof was still smoldering, the front door was no more, and yet bizarrely, almost defiantly, the tower remained standing proud. She couldn't make sense of what she was seeing. It was a nightmare. It had to be. Her beautiful home, her friend, her haven, couldn't have been subjected to something as terrible as this.

Beside her someone was retching. She turned to see Jasmine being held by Andee as she choked and coughed the bile from her throat.

"We have to get to Nana," Claudia told her. As she said the words it felt as though she was floating, disappearing into another dimension, and for an awful moment she thought she was going to pass out.

"We got here as soon as we could," Leanne cried, running up to them with Tom. "How's Marcy? Do you have any news yet?"

"The air ambulance has just left," Andee told her. "They've taken her to Swansea . . ."

"Why Swansea?" Claudia cried again. It was so far. How were she and Jasmine going to get there?

"It's the main burns center for the South West," Andee explained. "They'll be taking her straight there so she doesn't have to be moved again in case it turns out to be . . . necessary."

Understanding from these words that her mother's injuries must already have been deemed critical, even life-threatening, Claudia fought down a wave of panic. "I have to go to her," she gasped. "Jasmine, we need to get there."

The crowd of onlookers parted as Andee steered Claudia and Jasmine through to Graeme's car. A police officer was moving alongside them, but Claudia didn't register what Andee was telling him.

Once in the back of the Mercedes Claudia and Jasmine belted up and as though it were happening in a dream, she heard Graeme starting the engine and Leanne saying to Andee, "We'll stay here for as long as we're needed. Call me as soon as there's news."

"I will," Andee promised. "We might need you to bring a change of clothes tomorrow."

"Just let me know." To Claudia Leanne said, "Don't worry about anything here. We've got it covered. Just focus on your mum and tell her that we all love her."

Claudia swallowed, dimly aware of ash in her mouth, stuck to her skin, in her hair. "Thank you," she managed. "Thank you."

Graeme drove swiftly through mile after mile of countryside to join the M5. By the time they reached it Claudia had managed to contact someone at the Morriston Hospital, who confirmed that the air ambulance had arrived and her mother was being assessed.

"Do you know how bad it is yet?" Claudia made herself ask. "It's her daughter speaking."

"The doctor will talk to you when you get here," came the reply, and Claudia wanted to scream in frustration—and terror.

"That might take three hours," she explained, as Jasmine's hands closed around hers like a vice. "Is she conscious? Can you tell her we're on our way?"

"As I said, she's being assessed, but if there's an opportunity to pass on the message I will."

Before the woman could ring off Claudia cried, "Can I call again?"

"Yes, of course."

IT WAS PAST midnight by the time they arrived at the hospital, and rain was coming down in torrents. Hardly noticing, Claudia and Jasmine leapt from the car and ran in through the main doors.

Claudia explained to a lone receptionist why they were there and they were immediately directed to ER.

"Claudia?" a nurse asked, coming to meet them. "I'm Alex. Your mother's been taken to surgery. Don't worry, one of our top burns teams is here so she's in the best hands."

Claudia somehow thanked her, and tried to think what to do next.

"There's a waiting room for families," the nurse told her. "I'll take you."

Remembering Andee and Graeme, Claudia took out her phone, explaining that she needed to let her friends know where to find them. "They're parking the car," she added, feeling suddenly hot and nauseous and dizzy . . .

"Mum!" Jasmine cried, grabbing her as she swayed.

"I'm OK," Claudia murmured. "I'm fine."

"Sit down here for a moment," the nurse instructed. "You've had a nasty shock. Take deep breaths and I'll bring you some water."

Andee and Graeme found them in the waiting room, and as there was no one else holding vigil for a loved one that night they had the place to themselves.

"Can you tell us anything?" Claudia implored when nurse Alex returned.

"Someone will be out to speak to you shortly," she promised. Her expression was kindly and sympathetic, but grave. "There are tea- and coffee-making facilities in the corner there, feel free to help yourselves."

Graeme did the honors while Andee sat with Claudia and Jasmine, ignoring the vibrations of her phone and doing her best to reassure them.

The door opened and Claudia shot to her feet.

A tired-looking middle-aged man in green surgical scrubs and oversized clogs and with sweat pouring from his face introduced himself. He wasn't smiling, but he didn't appear frighteningly solemn either. "Andrew Brown," he said, shaking Claudia's hand as she stepped toward him. "Please excuse my appearance. It's important that we keep the operating room warm for burns patients."

"How is she?" Claudia asked brokenly.

"I'm afraid she's suffered extensive injuries to her face, neck, and left arm," he replied. "They're what we term deep dermal, possibly full-thickness burns into the bottom layer of the skin. It's difficult to say how deep—only time will tell—but it's serious."

"But she'll survive?" Claudia urged, tears starting down her cheeks.

"We're still waiting for results of the tests she was given on arrival to find out if she has any deeper organ injury, and how much damage the smoke has caused to her lungs. She was given a tetanus shot in the emergency department and PlasmaLyte—a salty solution—to keep the circulation topped up. At the moment we're cleaning the wounds and removing the nonviable matter . . ."

Jasmine clasped a hand to her mouth. "Can she feel anything?" she wailed, horrified.

He smiled. "She's anesthetized, fast asleep, pain-free," he assured her. "However, the depth of the burns means that her nerve endings are injured, so it could be that even if she was awake she wouldn't feel that much in those areas."

Not wanting to think about how it was going to be later, if there was going to be a later, Claudia said, "How much longer will she be in surgery?"

"She'll be moved to intensive care sometime in the next half an hour, but I should warn you that further surgeries will be required. However, one step at a time. We'll assess the situation in the morning and hopefully we'll have more to tell you then."

Claudia didn't know what more to ask; she was dizzy again and losing her thoughts.

"Will we be able to see her?" Jasmine asked.

"As soon as she's comfortable. She'll be heavily sedated and you might find the paraphernalia a little alarming, but try to bear in mind that it's doing a good job of . . ."

"Of what?" Claudia cried, without really wanting to know.

Patiently he said, "Of keeping her out of distress. She'll be intubated and ventilated to maintain her breathing, and we'll be passing fluids into her veins to keep her circulation flowing—at the moment all her blood vessels are leaky from the inflammation."

Not sure she could take any more, Claudia forced herself to listen as he continued.

"Dressing changes will happen every couple of days," he informed her. "You'll be asked to leave while that's happening, but otherwise visiting hours are quite relaxed during this critical time."

Wishing he hadn't used that word, Claudia tried to thank him, but her voice had become hoarse, and her legs were suddenly so weak she needed to sit down.

Seeming to understand this, he gave her a reassuring smile. "One of the nurses will be out to speak to you again when we move her," he said, and with a nod toward Andee and Graeme he left.

Claudia's distraught eyes found Jasmine's. "She's going to be all right," she said, sounding far more definite than she was feeling. "She'll get through this."

"I know." Jasmine's voice was small and childlike. "She's Nana. She doesn't let anything get the better of her."

Claudia turned to Andee.

"Don't go there," Andee warned, clearly reading her mind. "Just don't."

Claudia took a breath, wondering how Andee could tell she was blaming herself, but there was so much in her head now, so many terrible thoughts, that she had no idea how to articulate them, much less assemble them.

Handing her phone to Graeme, Andee said, "Can you return these calls?"

After he'd gone Andee sat Claudia down and held her hands again, as Jasmine leaned against her mother. "We need to focus on why this has happened," she said gently but firmly. "Let's start with why wasn't Marcy at the dress rehearsal with you?"

Claudia's head swam as she tried to think back. It felt like part of another world, something that had happened too long ago to remember. "She should have been," she replied. "She wanted to come. We were all in the car ready to go, but she's had a terrible cold these last few days. She decided as we were leaving that she was too sick to come with us, that she should try to get herself in better shape for the opening night."

Jasmine said, "I can't do the opening night now. We have to stay here with Nana, and anyway, Dad's violin was in the house."

Claudia turned to her, realizing to her horror that she was right.

For what seemed an eternity it was all she could think of, but as awful as it was, nothing—just nothing—mattered more than her mother right now.

# CHAPTER TWENTY-SIX

Once I realized you were inside the house I'd set fire to I seemed to wake up, panic, and I started to run. Coward, eh? Well, what do you expect of someone who'd do something like that?

I'd hidden the van at the back of a layby on the edge of the moor. I was still in it when the air ambulance took off, so close that the van shook like it might fall apart. No one saw me, they weren't looking. I suppose I was in a daze, shocked, spaced out, because honest to God I hadn't known that you were in the house. I saw you get in the car with the others, your granddaughter drove off, so you must have gone back inside while I went round to the shed to get my stuff.

It was the only explanation that made any sense.

I watched the helicopter carry you off until it wasn't much more than a few pinpricks over the estuary. I reckon I stopped thinking, or feeling, even breathing, I just remember that more than anything in the world I wanted you to be all right. Not for me, for you. OK, for me too. Next to that I wished to God that I'd never taken the job. I'd had a bad vibe about it from the get-go, so why the f*** had I allowed myself to get sucked in?

Then I was speeding off over the moor—there was no chance of getting back to town the way I'd come, the road was blocked by police and fire engines.

I've no idea how long it took me to get home, but I don't suppose it matters. I dumped the van outside my mate's lockup and ran to the house. My ma wasn't there, no idea where she'd gone. I texted BJ to let him know <u>job done.</u> A while after I sent another fessing up that someone had been inside.

I knew there was going to be hell to pay. I'd been told to torch a house, not to cremate one of the occupants.

I thought about you then, and your daughter and grand-daughter. I'd seen you a few times while I was staking the place out. You'd always looked decent enough people to me and I wondered again what you'd done to piss someone off so much that they wanted to incinerate your home. It wasn't any of my business, of course, but I couldn't help trying to work it out.

I didn't sleep that night, no point even trying. I paced up and down, drank some beer, scared like I'd never been before. Something real bad was going to happen to me for screwing up like this. I'd heard about kids who'd had half their tongues cut out to stop them talking, or were beaten up so bad they might as well be dead.

I'm not saying I didn't think about you, because I did, but there was nothing I could do about you now. The people deciding my fate were some of the worst. I needed to get myself and my ma out of there, to someplace we couldn't be found.

I got a text back from BJ about four in the morning. It said: <u>You did good. Lie low and speak to no one.</u>

So, they knew you were hurt, but I still did good.

# CHAPTER TWENTY-SEVEN

DCI Gould clicked off his phone and fixed Dan Collier with a fiercely intent stare. "It was arson," he said shortly. "The place reeked of petrol."

Dan pressed his fingers to his eye sockets trying to ease the tension that had been building up in his head since he'd heard the news. He was lucky to have gotten this meeting so soon after the event, although he guessed Andee had paved the way.

"So, the question is," Gould continued, "was the perp, or perps, targeting only the house, or did they know someone was inside?"

Dan said, "For me, the bigger question right now is, will Marcy survive it? And the next that comes to mind is, who the hell did it?"

Gould conceded the points.

"When I spoke to Andee first thing," Dan went on, "she confirmed that all three of them, Claudia, Marcy, and Jasmine, were due to be at the dress rehearsal last night, but Marcy stayed behind at the last minute. So a change of plan that whoever did it wasn't prepared for?"

Gould absorbed this thoughtfully. "Initial take from the scene," he said, "is that she heard something and went to investigate. It's probable that she tried to put the fire out but the smoke overwhelmed her."

Not even wanting to picture Marcy's fear and desperation, the horror she must have felt when she'd realized their beloved house was on fire, Dan said, "Have you been up there yet?"

"I came back about an hour ago. Both bedroom wings are intact, so's the tower, but most of the kitchen, sitting room, and part of the roof have gone."

Dan's heart folded around a visceral ache of despair. He frowned to try and ease the tension again. "Well, it's just a house," he stated, certain Claudia saw it as more than that, "and I'm sure it can be fixed. What really matters is Marcy. She's having a second surgery as we speak."

Gould nodded grimly. "Yes, Andee told me. I haven't met her, but . . . Dear God, this is a bad business."

It certainly was. "I should probably tell you," Dan said, "that I know who Claudia is and more or less why she and Jasmine changed their names, so I'm guessing someone's talking to the husband?"

Gould appeared unsurprised by the admission, or the question. "I've already spoken to Carl Phillips in London, so he's on it, but given that we know Huxley-Browne couldn't have done it himself, it's going to be a question of finding out who he got to act for him. Good luck with that. However, one of my guys here, Leo Johnson, is trying to track down this Miles Montgomery character who was asking around about Claudia a couple of days ago."

Dan stiffened. "I didn't know about that," he declared. "Did Claudia?"

Gould shook his head. "I was waiting to hear back from Carl Phillips before contacting her . . ." He propped his head onto one hand. "Jesus, if ever there was a wrong judgment call . . ."

Dan snapped, "So what leads do you have on this Montgomery bloke?"

"None so far, but given it's almost certainly a false name . . ." He clicked on his mobile as it rang. "Barry, talk to me."

As he listened his scowl deepened, but all he said was, "OK, keep at it and let me know if there are any other witnesses." Ending the call, he said to Dan, "One of the officers at the scene. Apparently a neighbor spotted a youth running away some time after the fire started. He didn't get a good look at him, but maybe someone else did. They're going door to door at the moment and forensics are all over it, obviously."

Picturing the scene in his mind, Dan said, "I guess you'll need to speak to Claudia at some point?"

"That's a given, but I don't expect she'll be back this way anytime soon. I'll have to send someone to Swansea—and if I had anyone spare it would help. Still, at least Andee's managed to establish that the name Miles Montgomery means nothing to her. I guess no surprise there, but the description we have of him—large and middle-aged—doesn't fit with 'a youth running away' from the scene. So this puts two possible perps in the frame—the one who carried out the attack and a likely handler, or conspirator. Knowing Huxley-Browne, I'd say this could be a pretty crowded frame. When did you last speak to Andee?"

"Just before I arrived here. She and Graeme are on their way back now. Leanne's staying for a while. She took some clothes over this morning. I'm driving there myself when I leave here, with Henry."

Gould said, "Good. Claudia's most likely still in shock, but try talking to her if you can. There's a chance she might be able to give us some names or information that'll help move things along."

CLAUDIA WAS IN the room she and Jasmine were sharing at a Premier Inn, close to the hospital. They'd checked in just after five this morning, and a while later Leanne had turned up with clothes and toiletries so they'd been able to shower and change. The phone chargers had been a thoughtful addition.

Leanne had taken Jasmine across the road for a bite to eat a few minutes ago, but Claudia, unable to face even the thought of food, had stayed here. All that mattered was getting her mother through this.

Marcy would survive, the surgeon had sounded confident about that when he'd spoken to them earlier. The tests on her vital organs had revealed no irreparable damage and the extent of the burns, though severe, wasn't considered life-threatening. However, they were almost certainly going to be life-changing, not only physically, but mentally, given the damage inflicted on her face. It was far too early to say exactly how disfiguring the injuries would be, but Claudia had seen enough burns victims on TV and in newspapers to know how they looked months, even years into the future.

Apparently skin grafts were due to begin on Marcy as soon as sometime in the next few days. At this moment she was undergoing further surgery for more of the charred and dead skin to be cut away, and merely thinking of it made Claudia ball a fist to her mouth to stop herself from screaming.

The only way to distract herself from the panic, and the guilt, was to focus on the certainty that this had been no accident. The fact that someone had been asking around about her a few days ago was enough to confirm that she'd been found, and the fire had been a message from Marcus letting her know that she hadn't escaped him, and never would. She had no idea how he had tracked her down; it hardly mattered, although his sister would have had a hand in it, and presumably they'd paid someone to carry out the crime. She wondered if Marcus had meant for her to be inside the house and the arsonist had got the wrong person. More likely the instruction was for the house and everything in it—most particularly the attaché case—to go up in flames.

Why couldn't he have just got someone to break in and steal it? Perhaps he had. She recalled the feeling she'd had lately that someone had been in the house, and now she was convinced that they had. She hadn't checked since they'd moved in to see if the case was still where she'd hidden it. So it was possible that Marcus, or his sister, already had it, and the horrific act of vandalism inflicted on the house was to punish her, to spite her and remind her who had all the power.

Or the case could have perished in the fire.

She didn't know, because she hadn't yet been told, the extent of the damage. She could hardly bear to think of it; it was like imagining a beloved friend injured and abandoned, helplessly waiting for her to return to begin the process of restoring it to glory all over again. At least it stood a chance, could even emerge from the tragedy more splendid than before, but that was never going to happen for her mother. The surgeon's miracles could only work so far, and suddenly she felt so overwhelmed by the horror of it all that she had to push it from her mind or she simply wouldn't be able to cope.

A WHILE LATER, unable to stand the hotel room or the waiting any longer, Claudia put on her coat to go back to the hospital. Her mother wasn't expected to be out of surgery yet, but she couldn't go on sitting around driving herself crazy with guilt and fear, and such murderous thoughts of revenge were making her nauseous. She needed some air, some space between herself and her conscience, although she knew she'd never find that. This was all her fault, her mother wouldn't be where she was if it weren't for their crazy attempt to start again—if it weren't for the fact that she, Claudia, had taken the attaché case and held on to it.

After texting Jasmine to let her know where she was, she left the room, and a few minutes later she was being buzzed into the Burns Intensive Care Unit in time to see her mother being brought back from one of the theaters in the middle of the horseshoe-shaped specialist center.

The surgery had gone as well as hoped, she was told as Marcy was settled on the ventilator while drugs to maintain her blood pressure were tapered down. Again, her entire head was swathed in dressings, apart from her eyes and mouth forming three shadowy gashes in the ghoulish white of the helmet. It was stifling in the cubicle, the way it had to be for burns patients, but Claudia hardly noticed the heat. She was transfixed by the discoloration around her mother's left eye where fluorescein dye, the nurse explained, had been used to check the depth of the burns. There was no sign of infection, she was assured, although it remained a concern, so drops would be regularly applied to reduce the risk. A further surgery was scheduled for tomorrow to take skin from her underarm in order to remake the left eyelid.

Claudia had never heard of such astonishing procedures before, and would have been happy to remain unenlightened.

"We'll be keeping her sedated for at least the next few days," the senior nurse informed her. "This will stop her fighting the ventilator, although the aim is to get her off of that as quickly as we can to avoid a chest infection."

Claudia didn't ask how much pain there was going to be once her mother was conscious; it was something that would have to be dealt with when it happened. For now, it was important simply to take one step at a time, and the fact that the second surgery hadn't uncovered anything worse than was already known—as if that wasn't terrible enough—must count as a blessing.

As the nurses worked quietly around the bed, Claudia sat down and took her mother's right hand between both of hers. The skin was as soft and unblemished by fire as her own, while the other hand was in a boxing-glove-size dressing that continued up to her shoulder. All blisters had been removed during surgery and the small amount of exposed skin on her neck glistened red and raw each time a soothing coat of paraffin was applied. Through the small frame of bandages around the mouth it was possible to see that her lips were swollen and taut and silvery, and each time a nurse gently moved her head Claudia was reminded that beneath the dressings her mother's burnt scalp was now entirely bald. What had been left of her hair on admission had been shaved off to avoid infection.

Time hissed and bleeped quietly by as Claudia tried to connect with her mother by telepathy, to assure her that she would get through this. *You mustn't worry about the house*, she told her silently, *or about anything else. You're all that matters.*

She was concentrating so hard that it was a moment before she realized there was a hand on her shoulder. Seeing it was Jasmine, she tilted her head to press the paper-gloved fingers to her cheek. Like her Jasmine was wearing a gown, a hat, and shoe covers, obligatory protection when visiting this ward. "Are you OK?" she asked.

"I guess."

They hadn't spoken about the violin again; there was nothing they could say to make the loss of Joel's precious gift any easier to bear.

"Leanne's still here," Jasmine said, "and Dan and Henry have just arrived."

Claudia didn't know what to say.

"Don't worry, they know they can't see her, but I think they wanted to lend some moral support."

Claudia nodded distractedly. It was kind of them, but her mind was suddenly more focused on the individual, or individuals, who'd come to her home and done this. Faceless and nameless they might be, but her hatred for them was consuming.

"How did the surgery go?" Jasmine asked, sounding as though she was afraid of the answer.

Bringing herself back to the moment, Claudia said, "Quite well apparently. Another is scheduled for tomorrow." She glanced up as a nurse came to check the bank of computers behind the bed. So much technology, all of it playing a vital role in keeping her mother steady and out of pain.

*She'll pull through*, the surgeon had said, *but it's going to take time*.

Pressing a kiss to her mother's good hand, Claudia stood up for Jasmine to take her place. "Talk to her," she said. "She'll want to know you're here."

After removing her protective clothing and disposing of it, Claudia went in search of Henry and Dan, who, in her bizarrely dislocated state, were feeling like people she used to know from a long time ago.

A nurse directed her to the BICU waiting room, which wasn't far from the secure doors to the ward, and as she entered both men rose to their feet. Henry looked so pale and shattered that she felt a bolt of irrational anger toward him. It wasn't that she didn't know the situation was serious, how could she not, but seeing it reflected in Henry's eyes was making it more real than she was willing to accept right now.

"Claudia, my dear," he said, coming to envelop her. "I hope you don't mind us turning up like this. I just had to be near, even if I can't see her."

"It's lovely that you came," she told him, aware of the slight shake in his arms.

She turned to Dan and allowed him to hug her too, but she could feel herself withdrawing even as his strength seemed to embrace her. He was a good man, decent beyond anything she'd known for years, but she couldn't take that sort of kindness now. She was still too traumatized, confused, and horrified to know how to respond to anything beyond what was happening to her mother.

"Leanne's gone to make some phone calls," Dan said, as if she'd asked.

Claudia nodded and gestured for them to sit down, as though they were in her sitting room and everything was normal and tea might be on its way.

The sitting room. *Don't go there. Not now.*

"The nurse told us," Henry said, "that the op today went well. That's a relief."

Claudia forced a smile. Everything was being judged differently now—relief came with the successful removal of more burnt skin, not with the finding of lost keys, or sinking into bed after a stressful day.

Now all she could think was: *How much is going to be left of her beautiful face? How damaged are her muscles, her tendons, her hand, her arm, her lovely skin?*

*How severe is the pain going to be?*

Henry said, "Can we get you some tea or coffee?"

She looked at him and wondered what she could possibly say to him, or Dan, that would make any sense of this. There was so much they didn't know, where would she begin? Did she even want to?

"The police are at the house," Dan told her. "It's already been confirmed that it was arson." He paused as Claudia flinched. "Did you have any idea that it might be?" he asked gently.

She let her eyes drift, not clear enough in her mind to know how to answer.

"Claudia," he said, taking one of her hands. "We know who you are, and we know who . . ."

She turned to look at him. "What do you know?" she asked stiffly.

Henry said, "Your husband . . ."

She rose to her feet. "How do you know?" she demanded, glaring at them. "How long have you known?"

Henry replied, "Andee will be able to answer your questions, she's the one who figured it out. DCI Gould at the station confirmed it . . ."

Claudia's eyes flashed. "I don't know him. He's making things up."

"Claudia," Dan said, gently but firmly. "We need to help the police find out who was behind this."

He was right of course, but she just couldn't seem to break free of the anger, the outrage that they'd all known who she really was and had never told her. Did he have any idea how humiliating that was? How patronizing and deceitful?

Was it even important?

All that mattered was her mother, but it was easier hanging on to this fury than it was to try and deal with her guilt.

"I think you should go now," she said sharply. "It was kind of you to come, but we can—"

Dan protested, "Listen, I understand how hard this is for you, but you have to help the police—"

"I don't *have* to do anything," she cried angrily. "My only job now is to make sure my mother gets through this and you two, who've pretended you didn't know who we really are . . . You can . . . You can . . ." As she started to break down Dan caught her, and held her, but she pushed him away. "Thank you for coming," she mumbled, struggling to control herself, "but I need to go now," and before they could stop her she left the room.

# CHAPTER TWENTY-EIGHT

Andee stopped as she reached the police tape that surrounded the coach house, her padded coat and scarf helping to keep out the cold. At least it wasn't raining, although the ground was awash with puddles created the night before by the firemen's hoses.

In spite of being familiar with many of the forensic team hard at work at the scene, she knew better than to breach the tape, or even to try and talk her way in. They had a job to do and she wasn't here to disturb them, or to press them for information. She'd come simply to gauge for herself, in the cold light of day and now that the fire engines and their crews had departed, just how much damage the blaze had caused. Until she went inside it wouldn't be possible to assess the full extent, but from where she was standing it was obvious that the central part of the house, kitchen dining area, and sitting room had taken the brunt of the attack. Her heart ached as she thought of how lovingly Claudia had put it all together, the exquisitely restored cornices and windows, the hand-crafted units, quirky patchwork sofas, splendid refectory table, and colorful mismatched chairs . . . All the care and pride she'd put into it gone in one random act of violence, or revenge, or whatever it had been.

Andee could see that what Gould had told her on the phone was correct: both bedroom wings appeared unscathed and the tower too was standing tall, apart from the scorch marks marring the limestone facade like forked tongues flickering around it. All six of the arched windows had been lost, glass shattered, metal frames buckled and burnt, but the stonework around them, blackened as it was, seemed solid. She couldn't see the back of the place from here, but she imagined—at least hoped—that the damage might be slightly less severe, given the fire had been started at the front.

The important thing was that the house could be saved. There was no doubt in her mind about that. If the will was there, and it surely was—or would be once the initial horror had passed—she saw no reason it wouldn't be possible to re-create what had been destroyed and turn it back into a beloved home again.

Claudia would want to know that. Maybe not today, but at some point soon.

Checking her mobile as it rang, she clicked on right away. "Hi, Dan, are you at the hospital?"

"Yes. Henry and I have just spoken to Claudia, but I'm afraid it didn't go well. She's furious that we knew who she was and never told her."

With a sigh, Andee said, "I don't suppose we can blame her for that, but she's still in shock. We need to give her some time to understand that there was nothing malicious on our part in keeping it from her. What's bothering me more, right now, is that I didn't tell her about this Miles Montgomery character right away."

"You can't go there," Dan cautioned.

"It's hard not to."

"Then ask yourself what she'd have done if you had? She'd still have gone to the dress rehearsal, because no one could possibly have known that the danger was so imminent, or going to take the shape that it did."

Knowing that was true kind of helped, and she was glad he'd been the one to say it, but she knew that, like her, he was having a very bad time with his conscience. Whichever way they looked at it they'd let Claudia and Marcy down. And in doing so had played a part in bringing about these horrific consequences. If they could change things, of course they would, but it was too late for that. Too late for anything. All they could do now was try to be there for Claudia and her family in every possible way, if they'd allow it. And perhaps as they dealt with their guilt—their responsibility—they should take a long hard look at the way they took decisions on behalf of others.

"Where are you?" he asked.

"Outside the house. I think the structure is sound, but obviously we'll have to get an expert to check it out. I haven't been inside yet."

"Do you know if they're insured?"

Waving to someone she recognized, she said, "I put Claudia in touch with the broker Graeme and I use, so I'm hoping the answer is yes. There's a house-to-house going on up here at the moment. Apparently someone saw a youth running away from the scene."

"Yes, Gould told me. Do you know if anyone else has come forward to say they did too?"

"Not that I've heard. I don't suppose Claudia gave you an idea of who she thinks might have done it? I mean apart from her husband, who we know is in prison."

With a sigh, he said, "She was in no state of mind to tell me anything, but I've just spoken to Gould and apparently someone's on their way over here to speak to her. Maybe she'll be a bit more forthcoming with them than she was with me. She won't be dealing with someone she thinks has deceived her."

Understanding how bad he was feeling about that, she said, "Being angry with us at the moment is probably easier than trying to handle everything else she's going through. Now tell me, what news of Marcy?"

"She's stable, apparently, and one of the nurses told us that the skin grafts are likely to start in the next couple of days."

"I guess she's still sedated?"

"She is. Hang on, Leanne's here. She wants to have a word."

A moment later Leanne was saying, "I've just been talking to Mum and when the time feels right we're going to ask Claudia if she'd like to stay with us at Ash Morley until the coach house is up together again. They can have the stables now that it's empty. It'll be one less thing for her to have to worry about."

"That's a wonderful offer," Andee responded with feeling, for being in the safety of Ash Morley surrounded by friends was exactly what Claudia and Jasmine were going to need in the coming weeks and months. "I guess we've no idea yet how long Marcy is going to be where she is," she said, "but the next time I speak to Claudia I'll ask if she'd like us to start moving things over there. How's Jasmine holding up?"

"Pretty well, considering. She's been calling people to let them know that she won't be taking part in the concert and why. It seems to help her to talk about it, at least for the moment. She told me earlier that her special violin was in the house. Apparently her dad gave it to her not long before he died."

"Oh God," Andee murmured, her heart contracting with pity, but as she turned to look at the house she experienced a beat of hope. "Tell her that if it was in her room there's a good chance it's OK. Or no, don't say anything yet. There's no point getting her hopes up until we know for certain. How much longer are you staying there?"

"I've booked myself into the hotel tonight. So have Dan and Henry, but I'll probably head back in the morning. Are you coming over again?"

"I expect so. I'll call Claudia first to make sure she wants me there. If she's angry about us knowing who she really is she might want . . . Hang on, this is her trying to get through to me. Tell Dan I'll call him back," and switching lines, she said, "Hi, Claudia. How are you?"

For a time there was only silence at the other end until Claudia finally said, "The fire wasn't an accident. It was arson and my husband was behind it. If you know who I really am, then you'll be aware of who he is."

"Yes," Andee responded softly.

"He'll deny being involved, but if you can . . . The police should speak to his sister."

"I believe someone is already doing that."

"Good, but it won't be easy to pin anything on her. They need to find the person who actually did it. He or she should be able to provide the link."

"Do you have any idea who it might have been?"

"I can't even tell you where to start. Do you know if my craft room is still intact?"

"I'm outside now, and there's a good chance it is."

"OK, there's an attaché case in there, hidden inside a sewing machine box. It contains a lot of money and some papers that I think could incriminate Marcus's cronies in the insider trading he was jailed for. If it's possible, please get it to whoever is leading the investigation."

"I'll go in as soon as I can and let you know what I find."

There was a moment's silence that neither of them filled, until Andee finally said, "I'm sorry I didn't tell you that I'd worked out who you really are."

"You didn't tell me, but you told Dan."

"I know and I was wrong to do that. I'm sorry. But, Claudia, we're on your side. Neither of us held back for any other reason than we wanted you to feel free to be whoever you want to be."

For a moment it seemed that Claudia was going to say more, but instead she ended the call.

# CHAPTER TWENTY-NINE

I knew what was happening to you because it was on the news most days that first week. And the week after. Thanks to social media it seemed to go on forever. Not that I normally engaged with all that, but I did then—and you got a shedload of coverage on the local newspaper's website as well. You made headlines nationally at first—"Sixty-Four-Year-Old Grandmother Victim of Arson Attack," that sort of thing. The nation was outraged, but it didn't seem to last. I reckon if it'd been your granddaughter who got hurt there would've been a lot more interest, but it's like people don't care so much about grannies and over-sixties, do they? That's what my ma said.

Then it came out that your granddaughter's violin had been lost in the blaze, one her dad had given her that was worth a good bit; she got plenty of coverage then. I saw her being interviewed on TV West and I thought to myself, must be nice to own something special like that, to have a dad who isn't an a***hole who didn't even hang around for the birth. A dad who'd think about what would make her happy when she got older and he was no longer around. I kind of get what she meant when she said she felt she'd lost the last part of him, and I forgot for a moment that it was because of me. Then I had this crazy idea about using some of the cash I'd made to try and get her a new one, but obviously I couldn't do that, could I?

My mum cried when she saw her on the news, then she flipped out the way she does sometimes, screaming and banging her head against the wall like she wants to bash her own brains in. I had to pin her down or she'd have managed it. I've always hated it when she goes off on one like that. I want to shout at her and shake her to make her stop, but I don't. I just hold on until the worst is past. Then I give her some vodka or weed and try to settle her down.

You won't want to hear this, but apart from her hysterics everything else was sweet for me. As far as the bosses were concerned, I'd done good and they were happy to pay out. As usual it wasn't as much as I was expecting, thanks to BJ and the cut he helped himself to. Anyway, it meant I could get my mum some new clothes for job interviews, like we'd planned, and a woman who lives in the next street—Julie—came in to do her hair. We bought a car, an old green Astra with a red driver's door, and we were just about to get the kitchen window fixed when the s*** suddenly hit the fan.

It turned out the cops had the briefcase I was meant to have removed from the house the nights I broke in. I still don't know what was in it, but when BJ came to beat the s*** out of me (he tried, failed) I got that some of the PCs I've delivered to in the past were suffering a lot of grief because of it. Actually, without making the connection, I'd already heard about some of the arrests on the news, high-profile stuff if you're into that sort of world—basically corruption on plenty of levels—so no wonder the PC at the top of my command chain wanted it back.

I couldn't feel sorry they'd been busted, who in their right mind gives a s*** about minted scumbags who'd pay to have you knifed in a dark alley if it was going to save their skin? But I'll admit to the proper heebie-jeebies about what was going to happen to me for screwing up. None of the bosses had been pulled in yet. According to BJ they were just the slamsex suppliers, had nothing to do with the insider stuff, but only a tossbag like him would believe that crap.

The only good part of it all was that I was totally under the radar. The cops weren't going to connect me with the torching, because they had no reason to. The only ones who knew were my ma, BJ, and the bosses who obvs weren't going to talk. Oh, and I guess Monty, the mate in prison who I'd consulted about how to pull it off, he must have had an inkling it might be me, given it happened on my manor. Also, I reckon Smithy, who I'd borrowed the van from might have wondered. If he did, or if Monty did, they never said, and I wasn't worried, because those of us who grew up on the estate never snitch on each other They didn't even speak up when a couple of kids we knew were hauled in to line up for an ID parade. Whether these kids were actually under suspicion I've got no idea, I just know they were on the radar for previous lightings, or spots of urban renewal as they termed it. At the end of the beauty pageant they walked, so no one got locked up that day for something they didn't do.

I don't suppose you're much interested in any of this though, are you? While it was all going on you were still having surgeries until you were transferred to the local infirmary for ongoing treatment. Apparently this meant your condition was no longer critical, but you were still a long way from being able to go home.

I knew most of this thanks to Richie something-or-other, who kept on posting stuff on the Gazette website. He just couldn't let it go, giving everyone constant updates on how you were doing, making a regular celebrity of you, and don't think I didn't understand what he was up to. He'd got it into his head that the job had been carried out by someone local, and so he was having a go at citizens' consciences, trying to make someone come forward with any information they might have about the scumbag (my word, not his) who'd done this to you. He kept on and on and I read it all, couldn't seem to stay away from it. I got a bit of a shock one day when he reported that someone called Miles Montgomery had been asking around about your daughter, Claudia, just before the fire. Apparently the cops were keen to know if anyone had heard of this bloke, or had been approached by him. I didn't have a clue who he was myself, but what it told me was that there was someone else who might know I'd been chosen for the deed, and that didn't make me feel very good.

Then I thought about it and decided that it wasn't in anyone's interest to feed me to the law; they wouldn't want me shouting my mouth off about who and what I knew. But the possibility that a bunch of muscles was going to shadow my doorstep and pulverize me for having screwed up hadn't gone away.

It was a stressful time, but I guess nothing in comparison to what it must have been like for you. My old lady kept going on about you. She was as fixated on this Richie's postings as she was on _Jeremy Kyle_ or _Love Island_, apart from when she was off her face. Then she cried a lot and got so scared and loud about what someone might do to me that I'd end up having to gag her before someone heard.

Then a new post from Richie of the _Gazette_ came up one day, and looking back I guess that was when my time properly started to run out.

# CHAPTER THIRTY

The outpouring of support for Marcy on social media and in the local news had remained constant throughout the six weeks she was at the Morriston Hospital in Swansea, and Claudia and Jasmine had read or listened to it all. It was a comfort in its way, the hundreds of posts and heartfelt responses, and they continued during the time of her transfer to the burns ward of Kesterly Royal Infirmary. So many people wanted to welcome her home and assure her that the whole town was wishing her well. It touched Claudia deeply that people who'd never heard of them before seemed to care so much and were calling them by their first names, even stopping her in the street to let her know how appalled they were by what had happened. Many even offered to help rebuild the coach house.

"My husband's a plumber, call anytime."

"I've got a flooring company, happy to sort you out for cost."

"If you ever need to chat, our Bible group meets every Wednesday."

"Have you heard about our burns charity? We help with rehabilitation. Please get in touch when your mother's up to it."

Marcy wasn't going to be up to it anytime soon, Claudia was aware of that, and right now she wasn't sure she'd want to take part anyway. She wasn't the person she'd been before the fire. Everything about her had changed: her appearance, of course, drastically, but her sense of caring about her life, her family, her recovery seemed to have gone too, as had her upbeat morale and the musical timbre of her voice. Most of the time she preferred not to talk. She simply listened as others spoke to her, rarely looking at them or even showing that she'd heard, although Claudia knew that she had. Damaged though her left ear was, it was still functioning as well as the right one.

Coping with the devastation of her mother's spirit was almost as hard as trying to help her deal with the pain. It was so bad at times that Marcy screamed and writhed as she fought the urge to rip and tear at the fiercely prickling skin. She was on strong medication—in the early weeks she'd been on morphine—but recently the care team had moved her onto still powerful but slightly milder analgesics. The sepsis she'd suffered while still at the Morriston had, mercifully, not so far recurred. Those had been terrifyingly dark days for Claudia, when she'd felt convinced they were going to lose her. However, she'd managed to pull through, and now Rohan Laghari, the lead consultant at Kesterly, was optimistic that the powerful cocktail of antibiotics she was still being fed intravenously would continue to prevent it happening again.

Sepsis was one of the biggest killers of burns patients, Claudia had learned, so she understood how fortunate they were that her mother had survived it.

Today another crucial stage in recovery was due to take place, and Claudia's heart turned over with dread and anxiety simply to think of it. Putting all the surgeries and pain aside, she suspected this was going to be one of the most difficult tests for her mother so far, although Marcy hadn't said as much, but then she said so little. For the past couple of weeks the medical team had been preparing her for mirror work, which spoke for itself, and it seemed everyone had a role to play, nurses, a clinical psychologist, a psychotherapist, and also the surgeons. With so many being involved, neither Claudia, her mother, nor Jasmine could be in any doubt of how seriously this vital next step was.

Claudia knew, because she'd asked, that every patient dealt with it in their own way. For some the disfigurement wasn't as bad as they'd imagined, while for others it was so much worse that they ended up on suicide watch. This was why the psychologist had spent so much time with Marcy lately, to help avoid post-traumatic symptoms developing into full-scale PTSD, but it was hard to tell how much Marcy had taken in given her reluctance to speak, or even to show any emotion.

Now, as Claudia got ready to leave the stables at Ash Morley, which had been her and Jasmine's home since the fire, her mind was filled with the shock she'd experienced the first time her mother's dressings had been removed in front of her. The scars had been so visibly inflamed, like a live disease ravaging one side of her lovely face, that she could only feel thankful that Marcy's eyes had been closed. She wouldn't have seen the horror that whitened Claudia's cheeks, but she must have heard Jasmine's gasp and strangled cry as she'd tried to stifle the shock. Marcy had never mentioned it, probably because she wouldn't have wanted to make Jasmine feel bad, but that terrible moment must have fueled her own dread as cruelly as it had her imagination.

Hearing a knock on the door, Claudia went to answer, and found Leanne outside in the drizzling rain.

"I wondered if you'd like me to drive you to the hospital today?" Leanne suggested as Claudia stood aside for her to come in.

"That's kind of you," Claudia replied, turning back into the cozy kitchen where she'd failed to cook or even eat very much since they'd gotten here, "but I'll be OK. It's going to be a bit of a performance so I'm not sure how long I'll be there."

Regarding her worriedly, Leanne said, "Are you sure you're up to this? You look exhausted."

"I couldn't let her go through it on her own. Even if she doesn't say anything, or look at me, I think it'll matter to her that I'm nearby." She took a breath. "Jasmine texted just now to wish us luck. I keep asking myself if I did the right thing, persuading her to go to the first night of the Proms with your mum and Abby. I don't want her to feel shut out, but it's going to be hard enough for my mother without worrying about Jasmine's reaction."

"Jasmine understands that," Leanne assured her, "and she'll be back tomorrow. She can go to see her then."

Claudia nodded, but her eyes were fixed on nothing as she experienced a fleeting connection with the world outside the bubble she and her mother were in. Thanks to everyone's kindness and help, the coach house, mostly under Andee's supervision, had already been cleared and cleaned and was now being rewired, replastered, and painted. She went herself, most days, helping out where she could, but her heart still wasn't in making decisions about colors and designs.

She was thankful, of course, for everything they were doing, and for the way Dan had dealt with the insurance company, making sure that all costs were covered. She told her mother all about it during her visits, probably going into too much detail, or rambling off the subject at times without really knowing where she was going. She never mentioned anything about the arrests that had been made as a result of the documents in the attaché case being found. They would be of no more interest to her mother than they were to her. What mattered in their world was finding whoever had started the fire and getting him, or her, to provide the connection to Marcus. Making either of them pay wouldn't undo what had been done, but they couldn't be allowed to get away with it.

MARCY HAD BEEN aware of almost everything that had happened to her since the early days of being admitted to the Burns Intensive Care Unit in Swansea. Although the ventilator tube had prevented her from speaking at first, she'd listened as each surgery was explained, from the first to clean the burns—how simple that sounded, how crucial and invasive it was—right through to the fourth, fifth, and sixth procedures that had mostly involved intricate and life-saving skin grafts.

The early ones, she'd been told, were called cadaveric allografts, meaning they'd used skin from a donor to cover her injuries; apparently they were the best form of dressing. However, the skin had no life of its own, so it fell off within two or three weeks. By then, the surgical team was ready to begin the autografts, which meant using her own healthy skin to further the healing process.

In order to restore her left eyelid, they'd transplanted a microscopic sliver of flesh from the inside of her right arm and apparently it had taken well. She already had partial, cloudy vision in the eye, but she'd been told it was unlikely the lashes or brow would grow back, owing to the destruction of the necessary follicles. As for the muscles required to make her blink, this was an ongoing process.

The hair on her head was a better story, for in spite of most of it being burnt off during the fire and the rest shaved off on her admission to hospital, it was starting to come through again. She knew it was in patches, for she could feel it with her good hand, but apparently there was a chance it would grow back completely. As yet she had no idea of its color, but she was expecting it to be gray, or possibly white, and as for the texture . . . She'd have to wait and see.

Her left hand was still encased in an enormous dressing, and everything down that side of her body to her hip was a raging, stinging river of pain in spite of the drugs. It was so intense at times that she longed to tear herself apart with knives to try and alleviate the agony and itching.

Right now, she was raised up against pillows in her hospital bed, tilted slightly to the right to ease the pressure on her injured left side and still attached to the intravenous antibiotics. Usually at this time of day the physio came to inflict her own brand of torture, but there was another sort on the agenda today. She wasn't ready for it, and knew she probably never would be, but she was unable to summon the words to argue against it. Easier to go along with what they wanted and not make a fuss.

She looked up as Ruth, the senior nurse, came around the privacy screen, her fair corkscrew curls pulled back into a band, and her smooth, round face radiating health and perfection. Marcy didn't resent her for that, only envied her. After all, it wasn't going to help her patients if she covered her looks with a mask or drew on a clownish expression to disguise them. Marcy suspected she would, if asked, for she'd come to believe that there wasn't much this bossy mother of three wouldn't do to help those in her care.

Of the many members of the burns team, Ruth was the one Marcy had developed the greatest attachment to, with the exception of her roguishly witty consultant, Rohan Laghari, whom she saw most days. He had no idea that she looked forward to his visits and held on to his every word, for she didn't engage with him much more than she did with the others. She didn't mean to be rude; she just couldn't bring herself up from the depths where she languished into the full light of comings and goings around her. Not even the psychologist was having much luck in reaching her, and if the truth were told, Marcy wished he'd stop trying.

"Are you sure about this?" Ruth asked, holding the mirror against her chest with the back of it facing Marcy. "We always prefer to do it with the full team present . . ."

"Please, let's get it over with," Marcy whispered hoarsely. *It's only my face*, she was telling herself, *and however it looks I'll find a way to cope with it.* The fact it might make her want to kill herself when she saw what she'd become was something she'd have to decide on later.

"I think I'll call Mr. Laghari," Ruth stated. "Just him. We don't have to tell the others."

Marcy shook her head. She was as prepared for the shock as she'd ever be; now she needed to get on with it, but not with everyone watching. She'd already explained to Ruth that she wanted it to be as private a moment as she could make it and would have done it alone if she'd been able to fetch a mirror without assistance. She didn't even want Claudia present—she especially didn't want her there—for she didn't want her daughter to see her reaction in case it was bad.

Taking a doubtful step closer Ruth put the mirror into Marcy's right hand.

Marcy held it low for a moment, steeling herself, then turning the glass over, she lifted it up so that the frame was surrounding her face.

Her heart stopped in shock. What she saw was so much worse than she'd feared. She was grotesque, a monster; how could anyone bear to look at her? How terrible it must be for Claudia and Jasmine. She couldn't even understand how the medical team was able to bear it. She felt so sick inside, so appalled and afraid that she wanted her life to end right that minute.

CLAUDIA SAT QUIETLY at the side of her mother's bed and covered her good hand with her own. She knew what had happened with the mirror, Ruth had told her as soon as she'd arrived; apparently Marcy had said nothing then, or since.

Claudia could feel her heart breaking as she looked down at her mother, face turned away to mask the devastation that she'd now seen for herself. Her right eye was open, staring at nothing, and she didn't in any way acknowledge that she knew Claudia was there.

"Why didn't you wait for me?" Claudia asked softly.

Marcy gave no answer, didn't even move. It was as if she hadn't heard, or had somehow transported herself to a place no one could reach her.

"It won't always be like that," Claudia said, trying to comfort her. "It's still early days . . ."

"Please talk about something else," Marcy croaked.

Claudia fell silent, unable to think of anything else. Perhaps it had been too soon for the mirror—was there ever a right time?—but her mother had seemed to want it, or she hadn't objected when her consultant, Rohan, had suggested they start preparing for it.

Now Claudia wished that they could turn back the clock, but not to before the mirror, that would solve nothing, to before the fire.

Useless wishes; wrenching grief; fear of the future; silent rage, with a consuming need to make those responsible pay.

Should she tell Marcy that the police still hadn't caught anyone, that a connection to Marcus hadn't been proved? She pictured him in his prison cell, satisfied with what he'd made happen to her and her mother, although no doubt furious and fearful about the arrests.

Maybe he was already plotting what else he could do to punish her for that. He knew where she was now and that frightened her, but she wasn't going to run away again. She couldn't while her mother was still in hospital, and when it finally came time for her to go home she would need to be quiet, to take whatever time was necessary to heal in both mind and body. That was going to be easier among the friends they'd come to know and trust.

Deciding her mother wouldn't want to hear about Marcus, or the fact that the police still seemed no closer to catching whoever had started the fire, she began talking instead about the coach house. She asked if Marcy thought she should try to re-create what had been there before—the same or similar patchwork sofas, the refectory table and colorful mismatched chairs—but she received no answer.

She changed the subject to Henry and how much he wanted to see her. At that her mother's uninjured eye closed, and Claudia realized it had been the wrong thing to say. She hadn't allowed any of their friends to see her since being admitted to hospital; there seemed to be a part of her that wanted to forget she even knew anyone else.

A while later Ruth came to check on them and Claudia gave a small shake of her head, letting the nurse know that she hadn't been able to persuade her mother to respond to her.

After Ruth had gone, Marcy said, in a voice that was barely audible, "Did Jasmine go to the Proms?"

Relief rushed to Claudia's eyes; her mother had spoken without prompting. "Yes," she replied. "They're staying the night, coming back tomorrow."

Marcy whispered, "That's nice."

She spoke quietly, Claudia knew, because she didn't want to emphasize the difficulty she had pushing words past the injured tissue inside her throat and mouth. The muscles there were still unable to work as they once had, so sometimes it was hard to understand her. It would improve, Rohan had assured them, but like the skin grafts and new eyelid it was going to take time for her body to accustom itself to the changes.

Claudia wondered if she should mention her mother's hair and how much better it was starting to look. Although it was still patchy, there was no longer any baldness, and maybe soon they could cut the longer strands to the same length as the shorter ones.

No, she couldn't go there, it was too connected to the way she looked.

In the end Claudia said, "I'm sorry, Mum, I know this is my fault. I just wish I knew how to make it up to you."

Marcy's eyes closed again and as she pulled her hand free, she said, "Have you seen Dan?"

Claudia's heart contracted. Her mother regularly asked this question, and though she had seen Dan it wasn't in the way Marcy meant. Others were always around, which she was thankful for in one way, but not in another, for she still hadn't apologized for the way she'd turned on him when he'd told her he knew the truth about her. So much time had passed since that awful scene, and while she wouldn't deny to herself that she wished she found it easier to talk to him, she wasn't going to admit it to anyone else.

"You should see him," Marcy told her. "You know he's a good man."

"You're my only concern."

Marcy didn't argue, she rarely did, but Claudia didn't doubt that she'd bring the subject up again tomorrow or the next day. It was a way of distracting herself from the awful reality that was her life now.

They fell silent for a while after that, until eventually Claudia got up to press a gentle kiss to her mother's unspoiled cheek. Her eyes were closed, so maybe she was sleeping.

Marcy said, "It's the fault of the person who did it, not yours."

Claudia didn't argue. "And I promise," she said, "we'll find him . . ."

"Don't make promises you can't keep."

Claudia looked at her and felt so overwhelmed by her own helplessness, her need to do something that might in some way help her mother to return to who she really was, that she had to leave quickly before she broke into a sobbing rage of frustration and despair.

# CHAPTER THIRTY-ONE

Andee, great you're here," Fliss declared, rushing over to greet her as soon as Andee came into the Seafront Café.

"I got here as soon as I could," Andee told her, stuffing an umbrella into the stand and unraveling her scarf. "Is everything OK? It sounded urgent when you rang."

"I think it is," Fliss replied, and gestured for her to go through the café to the back. "There's someone in the office you need to talk to."

After winding through the tables and greeting those she knew, Andee pushed open the kitchen door and continued on past the cooks to the large room beyond, where Fliss's desk, computer, and file cabinets fought for space among bulk packs of toilet rolls, coffee, flour, cooking oil, and any number of culinary products.

Sitting on a spindle-backed chair in front of the desk and hunched in against a shelf of paper napkins was a tiny scrap of a woman whom Andee recognized, but struggled to place.

"This is Maria," Fliss reminded her. "She used to work here."

Andee nodded, recalling now how this nervy little woman, had slammed out of the café sometime last summer, following an altercation in the kitchen. "Hello, Maria," she said kindly, sitting on the chair Fliss put behind her. "Fliss tells me you're upset about something. Is it anything I can help with?"

The woman's ruddy, pixyish face twitched slightly as she looked first at Andee, then at Fliss.

"Nothing bad's going to happen to you," Fliss assured her. "Just tell Andee what you told me."

Maria's frightened eyes returned to Andee and a moment later, in words altered by a strong speech impediment, she said, "I 'ad t'come. I couldn't go on . . . Is wrong and my duty to speak up."

"About what?" Andee prompted.

"About th' lady. Th' one who nearly die in that fy-ah."

Realizing she meant "fire," Andee became very still. "What do you know about that?" she asked carefully.

"I know who do it," Maria cried wretchedly, "and they goin' to get him for not doing it right."

Andee said, "Who are we talking about, Maria?"

"My boy. My Archie. He set ligh' to the 'ouse, but he dinnow she in there. I swear. They made him do it. They say bad things happen to me if he don'. They always do that to him. He a good boy. He care for his mum, but he shouldn't set fy-ah to that house. Those who made him do it comin' after him. They're goin' to kill him, my boy, and I can't let 'em do that."

Andee glanced at Fliss before saying, "I need to be sure about this, Maria. Your son Archie is responsible for the fire at the coach house on Westleigh Heights?"

"Thass wha' I say. Is him who do it, 'cos they made him."

"Who are they?"

Maria recoiled. "No tell tha'," she cried, her poor tongue mangling the words so badly they were almost impossible to understand. "I juss want keep ma boy way from them."

Realizing that she must have decided he'd be safer in custody than out on the streets, Andee said, "Where is he now?"

"At 'ome. He there when I leff."

"Does he know you were coming to talk to Fliss?"

Maria shook her head so fast and so agitatedly that Andee put out a hand to steady her. "You did right to tell Fliss," she said gently, "and you understand that I now have to contact the police?"

Maria wailed and nodded and bunched her fists to her mouth as she started to choke.

"I'll take care of her," Fliss said quietly. "You go and do what you have to do."

Getting to her feet, Andee touched a hand to Maria's wispy fair hair. Life really hadn't showered this wretched little creature with blessings, and now here she was in the middle of even more horror than she could properly cope with. "I'll be back soon and we can talk some more," she promised.

Maria nodded, but didn't look up until Andee reached the door. "Will I eff to talk to cops too?" she asked woefully.

Andee nodded. "I'm afraid so."

Maria howled with alarm and buried her face again in her hands as Andee let herself out of the room.

Immediately after calling Gould she rang Leanne to warn her that an arrest was likely by the end of the day. "Do you know where Claudia is?" she asked.

"Yes, she's just come back from the hospital. Don't worry, I'll break it to her and stay with her if she wants me to. Where are you?"

"At the Seafront Café. Gould's on his way to talk to Maria so I'm going to stay." After ringing off she was about to go back inside when Dan called.

"Hi, I'm wondering if we can put our meeting back half an hour tonight?" he said.

"We might have to postpone longer than that," she replied, and after alerting him to what was happening, she added, "If it does turn out to be Maria's son, and I don't think she's making this up,

I'm going to try and get Gould to assign me to the case as Marcy's victim support officer."

"To replace the one they already have?"

"That's right. She's so overworked they've hardly seen her anyway. I can organize my schedule to give them more time. As soon as you're free tonight give me a call, and if you're able to come to the house that would be great. There could be a lot to talk about."

# CHAPTER THIRTY-TWO

So, it was my old lady who ended up turning me in. I was pretty hacked off when I finally found out, although I knew why she'd done it. She'd got it into her head that I'd be safer in one of Her Majesty's houses than at home with her where she kept hiding behind the curtains and working herself into a state every time someone came near the house. She was convinced the bosses had a hit out on me.

So, the SWAT team turns up, all tooled up and kitted out like they're about to take down Osama bin Laden, and what am I doing? Me, I'm inside bingeing on Line of Duty.

Ironic that, don't you think?

I didn't even know they were there until someone kicked the door in and started shouting like a maniac. Surreal or what, when I was in the middle of watching the same scene, but scared the s*** out of me when I got that this was really happening.

I was shoved facedown on the carpet, hands wrenched up behind me, knee in the back, punch in the head. That's right, one of them snuck a pop and it made me see stars. Some Sherlock in a suit read me my rights, so I knew it was about the arson, and off we went.

To be honest, after all the tension and waiting and wondering, it was almost a relief when they stuffed me in the back of a car and drove off. I couldn't wave goodbye to the audience who'd gathered because I was cuffed, but I looked at them good and hard, letting them know to stay away from my ma. I wished someone would cart her off to the whacky shack, she'd have been safer there.

So, they had me, fair and square. I wasn't planning on making out they'd got the wrong bloke, DNA would prove I was there, but when I realized I was up on a charge of attempted murder as well as arson, well, I couldn't cop for that too. I didn't know you was there, if I had I wouldn't have done it, so nothing intentional about it. It was an accident. A bad one, I admit, and one I really wish hadn't happened, but that's what it was.

I needed a brief to help sort it out, but people like me get what we're given and the ambulance chaser who bobbed up for me had me down as guilty even before he came through the door. I had a proper struggle with him—it's no fun dealing with a***holes and he was one of the biggest.

I'm remanded in custody and soon after, surprise, surprise, I get a visit from BJ warning me to keep my mouth shut about the PC who'd wanted it done. I told him I wasn't planning on blabbing, but it might be in everyone's interest if someone made the attempted murder rap go away.

No one did. I just got a reminder that my old lady had no protection now so it would be in <u>her best interests</u> if I acted wise. My answer was to say I understood loud and clear, but no way was I going to plead guilty to something I didn't do.

OK, I did do it, but like I said, it was an accident and I want that understood by a jury so I don't get sent down for the rest of my natural. Of course, that's likely to happen anyway, because the max for arson and criminal damage is also life. I'd just rather not have two running one after the other and if the judge is of a mind to do that he can.

So, I made it clear to the dickhead who was representing me that I'd cop for arson and criminal damage to save a trial on the understanding he got rid of the attempted murder and maybe worked out a lesser sentence.

He said he'd get back to me and all these weeks later I still don't know where we stand on it, but I've heard nothing to say the charge has gone away. I guess someone'll tell me before my big day in court, but that's not going to be anytime soon, because it never is. Six months waiting turns into nine, turns into a year and you're given so many excuses, scheduling, sickness, change of judge, that you end up not listening anymore.

My ma visits as often as she can and brings me stuff that's allowed—no way am I getting her to smuggle in the kind of currency that would help me a lot in here. Drugs, cigs, blades . . . I can take care of myself, just about, but I know I'm being watched so one wrong move . . .

The last time she came she brought chocolate—it's useful—and the news that you're due to go home from hospital. When she leaves I return to my cell and think about that. I know your house is back up together because my ma's read all about it on the Gazette website, so I guess that's where you'll be going. I wonder what it'll be like for you after what happened, if it'll feel weird or scary, if you're nervous about it, how strange it'll feel being in the big bad world again after so much time in hospital.

I picture the house and the times I saw you coming and going, not a conventional grandma, younger and kind of fit I suppose for someone your age. I remember you reminded me of that actress who played Nanny McPhee, not when she was in the film, but in real life. Emma something-or-other, Thompson, I think.

Then I realize you probably don't look very much like her now and I feel as gutted about that as I have about anything else that's happened so far.

# CHAPTER THIRTY-THREE

M arcy was in the passenger seat of Claudia's car, both hands—
one manicured, the other mutilated—resting on the medical pack she'd been given before leaving the hospital. There was so
much advice on what should or shouldn't be done in so many different situations—all of which she'd been talked through in careful
detail during the past week—that she knew she'd never remember
it all.

Apparently she needn't worry because Claudia had it all written
down.

Marcy hadn't wanted to leave her hospital bed, had felt afraid of
being parted from Ruth and Rohan and the rest of the team who'd
taken care of her so tirelessly and tenderly for the past months.
They'd become her family, the people she trusted, who explained
and cajoled, teased and scolded, helped in every way, and knew
when to leave her alone. They didn't make her feel different, an object of pity, a freak, which was how it was going to be outside the
ward.

She'd become especially attached to Angus, the psychologist,
who'd been preparing her for today, and all the days to come. In
her raspy voice she'd called him a bully, which had made him laugh
with delight. She'd answered all his questions, though, and had
apparently passed most of his tests. Last week she'd told him that
she probably wouldn't have been able to face things if it weren't for
his counseling. She didn't actually know if that was true, but he'd

seemed pleased to hear it, and she could see nothing wrong in making someone feel good about the kindness they showed.

She glanced down at her left hand, free of its splint for now (to be worn at night), and felt, as she often did at the sight of it, sickened, appalled by the fact that it belonged to her. She wanted to flick her wrist and make it disappear. It was horrible, purplish and hideously scarred, with misshapen fingers that could no longer function as useful extremities. It was as though looking at it, hating it, caused an intense prickling to flare up like red-hot pins, and she grasped the sorry appendage with her other hand to try and stifle the pain.

The ravaged side of her face felt as it always did, raw and stretched tight like a drum, and she knew only too well how it looked: the grafted skin was still fiery red, her left nostril was tugged and flattened toward her cheek, and her left eye with its new lid and surrounding puckers looked as though it belonged to a pig. She never voiced that to anyone—Rohan and his team had performed miracles in many ways so she wouldn't have wanted to upset and insult them. They'd even transplanted tiny hair follicles from the back of her neck to help restore her eyelashes and eyebrow, but there was no sign of anything yet.

"Everything takes time," Rohan had told her the day after that particular op, "but you're doing very well, better than expected, so there's no reason to think you won't wear mascara on that eye again." His smile was infectious, while hers was so taut on one side that only the other side lifted, giving her, she thought, a drunken, even piratical look. Or probably something far more grotesque.

"And your hair," he'd pointed out with so much pride it could have been his own, "is growing back so fast and full I think you're going to look even younger than before you came in."

There was no chance of that, but he was right about how well it was coming through, quite gray unsurprisingly, but thick and even glossy, and perhaps she could agree with Jasmine that it was kind of funky. Not long enough yet to help mask any of the scars, but nothing was ever really going to do that.

"Are you OK?" Claudia asked, casting her a concerned glance as they began the ascent to Westleigh Heights.

"Yes," Marcy said softly. This was the fourth time Claudia had asked since they'd left the hospital, and Marcy suspected she'd ask again before they got to the house. She didn't mind, she understood that her daughter was nervous.

"Would you like me to pull over for a moment to give you a bit more time?" Claudia offered.

Marcy shook her head. It was going to take a lot more than time to make her feel ready to do this, so she'd decided simply to reassure Claudia when required, and actually in that distant place where her mind seemed to exist these days it was feeling like the right thing to do. She didn't want to make life any more difficult for her than it already was, especially not after how frightened she'd been following the fire, and how hard she'd worked to make the house ready for the big return.

Marcy wanted to say that she was looking forward to seeing what Claudia and the others had done to the place, but in spite of being able to speak more clearly now she still found it hard to summon many words. They seemed stuck somewhere deep inside her, cowering in a closed room along with her emotions, afraid to come out. She didn't have a complete understanding of anything yet, but she knew that it was as if the essence of her had been burned away in the fire, and there were no allografts or autografts to fix that. Only therapy, and she would continue with that, as promised.

"Almost there," Claudia said, trying for cheerful, but only managing anxious.

Marcy looked out at the trees, dense hedgerows, and high gates they were passing, the occasional dog walker and jogger, the recycling bins, mailboxes, and house names. She thought of the many times she'd driven up and down this road herself, feeling glad they'd found somewhere in this leafy area not far from town and close to the moor. She'd been certain it was safe, or as safe as anywhere ever was; she'd believed they were going to be happy in their new home.

She tried not to think about the arsonist who'd done this to her, the youth who'd been arrested and was denying the charge of attempted murder. Although no connection had yet been established between him and her son-in-law, she, like Claudia, was certain one existed. However, her counselor was right when he'd told her that it would do no good to dwell on the anger and hatred she felt toward them both. It wouldn't alter anything, would only slow her recovery and fill her mind with unnecessary negativity.

"From what I hear," he'd said, "you were Mrs. Joie de Vivre before you came into my life, a loving mother who'd never let anything or anyone get her down, so that's who we're calling on now. I know she's still in there, along with the world's best nana, so let's keep working on waking her up." He laughed delightedly. "That makes me sound like Prince Charming, doesn't it? Bet you never thought he'd arrive as a gay."

She would see Angus again, and the rest of the team when she went for her regular check-ups, clinics, and possibly more skin grafts during the coming weeks, months, and even years.

There was no end to this.

They were at the top of the hill now and soon passing Haylesbury Enclave where the new houses were complete and occupied but not visible from the road. Much as their own wasn't visible either. Marcy could feel her right fingernails digging into her ravaged hand and made herself stop. It was going to be all right. They'd caught the person who'd committed the crime, he wasn't going to be hiding among the trees or behind bushes waiting for her to return, he was locked away and hopefully he would never come out again.

She knew Jasmine was waiting for them to arrive, had probably been preparing the place for hours, and as they turned into the drive she saw the banner straightaway. *Welcome Home, Nana.* It was strung across the front of the tower, as colorful and cheering as Jasmine could make it.

Marcy felt strangely betrayed as she realized the house looked the same as it always had, as if a fire had never been near it.

If only her own damage had been so easy to repair.

*Don't think like that.*

Starting again she saw the house as it really was, friendly, hospitable, proud to be a home, although it was different because the front door was painted a deep burgundy red and it had been black before. There was a pair of bay trees on either side of it, and a new transom window above with rainbow colors in the glass.

She gazed around the garden, still a tangled mess of shrubs and brambles, but there were flowers now springing up through the weeds: bird's-foot trefoil, wood anemones, buttercups, corn cockle, columbine, thrift. There were hydrangeas and roses, snapdragons and sunflowers, evidence that someone had once planted the beds and probably nurtured them. And with so much valerian and verbena they should have plenty of butterflies and bees over the rest of the summer.

She was feeling nervous again and slightly nauseous. She didn't want to see anyone, would have liked simply to go to her room and close the door, but when Jasmine had asked if she could invite a few of their friends to welcome her home she'd agreed. It had to be gone through, and there was nothing to be gained from putting it off.

Their cars were outside on the patchy lawn, but she knew already who was inside: Andee and Graeme, Leanne and Tom, Wilkie and Abby, Richie, Dan, and Henry. Her heart tightened with dread as she thought of Henry. She'd almost asked Jasmine not to invite him, but it would have hurt him terribly if she had, and it was time for him to see what she was like now. She wouldn't blame him if he began making excuses not to see her again after today. It would hurt, of course, devastate her probably, but she was expecting it and as with everything else, she would find a way to deal with it.

By the time they stepped out of the car into the fragrant early summer air the front door had opened and Jasmine was coming to greet them. As they embraced Marcy glanced worriedly toward the house, wondering who was watching.

Jasmine said, "Everyone's on the deck at the back. It's such a lovely day we thought it would be nice to sit outside, and there's a new canopy to shade us from the sun."

*Avoid direct sunlight*, just one of the many instructions she'd been given to help ease her into the changed life she was about to begin. Two new beginnings in nearly as many years, the first so much easier than this.

She allowed Claudia to take her arm and they followed Jasmine in through the front door. To Marcy's relief she wasn't assailed by a terrifying flashback of trying to beat out the flames, or stilled by a horror of going any farther. She felt instead as though she was seeing an old friend for the first time in a while, and while it had changed in some ways, it was the same in others. Another large table had been found, the oak beams across the ceiling had been replaced and limed, and the pale flagstone floor was maybe a shade lighter, it was hard to tell. There were new mismatched chairs, although these hadn't yet been painted an assortment of colors the way the others had, and the walls were yellow, not purple. The kitchen units were identical to those that had been lost, made and fitted by the same craftsmen, Claudia had told her. The patchwork sofas were no more, but the new ones were just as inviting with their lively blue stripes, mint-green dots, and plumped-up cushions. There were no drapes yet, but Claudia had told her that she was no longer sure there should be.

It was the drapes that Marcy had tried to save. If she hadn't. . . .

Hearing voices outside, she glanced at the open French doors, noting that they too were the same as their predecessors, and as someone laughed her insides turned inside out.

"You don't have to do this," Claudia whispered. "It's probably too soon . . ."

It was, but Marcy needed to prove to herself that she really did have the courage for it.

The instant their friends realized the guest of honor had arrived they got to their feet to welcome her, and as she forced one of her tortured smiles into its hideous shape she felt tears burning her eyes. She hated that they were seeing her like this, felt ashamed and mortifyingly self-conscious, but at the same time she was grateful to them for caring enough to be here, and for everything they'd done to support Claudia and Jasmine. She wanted to tell them that, but the words wouldn't come.

"My dear," Wilkie murmured, coming forward with hands outstretched and nothing but affection and tenderness filling her eyes, "welcome home."

The others followed, embracing her with equal warmth, telling her how lovely it was to see her and showing nothing of the shock they must surely be feeling.

"Great hair," Leanne told her with a playful smile.

"Come and sit down," Tom insisted, holding out a chair.

"We're told you're allowed one glass," Andee said, as Graeme uncorked a bottle of Moët.

Marcy nodded. Yes, Rohan had said that, but no more, it didn't go well with the gabapentin she was taking to relieve the itching.

When her eyes finally found Henry's he was still standing beside the table, his gaze fixed on her as though she were an apparition (or a freak), and she noticed the tears on his cheeks.

*Please don't tell me you're sorry*, she wanted to say. *I understand it's even worse than you thought. You probably wouldn't recognize me if you saw me in the street.*

He came to her, cupped her tragic face gently in his hands, and looked so deeply into her eyes, both of them, that it was as if no one else was present. "I've missed you," he told her softly, "and one day soon I'll forgive you for not letting me come to see you."

Her awful smile trembled as he touched his lips to hers, and she didn't resist when he led her to the chair next to his.

Glasses were passed around and in order to hold hers she had to slip her right hand from Henry's, because her left wasn't able to hold a drink.

Graeme proposed the toast. "Marcy," he said, "I know I speak for every one of us here when I say how happy we are to have you home. You've been through a very traumatic experience, one that most of us here can't begin to imagine, but we want you to know that our respect and affection for you has deepened a great deal these past months—and given how profound it was before, that's pretty deep." As they all smiled and laughed, she was aware of Henry turning to look at her again and felt glad that he wasn't on her left side, then sick that it was even an issue. "We also want you to know," Graeme continued, "that each and every one of us will be there for you anytime you need us, whatever it might be for. You are and will always be our dear and treasured friend. To Marcy, welcome home."

As everyone echoed the last words Claudia said, "Can I just quickly add that as well as being a dear and treasured friend, she is a deeply loved mother and grandmother, and is, without any shadow of doubt, the most special person in the entire world. To you, Mum."

"To Nana," Jasmine put in, teary-eyed.

Marcy looked at her drink and tried to say some words of her own, but in spite of how grateful she was none came. It didn't seem to matter, for everyone was drinking and repeating the toast and seeming to understand that she might feel a little overwhelmed.

She did—and when she sipped the champagne, she felt dizzied and strange, as if the world around her was receding into a distance, or she was detaching and moving away. She realized it was the alcohol, not having had any in months, but even when the conversation started up again the feeling didn't quite go away.

It was Wilkie who finally grasped the nettle and asked about her ongoing treatment, and Marcy was relieved; she didn't want her condition to become the elephant in the room, always there, never mentioned. However, she didn't want it to be the only thing anyone ever discussed with her, so she made herself a promise that after today she'd try to change the subject soon after it came up.

For now she left it to Claudia to explain about her physiotherapy, how her hand and neck needed to be splinted at night to prevent too much tightening of the skin, and the possibility that her new left eyelid might retract over time, and if it did the graft would have to be done again.

"Where do they take the skin from?" Leanne wanted to know.

Glancing at her mother, Claudia said, "The first time they took it from under her arm, but the second time it came from her other eyelid. Isn't that amazing, because looking at her other eye—what they call the donor area—you'd never know, it's healed so quickly."

It was still noticeable, Marcy was aware of that, but when compared to the rest of her face it was a smudge in a devastated drawing.

The conversation inevitably turned to other cases of plastic surgery that had been performed on friends or relatives, or read about online. Though Marcy listened, and allowed Henry to hold her hand again, she wasn't really there. She didn't seem to be anywhere, she realized as she gazed out at the jungly back garden, where two lovely palms were being choked by the unchecked spread of the trees around them. Was she really feeling like one of them now, as if she was being overpowered by her family and friends?

She wasn't sure how long everyone stayed, maybe half an hour, perhaps longer; she only properly registered them again when they started to leave. She felt rude and bemused and so bone-achingly tired that it was hard to make herself stand up.

She'd been warned about how exhausting this first day would be. She'd been warned about a lot of things, such as how she wouldn't be able to dress and undress herself (Claudia was already aware of that). She'd also need help in the shower and with rubbing E45 (from the fridge) into her burns. There was no special diet, other than abstaining from alcohol, but there was an ongoing concern about her post-trauma symptoms, so she must call Angus if she felt herself falling into a black hole.

She was heading there now, and she wouldn't have minded sink-

ing into the darkness and never coming back up again, but Henry
was holding on to her hand as though to stop her from slipping away.
She wanted to tell him not to let go, but it would make him feel responsible for her, maybe even nervous, and though he'd do it gently, she was sure, he'd probably prefer to start the process of pulling
away.

# CHAPTER THIRTY-FOUR

Three days had passed since everyone had gathered to welcome Marcy home, but this was the first time Andee and Dan had been able to get together. They were sitting in the small courtyard garden behind Andee and Graeme's house enjoying a glass of wine, while Graeme fixed a salad and listened to their conversation through the open doors.

"I think she's convinced herself that she looks worse than she does," Andee was saying, "the way she kept her head down as if it might upset us to see her . . . It was heartbreaking, and she hardly said a word while we were there."

Dan said, "Henry tells me he's visited a couple of times since and she's said a few words to him."

"Well, that's a relief. Claudia assures me that she talks to her and Jasmine too, but nothing like the way she used to." Andee sighed deeply. "You can imagine how worried Claudia is, but at least Marcy is still seeing the psychologist, so hopefully he'll help to rebuild her confidence."

"And," Graeme said from the doorway, "she'll start to believe that no one is going to shun her, or think any the less of her for not looking the same as she did before."

"Hear, hear to that," Dan responded, raising his glass. After drinking he said, "Henry's visits, the psychologist, her friends' support, all excellent therapy, but Andee, you, and I both know that there's something more we can do."

Fairly certain she knew where this was going, Andee waited for him to continue, needing to hear it in case she was wrong.

"What I'm going to suggest," he said, "is pretty unconventional, in fact definitely not out of the playbook, but Marcy is our friend, we want to help her, and as we have certain skills that could be put to good use I feel that not to use them—or at least try to use them—wouldn't do much for our self-respect."

Understanding exactly what he was saying, Andee replied, "So, you're suggesting we start work on a restorative justice program for her and Archie Colbrook?"

He nodded.

"Just a minute," Graeme interrupted. "You want to get Marcy together with the arsonist? Is that really wise? I'm not sure I can see her going for it."

"It wouldn't happen right away," Dan assured him, "and it won't happen at all if she doesn't want it to, but there might come a time when it could prove beneficial. At this stage it will simply be for me to try to make contact with Colbrook to find out if it's a process he'd be willing to engage with."

Graeme said, "And if he is, and she isn't?"

"Then it would be like any other restorative justice case, it wouldn't go any further. We can't approach Marcy first because if he doesn't want to engage it would make matters worse than they already are, and we definitely don't want that."

"It could take weeks, months," Andee explained to Graeme, "to get Colbrook to the point where everyone feels it might be helpful for Marcy to meet him, and by then Marcy could be in quite a different place to the one she's in now. Are you going to mention it to Claudia?" she asked Dan.

He shook his head. "It's important to be certain that Colbrook is on our side before we say anything to anyone, even his mother. Have you seen her recently, by the way?"

"Only yesterday. She's working at the café again, washing up and general chores. She's so devastated by everything that Fliss is trying to get her GP or social services to help with some kind of support. She's also letting her stay in a room upstairs because she doesn't want to go home."

Shaking his head regretfully at that, Dan said, "So I know where to find her, should I need to. My next step though is to talk to Gould, to get his take on the usefulness of the proposal. If he supports it, I'll contact Colbrook's lawyer to try and get access to him. I'm told he's on remand in Sellybrook, so not much more than an hour by car."

"And my role will be to support Marcy," Andee said, "should we ever manage to get them together?"

"Indeed. You're already doing that as her victim support officer, so it makes sense for you to be her RJ practitioner, assuming we get that far."

"How are you going to persuade Colbrook that this is good news for him?" Graeme asked, coming outside to top up his wineglass.

"The key," Andee replied, "is tapping into a person's natural empathy. The process can't work without it, and at the moment we have no idea if Archie Colbrook possesses it."

"I like to think everyone does, to some degree," Dan declared, "but I've been proved wrong in the past. Gould will probably be able to fill me in on what sort of character we're dealing with in Colbrook's case."

"You mean apart from one who sets fire to other people's property while they're inside?" Graeme didn't mince his words.

Unable to argue with that, Dan said, "I don't think there's much doubt in anyone's mind that he was paid to do it, although as far as I'm aware he hasn't admitted to that."

"He'll be afraid to," Andee put in.

"Indeed, so maybe engaging with him, not as a criminal on remand, or a legal client, but as a human being, we'll end up with the link to Huxley-Browne we're looking for. I realize it won't turn back the clock, or heal Marcy's injuries, but if she's able to feel that justice is being done it could go a long way toward helping her to move on."

"It could also," Andee added, "satisfy Claudia's need to make Huxley-Browne pay." Her eyes moved to Graeme, inviting any further thoughts he might have.

"OK, if you're giving me a vote," he said, "I'm in favor of at least talking to the lad to find out if this can go anywhere."

Turning back to Dan, Andee said, "Would you like me to see Gould with you?"

He shook his head. "Thanks, but I think I can handle him. We've just got to hope that he's willing to start paving the way, because it won't be possible without him."

# CHAPTER THIRTY-FIVE

Funny we should reach this point now when I've already written so much to you, mostly about my background and how I came to . . . well, we know what I did so no need to spell it out. Not saving myself here, saving you from having to hear it again.

Anyway, I've already told you about my arrest, so now here's an account of my first meeting with Dan. I know I touched on it before, but this is it in the order of things happening.

By the time he turns up at Sellybrook I've been on remand for a few months and my trial date's already been put back twice, so still no real idea of when it's going to happen. I don't fret myself about it, nothing to be gained from that, it's more helpful in my circumstances to focus on the day-to-day and keeping out of trouble. I don't go looking for it, but there are times when it finds me. You've just got to look at someone the wrong way in here and your head's getting stuck down a toilet, or your balls are being crushed in a meaty fist. It's not a good idea to beat anyone at table tennis, or to support a different football team, or to ask someone's name, or to take a shower on your own, because you're never on your own for long.

No music in here, I miss that more than anything—not

that I'm expecting you to shed any tears for me, just saying, is all.

Anyways, there I am in my cell one morning, hurting badly after a smacking from a couple of GBH-ers who'd taken against me, when I suddenly get dragged out to see a visitor and it's not a visiting day. I automatically think it's my jerk of a lawyer, finally turned up again, or the cops wanting another little chat about how I can help them fill in the big picture.

As I truck off with the Blimp—one of the screws—I'm hoping I might be about to hear that the charge of attempted murder has been reduced to attempted manslaughter, if there is such a thing, or even that it's been dropped altogether. OK, I wasn't holding my breath for it, but it was in my head.

I end up in this room I've never been in before that's a bit like the ones you see in cop shows for interviews, only bigger, and I can hardly believe it when I see who's waiting for me.

It's only Superman.

Or the Clark Kent version of him, with reddy-brown hair and black-framed glasses, and OK he's not as muscular as the real deal, or as tall, but he's deffo got a look about him that says he might like putting his pants on over his trousers.

Joke. He doesn't look like that sort of twonk at all.

He looks kind of ordinary I suppose, and friendly, because he gets up and shakes my hand, says thanks for agreeing to see him—no one asked—and would I like to sit down?

I see no reason not to, I don't have anything else to do,

and with any luck this isn't going to be about ratting out the PC or BJ.

He tells me his name, Dan Collier, and when he says he wants to talk about you, because of the way he says it I straightaway want to run. I don't, mainly because there's a screw outside the door to stop me. I think he must be a cop, or . . . Actually, I don't know what else I thought he might be . . . A vicar?

Even after he explains what he does I'm still not sure I'm fully clued in. Restorative justice has never been on my radar before, but I listen to what he has to say, and I kind of get it, but I just don't see it working. So I tell him he's wasting his time and probably ought to give up now and go home.

He doesn't argue or anything, or get worked up when I start tapping my hand to let him know I'm bored (what a muppet I was then). He just keeps going, talking, talking, or he stops and looks at me like he's expecting an answer to something he's asked. When he doesn't get one he starts up again. Next thing he's answering his questions himself as if it's me doing the talking, and I'm starting to feel a bit like one of those ventriloquists—you know, I keep my mouth shut and all the words come out of him.

It starts to get entertaining after a while, and I end up laughing at something, can't remember what, and by the time he gets around to asking me about the attempted murder charge I don't mind telling him what a toerag my lawyer is and that no one's told me anything almost since I got put in here.

I'm gobsmacked when he says he'll look into things for

me, because it sounds like he means it, so I ask him if he's
a lawyer. Turns out he is, just not the sort I need, but he
tells me not to worry about that, he'll be back again soon
and by then he should have my legal representation better
sorted.

So, he is Superman.

I don't see him for another week, but in that time a
different brief turns up to chew things through with me,
a woman this time, who puts on a good show of being interested and has some encouraging things to say, although
I know what's really going on. She's chasing her legal aid
fee, just doing it with a better attitude than the other
one. I definitely qualify for legal aid, by the way, because
neither me nor my ma are over the earning threshold, not
even combined, which is a good thing, because I wouldn't
want to think of how many life sentences I might get if
I had to stand up there and defend myself.

A few days later I get a second visit from SuperDan.

This time we talk about all kinds of different stuff, like
he's trying to get inside my head and find something buried deep that's not there. I don't suppose I mind, he's not
the kind of bloke you feel bothered about knowing your
shit, or some of it anyway.

I'm not sure how many times he comes before he first
brings up the subject of me writing to you, probably two or
three, but I do know that when he said it I told him he
was off his head, it was never going to happen. I mean, if I
start blurting out stuff like sorry and regret, then it would
be like me telling everyone I'm guilty. (OK, I am, of arson,
but I think you get my drift.)

He just sits there and looks at me like he's waiting for me to morph into the person he wants me to be, and I look at him like he's a knob, because he is. But he's also Dan, so I end up saying I'll give it a go, and then he'll see that it's a menstrual period, which is a way of saying a waste of time.

It was that at first, a mega lost cause, mainly because I'd never written anything down before, I mean outside of lessons at school. Texts were my thing, and maybe the odd phone call or IM, not pen and paper. He tells me just to write the words the way I speak, so that's what I do, trying not to cuss and swear too much, but he says not to worry about that. If it's really bad he'll get me to explain what I mean in another way, and if he thinks some of my language is obscure—his word—he'll get me to explain that too.

It takes some getting used to, I can tell you, but once I get into it, it turns out to be something I find myself looking forward to doing. Weird, huh? It also means I get to see Dan on a fairly regular basis and if he can't come I send in my homework, as I call it, and he brings it with him the next time he comes so we can discuss it.

During all this time he doesn't mention much about what's going on with you, but I know he's building up to it and I'm bracing myself. Finally, he gets around to telling me that even though you've been out of hospital for a good while, you're still not doing all that well. He says physically you're healing the way you should, although you'll always have scars, but upstairs you've still got the curtains pulled. I feel myself shrinking up inside when I hear that, like I need to get away from it, but there's also a lot I want to say to you, I just don't know how to find the words.

He wants me to write one more letter after this one before he starts what he calls the next stage of the process, whatever that is, but I've decided not to. He doesn't understand why, so I tell him that I need to know what you think of my other letters before I start trying with all the sorry stuff. OK, I get that it doesn't work like that, it's not my place to call shots in this, but truth is, I'm scared. Big admission for me, that. It's true though. I'm scared that there's nothing I can do or say that'll make a difference for you and that'll be like hurting you all over again.

I know he's going to tell me that the best way I can help you is to name the PC who ordered the hit. The trouble is, that's like asking me to choose between you and my ma.

# CHAPTER THIRTY-SIX

"Are you OK? Not too tired?" Claudia asked, opening the front door for her mother to go in ahead of her.

"Not tired at all," Marcy replied softly, and after unbuttoning her coat she hung it on the stand while Claudia made a point of not watching her; she knew that it bothered her mother to have her single-handed efforts to help herself monitored as if she were a child. Actually, she was doing quite well on that front, and it wasn't as if her left hand didn't function at all, it just hadn't regained much of the dexterity it had enjoyed before.

After hanging her own coat, Claudia went to put on the kettle while Marcy stood at the middle arched window, staring down their short drive toward the road. The gates were operational now, opening and closing with a remote control, and a large drystone wall had been constructed on either side to seal the boundary. Clearing the front and back gardens was an ongoing project, and to Claudia's relief it was something her mother was taking an interest in.

Right now she was waiting for Henry to arrive, which he would in the next few minutes since he'd already called to say he was on his way. He'd be eager to know how they'd got on at the burns clinic today, in fact he'd have taken Marcy himself if Claudia hadn't made it clear a while ago that she needed to be there for these appointments. If she wasn't she was afraid her mother might not tell her everything, and it wouldn't be possible for her to stay on top of things if she didn't have all the information.

"Is that him?" she asked, hearing the crunch of tires approaching the house. Henry had his own remote control for the gates.

"Yes," came Marcy's reply, and she turned from the window to help with the tea, unhooking one mug at a time while keeping her left hand in the pocket of her dress. Her hair had grown almost to chin level by now and had been styled with a right-side parting to create a full sweep of her bob down over the injured side of her face. Unlike the pretty scarves she wore around her scarred neck it didn't mask very much, but at least it covered what remained of her ear— and the color, since being highlighted, suited her well. She was still beautiful if caught in the right profile and in the right light, but the damaged side of her face was a constant and brutal reminder of what she'd been through.

Henry let himself in through the front door, banging his gloved hands together and stomping his feet on the doormat as if he'd just arrived from the Arctic. It was cold out, but not that cold. "I've brought cake," he told them. He grinned, "And I've left it in the car. I'll be right back," and he disappeared outside again.

"I'm guessing lemon tart," Claudia said, pouring hot water into the teapot.

Marcy said, "Definitely something with lemon."

It turned out to be a drizzle cake, one of Marcy's favorites, and after enjoying a slice with them while updating Henry on her mother's progress, Claudia left them to the *Times* crossword—something they did together most days—and disappeared into her craft room.

With the door closed and the radio on she sat down at the table and buried her head in her hands. She couldn't say why today was feeling so much harder than any other, she only knew that right at this moment she was so pent up with frustration and guilt and anger that she wanted to scream and rant and bang her fists to her head as if to break her skull. She had brought this on her mother, almost as if she'd set fire to the place herself, and though Marcy had never uttered a single word of recrimination that was only because she hardly spoke at all.

Ignoring her phone as it rang, in spite of it being Andee, she clasped her hands to her face and sobbed. It was during episodes like this that she had no idea what to do with herself, where to turn or how to bring herself back from the brink. She was so caught up in self-loathing, and the fear that Marcus would strike again to punish her for handing over the attaché case, that she felt physically sick with it. She needed him to be named as the person behind the arson attack, to be imprisoned for it, to be publicly shamed. No punishment was too great for him; were she able she'd order a hit on him herself to make sure he never came near them again.

There were times when things got so bad that she had to drive out to the moor to find a lonely spot where she could cry and shout and beg for answers from a God who clearly wasn't listening. Or maybe He was, for it was one terrible Monday afternoon a couple of months ago that Dan had found her in a remote layby slumped over the steering wheel of her car, so tormented by grief and fear that she didn't even hear him come to a stop beside her. She only knew he was there when he pulled her gently from the driver's seat into his arms and held her in a way that had, as the minutes ticked by, seemed to give her as much of his strength as she needed to get past the almost uncontrollable upsurge of despair.

Later, when he'd driven her to a pub so they could continue to talk, he'd explained that he'd called the house to update them on the insurance company's latest payout and had found her mother worrying about where she might have gone. So he'd driven around looking for her until he'd finally spotted her car, which, given the size of Exmoor, was nothing short of a miracle—aka divine guidance.

"You can't cope with this on your own," he told her, coming straight to the point in a tone that brooked no dissent. "Nor can you carry on blaming yourself for something you didn't do. The responsibility for what happened to your mother lies squarely with those behind the fire."

"But if I hadn't brought her here . . ."

"The responsibility is *not* yours," he said emphatically, "but your mental health is, so what you must do for yourself, and your mother and Jasmine, is talk to someone who knows how to help you."

Because she'd known he was right, she'd booked an appointment with her GP the next day, but when she finally got to see him she discovered that the wait list for an NHS psychotherapist was months. So instead of going that route she contacted a recommended private therapist instead.

It was his voice that she could hear inside her head now as she sat in her craft room with everything crowding in on her. It somehow broke through the chaos, a whisper in a storm at first, but calm and comforting, telling her to cry and rage all she needed to until she was ready to begin one of the exercises he'd given her. She always chose the same one, for it was simple and worked every time. All she had to do was picture herself in a place that felt restful and nurturing, somewhere she'd been before or maybe somewhere she'd like to go. She could be alone, or with someone she trusted, a friend or relative who brought no negativity at all into her world. At first it was always Joel or her father she turned to, but lately she'd found herself thinking of Dan and the way he'd held her that day on the moor. Even in memory it felt like a safe haven, and holding it close in her mind could be almost as soothing as the times he'd held her since.

They weren't dating, or calling each other every day, or making promises they might not be able to keep, but over the past couple of months he'd often joined them for picnics on the moor, or hikes along the coastal path, or a trip to the cinema. It was always some-where Marcy wouldn't have to cope with too many people looking at her. Henry usually organized the excursions and more often than not it was just the four of them, although Jasmine occasionally came too, or Andee, or Leanne. At the end of the day, or evening, Dan would sometimes hold Claudia just a little bit longer than a friend might before going on his way, as though reassuring her that he was there if she needed him. It helped so much, and she wondered if he had any idea of that.

Maybe she should tell him, but if she did he might feel pressured to do it more often and she didn't feel able to cope with that. She needed everything to be sorted out before she could get on with her life, and arresting the thug who'd carried out the attack—may he rot in his prison cell—might be a step in the right direction, but it was a long way from being enough.

Vaguely registering Richie's arrival—Henry or her mother must have let him in—she stayed where she was, in no mood to see any-one if she didn't have to. He'd become a regular visitor to the house since Marcy had come home, although he'd ended the newspaper blog a while ago—Marcy had asked him not to post updates on her progress. She just wanted to fade away from public recognition. However, before giving it up, he'd persuaded her to authorize a short thank-you message to everyone who'd lightened the darkest of her days with their kind words.

He came now simply because he knew Marcy wasn't going out much, so he brought chitchat and the kind of books and magazines he thought might interest her, in spite of knowing she could get most things online. It was where she did all her shopping these days, clothes and cosmetics, a garden swing seat for Claudia's birthday, and an Il Cessol Stradivarius copy for Jasmine to replace the one lost in the fire. It was very similar to the one Joel had given her, and in its way just as precious.

Jasmine often played for her, and when she did Marcy would sit quietly enjoying the beautiful sounds her granddaughter brought to life in the music, the sigh of wind in trees, footsteps in the snow, laughter, birdsong, rain.

In a physical sense Marcy's recovery continued to be as good as her medical team had hoped for, only two further grafts since her discharge, and though she still wore splints on her neck and hand at night to stretch the skin, she wasn't using them as much during the daytime.

The problem that remained was her mental state, her morale, or whatever it was that had stopped functioning the day of the fire. Although she still saw the psychologist once a fortnight Claudia had no idea what she was telling him, although he'd admitted to sharing Claudia's concerns that the post-trauma symptoms hadn't gone away. But he didn't feel they were getting worse, so all they could do was continue monitoring the situation, and Claudia must feel free to contact him if anything happened to worry her.

That was half the trouble: nothing ever seemed to happen, it was as if her mother had become stuck somewhere out of the reach of normal life. Perhaps she was feeling stifled or submerged by the fear of anything like it happening again—or the horror of seeing herself in the mirror each day. She never talked about it, she didn't complain or seem to fret or feel sorry for herself either. She just went through the motions of each day doing whatever she thought was expected of her, and no more.

"It's driving me mad," Claudia wailed into the phone when Andee rang again. "I know that's a terrible thing to say, but it's true. Sometimes I even want to shake her, or slap her to try and bring some life back to her, but of course I'd never forgive myself if I did. I'm never going to forgive myself anyway. It's all so horrible, we're going out of our minds in our different ways, and now Jasmine's telling me she's not going to college next year if we're still like this."

With a sympathetic murmur, Andee said, "You sound tired as well as strung out . . ."

"Actually, I'm better now than I was a few minutes ago," Claudia quickly assured her. "I've done my mental exercises so I'm just sounding off, no danger of an explosion or rush for the pill jar."

"That's good to hear."

"It never gets that bad," Claudia babbled on. "I was just making a joke, but obviously not a funny one." It did get that bad, but thankfully her exercises and conscience always managed to settle her down again. What on earth would her mother and Jasmine do if she wasn't there to take care of them?

"Where is she now?" Andee asked.

"Richie's just left, so I guess she's back to doing the crossword with Henry. I don't know how we'd cope without him. He's so patient and it never seems to upset him that she doesn't engage much, he just chats away as if everything's normal, thinking up things to do that don't run a risk of her being stared at. I swear if it weren't for him I'd probably have lost it completely by now. Anyway," she continued with a laugh, "I'm sure you didn't ring up to listen to me ranting on like a lunatic, but if it's about the bedspread for Angela Cairns—"

"It's not about that," Andee interrupted, "and anyway there's no rush for it, she's going to be in the States until after Christmas so you can reprioritize the workload. No, I'm ringing to ask if you'd like to come here for supper tomorrow evening? Graeme's away so I'm afraid I'll be doing the cooking, although Dan has gamely offered to help out."

Claudia immediately felt better, even something close to light-hearted. "That sounds wonderful," she replied. "Do you mean all three of us?"

"Of course, all three of you. And as Henry's there, perhaps you can invite him along too."

AT SIX THE following evening Andee sat down with Dan in the home office she shared with Graeme to go over everything they needed to have straight in their minds before Marcy, Claudia, and the others arrived.

"OK, the floor is yours, SuperDan," she encouraged. "Speak what's in your mind so we can go through it."

With an ironic smile, he said, "Obviously this is all about Marcy. She is, and will remain, our priority, but as Archie's RJ practitioner, I also have a responsibility to him, so I'll talk about him first. I'll come on to the letters he's written, but for now Helen, the lawyer you recommended, isn't optimistic about getting the attempted murder charge reduced to severe assault. She's still talking to the Crown Prosecution Service, so hasn't given up yet, and I've offered to speak to them too should it prove relevant further down the line."

"I take it Archie knows he's going down anyway for the arson? He must do, he pleaded guilty. Does he understand that the chances of reducing the attempted murder charge aren't good?"

"Probably, but we haven't discussed it in any detail. That's his lawyer's job, and I don't want him thinking that Restorative Justice is an easy way of manipulating the system to work in his favor. His remorse has to be genuine, actually I'm sure it is, but we're not yet in a place where he's presenting it well."

"But you believe he'll get there?"

"Absolutely. I wouldn't have wasted all this time on him if I didn't, nor would I have suggested a meeting with Marcy and Claudia. If it goes the way we're hoping, it could have a profound effect on Archie—Marcy too, of course. In his head he's got to know her while he's been writing to her, he feels attached to her, so to hear that his letters have been read and not rejected could strengthen his remorse to a point where he finds it easier to express."

"*If* they get read, and it's a big if. I guess you're prepared for this to backfire horribly? The very fact that you've been engaging, in a sympathetic sense, with the boy who caused her injuries could turn her against you and him for good."

"It's a risk I'm prepared to take, because I believe that beneath all the negative feelings she's experiencing right now, her natural empathy is alive and well. And it's that, more than anything, that'll help her to start moving past the trauma. Would you agree with that?"

"We wouldn't be having this conversation if I didn't. So now, do you want to hear what I think of the letters?"

He gestured for her to go ahead.

Opening the file they'd been scanned to on her laptop, she said slowly, thoughtfully, "He writes more honestly than I expected him to, and probably better than he imagined he could, but is he winning my heart?"

Dan waited, keen for an honest answer.

"Not entirely," she confessed, "although I think my feelings about it don't really matter, it's Marcy and Claudia he has to reach and the way to do that is for him to confirm a connection to Huxley-Browne. If you or Helen had persuaded him to do that there would be a much better chance of these letters even getting into their hands."

With a sigh he said, "You're right, and I'm still working on it, but if I push too hard it could make him clam up altogether."

"We know threats have been made against his mother to keep him quiet, so how to get around that?"

"Good question," Dan said. "He talks in his letters about the supply of chemsex drugs to PC clients and we know Huxley-Browne and his cronies were users. I'd say it's very probably the middlemen, the suppliers, this BJ character and the gang bosses, who've made the threats either on Huxley-Browne's behalf, or their own."

"Or both." Andee returned to the letters. "Have you told Archie yet that you're about to show these to Marcy?"

"He knows it's imminent, but I don't plan to discuss it with him until we have a clearer idea of which way it's going to go."

Andee glanced up at the sound of voices outside. "Looks like we're about to take our first step in finding out," she told him, and closing the files on her laptop, she went to open the front door.

# CHAPTER THIRTY-SEVEN

Tell me you're not serious," Claudia cried, her eyes blazing with fury as she rounded on Dan. "Is that what this evening is about? You got us here on the pretense of a friendly dinner and all the time . . ." She clasped her hands to her head in raging disbelief. "I can't believe you'd do this. Don't you think we've been through enough? Look at her, *that's* what that animal did to my mother and yet you seem to think it's all right to talk to him about it, to get him to write her letters as if he's some kind of . . . *fucking pen pal* . . ."

"Claudia," Andee said softly.

"Don't touch me," Claudia growled, snatching her arm away from Andee's soothing hand. "*We*, me and my family, are not your project, do you understand that? We don't want you interfering in our lives, because you clearly don't understand the first thing about what's happened to us if this is what you're going to do. All you apparently care about is some vile human being who goes around setting fire to people's houses and almost killing them. No one made him do it. You do realize that, don't you? He could have said no, walked away, done the right thing, but he didn't. Apparently he even watched us coming and going like a bloody stalker deciding on the best time to strike, and please don't tell me that proves he didn't want to hurt anyone, because it's too late for that. He's where he deserves to be, where I hope he'll stay for the rest of his rotten life, and if you think either of us is going to read his bloody letters, much less ever forgive him, you're out of your minds."

Casting a glance at Dan, Andee said, "Claudia, I understand how you feel, really I do . . ."

"No, you *don't*. If you did you wouldn't have done this. Listen to me, we want nothing to do with that monster, and I can't believe you ever thought we would. Haven't you seen how hard we've been trying to put our lives back together, to move on from it and try to forget it ever happened? Except we'll never be able to do that, will we? One of us will bear the scars forever, in our own ways we all will, and now you seem to think that adding this to our pain is a good idea. Just what kind of people are you? We thought you were our friends, we trusted you, and yet all the time you've been using us as . . . *experiments*, pawns, seeing if you can fix us with one of your do-gooder schemes. How dare you? How could you even have thought we'd want to be involved in this?"

Andee was watching Marcy and Jasmine sitting together on the sofa, Marcy staring down at their joined hands, while Jasmine watched her mother, her eyes dark with anguish as she flinched and frowned at the tirade. It was bad, far worse than Andee had expected . . .

Henry said, "Claudia, maybe we need to . . ."

"Don't!" Claudia snapped at him. "I'm not interested in what you have to say, I just want to get out of here. Mum, Jasmine, find your coats. There's no point staying now that we know why we're here."

"Claudia," Dan protested, "you've got the wrong idea . . ."

"No, *you* have," she hissed at him, "and you've also got the wrong people. Please don't speak to me again or come to the house. False friends are not the kind we want anything to do with. Mum? Are you ready? Jasmine, help her up."

As Jasmine tried to take her grandmother's arm Marcy gently pulled it away, letting her hand flop back into her lap. Without looking at Claudia she said quietly to Dan, "I'd like to read the letters."

Claudia stared at her in disbelief. She was so stunned she didn't know what to say or do. She tried to speak, but no words came out.

Jasmine said softly, "Sorry, Mum, but I think I would too."

Claudia reeled. She couldn't take in what was happening. She'd been so sure the other two felt the same way she did, that they shared her hurt and outrage, that they were glad she was speaking up for them, but apparently not. How could they want to go through with this? It didn't make any sense to her, none at all . . .

She needed to leave, to walk out and never come back to this house, but she couldn't go without them.

Tightly, brokenly, she said, "I'll wait in the car."

DAN FOUND HER standing beside the BMW a few minutes later, staring blindly toward the closed gates of the Botanical Gardens. It was dark, there was no one around, nothing to see or hear apart from the distant rumble of traffic.

She didn't hear him come, had no idea he was there until her senses picked up on him and turning her back she started to open the car door.

"Please wait," he said, putting out a hand to stop her. "I understand that you're angry and probably feeling betrayed, but I promise you it was never anyone's intention to hurt you or your family."

"Intention or not, you've succeeded."

"Yes, we have, and for that I'm truly sorry."

She stiffened. She couldn't accept the apology; there was nothing about this nightmare that was possible to accept.

"Can you try to think of it as something that might help your mother, even if you don't want to engage yourself? She's said she wants to read the letters . . ."

"And what good do you think they're going to do?" she demanded, spinning around to face him, eyes swimming in tears, skin blotched with heated emotions. "Whatever that verminous toad has to say it isn't going to heal her . . ."

"It could help her to understand why it happened and—"

"We know *why*, Dan. He was paid to do it; he's already admitted that. He took money to harm people he doesn't even know. He didn't give a damn about us. All that mattered to him was his *payday*. So, unless he tells us who was behind it . . . Has he? Is it in his letters?"

Dan shook his head. "I'm afraid not."

"So, what the hell is the point of them?"

He dropped his head for a moment, pushing his glasses up his nose as he gathered his words. "I asked him to tell Marcy—and you—about himself," he explained. "I thought it was important for him to try and put across to you a sense of who he is and what's made him the person he's grown into."

"And why the hell would we care about that?"

"It's not so much about caring as understanding that he is a person, a victim, if you like, of his own circumstances, just as you are of yours. He hasn't experienced any of the privileges or benefits that people like you and I take for granted. He's struggled in more ways than even I know, or probably want to know. In spite of being exploited from a very young age he tried to get an education, to lead a normal life, but living where he does in the kind of environment that shuns traditional learning, authority, all the norms . . ."

"Spare me the sob story. He's a cliché . . ."

"Come on, you can do better than that."

Maybe she could, but maybe she didn't want to. "If you're trying to make me feel sorry for him," she snapped, "then it's not going to happen."

"That's not what I'm asking, nor am I trying to make excuses for him. What he did has caused immense harm to you and your family, no one is ever going to deny that, least of all me—or him. My aim here is to try and help you to understand that all the rage and hatred you feel toward him is more damaging to you than it is to him. In your different ways you and your mother are still suffering profoundly; most of it is locked up inside you and that's making it worse. You only have to look at your mother and see the way she is . . ."

Claudia turned her head abruptly away.

"I believe," he continued carefully, "I hope, that if you can gain an insight into the person who did this to you and why he did it . . . OK, I know he was paid, and that he needn't have done it, but if you read his story, told in his own words, it might help you to understand him . . ."

"I've already told you . . ."

". . . and that could be extremely beneficial for you, and for your mother. I think Jasmine needs it too, but Marcy is the one who is finding it the hardest to overcome what happened. It's not just her injuries, although obviously they're a big part of why she hardly goes out in public, it's the suppression of her spirit, her inability or unwillingness to communicate or to *feel* that is the biggest concern. We both know what a lively and confident woman she really is, and I accept that the kind of trauma she suffered can change a person, but I am not ready to accept that it's changed her. She's still there, I'm sure of it, and I know you are too. We have to support her, Claudia, and the fact that she's prepared to read the letters suggests to me that she's ready to do even this if it's going to help her."

Claudia lowered her eyes, not wanting to look at him anymore, not even sure she could go on listening in spite of the glimmers of hope he was offering. She wanted to resist him, to carry on ranting, accusing him of betraying her trust, insisting that he didn't know what was best for her mother, or for her. The words, the anger, were all there knotted up inside her along with the hatred of Archie Colbrook and all the evil things she wished on him. And yet, making its way into all that pent-up rage and venom was the inescapable realization that Dan could be right.

Minutes ticked by. There was so much she wanted to say, to ask, to feel even, but everything was so jumbled and uncertain that she couldn't try. She simply stood where she was, stiff and cold and finally yielding to him as his arms went around her and he held her the way he had the day he'd found her on the moor, soothing her loneliness and despair with his quiet, undemanding strength.

"It's starting to rain," he said after a while. "We should go back inside or sit in the car."

She chose the car and it was only when she found herself on the passenger side that she realized they were in his BMW, not hers. It hardly mattered, they weren't going anywhere, although perhaps she wished they were, somewhere a long way from here where she might be able to think more clearly, or even pretend that life didn't require so many impossible decisions.

"Will you tell me what's in the letters?" she asked, after he'd started the engine in order to turn on some heat.

He didn't answer right away, instead he removed his glasses, wiped them with a cloth taken from the glove box and put them on again. "If I did," he said in the end, "I'd be using my words, and I think it's important for you to hear Archie's."

"Please tell me there's nothing in them that's going to upset Mum, or frighten her . . ."

"I wouldn't let her read them if there was. You must know that."

Yes, she did, but she still had to ask. He might not have handled this well, at least in her opinion, but he wasn't a cruel man, far from it. "And where is it all supposed to lead?" she asked. "I know you think it'll help us to know something about him, but is your real purpose to get his sentence reduced or even . . ."

Stopping her before her presumptions could run into territory that would hurt and anger her again, he said, "When I started this it wasn't necessarily to help Archie, it was mostly about Marcy and you. It still is about you both, but I'm not going to deny that if some good comes from these letters and any subsequent communication you or Marcy might have with him, I will write a report for his defense team to use in any way they can."

She sat with that for a while, imagining all kinds of scenarios that she wasn't liking at all, until she said, "Is there a chance he'll get off completely?" She wouldn't be able to bear it if he did; it would feel as though Marcus had won and she simply couldn't allow that to happen.

"No," he replied. "He's already admitted to the charge of arson and criminal damage, so he'll serve a prison term for that, and it's highly likely that when the attempted murder case goes to trial he'll be found guilty."

She swallowed dryly. "And you don't think he's guilty of attempted murder?"

"What I think doesn't count, it'll be up to a jury."

She turned to him. "That doesn't answer my question. I want to know what you think."

Not taking his eyes from hers he said, "I don't believe it was his intention to harm anyone. So I wouldn't consider it wrong to reduce that particular charge to one that's more fitting. As far as sentencing goes there won't be much in it, and as he'll go down anyway for arson you can be sure he won't be back out on the streets this side of his thirtieth birthday."

She fell silent again, unable to determine exactly how she was feeling now, apart from oddly remote from it all. As if they weren't talking about her and what had happened to her mother. But they were, and Marcy could have lost her life in that fire, would have if the emergency services hadn't turned up when they did, so there remained no doubt in her mind that a charge of attempted murder was the right one to pursue.

Breaking the silence, he said, "We're getting a little ahead of ourselves with all this talk about charges and prison sentences. What we need to focus on right now is how to make all this more bearable for you, Jasmine, and your mother."

Although she could hardly argue with that, her voice was edgy as she replied, "And you think getting to know Archie Colbrook will do that?" For some reason it didn't sound as horrific as she'd expected it to, although that still didn't make it a good idea. "Do we have to meet him?" she asked. "I don't think . . ."

"We're not there yet," he came in gently. "I haven't even broached the possibility with Archie, but I know he'll be willing if you and your mother are."

She wasn't, she knew that without having to think about it, but could she say the same for her mother? "I have a feeling she will be," she said, "depending on what's in the letters, of course."

"There really isn't any reason to be afraid of them," he assured her.

She let her eyes drift to the dark night, lit by streetlamps and the glow of the sign over the Botanical Gardens. She was picturing a nineteen-year-old thug in a prison cell writing to someone he didn't know because he'd been told to, not because he wanted to. She saw him in the dock being accused of his crimes. She thought of Marcus, safe and triumphant in his own prison cell, his only regret that it wasn't her who'd been scarred for life.

After a while she turned to Dan and seeing the earnestness of his expression, sensing his determination to help, she felt a little of her resistance starting to fall away. All that mattered to her in the world was her mother and Jasmine. But since they'd been here in this town they'd discovered that they weren't on their own anymore. They'd made friends who'd given them support in so many ways that they'd come to trust and believe in them. They had nothing but Marcy's best interests at heart, hers and Jasmine's too, and maybe it was time to accept that. She couldn't feel sorry for the way she had exploded when Dan had explained what this evening was really about—really, what had they expected?—but he hadn't deserved all the things she'd yelled at him. She wanted to explain this to him but wasn't sure where to begin. Instead, she said, "I'll read the letters."

He smiled. "I don't think you'll regret it," and pulling her to him he pressed a gentle kiss to her forehead.

As MARCY PUT the last letter aside her hand was shaking slightly, and her shoulder ached from having held it in the same position for so long. She was aware of the others watching her, waiting for her response, but she simply let her eyes lose focus as her thoughts weaved her back through his story, seeming to keep her attached to him in a way that wasn't easy to escape. His home, his mother, the men who'd exploited him . . . It was as if she'd just dreamt about him, and the oddness of it was still playing out in her mind. She didn't have a clear picture of him, in spite of the photos she'd seen in the press. That person, grim-faced and hollow-eyed, a youthful degenerate who evinced no conscience or remorse, no decency or compassion, wasn't the one who'd spoken to her from the pages he'd filled. She wasn't sure who had, she only knew that he'd left her feeling more confused than vengeful, and uncertain about where to go from here, if they should go anywhere at all.

"Are you OK?" Andee asked softly.

Marcy glanced at her and nodded. Yes, she was all right, but she was also disturbed by the connection she continued to feel to Archie Colbrook. His crime had created a link between them that was like no other she'd experienced. He seemed to understand, as she now did, that for good or ill they would always be a part of each other's lives. In the coming hours and days he would be waiting for her response, maybe wondering if he'd done the right thing in writing to her, or if he'd wasted his time. Was he nervous, or did it not really matter to him what she thought of his efforts? His purpose could have been entirely self-serving, an attempt to put himself in a good light with Dan, judge, and jury . . .

There was no denying that a part of her wanted to wreak the bitterest revenge on him, to burn *his* face, even kill him for what he'd done to her. It was a raging, dark, ugly part of herself that lay hidden and chafing beneath the shell of zombie-like calm she had been using to protect herself. It scared her, and she knew it could probably destroy her if she allowed it to take her over with its surges of fury and frustration, or its hunger for retribution. If it did, she was afraid she'd end up losing herself along with everything else.

Picking up the letters, she stared at them as if they might communicate answers to the questions she still had, as if in some way they'd give her the inner strength she needed to defeat her worst instincts.

She would read them again, but before that she would give them to Jasmine and hopefully Claudia would read them too. It was important to know what they thought, Henry too, before she made up her mind about what she wanted to do.

# CHAPTER THIRTY-EIGHT

So, Dan gave you my letters, you read them and decided you're not going to write back. That's cool, I get it. If I was you I wouldn't write back to me either. What could you say that a polite person like you would want to put into writing? You might not even know the words to tell me what you think of me.

I could help you with that.

I have to admit I'm way more gutted than I expected to be by your decision and I knew it was going to be a knock-back if you didn't want to engage, just not this big of a one. Suddenly being in prison feels a whole lot worse than it did before—and it was never good—but I expect you'll be glad to know that. It's what I deserve.

I don't think Dan saw right away how much it tore me up when he delivered his news because he just goes on talking about other stuff until he realizes I'm not properly taking it in.

He bangs the table to get my attention, and starts over again.

It takes me a while to get what he's saying, because it feels like he's making it up, or I'm just hearing stuff I want to hear so I don't have to handle the truth. "She's not going to write you a letter, Archie, instead she wants to see you."

I feel totally blown away by that, and so close to a proper blub that I have to hide my face in my hands. I really didn't expect that, honest I didn't, and there's no way I'm going to turn it down. I wouldn't do that to you even though I'm already scared s***less.

SuperDan then starts going on about how it's going to work, but I'm asking myself what it might have been about my letters that made you want to see me. It would be helpful to know that, because if I said something right I can be sure of doing it again. Dan says he doesn't know, because you haven't discussed it with anyone. You just told him you want to see me and that surprised him, he said, because he hadn't expected it to happen that soon. He wasn't sure it would happen at all, but now it's going to, although no one knows where or when yet.

So here I am writing to you again and this time I'm going to try and say at least some of the stuff I know Dan wants me to. It's not like I don't feel it, honest, it's just I'm not used to expressing myself in a way that would lose me a lot of cred if anyone of my kind heard it. I think even my ma would have a turn if she got to read this letter, and she don't need any more turns, that's for sure. It would set her off crying again, like everything to do with me does—did I already tell you it's how we spend most of her visits? I'm glad she comes though so I can see she's all right and she seems to be, so far. Fliss at the caff has taken her on again, and now she has a few bob for petrol, she can drive our old banger up here and back. 'Course I worry about her on the roads, she's a crap driver and handy with the horn, but that's my ma for you, crazy and sad and kind of indestructible.

Anyways, I'm going to start my out-of-character stuff with a really big thank-you for reading my letters. I know there was never any guarantee you would, but after I got a bit more used to doing them I really felt as though I was talking to you, so I always hoped you'd see them one day. Dan says your daughter's read them too, and your grand-daughter, so I also want to say thanks to them. You might all still hate my guts—probably a given—and the reason you want to see me could be to spit in my face—probably another given—but even if that's true I'm still grateful for you taking the time to read what I wrote.

Now here comes the really big one and I'll probably mess it up, but I get that it's important to try, so here goes.

With all my heart and soul I'm sorry for what I did to you and your family. I regret it more than anything I've ever done in my life, and I'll never stop regretting it. Please don't think this is me angling for forgiveness. I get that would be too much to ask so I'm not going to try. I just need to tell you that I'm sorrier than anyone has ever been about anything. I am a hundred percent genuine with this. It doesn't have anything to do with me trying to sway a judge or to get my AM charge reduced. In fact, now I know you want to see me it's changed a lot of things for me, so I've told my solicitor that I want her to stop trying for a lesser charge. I could have killed you even though I never meant to, and so it's only right that I face up to what I did and do the time. This means there won't be a trial because I'm going to change my plea to guilty so you won't have to go through that ordeal.

I hope that proves to you how sorry I am.

If I could do what I know you really want I swear I would, but if I do it'll be my ma who suffers and I just can't allow that to happen. I hope you understand and that me spending the rest of my natural in prison will help to make up for it.

# CHAPTER THIRTY-NINE

Andee said, "I guess you've read the letter from Archie that I dropped off yesterday?"

Claudia glanced at her mother as she passed Andee a cup of tea.

"You're looking worried," Andee told them. "Can I ask what's bothering you about it?"

Sitting down next to Marcy at the table, Claudia said, "I guess the prospect of seeing him is starting to feel more real now, and we're concerned about whether it really is a good idea."

Since it wasn't unusual for victims to experience misgivings as the day of confrontation came closer, Andee waited for her to expand.

"It's going to be hard for Mum," Claudia said.

Andee nodded, fully appreciating that, and as she looked at Marcy she felt the same overwhelming pity and regret she always did at the sight of the scars. "Tell me," she said gently, "what was it about his original letters that made you want to see him?"

Claudia started to answer, but Marcy raised a hand to stop her. "I sensed his loneliness," she said.

When she realized there wasn't any more, Andee said, "And you don't feel that now?"

Marcy swallowed, and made herself continue. "I still feel it," she said, "but . . ." She swallowed again, and her eyes went down as she said, "Claudia and Jasmine think I've forgiven him already, but I haven't. I don't know if I ever can, or if seeing him will do any of us any good in the long run."

"I've already told you, Mum," Claudia said, "we don't have to go through with it. You don't owe him anything. None of us do."

Because she had to, Andee said, "Claudia's right. You must think of yourself and what you truly believe will work best for you."

Marcy glanced at Andee's phone as it started to ring.

"It's Dan," Andee told them, and clicked on. "Hi, are you with Helen?" she asked.

"I've just left her office," came the reply. "She's got a call booked in with the prison governor about a special visit for tomorrow afternoon. She knows him personally, so that should help. Have you found out yet why Claudia and Marcy wanted to see you?"

"I'm with them now. We're discussing a few concerns that have come up since Archie's last letter arrived."

"Oh?" He sounded worried, as Andee knew he would. "Are they backing out?"

Aware of them listening, she said, "We'll carry on talking it through and I'll call you later." After ringing off she told them, "The arrangements for a visit are going ahead, nothing's confirmed yet, but it can always be stopped."

Claudia looked at her mother.

Seeing Marcy at a loss, Andee continued carefully. "What do you think of him pleading guilty to attempted murder?"

"Has he discussed it with his solicitor?" Claudia asked.

"I don't know."

"Then we can't be sure he means it."

"We can always find out." When Andee received no response to that, she said, "Would you like me to ask Dan to come and talk to you?" It wasn't the way it was supposed to work, the offender's practitioner engaging with the victims, particularly not at this stage, but since they'd hardly followed a conventional path so far it seemed pointless to start now.

Marcy raised her eyes from the table and gave Andee a half-smile. "Maybe we need to sleep on it some more," she said.

As Andee drove away a few minutes later, she was asking herself what difference Archie's regret, apology, or even his change of plea was really going to make to Marcy. Would any of it help her come to terms with what the fire had done to her face and hand, or alter how humiliating and painful it was to be stared at, avoided and pitied? She would still have to look in the mirror every day and see a hideous travesty of her former self looking back. Not that any of her friends ever thought of her that way, but it was inevitably how Marcy would see it, and how the hell must it feel to know that time was going to be no healer?

Connecting to Dan, she said, "It might be a good idea to prepare Archie for it not happening."

His reply was slow in coming and she could hear the disappointment in his voice. "I'm guessing you're no longer at the coach house?"

"I've just left. They're going to think about it some more, but it's not looking good."

"What's the objection?"

"I think it's still Claudia who has the biggest problem with it. She's afraid it's not going to help her mother the way we all want it to, and we can't blame her for that. Not after what they've been through. To be honest, I'm starting to have doubts myself. Are we really so sure this is the right thing to do?"

There was a long pause, and then—with a humorless laugh—Dan said, "I guess we'll find out soon enough."

# CHAPTER FORTY

When Dan warned me a couple of weeks ago that our meeting might not happen, tbh I wasn't all that surprised. Not that I'd been planning how I'd cope if it didn't turn out—making plans in here is a part of the lies you tell yourself—but I have to admit I went back to my cell feeling like I'd got proper kicked over for what I'd done, because nothing else—apart from a death sentence—could have made me feel that bad, and I even wondered if an end to it all might be better.

But then SuperDan turns up three days ago and tells me it's all on. I'm not sure who's more chuffed, me or him, but for the first time we high-five (didn't like to tell him no one really does that anymore) and his happiness shows me that he actually cares. OK, a lot more about you and your family than he does about me, but it still feels good to have someone a little bit onside.

I'm waiting in my cell now for someone to come and get me. You must be on your way here, or maybe you've already arrived. I don't know how you're feeling, but me, I'm totally brickin' it. I've never felt this nervous about anything in my life. I honestly don't think it can be this bad waiting for a jury to come back when you're in the dock, but I'm not going to know about that now. My solicitor's been told I want to plead guilty on both charges; I'm just waiting to hear about what happens next. Apparently I'll still have to go to court, but probably only for sentencing.

Happy days!

Anyways, I'm only thinking about that so I don't have to fret myself over how the next hour is going to pan out, or worry about taking too much of the stink of this place into the room where we're meeting. I'm not sure where that is, I've been told it's here in the prison, but not any part of it I've been before—and there'll still be guards around to make sure I don't try anything handy.

One last thing before they come for me: if this doesn't go well I want you to know again how really sorry I am and that I wish with everything in me that I could undo it, or find a way to make it up to you. I could say something about my ma here, and my need to protect her, but you already know it so I'll leave it there.

PS: I'm trusting you're not going to say or do anything to change my mind about things, just can't see it, so not sure why I wrote that.

# CHAPTER FORTY-ONE

They were in a kind of conference room with a large rectangular table taking up most of the space, whiteboards and a TV screen on the burlap-clad walls, and a long teak sideboard beneath windows that overlooked a well-stocked kitchen garden. They'd been led here by the deputy governor's assistant, a chatty woman who'd explained that this was the admin block and quite separate from the main building, although they might spot a few inmates working among the vegetable patches outside.

"They won't bother you," she'd assured them as she'd pushed open the door to this room and waved an arm as if she were introducing them to the royal suite. "No one will interrupt you in here. It's very private and comfortable—I'm told it's even soundproofed, but I'm not sure anyone's ever put it to the test."

Dan thanked her on behalf of them all, and after she'd gone to chase up coffee and biscuits he and Andee exchanged ironic glances. This was quite a luxury in comparison to some of the places they held RJ meetings—and in a prison? Who'd have thought it?

The seating arrangements were easily sorted, with Claudia, Marcy, Jasmine, and Andee on one side of the table, Dan on the other with Archie when he arrived.

"I'm going to lower the blinds a little," Andee said, "or we'll be looking into the sun and it's important for you to see more than the silhouette of the person you're talking to."

Marcy watched her adjusting the shades and nodded when she'd achieved the right level. Although everyone had a role to play here today she knew that the main focus was going to be on her and Archie Colbrook, and while she accepted that, it was still making her nervous.

Beside her, to her left, Claudia was checking again that her mobile was off, and after putting it away she reached for her mother's injured hand. It was OK to touch it now; it didn't hurt as much, although the itching could still be its own form of living hell. They'd joked the other day about getting half-price manicures now that she only had properly formed fingernails on one hand.

"What about half-price makeup too?" Marcy had added, but that little witticism had fallen flat as she should have known it would. There was nothing funny about her raw, scarred face and porcine eye, nothing to laugh at there at all—only oceans of desperate tears to shed in the privacy of her room. Still, the fact that they'd been able to raise at least one smile about her new look was surely a step in the right direction.

"If you want to leave at any time," Claudia whispered, "you know you can."

Yes, Marcy knew that, but she couldn't imagine herself just upping and walking away now that they'd come this far. Unless things went horribly wrong, of course, in which case she might have to. Turning to Jasmine, she gave her a reassuring smile in spite of knowing how grotesque it was; hopefully the tone of her voice would convey her feelings. "You speak if you want to," she told her. "Just because you've opted not to doesn't mean you can't change your mind."

Jasmine leaned in to hug her. "I want this to be all about you," she told her, "and Mum as well, so unless it feels that I ought to say something, or he asks me a question, I'll just listen."

Marcy looked across the table to where Dan was checking

something on his laptop, and knowing how much he wanted this to go well, for everyone, she felt a surge of gratitude toward him. She wondered how Claudia might be reacting to seeing him on the other side of the table, taking up position with the enemy so to speak, although she'd known it was going to happen so perhaps it wasn't upsetting her.

Turning to her, Marcy whispered, "Are you OK?"

"Yes," Claudia replied. "Are you?"

"I'm fine. I wonder how he's feeling right now."

Dan said, "Nervous, I'm sure. Well, he'd probably use a different expression, but it would have the same meaning."

Marcy couldn't help imagining what words Archie might reach for, but she soon let it go as she began asking herself again if they were doing the right thing in coming here. After his last letter, his apology, she'd felt that it might be enough; she didn't need to have any more to do with him, for no amount of talking, explaining, trying to understand each other, or whatever else might come up was going to change what had happened. Her face could never be properly repaired. She was disfigured now for the rest of her life. So, what was the point of it all?

"The point," Henry had told her, "is that you've been talking more since you read his letters. I don't know why or how, but they seem to have reached something in you that the rest of us haven't managed to. Isn't it worth finding out if seeing him really could help?"

Marcy had been surprised by that answer, for she'd expected him to be as wary as Claudia over this meeting; however, when she'd reported back to Claudia, her daughter had agreed, albeit cautiously, with Henry. So had Jasmine.

"It feels like a properly positive step," Jasmine had said, "and if Andee and Dan are behind it I really don't think we need to worry."

"A lot can be to do with chemistry," Claudia had continued, surprising Marcy further. "Don't look like that, I've been reading about RJ online. If you absolutely take against him the minute you see him, we'll know there's no point going ahead with it, but I don't think you will, not after the way you reacted to his letters."

Marcy began thinking about the letters now, and the parts that had affected her the most. She was remembering letting go of her anger and vindictiveness at the unexpected tenderness she'd felt over their transparent bravado, when her heart suddenly lurched. The door was opening.

A woman came through with a tray of refreshments. Marcy watched her set it on the sideboard, then felt Claudia's hand tighten on hers. She turned back to the door and her heart stilled again. A young man was filling the space and looking vaguely like the mugshots she'd seen on the news, but only vaguely. He was tall and clean shaven; his dark hair was combed back from his forehead, and his brown eyes as he looked at Dan showed the same vulnerability she'd picked up in his letters. There was no air of arrogance or cockiness about him, no sense of boredom or irritation; almost nothing of what she'd primed herself for, not even any tattoos or piercings.

"Everyone," Dan said, placing a hand on the boy's shoulder as he turned to address the room, "this is Archie."

Marcy, Claudia, and Jasmine watched as Andee went to greet him, introducing herself as their supporter, shaking his hand and thanking him for coming. As she returned to her place Dan led him to the other side of the table and before they sat down he continued his introductions.

"Archie, this is Claudia Winters."

Archie started to reach out a hand but pulled it back when Claudia simply raised hers in greeting.

"This is Claudia's daughter, Jasmine," Dan continued.

He didn't attempt to shake this time, simply gave her the same sort of awkward salute that she gave him.

"And this is Marcy Kavanagh," Dan said.

As Archie's eyes came to her Marcy ached inside to see his shock, horror—and was it panic? She obviously looked even worse than he'd expected, and he didn't know what to do or say. She suspected he'd run, if he could.

Although she'd expected him to react to her scarring, and had been bracing herself for it, now that it was happening she had no idea what to do. Until, as though it had a will of its own, her right hand reached toward him offering to shake. He took it, tentatively, and managed a wrenchingly self-conscious hello.

Dan put a hand on his shoulder and held it there, gently easing him into his chair as Andee dished out the coffees.

Finally, Dan said, "OK, I'll start off with a few easy rules to get us going. First, try not to interrupt when someone else is speaking. Second, if anyone feels they need time out at any point, just raise a hand and it can happen. Next, all our phones should be switched off—I think we did that before we came in. Lastly let's do our best not to swear—Archie."

Though it was meant as a gentle tease, Archie looked so alarmed that it was as though he thought he'd already disgraced himself. "No, no, definitely not," he promised, lifting his eyes to Marcy before quickly lowering them again.

Telling herself that this reluctance to fully engage could be as much about nerves as repulsion—or guilt—Marcy found herself saying, "I'll do my best to hold it in too."

She almost felt Claudia's and Jasmine's eyebrows rise.

Apparently amused, Dan said, "In these meetings it's usually the person who's caused harm that speaks first, so unless you, Marcy, or Claudia have anything you'd like to say upfront . . ."

They shook their heads.

". . . I'll help Archie to kick off by asking a few questions." Turning to address Archie, he said, "We're all aware that the reason we're here today is because of the crime you committed, and that someone ordered you to do it. You've already explained to me, and to Marcy in your letters, why you don't want to discuss a third-party involvement, so I won't press you about it during this meeting. What I want you to do is talk us through the events of the night of the fire, from your perspective. I realize you've written this down, but I think it'll help Marcy and her family to hear you tell it. Maybe you can start by describing what you were thinking as you prepared to set the fire."

Marcy watched Archie's Adam's apple bob up and down in his muscular neck as if it were as eager to get out of here as he was. His cheeks bloomed with color and he was unable to look at anyone when he finally stumbled into an answer. "Uh, um . . . I guess I wasn't thinking about very much really," he said to his hands, "only what I had to do, and if the advice I'd been given was sound."

Dan said, "We know you watched Marcy and her family get into the car; what were you thinking then?"

Archie's eyes flicked tentatively to Marcy as he said, "I was thinking the same as I did when I was staking the place before the times I broke in, that it was a shame someone had it in for you because you looked like nice people."

Marcy wanted to ask who had it in for them, but as she'd been advised not to interrupt, she held on to it for now.

"Even though they looked like nice people," Dan prompted, "you still went ahead and carried out the instructions you'd been given. Maybe you can tell us what those instructions were?"

Archie's head was still down, the muscles in his arms tightening as he pressed his hands together. "They were to torch the place," he said. "I knew there might be something inside that needed to be got rid of, and because I hadn't been able to find it when I broke in . . . I . . . I was told to make the place go up in smoke as a kind of insurance."

"And how did you feel when you were smashing the windows and pouring petrol through them?" Dan asked, matter-of-factly enough to make Marcy flinch.

Archie's eyes were still on his hands as he said, "I felt scared of being caught, and of setting fire to myself. I'd been warned about how that might happen. I was also scared of screwing up because of what might happen to me and my ma if I did."

Dan said, "Had anyone actually told you what that would be?"

Archie shook his head. "Those things don't get put into words, you just know they're bad."

Accepting that, Dan prompted him to continue with how he'd felt while committing the crime.

"I suppose," Archie said, "apart from scared and everything, I felt kind of weird about it all, because it wasn't something I wanted to do. I just thought I had to . . ." He took a breath and wiped a shaky hand over his mouth. "Looking back, I reckon I wasn't allowing myself to think much at all. I just went through the motions . . . Obviously I wish now that I'd had the courage to tell them what to do with their money and their orders and their threats. I wish they didn't always target my ma the way they do. I used to try to make out she don't mean anything to me so they'd leave her alone, stop using her to force me into stuff, but they did it anyway." He took a moment, making his knuckles turn white as he bunched his hands together on the table, a kind of power-up, Marcy thought, to make himself continue.

"She's not right, you see," he said, "I mean in the head. She's not mental or anything, well, I suppose she is a bit, but she understands things and she's got feelings like anyone else." He took a breath and then another, showing that talking about his mother affected him deeply. "She tried to stop me from going that night," he told them. "She said it didn't matter what they did to us we couldn't go round hurting other people just to save ourselves. I saw straightaway after that she was right. No way did you deserve what I did to you. I swear I didn't see you going back into the house. On my ma's life I'd never have done it if I had. I wish I hadn't done it anyway . . ." His voice fractured as he pressed his bunched hands to his head.

"It's OK, son," Dan said comfortingly, "this is a big thing you're doing and it's bound to bring up a lot of emotions, probably more than you're expecting."

Marcy watched the lad take gulps of air and press his fingers into his eye sockets as though to stem the tears. She wondered how it might have felt to hear Dan call him son. Had anyone ever called him that before, with affection? It was no surprise, with everything happening, that he was having such a struggle to rein in his emotions. If she allowed herself to think too much about it she'd have trouble reining in her own.

"Tell us what happened after you started the fire," Dan said, when Archie was ready again.

"I can't really explain what happened after," Archie answered. "I mean, I knew it was happening, and I got myself clear the way I'd been told to, but when I got into the trees it was like I couldn't make myself stop watching. It was nothing to do with making sure the whole place went up, I wasn't even thinking about that . . . I just couldn't make myself run like I was supposed to."

"How long did you stay?" Dan asked.

Archie shook his head as though he were trying to recall a dream. "If this doesn't sound too weird," he said, "it was like I was hypnotized or something, you know kind of in a trance. I heard someone shouting that they'd called 999 and I even thought for a minute it was me doing the shouting.

"I was still there when the fire engines turned up. I watched them rolling out the hoses, breaking in through the door, spraying the roof . . . It was only when I heard someone shouting . . ." He lost his breath and after a tense moment he stole a quick glance at Jasmine. "I heard you shouting," he told her. "As you got out of the car, I heard . . . and that's when I realized someone was inside the house."

As he fell silent Marcy wondered if he had any idea of the terrible impact his words were having on her and her family, being told that he'd been there watching the tragedy he'd caused to unfold. In truth, she wasn't entirely sure how she did feel about it. Would it have been better if he'd just run away? Or did it make it worse that he hadn't?

Realizing that there were no easy answers, and probably still wouldn't be even after today, she took a sip of her coffee, now cold, and waited for him to continue.

Assisting him, Dan said, "At what point did you leave the scene, Archie?"

Archie frowned as he thought. "Just before, just after the air ambulance turned up. I can't really remember now. I know it landed on the moor. My van was there, hidden in a layby. I got to it, but there was no way I could get into town through all the fire engines and stuff, so I went in the opposite direction."

"To where?"

"I went home eventually. I took the long way round."

"Did you call anyone to let them know you'd completed your task?"

He nodded. "I texted. I admitted I'd screwed up, that someone had been inside . . . I knew it was going to be the end for me. I thought about running, taking my ma with me, but then a message came back . . ." He glanced awkwardly at Marcy.

Guessing he didn't want to repeat the words that had told him it was OK that someone had been inside, and knowing that she didn't want to hear them, she said, "What happened next? Were you paid?"

His head fell forward as he nodded.

"Can I ask how much?"

"Five grand," he mumbled.

She felt strangely dizzied by that. She hadn't considered the price of burning down their home before, wouldn't have had any idea of the going rate for such a monstrous crime, but that it was so little . . . But not little to him. To him, as he'd told her in his letters, it had opened up a small world of possibilities.

Moving them on, Dan said, "Then what happened?"

Archie shrugged. "I tried not to think about what I'd done, but it never went out of my head, and we kept hearing about it on the news. My ma fixated on it, got herself into a terrible state, even threatening to kill herself and me." He broke off, took a breath, and started again. "I kind of knew she'd end up reporting it. In a way it was a relief when she did. Not that I want to be stuck in here, don't get me wrong, but it's where I belong so . . ." He shrugged again and began jigging a knee up and down so fast it was as though he had no control over it.

Dan put out a hand to stop him. "Before we take a break," he said, "is there anything else you'd like to say to Marcy and her family?"

Archie nodded, and swept a tumble of hair from his forehead as he forced himself to meet Marcy's eyes. "I want to tell you again," he said, "that I'm truly sorry for what I did. I can't imagine what it's like to have gone through what you did, but if I could make it like I went through it instead and you were OK, I promise I would."

Marcy held his eyes, watched him swallow more emotion, and continued to watch him as he finally looked away. Words were so easy; anything could be said or promised when there was no possible way of following through. And emotions could be feigned, as could tears. It was true he looked and sounded genuine. She couldn't imagine Dan bringing them this far if he didn't believe in him.

For the moment she seemed to have lost touch with her own emotions, but she realized that what she needed more than anything, for Claudia's sake and her own, was for Archie to confirm that Marcus had been behind it. It was the only way for real justice to be done—and for them to ever have a chance of moving on.

# CHAPTER FORTY-TWO

Fifteen minutes later Marcy and the others returned to the meeting room, passing the guard outside who nodded stiffly as they went in. Dan and Archie were already seated at the table, as though they'd not left it. They had probably spent the entire time discussing what the next hour or more might bring.

Although Dan's expression was relaxed as he looked up, Marcy noticed that Archie's remained tense; he seemed paler now, and even edgier than before.

As they resumed their seats Claudia and Andee opened their tablets to the notes they'd made while preparing for today. During the break they'd added to them, but Marcy didn't need any prompts to guide her through the next few minutes. She knew what she wanted to say, and had informed the others while they were outside, so after Andee had spoken a few words to set them back on course, Marcy began her piece, speaking quietly yet clearly.

"It's been explained to us," she said to the top of Archie's head, bowed, she understood, in shame, "that we can take this opportunity to tell you how your actions have impacted our lives. We can go into as much detail as we like about how the fire and my injuries have made us feel as individuals and as a family, and about how afraid we've been and remain because of the person we believe to be behind what you did." She paused, allowing her allusion to Marcus to sink in, and to see if Archie might respond.

When he didn't, she continued. "I will admit that a part of me—a strong part of me—has an almost constant need to express all the anger and hatred bottled up inside me, all the resentment and self-pity I feel about what's happened to me, especially when I look in the mirror. It's my own personal horror show, one I can never escape, and never will be able to. Somehow, I have to learn to live with it and it isn't easy. I don't talk about it with my family, because I don't want my negative feelings spilling over them and turning our lives into a perpetual struggle with bitterness and spite. I do discuss it with my therapist, and together we're working on helping me get to a better and calmer place. He was—is—fully supportive of my decision to meet with you, and he's advised me not to hold back. I really didn't think I would, but after listening to you I've decided that you already feel bad enough about what you did and making you feel worse isn't going to help any of us."

As his head came up, she met his confused and wary expression with one of cool compassion. She'd meant it, they didn't need to make him squirm with guilt and shame—he appeared to be doing that without any help—and she certainly didn't need to indulge herself in a diatribe of self-pity. This meeting, as they'd been advised, must be about how they could go forward in a way that was going to benefit them all, and attacking him verbally and emotionally simply wasn't going to achieve that.

What could, perhaps, was to be mindful of the fact that he'd probably never had anyone to believe in him before, at least not in the way he needed.

If she gave him a chance, would life give her one?

She knew it didn't work like that, but how on earth would it help either of them if she turned her back on him?

Now it was Claudia's turn. "I realize," she began, sounding more composed than Marcy knew she felt, "that you didn't know who we were before you broke into our home and then set fire to it, but I think you do now?"

Seeming baffled by the question, he glanced at Marcy and Jasmine before saying, "Yeah, I guess so."

"I don't mean just our names," Claudia told him, "I'm talking about who I really am."

He frowned, but she knew he was aware of her true identity, because Dan had told him in the hope of getting him to admit that Marcus was behind the crime.

Her mouth was dry, her heart beating too hard, but she needed to try and break through his defenses. "You said just now that you thought it was a shame someone had it in for us because we seemed like nice people. Do you know who that someone is?"

He shook his head, but she knew he wasn't being truthful.

"Have you considered," she said, "that he could harm us again using someone else? That's why we need to be certain about who gave you your instructions."

His head went down, and when it became clear he wasn't going to respond Jasmine suddenly said, "We all know it was my stepfather, and he's due to be released in a few weeks. If you can confirm that he gave you the orders . . ."

"I've already said in my letters, it was BJ," he told her.

"But BJ was acting for him?" Claudia prompted.

"I don't know. I didn't ask."

Claudia sat back in her chair, allowing Andee to take over.

"Why don't you tell us who BJ is?" Andee said encouragingly.

He took a short breath and gave a shrug. "He's just BJ. It stands for Big John."

"But he has another name. A real name."

He didn't answer.

"Jason Colbrook," she stated. "He shares your surname. I thought at first he might be your father, but he's your mother's brother, isn't he?"

Still he didn't respond.

"BJ is your uncle," she continued, "a man who regularly beats up his disadvantaged sister, procures her for other men, steals from her, and who recruited her son, his nephew, into drug dealing and worse. This is who you're trying to protect?"

"Not him," Archie protested, "my ma. If he ever found out about any of this, she's the one he'd go for."

"But he can be stopped, Archie. If you help us with this, we can make sure he doesn't go near her again."

"If you're talking about locking him up, he'll just get someone else to do it. That's how they work."

She regarded him skeptically. "Do you really believe that? Think about it. He's not a big player from what I hear, so why would anyone want to be involved in his business if he's no longer of any use to them?"

Archie swallowed dryly.

"There are any number of offenses he can be charged with," she told him, "that don't need to include his involvement in the fire so there would be no reason for him to link you to his arrest. All we need are a few words about the drug dealing that a dozen or more others would know about, or the trafficking. It's all known, Archie, we just need dates, times, locations. Doesn't matter if they're historical. It'll take him out of circulation and make your mother safe."

He still didn't speak, but the fear was retreating from his stare.

"The same goes for Marcus Huxley-Browne," Andee continued. "Your bosses, the gang members who run your uncle, aren't interested in him anymore. As soon as it was discovered that none of their names were in the attaché case you were ordered to steal—meaning it contained no proof that they'd supplied Huxley-Browne with illegal substances—he lost all his leverage."

Archie was looking wary again. "He's a PC. It means he knows at least some of the bosses' business model, and who they are. He can still do damage."

Marcy tensed. This might not be an admission of Marcus's involvement, but it was close.

"His knowledge gives him power," Archie added.

Andee said, "So the order did come from Huxley-Browne?"

"That's not what I'm saying," he protested. "I don't know who was behind it. I only know what BJ told me and he never mentioned no names."

"If you can link Marcus Huxley-Browne to the crime you committed he will be charged and kept in prison pending trial. Can you do that?"

He shook his head. "I'm not saying he had nothing to do with it," he told her, "but I've got no way of proving it. Like I said, my instructions came from BJ."

"Did you ever make deliveries to Marcus Huxley-Browne?" she asked.

He stiffened, but ended up giving a short nod.

"To his home, or his office?"

"Mostly his office, but a couple of times to his home."

"The one in West London?"

He nodded again and looked suddenly panicked. "Listen, I'm not telling anyone I delivered to him . . . I don't need any more on my rap sheet . . ."

"This isn't a police interview," Andee reminded him. "We're just establishing that you know who Huxley-Browne is and that you and your uncle had contact with him over a period of time for reasons unconnected to the fire."

Looking panicked again, Archie said, "You're asking me to be a snitch and I just can't do that. Sorry," he said to Marcy, "I get where you're coming from but if you knew what happened to snitches in here . . . Someone would put the word out and . . ." His voice trailed off as his eyes returned to his hands, leaving them to imagine what kind of horrors and abuse he might face if he helped them.

Andee was not ready to give up yet. "If we can't keep Huxley-Browne in prison by connecting him to the fire, he'll be free in a few weeks, and if he does still wish Claudia harm, he could try to approach her. We have to do what we can to stop him. Would you agree with that?"

Archie's eyes went to Claudia, his face pinched with anxiety and indecision.

"Archie, look at me," Marcy said softly.

He flinched, clearly knowing why she wanted him to meet her eyes, but he couldn't do it.

"I understand about your mother," Marcy told him, "but if your uncle is taken into custody, we really believe she can be kept safe. We just need you to do the same for us by admitting that my son-in-law was the one who ordered the crime you committed . . ."

"I can't because I don't know . . ."

Andee said, "But you do believe it was him?"

He said nothing.

"If I can persuade you to confirm that you've had dealings with Huxley-Browne in the past," Andee continued, "I can talk to a detective . . ."

"No, just not going to happen," he cut in, jerking back in his chair.

"The detective I'm referring to," Andee pressed on, "knows all about Claudia and why she left her husband. He hasn't in all this time revealed her whereabouts, because he considers her safety to be more important than exposing why she left. This means there's no evidence that Claudia was ill-treated, so he can't do anything to protect her once Huxley-Browne comes out. But if there's even the slightest suspicion that her husband was behind the fire it should be grounds for an investigation at least, and could also be enough to get a restraining order put on him."

To Claudia Archie said, "It's not that I don't want you to be protected, I swear I do, but if it ever got out that I . . ."

"Archie," Andee interrupted, "you need to get your head around the fact that the people you're afraid of are no longer a threat. They're not interested in you anymore. You've served your purpose, and as long as you don't drag any of them into this they won't care if you take down Huxley-Browne."

He didn't look convinced.

"You know how these people work," Andee reminded him, "so you've got to know that whatever knowledge Huxley-Browne has, he can never use it, not if he wants to stay alive."

Taking some time to digest this, Archie said, "Why should I believe you about my ma?"

"Because," Andee replied, "your uncle's the only one who ever posed a threat to her. No one else has ever come after her, have they?"

Archie's wide eyes confirmed this was true.

"So as soon as we get him off the streets she'll be safe. Now we need to do the same for Claudia and her family and make them safe too."

Archie clasped his head in his hands and Dan said, "Can we give him a few minutes? There's a lot to take in and . . ."

"Sure," Andee said at once. "We'll wait outside. Just let us know when you're ready."

As THEY WAITED, Marcy sensed so much stress and frustration building up in Claudia that she was afraid of what might be said when they went back into the room. She wished she could soothe it, that she could sort herself out too, but time out for Archie wasn't proving to be a good time out for them.

As though sensing Marcy's agitation, Andee said, "I understand how difficult this is, but please try to remember the kind of life he's led. Just about every minute of it has been spent living in fear of one sort or another, and it won't be any different for him where he is now. It's probably worse. He has trust issues the like of which we can't begin to imagine, hang-ups, anxieties, complexes, but I think you'll agree that he seems to want to do the right thing. He just has to find his own way there."

To Marcy's relief Claudia nodded, and closed her eyes as Jasmine put an arm around her.

Marcy said to Andee, "If you hadn't found out about his uncle . . ." She shuddered. "What he's done to his own sister and nephew . . . If ever anyone deserved to be taken off the streets . . ."

"Mum, you're making this about Archie," Claudia protested, "when it's about us, and what's been done to us. He's the offender, remember, we're the victims. OK, I understand he wants to protect his mother, but after what happened to you, don't you think we should be making ourselves a priority, not him?"

"Of course," Marcy agreed, "but isn't the purpose of us being here to try and make some sort of peace with what's happened, so that we can all move forward?"

Claudia was about to respond when the door opened and Dan beckoned them back inside.

Once they were seated Dan murmured something quietly to Archie before Archie fixed his eyes to Marcy's. "I'll tell whoever needs to know," he said, "that I've had contact with Marcus Huxley-Browne in the past and I'll also say that I think he was behind the fire."

Marcy gave a blink of surprise; beside her Jasmine hissed a yes under her breath; she didn't know how Claudia was reacting, because her gaze was still on Archie.

"I can't say it for certain," he continued, "because I don't know. I've never had any direct contact with him over it, I just reckon you're right, it was him."

After clearing her throat, Marcy said, "Thank you for that, Archie. It means a lot to us that you're willing to help keep us safe from my son-in-law—and I hope you believed Andee when she told you that everything will be done to make sure your mother is safe too."

His eyes went down, and seeing the way his mouth twisted and tightened she realized he didn't believe it, but he'd given them this anyway.

Dan said, "I think we've accomplished what we set out to do today. Does everyone agree?"

They all nodded, apart from Archie, who didn't look at anyone as he got up to leave the room.

A WHILE LATER, as Andee drove them away from the prison, Marcy realized she was feeling so low that she almost regretted coming. It had been a strain on them all, but on Archie too, she thought, and how was he feeling now about giving them this tenuous connection to Marcus?

She sighed and pressed her fingers to her forehead. "So, we all get to go home to our comfortable lives and families, while he goes back to a prison cell with no one to talk to or even to care how he's been affected by the day—or to bother about what harm comes to him."

Jasmine murmured, "I know what you mean. I'm having a problem with it too."

"But what can we do?" Claudia demanded. "We could hardly take him with us, and at least he has the solace of knowing he did the right thing in the end."

"If he believes that," Marcy said.

"I think he does," Andee assured them.

Marcy sighed again and her thoughts drifted to the way he'd looked when he'd left the room, young, lonely, trying to put a brave face on it all . . . He was nineteen, for heaven's sake—a young man, but in some ways still a boy. Moreover, this was probably the only time they'd see him; there was no reason for any more letters and why would there be any further RJ meetings? As Dan had said, they'd accomplished what they'd set out to, so there was no reason for any more contact.

"I'm not sure," she said, "what I was expecting at the end of today, but it feels like . . . there ought to be more."

Jasmine said, "So you don't think we'll visit him again?"

"I think you need to give it some time," Andee advised. "These meetings often take a while to process . . . Hang on, it's Dan," and clicking on to answer her phone she said, "Hi, is everything OK?"

"Fine," he replied, his voice clearly audible over the car's Command system.

Marcy asked, not able to help herself, "How was Archie when you left him?"

"Pretty subdued, but I'm sure he was glad he'd managed to try to make things up to you in the end."

"While we," Claudia said, "are feeling bad that he did."

"Does he believe his mother's going to be safe from the uncle?" Jasmine asked.

"He won't be fully on board with it until there's been an arrest."

Marcy said, "Is that likely to be soon?"

"Over to Andee for that. She's the one with the police contacts," Dan pointed out.

"I still haven't spoken to anyone," she reminded them, "but I will as soon as I drop you guys off."

"And what about Marcus?" Claudia asked. "Do we know what's going to happen with him?"

"That's more complicated, but now Archie's saying he thinks the orders came from him it could start an investigation. What will come of it . . . Well, I guess we'll find out."

After a moment Marcy said, "Wasn't today supposed to be about forgiveness?"

"If you wanted it to be," he answered, "although Archie made a point of not asking for it."

"I know."

Andee glanced at her.

"I'm realizing," Marcy said, "that it's easy enough to say the words, but . . . I can tell you that I don't feel any hatred toward him now, or a need for vengeance, but as for forgiveness . . ." She only had to remind herself that he could have walked away, turned the job down . . . "Maybe I need to work out what it really means before I can be sure it's something I'm able to offer."

# CHAPTER FORTY-THREE

So here I am writing to you again like I don't know how to stop. No Dan pushing me into it now. I suppose it's something I've got used to doing and it doesn't feel right to just give up on it.

I don't know what it was like for you meeting me today, I can only tell you what it was like for me meeting you. It did me up proper at first. I guess you saw that. Sorry if it hurt your feelings or embarrassed you; I honestly didn't mean to. Seeing what the fire had done to you and knowing it was because of me . . . . I've hated myself for stuff I've done before, but nothing's ever made me feel as bad as I did then, and still do now. I can't see anything else ever will.

When it came your turn to speak it was hard for me at first to take in the things you were saying. I was ashamed to be in the same room as you, and couldn't understand why you'd want anything to do with me.

Then you go and decide that you're not going to make me feel even worse than I already do, even though it was your right—that's what these meetings are all about, I think. You get to describe how I've screwed up your life, and to twist the knife to make sure I never forget it. But you opted out of that. I'm still trying to take it in, that you'd give up the chance of killing me in the only legal way possible.

So, if you're wondering what made me give it up about your son-in-law in the end, it was you showing me how decent people behave. Not only that, you'd already thought about how my ma could be protected. No way could I hold back on you after that, I just needed to get it straight in my head. That was why I had to have some time out. Amazing how Dan understands these things.

I'm really sorry I couldn't tell you anything definite about Hux-B, but I just don't have it. I just know it came from him. Tbh, I knew it the minute I saw your daughter, Claudia, outside the house. I'd seen her before while I was making a delivery. I don't think she ever saw me, but I remember her and how scared of him she seemed. I thought he was a POS then, I don't want to offend you by spelling out what I think of him now. I hope with everything in me that the cops find the trail that leads to him, but I know it won't be an easy one. It's not likely anyone's going to take my word for anything, and BJ won't rat him out, so I can't say what happens next. (Do you really think, by the way, that they'll be able to pull BJ in for something else without it being linked to me? Sorry if that sounds selfish, but survival instinct and all that.)

This is going to sound weird now, but when I think back on today and the way you handled the whole thing, it just keeps blowing me away. You're something else, you really are.

I don't suppose you'll be wanting to hear from me again, and I guess Dan won't be coming anymore, so time for me to get on with the other stuff I've got going on with my lawyer, the sentencing, and everything.

Thank you again for coming to meet me and for reading

my letters. I'm sorrier than I know how to put into words and I hope . . . Not sure what I hope really . . . Good stuff for you, obvs, for me too, if that's all right.

Please tell Claudia and Jasmine (hope you don't mind me using their names) that I'm grateful to them for coming too, and I'm sorry for what they've had to go through. I wish I knew how to get Jasmine a new violin, but I've got no money and being stuck in here isn't going to put me in the way of any. It wouldn't mean much coming from me anyway, I get that.

You people so didn't deserve anyone like me coming into your lives, or that psycho Huxley-Browne. I hope no one like us ever crosses your paths again.

# CHAPTER FORTY-FOUR

They're here," Marcy declared, as a car turned into their drive and stopped in front of the gates.

Claudia pushed the release button while watching her mother with a worried expression. "Are you OK?" she asked. "You're looking quite pale today."

"I'm fine," Marcy assured her. "Please don't fuss."

Claudia wanted to say more, but with Andee and Helen Hall, the town's leading criminal lawyer, about to arrive, now wasn't the time to get into how Marcy had been retreating into herself again since the meeting with Archie. She hadn't even commented on the letter from him that had turned up yesterday with a fully credible apology and equally genuine-sounding appreciation of the way Marcy had chosen not to skewer him during the visit. However, Claudia could tell that it had affected her.

She'd try to broach the subject again once Andee and Helen had gone. For now, as her mother set a tray of tea on the table, she went to let the visitors in.

The introductions were soon made and Claudia found herself warming to Helen Hall, who was very like the photo on her law firm's website with her mop of curly red hair, freckles, and sharp green eyes.

Andee said, "As you know, Helen's come along to talk us through why things aren't happening in quite the way we'd hoped, regarding the information Archie gave us last week about Marcus."

Helen smiled a thank-you to Marcy as she passed her a cup of black tea. "The problem we have," she began, "is that Archie's allegations aren't carrying any weight. This wasn't wholly unexpected, of course, given who and where he is—and the fact that there is no proof of a connection between him and Huxley-Browne really isn't helping. To be blunt about it, his claim, at the moment, is being viewed by some as a ploy to try and shift some blame in order to reduce his sentence when the time comes."

Claudia's mouth turned dry. "But surely someone's asking why he would randomly pick on Marcus to accuse?" she protested.

"Questions that deserve answers," Helen acknowledged, "but I'm afraid none are yet forthcoming. Your champion in the Met, Detective Inspector Carl Phillips, has tried to open an investigation in response to the claim, but so far he's getting nowhere. There's no interest in allocating funds to a case that is seen to belong to another force, and here in Kesterly they don't have the manpower to set up an inquiry that would largely have to take place in London." She took a sip of tea, leaving a pale pink mark on the cup's rim. "There's also no evidence of your husband ever being abusive toward you," she continued gently, "and without it I'm afraid a judge simply won't—can't—issue a restraining order."

Claudia's face was pinched and angry as she looked at her mother. Marcy lowered her eyes, at a loss for anything positive to say.

"Things could change," Helen stated encouragingly, "and they often do, so I want you to know that we're not giving up."

"I'm expecting to hear anytime now," Andee told them, "that Archie's uncle, the infamous BJ, has been picked up. The charges will be drug and trafficking related, so there's a chance he might be willing to throw Huxley-Browne under a bus over the fire in exchange for a few charges being dropped, or a lighter sentence."

Helen said, "I'm truly sorry I'm not yet able to tell you what you want to hear, but there's still a way to go before your husband is released."

Claudia said, "Seven weeks—not that we're counting."

With a sympathetic smile Helen checked her mobile as it vibrated on the table. "I have to take this," she said. "I hope you don't mind. It's about another case," she added, clearly not wanting to get hopes up unnecessarily.

As she went through to the sitting room, Andee said, "Have you seen Dan's report of our meeting with Archie yet?"

"He's bringing it over later," Claudia replied. "Have you?"

Andee smiled wryly. "I helped write it. I think it's thorough, and fair. There's no doubt in our minds that Archie is genuinely remorseful—and from the conversations we've had with you guys, we've gone with the assumption that you agree with that."

Claudia looked at her mother. "I think we do?" she prompted.

Marcy said, "Who does the report go to?"

"That usually depends on who's requested it," Andee replied. "The police, social workers, parole officers . . . In this case, because Dan and I initiated it ourselves we'll probably give it to DCI Gould for him to sign off on before presenting it to the Crown Prosecution Service. Of course, Helen, as the head of Archie's legal team, will have a copy too. It should prove an important and useful document for her."

Returning to the kitchen, Helen said, "My apologies for that, but it does mean I have to get back to the office. You have my number if you need to call, and once again, please don't give up. I'm sure we'll have better news soon."

Marcy said, "Before you go, can I ask you about Archie?"

"What would you like to know?" Helen replied kindly, "keeping in mind lawyer/client privilege, you understand."

Marcy nodded. "Of course, and I'll try not to put you in a difficult position. We've had another letter from him. Dan brought it yesterday."

Helen nodded, showing that she was aware of this. "Does it contain something that's bothering you?" she asked, concerned.

Marcy said, "I'd just like to know if you've managed to get his charge changed or dismissed yet?"

"You mean the attempted murder charge? We're still waiting to hear back from the CPS on that. I'm afraid these things often take longer than we'd like them to. At this rate we'll be in court before we get a response, and what a jolly fiasco that would turn out to be."

Marcy was aware of Claudia watching her curiously, clearly wondering why she was asking. She hadn't discussed this with anyone yet, but her mind was made up, and perhaps this was as good a time as any to tell them what she'd decided. "I think he should stand trial," she said to Helen.

Helen's surprise showed, as did everyone else's.

"You mean for attempted murder?" Andee asked.

Marcy nodded. "Yes. Please will you tell him that I want him to stand trial for attempted murder."

# CHAPTER FORTY-FIVE

It came as a big surprise to me when Dan requested a visit—I mean the kind of visit you usually get from mates or family, not the kind we usually have. I hadn't been expecting to see him again until we went to court, and I wasn't even sure if he'd be there then.

I can't tell you how chuffed I was when the request came through, and by the time the day comes round I'm so pumped I can hardly wait to see him. I'm all prepared to give him my news (I don't have any), and to tell him that next time he should come for a sleepover. Then I get to the visiting room, and talk about gobsmacked! Claudia's only sitting there with him. I don't get it at all, why would she come and see me?

When they get round to dropping the bombshell—that you want me to stand trial for trying to murder you—so much stuff spins round in my head, really bad stuff that I'm proper ashamed of now. But man, I was gutted. I swear I hadn't seen it coming. Even though I hadn't heard anything from you I never thought you still hated me. I thought we'd moved on from that, but then I realized that the reason you hadn't wiped the floor with me during our visit was because you'd decided on another way of doing it.

I was so backed up with all the s*** giving me grief

in my head that it took a while for me to catch up with what Claudia was saying—and by the time she'd finished I'm like totally done up. You want me to stand trial because you think there's a good chance a jury might not find me guilty of attempted murder—and if they don't it all goes away. But, if my lawyer presses for a lesser charge, the jury might be more inclined to accept it, and a guilty verdict will add it to my sentence for arson.

So suddenly, weirdly, attempted murder is looking like my best bet.

They're not kidding it's a gamble, but Dan thinks I should go for it, and apparently my lawyer's up for it too. (She was going to come and tell me herself, but then Dan and Claudia asked if they could do it. I guess you already know that.)

Anyways, because it's you who's asking, I'm going to go for it. It's a done deal that I'll be in here for a good long time for the arson, so if things don't work out what's the difference? Only thing that bothers me is, if there's going to be a trial, what'll that mean for you? Will you have to give evidence?

Dan tells me that's all under discussion, and what I need to focus on is the part I have to play. Helen's coming sometime soon with a barrister to talk me through it all, so it seems everyone's ahead of me. No surprise there.

It's not till after they've gone that I realize I forgot to ask about Huxley-Browne. Has anything happened there yet? I heard through the grapevine that BJ's been remanded on drug charges, so he'll be proper brickin' it by now, and trying to get messages out letting everyone know they got nothing to worry about, he's no snitch. Bet he is if there turns out to be something in it for him. I'm still scared it's going to come back on me, but hey, it's done now, can't change it, I'll deal with it when I have to. I've got other things to be thinking about now, like going over everything again in my head to make sure there's nothing I'm missing.

# CHAPTER FORTY-SIX

"A re you ready, Mum?" Claudia called from the front door.

"Coming," Marcy called back. "I'll just get the present. Be right there."

With a sigh of exasperation Claudia read the text that had just arrived.

*Am I meeting you at the restaurant? Dx*

She texted back. *That was the plan.*

*Great. On my way. See you there.*

Tonight there was a big birthday celebration for Henry at the Crustacean, with all their closest friends invited. It had been her mother's idea, and she was still fighting with Henry over who was going to pay for it. He'd lose because Claudia had already taken care of it, but she hadn't bothered telling them that yet, since their squabbling was good entertainment. It was also the best feeling in the world to see her mother coming out of her shell again and even looking forward to things.

However, to say she was looking forward to Archie's trial might be overstating it, but she'd been preparing for it with Helen for the past week or so, and remained determined to make an appearance on the stand on behalf of the defense. Naturally the prosecution had called her, it made sense for them to do so, but when she'd told them what she was, and was not, prepared to say they'd quickly dropped her. Quite why they hadn't also dropped the attempted murder charge only they knew, although it presumably meant they remained confident of securing a guilty verdict.

Turning at the sound of a car coming through the open gates Claudia frowned into the darkness, trying to recognize it in the headlights.

"Who's that?" her mother asked, joining her at the door.

"I don't know, but whoever it is they need to stop . . . *Now!*"

The dark green Astra ended up inches from the driver's door of Jasmine's Mini, headlights blazing and causing sparks of alarm to shoot through Claudia.

Putting an arm across her mother she was about to push her back into the house when a scrawny little woman in a yellow parka and green wellies all but tumbled out of the Astra.

"Ell—oh!" she shouted, hurrying awkwardly toward them. "I'm Archie's ma, Maria. Sorry to bother you. Ah you Ma-cee Kavnuh?"

As she came closer, they could see the twist of her mouth and crooked bones in her face, and realizing who she was, Marcy threw a surprised glance at Claudia as she stepped forward.

"Hello, Maria," she said. "I'm Marcy. Is everything all right?"

"Yeah. Ev-thing fine. Just want to ask please can I clean fo' you to say sorry fo' wha' my boy did, een tho he din mean to. No charge. Can come any day tha' sues you."

Marcy wasn't sure what to say, could only connect with the strangeness of being approached like this.

"Maria, I think—" Claudia began.

"Is ma way to make up to you," Maria interrupted. "He can' do himself because of bein' in prison."

Claudia said firmly, "We're about to go out, but we'll discuss your offer and give you an answer soon. Is that OK?"

Maria's lopsided mouth broke into a smile, and her eyes were bright with gratitude as she said, "Thas OK. I can wait. Thank you, thank you," and went swiftly back to her car.

Claudia and Marcy watched as she crunched it into gear and

prayed as she revved up that she would find reverse. She did, but they remained silently staring as she shot backward down the drive as if she'd just been sprung from a bow.

"What the f—" Jasmine cried, finally able to leap out of her Mini.

"We'll explain on the way," Claudia told her. "We need to go."

TWENTY MINUTES LATER, after agreeing to talk more about how they should respond to Maria's unexpected offer, they ran into the restaurant to find they were the last to arrive. A worried Henry spotted them first and hurried over to greet Marcy, who'd left his gift in the car so they went off to get it.

"Hey you," Dan said, coming to plant a kiss on Claudia's cheek. So familiar and so typical of the public greeting he gave her now that they were five official dates into a relationship.

"Hey you," she murmured back. "You're looking very dashing." He was, in his dark suit and pale blue shirt (no tie), but for her it was always the glasses that did it. And him, just for being him.

"And you're looking ravishing," he told her. "I don't think I've seen that dress before."

With a playful smile she said, "There's a lot you haven't seen before, but if you remembered to pack for a sleepover . . . ?"

His eyes narrowed in his version of seductive as he looked into hers. "I did," he replied, leaving her in little doubt of how pleased he was to have done so.

"Good, because it seems everyone's going in different directions from here—Jasmine's off clubbing with Abby, and Mum's going home with Henry."

His eyebrows shot up. "Seriously?"

"Seriously. Mum decided Henry shouldn't be on his own on his birthday, so she drove her things over there earlier and came home again to get ready."

"Wow," he murmured. "So, it's going to be just us at the coach house tonight."

"Just us. Oh, but remind me to tell you about the visit we just had from Archie's mother. It was . . . I'm not actually sure what it was, or how we should deal with it, but now's not the time. We should mingle."

Since all the regular crowd was there, and everyone was so fond of teasing Henry, it quickly turned into a rowdy and even raucous evening. Claudia was so happy to be a part of it that she all but forgot about the clock ticking down on Marcus's release. However, this was no time to be thinking about it, they were safe here, in this restaurant among friends, and knowing what the evening held with Dan was making everything feel like a wonderful dream coming true.

It was after the main course had been cleared that Richie came to sit beside her, taking the chair that Graeme had just vacated. "You know, I'm going to be covering the trial next week?" he asked quietly.

"Of course," she replied, her smile fading at the reminder. "We'd expect you to."

"So, would it be OK to ask your mother for an interview before it starts? You know, to find out how she's feeling about taking the stand?"

Simply hearing it put into words made Claudia's heart contract with nerves. "You should ask her, but to be honest, I'm starting to wonder if I'm more uptight about it than she is."

With a smile Richie said, "She's a remarkable woman. There aren't many who'd do what she's doing—with scars, or without." He stood, waving to a friend.

"Between us, I wish she'd change her mind, but I can't see it happening. Now, it looks as though the cake is about to arrive."

As it was wheeled in full of sparklers and candles, the whole restaurant broke into "Happy Birthday," and as Henry, beaming with delight, prepared to say thank you, Claudia felt Dan's arm go around her.

Leaning her head on his shoulder she whispered, "How long before we can go?"

He was about to respond when Richie popped back. "I meant to ask," he said, keeping his voice down as Henry launched into a speech, "has Marcy visited the prison at all?"

"No," Claudia replied. "She hasn't wanted to use up his mother's time with him, and I think she's worried about how the other inmates might react when they see her."

"Got you," Richie responded. "She's met with the lawyers by now though?"

"She's spent a lot of time with Helen Hall and the barrister, Gordon Lock. We're told he's a Queen's Counsel with an impressive reputation."

"I hear the prosecution are putting their own QC up against him."

She nodded, feeling anxious and fearful. Her mother was extremely brave to be doing this, especially when she had zero experience in a courtroom. Claudia just hoped to God that the prosecuting lawyer didn't end up tearing her still fragile confidence to shreds. "If things don't go as we'd like them to," she said to Richie, "you'll treat her well in your reports, won't you?"

"You have my word on it," he promised, "but I'll lay money they'll find him not guilty once they've heard what she has to say."

"And that," Claudia said to Dan as Richie returned to his own seat between Jasmine and Abby, "is what's making me more nervous than anything, the way everyone seems so certain that she, all on her own, is going to swing things in Archie's favor. The pressure on Mum is enormous. She won't talk about it, she says there's no point if I try to bring it up, but I know she's worried and I think quite a big part of her is actually regretting saying she'll do this."

"She can always pull out," Dan told her seriously. "It's still possible for the verdict to go in his favor even if she doesn't take the stand."

"That's what I've told her. I've even tried warning her that the prosecution could accuse her of trying to manipulate the jury with sight of her injuries."

"Believe me, no sane lawyer would do that to a victim who is brave enough to stand up for her attacker when she's clearly scarred for life. I think you need to try and stop worrying, trust her to know what she's doing, but make sure she's aware that if she does want to change her mind no one, I mean no one, will think worse of her for it." His eyes seemed to enlarge behind his glasses as he added, "I only wish the real guilty parties were facing trial, but we haven't given up hope of that yet."

Her brow was still furrowed.

Pressing a kiss to her head he murmured, "Would it be possible to put this aside now and be just us?"

With a smile as she returned to the present she said, "Of course," and for once it wasn't hard to let go of the tension inside her, not when she had so much to look forward to later.

THE FOLLOWING AFTERNOON Marcy returned to the coach house from Henry's, and as her eyes met Claudia's across the kitchen it was clear that they were both finding it hard to stop smiling.

"So, it went well for you, with Dan?" Marcy asked casually as she dropped her overnight bag and shrugged off her coat.

"It did, thank you. And from the look of you I'm guessing it went well for you, with Henry?"

Marcy laughed. "I'm glad Jasmine's not around to hear us, I can just imagine what she might say, or maybe I'd rather not," and going to fill the kettle she began making tea.

"So, are you up for discussing Maria's offer?" Claudia asked, as they took their mugs through to the sitting room.

Marcy felt a strange tightness inside as she thought about it, and wasn't sure whether it was resistance, or guilt, or even annoyance at having to deal with it. She'd far rather carry on thinking about Henry and replaying what a big step it had been for her to stay with him last night. And how tender he had been. Then she pictured the tiny woman's pleading face, and found herself wondering how she must be feeling now, with her son in prison and her conscience trying to make amends for his crime.

With a sigh, she drank some tea and put her mug on the table. "So, what are your thoughts?"

"Well, frankly," Claudia began, "I think it would be extremely odd—to put it mildly—to employ the mother of the person who set fire to our house. It doesn't feel right at all, in fact it feels distinctly wrong, but at the same time I can't help feeling sorry for her."

Marcy smiled reflectively. "I know what you mean. And let's not forget, she's not to blame for what happened. She's just a mother trying to do her best, the way any mother would . . ."

They sat quietly for a while, mulling over Maria's brief and unexpected visit again until Claudia said, "If we tell her no, how are we going to feel after?"

Marcy sighed. "Knowing us we'll worry about having hurt her feelings."

Being in little doubt of that, especially where her mother was concerned, Claudia said, "But we don't owe her anything."

"You might say that, but don't forget if she hadn't turned in her own son, we'd probably still have no idea who actually set fire to the place."

Accepting the truth of that, and actually admiring the courage it must have taken for Maria to do what she did, as well as all the distress it must have caused her at the time and since, Claudia said, "You're right, we are indebted to her for that, and we always will be, but if we do take her on it'll mean that she—and by extension, Archie—will always be with us, and I don't think we want that, do we?"

Marcy shook her head as she thought. It was hard to imagine ever being past this time in their lives, of reaching a point when not everything would be about the fire, or her injuries, or Archie's trial. "I'm wondering," she said, "if we should make this a part of the forgiving process . . ." She broke off, not entirely sure if she meant what she was saying, if she even knew what the process was or how she felt about it. Of course, she knew the dictionary definition of forgiveness, and what it should entail, but words were easy, anyone could speak them, whereas actually connecting with that level of understanding and exoneration, making it real and relevant . . .

"No one's saying you have to forgive anything," Claudia told her gently.

Marcy's eyebrows rose. "Isn't that why we entered the RJ program?"

"Maybe. Yes, I suppose it is, but I know I'm still having a really hard time with it myself."

Marcy frowned. "So, you're not starting to forgive Archie?"

Claudia said, "I want this to be about you, Mum, not me. If forgiving, or working on forgiveness, helps you to move forward I'll support you all the way, but it doesn't mean that I feel the same."

Marcy regarded her intently and allowed several minutes to pass. "I think," she said eventually, "that what you're actually having a difficult time with is being able to forgive yourself, but it wasn't your fault, Claudia. None of it."

"You say that, but if I hadn't married Marcus . . ."

"You had no idea this would happen, none of us did. For heaven's sake, you can't carry that sort of guilt around with you forever, especially when it doesn't belong to you. And if I thought you couldn't let it go that would make everything a whole lot harder for me."

Claudia's eyes went down as the warning assailed her conscience, though she wasn't sure it was making any difference. Sometimes she only had to look at her mother to feel a consuming, raging need to punish herself for having brought her to this.

"Claudia," Marcy said firmly, "I am truly coming to believe that the only way either of us is ever going to be able to move on is through some kind of forgiveness, and that has to include you forgiving yourself. OK, I know it's hard, I'm not finding it easy either, to empathize with Archie. God knows, a big part of me wants to say to hell with it, why should I forgive anyone after what's been done to me? Let them suffer, let all the wrath of the gods rain down on them, but if I do that, I'm the one who's going to end up a bitter and vengeful old woman. That's not who I want to be, it really isn't, but I'm sure it's what will happen if I hang on to all the terrible things I feel. They're corrosive, Claudia, even more damaging in their way than the fire. And it's the same for you. You need to exorcize all the ugliness that's come from knowing Marcus, because if you don't he'll always be with you."

Claudia's eyes widened in astonishment. "You're surely not asking me to forgive him," she protested.

"No, not at all. I understand that's far too big an ask, for either of us, but going easier on yourself, being more understanding of your mistakes—that you couldn't possibly have known were mistakes at the time—is every bit as important for you as it is for me. As a family we need to move on in as healthy a way as we can, and holding on to negative and destructive feelings about ourselves isn't going to help us to do that."

Claudia knew she couldn't deny any of this, she didn't even want to try, since she was perfectly aware that arguing a case for her self-loathing was as counterproductive as it was stupid. It was simply . . . It was simply what? It was so hard to know how she felt about anything, apart from responsible and brokenhearted about what her mother had been through, and would never escape. "I guess," she said quietly, "that we have to accept that it's going to take me longer to get the hang of forgiving than it seems to be taking you."

Marcy's tone was wry as she said, "Believe you me, I'm not there yet, I'm just going through the motions of it in the hope that it'll become a reality. And actually, so far, it seems to be working."

"You wouldn't be doing what you are for Archie if it weren't."

"Maybe not, but surely you can see that he's as much a victim in all this as he is an offender."

"I suppose it's one way of looking at it."

"I've decided it's the only way and not for him, for me."

Going to sit beside her, Claudia took her damaged hand between both of hers and raised it to her lips.

"It was Dan who first told us," Marcy went on, "that it's often harder for the families of victims to forgive than it is the victim themselves, and it seems he's right."

Claudia gazed into her mother's eyes seeing past the injuries to the beauty inside her. "I don't deserve two such wonderful people in my life," she said softly, "but I'm very glad I have you both."

"And we're very glad, and very lucky, to have you. Now what we still have to decide is, what should we do about Maria? Should we take Maria on, or shouldn't we? Would it be a step forward, or will it keep us rooted to where we are?"

# CHAPTER FORTY-SEVEN

I don't understand it," Marcy cried, looking from Helen to Andee and back again. "Can they do this? We're due in court next week. Why have they waited until now to change the indictment?"

"It's almost certainly because they're no longer confident of getting a conviction for attempted murder," Helen replied. "In my opinion that was a wrong call from the start, but now their barrister's got hold of it they've apparently woken up to what they're much more likely to be able to make stick."

As Marcy fell silent, Claudia said, "So tell us again what he's being charged with."

Consulting her tablet, Helen read aloud, "'Count one: aggravated arson with intention to destroy property.' He's already pleaded guilty to that so no issue there. It's count two that's the problem: 'Aggravated arson being reckless as to whether life would be endangered.'"

Marcy said, "Is that as bad as it sounds?"

Helen's expression was far from encouraging. "Attempted murder speaks to intent, and presenting a defense to demonstrate that there was no intention to take a life, which is what we were planning, is quite different from trying to convince a jury that there was no recklessness involved in the arson. Arson by its very nature is reckless."

Marcy and Claudia looked at each other as they digested this new turn of events. "Have you told him?" Claudia asked turning back to Helen.

Helen nodded. "I spoke to him earlier. He's still taking it in. We're due to speak again later to discuss his plea."

"What will you advise him to do?" Marcy wanted to know.

Helen shook her head and sighed. "If he pleads guilty to the second count as well as the first, the judge could be inclined to impose a lesser sentence."

"So how long could it be?" Marcy asked.

"Worst-case scenario? Fifteen years."

Marcy hadn't realized until now quite how certain she'd felt that Archie would be found not guilty of attempted murder; this new charge was throwing her completely.

"Is there any chance of him being found not guilty on the second count?" Claudia asked.

Helen was clearly doubtful. "Criminal trials are as unpredictable as juries," she replied, "so anything's possible, but would I advise him to enter that plea? Frankly, I don't know if it's the right call. I'm due to discuss it with Gordon Lock, his barrister, when he's finished in court for the day. I'll be interested to hear his opinion."

Speaking for the first time, Andee said, "Something that is in Archie's favor is the fact that the two counts are separate. If they were tied together as one, which they can be in a case like this, there wouldn't be a chance of him being found not guilty."

"This is true," Helen confirmed, "and it's the only reason I would counsel him to go ahead with a trial, slim as the chances are of him getting the verdict we all want."

Claudia turned to her mother. "What do you think he should do?" she asked, aware that this was too big a question for someone who knew next to nothing about the law.

Marcy was trying to picture Archie in his cell. What was he thinking now? How afraid was he? Did he have anyone to talk to about how the door seemed to be closing on the rest of his young life? Probably not, until Helen called him again, and it was too late now to organize a visit to the prison.

Realizing they were waiting for her reply, she said to Helen, "I appreciate you have to leave now, but, Andee, can you stay? We need to talk this through with someone who has a better knowledge of how the law works than we do."

"Of course," Andee said, "I'll do my best, but remember, I'm not a lawyer."

Helen was already preparing to leave. "I'll call as soon as I've spoken to Gordon," she promised, and after a quick apology for not being able to stay, she went off.

By the time she rang in the early afternoon, Marcy, after a long discussion with Andee, had come to a decision. There was absolutely no way of knowing if it was the right one, but unless the barrister strongly advised against it, the only chance Archie stood of avoiding a truly punishing sentence was to plead not guilty on the second count—the one that included a reckless disregard for life. It would then be his defense counsel's job to persuade the jury that he had in fact made certain that the house was empty before he'd set it alight.

"Gordon thinks it could be worth the risk," Helen told her, and as Marcy heaved a sigh of relief she gave a thumbs-up to Claudia and Andee.

"Of course, the ultimate decision has to be Archie's," Marcy said to Helen, "but when you speak to him please tell him that I think we should continue along the same path, in spite of the change. He should still plead not guilty."

FOUR DAYS LATER Marcy opened the front door of the coach house for Dan to come in, and as she removed his coat Claudia appeared from her craft room. "Hi, am I too early?" he asked as she came to greet him.

"It doesn't matter," she replied. "Have you heard anything from Archie since the change of indictment?"

He shook his head. "Have you asked his mother about his decision?"

Wryly, Marcy said, "She's too busy with her trial cleaning for chitchat, but she says that she'll be in court cheering her boy on, not literally I hope, but you never know."

Taking the gin and tonic Claudia had made for him, Dan said, "I got your email earlier. Still no plans to question Huxley-Browne about the arson?"

Claudia shook her head dejectedly. "Carl Phillips says he's doing all he can," she replied, "but there's still only Archie's word to go on and it's just not enough."

"So the uncle—BJ—isn't proving useful?"

"Not yet," Marcy interjected, "but there's still time. Marcus isn't due for release for another three weeks. Anything can happen in that time."

Dan slipped an arm around Claudia and pressed a kiss to her forehead. "Marcy's right about that," he told her. "You've only got to look at this new indictment for Archie. We didn't see that coming—although maybe not a good example when it's not exactly going our way."

Putting on a smile, Claudia decided to change the subject. It was the only way to sideline the feeling of Marcus coming closer as each day passed. "We're going to Henry's for dinner," she said. "His son and daughter-in-law have turned up unexpectedly and he wants us to come and meet them." She turned to her mother with teasing eyes. "And I'm reliably informed by the Fitbit fanatic here that it's no more than seventeen hundred steps to his place, so we can walk."

Marcy's eyes rounded in protest. "In the dark? I don't think so."

Amused, Dan said, "Don't worry, I'll drive," and after taking a sip of his drink he read Archie's letter again. "There's no time to get a visit in before next Monday," he said, "so unless he calls me, or another letter turns up, this could be all we're going to get from him until we see him in court."

Marcy regarded the letter with a heavy sense of foreboding. "Something's not right about this," she murmured. "I just wish I knew what it was."

# CHAPTER FORTY-EIGHT

The following Monday Marcy, Claudia, and Jasmine arrived at the court in good time, leaving Henry to park the car while they cleared security and found Andee in the main lobby with Dan and Helen.

"Is Archie here yet?" Marcy asked as they greeted one another.

"He's just arrived," Helen replied. "How are you feeling?"

"I'm fine," Marcy lied, as Claudia said, "She's worried," and Jasmine said, "This is a big deal for her, coming out in public like this."

Marcy regarded them helplessly. "Anything else of mine you'd like to share?" she asked snippily. Without waiting for an answer she said to Helen, "When you see him please tell him we're here and that nothing's changed, I'm still going to speak up for him."

"Of course." Helen squeezed her arm to show that she understood what this was costing Marcy.

"Can you also ask him," Claudia said, slipping a hand into Dan's as he came to greet her, "why he hasn't been in touch since the indictment changed?"

"Don't pressure him," Marcy scolded. "He's got enough to think about." Addressing Helen again, "Of course, if it all goes wrong it'll be my fault . . ."

"Nana, for heaven's sake," Jasmine protested. "He made the decision himself to plead not guilty . . ."

"But I encouraged him . . ."

"He also has a legal team," Helen came in gently. "Now, I ought to go down there, so if you'll excuse me I'll see you in court."

As she walked away Andee said, "Has anyone seen Archie's barrister?"

"He's in the robing room," Dan told her.

"What about Maria?" Marcy asked, searching the busy lobby and the queue coming through security.

"No sign of her yet," Andee replied, as Henry joined them, "but I'm sure she'll be here. Now you understand it's possible you won't be called today?" she said to Marcy.

"Yes, Helen explained that, but I can sit in court?"

"Provided the judge doesn't ask witnesses to wait outside."

Although it was starting to feel too much already, Marcy kept it to herself, certain the rising panic would dissipate before it reached a peak.

Dan said, "Here's Maria," and going over to security he waited for her to come through before bringing her to join their group.

"Are you OK?" Marcy asked, her nerves clenching again at the sight of Maria's pale face and red-raw eyes.

"Yes, din sleep so well. Is he 'ere?"

"Apparently, yes," Claudia told her. "Helen's gone down to see him."

Maria's eyes filled with tears as she turned to Dan. "They gon' lock 'im up for good?" she asked brokenly.

"I'm sure that won't happen," he soothed, sounding more confident than any of them felt. "Come on, there's time to get us all a coffee before we go upstairs."

Twenty minutes later they were taking their seats at the front of the public gallery, and as Marcy looked down into the well of the court she felt another surge of anxiety at the prospect of standing there in front of everyone with her terrible face on full display.

She took a breath and made herself think of Archie, and how awful it was going to be for him when he was brought up from the cells and seated behind the bulletproof screen. And how hard it was going to be for his mother seeing him there. Hopefully Maria wouldn't cry out, or make any sort of fuss that would end in her being ejected from proceedings.

As though sensing her mother's turmoil, Claudia reached for her hand and gave it a comforting squeeze. A smile of gratitude flitted across Marcy's face, making her aware of the tightness of the warped, silvery-red skin that was so unlike anyone else's.

Claudia watched Dan entering the court below with Helen Hall. Gordon Lock the barrister was with them, a tall, imposing figure with hawkish features and thick gray hair just visible beneath his horsehair wig. He was not someone it was easy to imagine summoning forth sympathy and understanding from a jury. However, looks could be deceiving, and Helen Hall had told them that Archie was extremely fortunate to have this man on his side.

*Why*, she asked herself for the thousandth time, *were they rooting for someone who'd caused such terrible damage to her mother?* It felt wrong in so many ways—but she tried to remind herself that Archie, in his way, was as much a victim of Marcus's as they were.

As Dan glanced up, she gave him a smile and thought of how lucky she was to have him in her life. Just please, when this was all over, don't let Marcus do something to ruin things. *He's not going to be released*, she told herself firmly. *The uncle, BJ, will tie him to the arson and he'll be remanded back into custody before he even makes it onto the street.*

The jury was brought in and as Marcy watched them, seven women and five men of varying ages and ethnicity, she was trying to imagine how they were going to react when they saw her face for the first time. It would be perhaps the most damning evidence of all against Archie, probably enough to make up their minds there and then for a conviction. After all, what more would they need to see to feel certain that he'd behaved recklessly enough to endanger life? However, once they'd heard the testimony she, Claudia, and Helen had prepared, it might persuade them to look at things in a different way.

It was the best she could hope for and in spite of how she was feeling right now, she remained determined to go through with it.

"Here he is," Jasmine murmured, and as Maria let out a wail all eyes went to Archie being escorted into the dock by two prison officers. He was wearing a navy suit that Dan had helped Maria to choose for him, a cream-colored shirt and a tie that didn't look comfortable around his muscular neck. He kept his eyes down, and didn't even look up when one of the officers spoke to him.

This was Marcus's doing, Claudia kept thinking. His compulsion to control and punish her, and remind her that even where he was he could still reach her, had brought this tragedy into their lives.

But Archie should have, could have walked away, and that was the case the prosecution was going to make, a case against which there was really no good argument to offer.

As soon as Mrs. Justice Kerr was seated, proceedings got underway with the reading of the indictment. As they'd known he would, Archie responded guilty to the first charge—aggravated arson with the intention to destroy property; and not guilty to the second— aggravated arson being reckless as to whether life would be endangered.

The Crown's opening statement followed, a bitter excoriation of Archie's background and character along with countless instances of his—no other way to describe it—reckless disregard for human life that culminated in what had happened to Ms. Marcy Kavanagh. It was such a merciless taking apart of a young man and his failure as a decent and worthy member of society that Jasmine had to take Maria outside before someone forced her to go for sobbing so noisily.

"I di' my best," Maria choked, as she went. "I swea' di' my best."

Marcy only wished she could have left with them, for next came the wholly unedifying experience of hearing herself and her family being spoken about by the prosecution with such crowing pity, indignant righteousness, and outrage that she kept wishing it would stop. There was no doubt, however, that it was resonating well with the jury.

At last prosecuting counsel finished his opening and Gordon Lock rose to his feet. In spite of how fierce he looked and the arresting power of his voice, his calm presentation of a young lad reformed and ready to accept responsibility for his actions, as well as the steps he'd taken to show his remorse to his victim, was persuasive, Marcy thought. Whether the jury shared her view was impossible to tell.

At twelve thirty they broke for lunch, and reconvened at two, when witnesses for the prosecution began to take the stand: police and fire officers, Rohan Laghari the burns consultant, all, in their own ways, adding to the condemnation of Archie and his actions.

Finally, it was over for the day, and after Marcy, Claudia, and Jasmine parted company with everyone in the lobby, leaving Dan to make sure Maria got the right bus home, Henry drove them back to the coach house.

As soon as they arrived Marcy left the others to discuss the day's events and took herself to her room. She needed a few minutes alone to assimilate and hopefully conquer the building dread of taking the stand the following day.

In her previous life, before the fire, she wouldn't have thought twice about getting up to address a room full of strangers. She'd had confidence then, and courage, and always a belief in what she was saying. She hadn't questioned herself, and she certainly hadn't thought about her looks, other than to make herself presentable before the event began.

She wasn't that person anymore, physically or mentally, and yet until today she'd thought she was making good progress in overcoming her insecurities. She'd truly believed she was calmer, or at least less horrified by her own looks; she'd even been able to mix with friends in public places. And wasn't entering into the RJ process with Archie proof that she still held the same values she always had? She'd always believed in redemption—easy when she hadn't had to put it into practice—and even after everything that had happened, perhaps especially after what had happened, she still had faith in a person's ability to change for the good. She had no doubt of it in Archie's case; he was genuinely sorry for what he'd done, to the point that he was ready to go to prison for destroying her property.

He was doing the right thing in admitting to the first count of arson, but he really didn't deserve to be found guilty on the second count. It would be so easy for the jury to believe he'd been reckless, but she was fully convinced that there had been no intention to cause her harm. She just didn't know if she had it in her to stand up in court to say so.

Going through to the bathroom, she stopped just inside the door and bowed her head. The mirror was still her enemy, brutal and unforgiving, the harshest of truth tellers, the place where there was nowhere to hide. It would be like that for the rest of her life; and it would be the same in court tomorrow. All eyes would be on her, scrutinizing her scars, flinching, pitying, inwardly recoiling, and probably thanking God that they didn't have to look at her for long.

Why would she put herself through the distress of it when Claudia, or Gordon Lock, could speak for her?

Unable to face her reflection, she turned away and picked up a towel to dry her eyes. She hated self-pity and usually did everything she could to avoid it, but now that it was here she couldn't make it go away. Trying to carry on as if nothing had changed wasn't helping her tonight. Nothing was and nothing could, because her conscience, her confidence, and her heart were in such terrible conflict that it was impossible to find a way forward.

"Mum," Claudia said softly.

Marcy didn't look up, but when Claudia's arms went around her she simply sobbed into her shoulder.

"It's all right," Claudia whispered, stroking her hair. "You don't have to do it. Everyone will understand."

# CHAPTER FORTY-NINE

I didn't see you in court today, but Helen told me you were there. She also said that you've been worried because you haven't heard from me since the indictment changed, so I'm writing this now for her to give you tomorrow before court starts.

I promise, I didn't mean to cause you any stress by not being in touch, I just didn't want to put any pressure on you about the trial. I thought if I gave you some space you might be able to work out whether you really want to get up and say something. I get that it won't be easy for you and there's no reason why you should do it because you definitely don't owe me anything. Not even close.

Please keep that in mind.

What did you think of the way it went today? Not great, was it? I was warned the Crown's opening would take me apart, and it sure did that. Proper little psycho me, in case anyone didn't know. You can probably imagine what the jury's thinking already, keep him locked up and throw away the key. I know I'd be thinking that if I was them.

I thought my Queen's Counsel when he got up sounded like he was talking about a totally different person to the nutter me, didn't you? Someone who's always taken care of his mother, who was forced into criminal ways by a family member . . . Well, I suppose that was me, but all that stuff about readiness to accept responsibility for my actions, the understanding of the damage I've caused, the remorse I've shown . . . I thought a halo was going to appear over my head by the end of it. God knows what the jury thought, but I don't expect they were impressed even though I guess it was basically true.

And what about the judge? She reminds me a bit of a woman I used to deliver to, though obvs it's not her. The user-cruiser I'm thinking of was one of the PCs who worked in the City. Wonder what she's doing now, if she's still coked off her head and trying to seduce the errand boys.

Anyways, like we were told, the prosecution's not bothering with many witnesses, just the police and fire officers who we saw today to confirm right away it was arson. I wondered why they bothered when I've already admitted it was and that I did it. I kept trying to imagine how you must be feeling when the surgeon got up to talk about your burns and how bad they were. It must have been hard, especially when he admitted that if the emergency services hadn't got there when they did you might not have made it.

I was gutted myself and wanted to put my hands over my ears, but you can imagine how that would have gone down with the jury.

It doesn't take much of a brain to work out that getting a conviction is going to be a walk in the park for the other side. My brief says everything'll change when you start speaking up for me, but I've been thinking about that a lot, and it sounds like too much pressure to me. I don't think you should have to go through it. You've already been through enough. Putting yourself up there for people to stare at and get so fixated on your burns that they might not take in what you're saying is not what you need. So that's why I'm asking you not to do it. Mr. Lock can tell them everything, and that way you can avoid getting up there in public to try and save the worthless kid who caused you all the harm, who doesn't deserve it anyway.

You've done so much for me already, and now it's time for me to cut you loose from feeling you have to do any more. It's right that I should get sent down for being reckless about endangering life. It's a no-brainer, everyone heard it today, and we both know it's true.

Before I end this letter, I want to say thanks for letting my ma sit with you today (Dan told me it was going to happen so I'm presuming it did). I heard her a couple of times and was sure she'd get thrown out, but I don't think she did. I'm going to talk to Dan and Helen about her being somewhere else when I get sentenced to the full stretch because I think that might be too hard for her to take.

Anyways, thanks for believing in me. I don't deserve it, but thanks anyway.

Be seeing you,
Archie

# CHAPTER FIFTY

Andee was waiting to greet them in the lobby the following morning. "Dan's talking to Gordon Lock," she told Claudia as they embraced, "and Helen's just gone to check if Archie's arrived. Are you OK?" she asked, peering worriedly at Marcy.

As Claudia started to answer Marcy said, "Why don't we get a coffee?"

"Miss Kav'na!" a voice called from the screening station.

They turned to see Maria clearing security with another woman following close behind. The stranger was plump with a nest of mussed blond hair, dark at the roots, and a proprietorial air toward Maria that seemed almost aggressive.

"This ma nay-buh, Raquel," Maria told them.

"Everyone calls me Raq," the woman added, reaching out to shake Marcy's hand.

"Good morning," Marcy responded, aware of Raq staring openly at her damaged face, almost as if inspecting it.

"Blimey, made a right mess of it, didn't he?" Raq declared with a sniff. "Still, from what I hear he's going down anyway. I told Maria he had to—"

"He not tryin' to get off," Maria broke in indignantly. "He said he did it and I tol' you not to come if you was goin' to say fings like tha'."

Suspecting this neighbor had bullied Maria into letting her come so she could gather gossip and share it around the estate later, Marcy glanced at Andee, certain she'd have a way of dealing with this.

Apparently Andee did. Stepping forward she took Raq's arm and began walking her to the door, saying, "It was lovely of you to make sure Maria got here safely, we all need good friends in difficult times, but we can take over now."

As Raq tried to protest Maria muttered, "Nosy cow. Din know how to get rid of her."

Claudia said, "We're just about to get a coffee if you'd like to come."

Holding back, Maria said, "Has anywuh see Ochie this mornin'?"

"Helen's down there," Marcy assured her, and spotting Henry coming through security, she added, "You go ahead to the café, I'll join you in a minute."

As Henry reached her he gave her an encouraging hug and held her by the shoulders as he searched her eyes with his. "Have you told anyone yet?" he asked.

"There hasn't been an opportunity, but Andee's just there, seeing that woman off . . ."

"And here's Helen," he added, spotting the lawyer on her way toward them.

After greeting Henry, Helen turned to Marcy. "Archie's very keen that I give you this before we go into court."

As Marcy took the letter her insides swirled into a chaos of nerves and concern, and a wrenching disappointment in herself for not having enough mettle to follow her conscience. She almost didn't want to read the letter, but how could she not?

By the time she'd finished Andee had returned to the group, and Henry was taking out a handkerchief for Marcy to dry her eyes.

"Is everything all right?" Andee asked apprehensively.

"A letter from Archie," Helen explained.

Marcy passed it to Andee and as Andee read it she explained what it said to Henry. "He thinks I shouldn't address the jury," she told him. "He says he understands how hard it'll be for me, so, to use his words, he wants to cut me loose from feeling that I have to do any more."

Henry searched her eyes carefully, apparently sensing what was going through her mind.

"It sounds as though he's giving up," she murmured, and knowing she couldn't allow that to happen, that she'd forever feel ashamed of her cowardice if she didn't speak up for him, she added, "I think we'll forget about everything we discussed last night."

Henry's expression showed his understanding, although he still looked worried.

"I'll be fine," she assured him, telling herself she would. "If you could go and explain things to Claudia and Jasmine, being careful of what you say in front of Maria, I'll have a quick chat with Andee and Helen before we go in."

THE MORNING WAS taken up with character witnesses for Archie—an old sports teacher who described his young student's gift with a football, and how sorry he was that Archie hadn't attended school regularly. An ex-headmaster who spoke stiffly, although positively, about Archie's willingness to learn and ability to stay out of trouble while in school in spite of the company he kept. Then came the owner of a car-repair shop who Archie had occasionally worked for and who'd have been happy to take him on as an apprentice if Archie had wanted it. It was generally known by all three men that Archie's home life was chaotic, possibly even abusive, but none could claim that they'd stepped in to help in any way.

Then it was Dan's turn to take the stand and explain who he was and the kind of work he'd carried out with Archie since his arrest.

Marcy was sure she detected an air of incredulity about the jury as they listened, as though they'd never heard of restorative justice before and weren't too sure what to make of it.

It was after lunch that Gordon Lock stood up to inform the jury of how unusual it was for the defense counsel to call someone who would ordinarily have been a witness for the prosecution.

"There is no doubt," he expounded, fixing them with his hawk-like eyes, "that Ms. Kavanagh was grievously harmed in the fire, as you will see when she takes the stand. That tragic reality is not being contested here today. What we are going to examine is whether or not the defendant acted recklessly so as to endanger life."

He took a moment to glance down at his notes. "Normal procedure," he continued, "would be for me to question Ms. Kavanagh about the night of the fire and what she remembers about it. Instead she is going to tell you of the experience in her own words, and at the same time she will offer you an insight into how she views the events—and the defendant. I would ask you to keep in mind as she speaks how difficult it is for someone with injuries such as she has to allow themselves to be exposed to your scrutiny." He turned to the judge. "Thank you for your indulgence in this matter, your honor, and now I call Ms. Marcy Kavanagh to the stand."

As Marcy was escorted to the witness box and handed the Bible, she'd never felt so conspicuous or nervous in her life. There was a sickening dread inside her, a shake to her hands, and the stares from all quarters were overpowering. As she swore to tell the truth, the whole truth, and nothing but the truth, she was aware above all of Archie's eyes on her. No doubt he was wondering if she'd got his letter and if she had why she was doing this. She wanted to look at him, to try to communicate with him on some level, but by the time she raised her eyes his head was down.

*Don't give up*, she willed him. *Dan has already said his piece, and now I'm going to do what I can to try and win these people over.*

Feeling a dry, painful throbbing through the left side of her face as if it were coming alive to its limelight, she turned to the jury. Her notes were in her hand if she needed them, and she felt certain she would.

"Ladies and gentlemen," she began, surprising herself with how clear and even strong her voice sounded, not at all the way she was feeling, "thank you for listening to what I have to say today. As Mr. Lock has already told you, it's unusual for someone in my position to speak up for the person who's caused them harm, but this is what I am going to do.

"I will admit to you that for quite a long time after the fire, when I was hospitalized and suffering terrible pain, I wished nothing but ill to the person who'd started it. I'm sure I felt much the same as anyone would after almost losing their life as they knew it and their home, and whose family had been caused so much distress. When I was told he'd been arrested I wanted him to pay in the severest of ways for what he'd done. And yes, there was a part of me that wanted to set fire to him, so he would experience the agony and devastation of full-thickness burns for himself."

She cleared her throat and touched a hand lightly to her mouth. "You've already heard about the restorative justice process from Dan Collier, and it probably won't surprise you to hear that my family and I would have been utterly repelled by the suggestion of engaging with our attacker, had it been presented to us at any other time than it was. In fact, I believe we would have remained completely resistant to it had I not been given letters written to me by Archie Colbrook, explaining who he is and how he came to try to burn down our house."

She hadn't expected those words to cause a small murmur in the room, so she paused, trying to gauge what it meant, until Gordon Lock nodded for her to continue.

"As I read about Archie in his own words, I gained an insight into a world that I knew very little of, although we hear about it on the news, of course. It just doesn't usually have much to do with our own existence. His is the kind of world where poverty and corruption are realities, not just news stories, and where it's hard for children to flourish even with two parents. Archie has only a mother who loves him very much, as he does her.

"So, through these letters our attacker was coming into a different sort of focus. He was no longer an evil stranger who had appeared from nowhere to try and destroy us, he was a person, a boy really, who'd been exploited and forced into crime at a very young age. He might have had the courage to try and resist his handlers, as he calls them, and to get on with his schooling, but for the threats made to his vulnerable mother. She was even beaten in front of him if he didn't agree to do as they wanted."

She took a breath, and sipped from the glass of water in front of her. "I believe," she continued, "that were it not for the man who exerted the most malevolent power over him that Archie would have gained the education he needed, and wanted. You've heard about his potential and willingness to learn, so who knows what he could have achieved with the right opportunities. He might even have found a way to get himself and his mother out of the negative environment they were in.

"Unfortunately, it didn't happen. He remained trapped in the grip of a man from whom he had to defend himself and his mother in any way he could. It was to try and keep his mother from harm that he carried out the trafficking that was forced on him, whether it was drugs, weapons, or mobile phones. Then one day he was ordered to break into a house to steal an attaché case believed to be inside. That house was—is—mine and my daughter's. My granddaughter also lives with us. When he broke in Archie was unable to find the case and that was when he was instructed to burn the place down."

She needed to give herself a moment now, for she wasn't really connecting with the rest of the courtroom any longer, only with what she was saying, and possibly with Archie.

"Before I say any more about the arson," she continued, "I want to tell you about the way Archie's letters seemed to unlock something inside me. Until I read them my psychological recovery hadn't been going well. I was unable to relate fully to my family, or to anyone else. I had difficulty finding words, so for the most part I stopped trying. I understood that I was suffering the after-effects of trauma, but even so I remained shut down. I couldn't see the point of trying to release myself when I looked the way I did. I was no longer me on the outside, and every time I looked in the mirror I felt sure I could never be the same on the inside either.

"I can't really explain why having contact with the person who'd caused me so much harm became the catalyst for the next stage of my recovery, I can only tell you that it did. Perhaps it was because I realized that hating him and wishing him harm was never going to help me; it was simply going to continue to make me less of a person than I'd been before. I was moved enough by his letters to see him as a young man who wasn't only sorry for what he'd done, but who, like me, was a victim of those who'd ordered the fire, and who, again like me, was probably going to suffer the consequences of it for the rest of his life. He had a conscience and he had a mother, and that made him so much more than just an arsonist."

Sipping more water, she took another glance at her notes and raised her head. "I am fully persuaded," she said, "that when Archie Colbrook acted that night it was with no malice toward me and my family. In fact, I believe without reservation that when he claims that he watched the house beforehand to make sure we'd left, he is speaking the truth. We did leave, but because I was unwell we only got to the end of the drive before I decided to go back.

"It is perfectly possible that Archie didn't see me return. It was dark, and if he was at the back of the house it would have been impossible for him to know what was happening at the front. Also, when I went inside I didn't turn on any more lights. We'd left some on, so there was nothing to alert him to the fact that anything had changed.

"What I'm saying is that I don't believe he acted with a reckless disregard for human life. It's the person who wanted the attaché case who should be held to account for this crime, but we aren't able to do that here, today. Please don't think I'm saying that Archie shouldn't also be held to account, he is the one who set the fire and though I know he deeply regrets it, he understands very well that he has to bear responsibility for it. This is why he has pleaded guilty to the first count of arson. He is not trying to run away from what he's done, unlike those who are hiding behind him."

She took another glance at her notes and looked at the jury again. "I will end now by saying that I strongly believe in the power of forgiveness, and in meeting Archie and forgiving him I have learned how positive that has been for my mental health. I've also learned how important it is to hear the other side of a story: to find out who someone is and why they behaved the way they did. Now, when I think of Archie I think of a young lad who had a difficult start in life, but who would have achieved so much given the right opportunities—and perhaps he still could, given the right outcome from this trial. Finding him not guilty on the second count could give him a belief in the justice system, and also a belief in himself that will enable him to turn his life around.

"I'm told that copies of the letters he wrote to me will be made available for you to read when you leave the court to deliberate your verdict. As you get to know him in his own words, as I did, I hope you'll agree that his honesty speaks to his integrity, and that his remorse is as present in the very fact that these letters exist as it is in what he says. It took as much courage for him to engage in the restorative justice process as it did for me. I am glad I did, and I know that he is too. It has given me a lasting belief in the power of compassion and in redemption. Thank you for listening."

The room fell into silence, and she wondered if anyone could hear her heart pounding. For a bizarre moment it sounded as though someone started to applaud, but it suddenly stopped. She looked at the prosecutor, waiting for him to get to his feet to start taking apart everything she'd said. He probably wouldn't do it in a cruel or aggressive way, she'd been advised, as that wouldn't get the jury onside, but it was their job to secure a conviction for the endangerment of life, and the true letter of the law said that they should have one.

Finally, the bewigged and bespectacled middle-aged man rose from his chair and announced to the judge that he had no questions. Marcy blinked and looked at Gordon Lock, who gave a brief nod. A moment later she was being escorted from the witness box.

It was over. She'd said what she wanted to say, told Archie that he was worth fighting for, and now she was ready to go home.

# CHAPTER FIFTY-ONE

You blew me away today in court. I thought after Helen gave you my note that you'd feel glad to be off the hook, I know I would have if I was you. But even if you did feel that way you still got up there and did it. I just can't get my head round you speaking up for me like that, <u>me</u>, someone who's brought nothing but grief to your life.

I want to say thank you — I am saying thank you — but it doesn't seem big enough. Nowhere near. I've got to think of something else, something that tells you properly just how filled with respect and gratitude I am. And impressed by the courage it must have taken for you to get up there like that in front of everyone.

I think the jury was pretty blown away by all you said too. Definitely not what they were expecting. Makes me wonder what they're thinking about tonight, but I'm afraid of going too far with that. Obvs I'm still going down, we know that, but what you did today could make all the difference between a fifteen stretch and the five years Helen reckons is the best-case scenario for the other charge.

Mr. Lock says there could be a verdict as early as tomorrow. Honest to God I didn't expect to be this keyed up when it came time to finding out how much longer I have to be in here, but I'm going to get whacked if I don't stop pacing soon. I just hope they don't end up transferring me to a prison that'll be too hard for my ma to get to.

Anyways, whatever the outcome tomorrow I'll never forget what you did. Getting to know you has been the best thing that's ever happened to me. I'm just sorry it came about the way it did.

Thank you, Marcy (hope you don't mind me using your name, first time). ☺

Archie

# CHAPTER FIFTY-TWO

By the end of the following morning both sides had delivered their closing statements, with the Crown reminding the jury that the defendant had committed a very serious offense that they'd seen for themselves had had a devastating—and lifetime—effect on one of his victims. There could be no doubt of a reckless disregard for life: the emergency services, paramedics, and Ms. Kavanagh's surgeon had all agreed that it was a miracle she hadn't died that night. And in spite of Archie Colbrook's remorse and engagement with Ms. Kavanagh being admirable, wouldn't it be a very wrong and even dangerous message to send to anyone considering a similar offense if the proper verdict of guilty was not returned?

Gordon Lock's summation was shorter and focused almost entirely on Marcy's statement to the jury, using it to remind them that even she, the most gravely injured of the victims, believed that Archie would not have set fire to the house if he'd known she'd gone back inside. Therefore, it surely wasn't possible to find him guilty of having no regard for life if the victim herself didn't believe it to be the case. He went on to paraphrase Marcy's comments about the importance of forgiveness, and to emphasize that the kind of remorse demonstrated by the defendant had so impressed her that it must surely count for something with them.

Before sending the jury to begin their deliberations the judge reminded them that they did not have to reach a verdict on the first count, only the second, that of being reckless so as to endanger life.

She then took some time talking through several points of law before asking them to select a foreman to speak on their behalf.

Moments later she was gone and everyone was leaving the court.

"I can' ea'," Maria wailed as Andee suggested they get some lunch.

"I'm not sure any of us can," Claudia murmured, taking her mother's trembling hand.

"Is that it?" Marcy asked. "We don't come back again until the jury returns?"

"That's right," Andee confirmed, glancing up as Dan came to join them.

"'ave you see ma boy?" Maria asked him.

"No, I can't go down to the cells," he replied gently, "but Helen and Gordon will go to talk to him. Please try not to worry too much. I know it's hard, but . . ."

"'ee migh' get fifteen," she reminded him desperately. "Can we 'peal if he does?"

"Let's cross that bridge when—if—we get to it. I think for now we need to get some air."

THE JURY RETURNED just after three o'clock, having taken only an hour to come to a decision, which no one could decide was good or bad news.

Maria was seated between Claudia and Marcy in the front row of the public gallery and as Archie was asked to rise for the verdict they each took hold of one of her hands. Her tiny frame was shaking so hard that Claudia wanted to put her arms around her. In the row behind, Dan and Andee both placed hands on Maria's shoulders, while Jasmine buried her face in Marcy's arm.

The room was so tense as the foreman of the jury was asked if the decision was unanimous that his voice as he said "Yes" was almost startling.

"On the charge of aggravated arson and being reckless as to whether life would be endangered how do you find the defendant?"

Maria whined under her breath.

"Not guilty," the foreman announced, and Maria shot to her feet, punching the air. Before she could cry out Andee gently gagged her and the others tugged her back into her seat.

Whatever happened now Archie wasn't going to prison for life, but as the jury was thanked and dismissed, tension gripped them again. The judge was ready to pass sentence for the first count, arson with the intent to destroy property.

She spoke first about the consequences of committing crimes ordered by others. "It is you who are here in the dock today," she told Archie sternly, "not those who paid you to commit the offense, and it was always going to be you, because you did not have the good sense to report to the authorities what you were being required to do. I understand the threat to your mother and the need to protect her, but you did not give the police or anyone else the opportunity to assist her safety. As a result, Ms. Kavanagh's home was severely damaged by the fire you set. I don't mention Ms. Kavanagh's injuries here as they were the subject of the second count.

"There is no doubt in my mind, or in law, that there must be a custodial sentence for the crime you have committed. After studying my options and taking into consideration the restorative justice process that was undertaken—and the eight months you have already spent in custody—my judgment is that you shall receive a two-year prison term . . ."

"No!" Maria cried. "Don' sen' him away."

The judge eyed her meaningfully, but waved down an attempt to eject her. "A two-year prison term," she repeated, "to be suspended for two years and carry with it a community order . . ."

"What?" Maria said, turning to Dan in confusion. "I don' . . ."

"He's coming home," Dan whispered.

Maria stared at him, wide-eyed with shock, and was suddenly back on her feet. "Ochie!" she shouted at the top of her voice. "Ma boy is comin' 'ome."

"Mrs. Colbrook," the judge warned.

Marcy and Claudia pulled her back into her seat, and with tears in their eyes they hugged her hard enough to break her birdlike limbs.

"He comin' 'ome," Maria sobbed. "Ma boy is comin' 'ome."

"Not what we expected," Gordon Lock admitted when Marcy and the others found him and Helen in the lobby, "but of course we hoped for it. A wise decision on the part of the judge. It would appear that she believes, as you clearly do, that the lad has potential and it won't be realized in prison. Now, if you'll excuse me, I have a train to catch."

"Than' you," Maria called after him.

He turned, smiled, and waved, before disappearing through the revolving doors into a future that didn't include any of them.

"What do we do now?" Marcy asked.

"We go to get Archie," Helen declared, and holding out an arm for Maria to hook on to she led the way back into court.

Marcy said to Dan, "It feels wrong to walk away as if we're strangers now. What usually happens in these situations?"

"This isn't like any other," he told her wryly, "but we don't have to walk away, we can at least wait to wish him well."

"Should we celebrate?" she said, turning to her daughter, who was already looking hostile to the idea. "Do you think they'll want to come to ours?" She grimaced slightly at the bizarreness of inviting the arsonist back into their home.

"No," Claudia said shortly. "It's out of the question, Mum."

Marcy shrugged, not arguing.

"There you all are," Richie declared, coming to join them with his voice recorder in hand. "What a story, huh? Didn't see the suspended sentence coming, I guess none of us did. So now I'm going to need some quotes to get up on the website. Who's up for it?"

Henry quickly said, "Speaking on behalf of the family, the judge is to be commended for her understanding of how important it is to give second chances to those who deserve them."

Apparently satisfied with that, Richie turned to Dan. "A great triumph for restorative justice today?"

Dan's expression was sardonic as he said, "I'm happy to give you an in-depth at some point to make sure we've got everything straight, but for now: I'm extremely pleased by this outcome."

"And what next for Archie, do you think?" Richie prompted.

"Why don't you ask him?" Marcy replied, and Richie turned to find Archie himself, with his mother clinging to one arm and Helen on the other side of him, coming toward them.

He seemed taller, Marcy thought, and perhaps less gaunt, smarter too thanks to his suit, although his eyes remained wary and hesitant, as though he wasn't quite able to believe this was happening.

Going to him, Dan wrapped him in an embrace. "Well done," he said warmly. "We're all pleased with the verdict." Standing back to look at him, he added, "I trust you are too?"

Archie broke into an unsteady laugh and Marcy realized this was the first time she'd seen him smile. He was a very handsome young lad.

His eyes finally came to hers, and not hesitating for a moment she walked toward him, arms open to embrace him.

"I have to be honest," she said, through the lump in her throat, "never in my life would I have imagined a day like this, much less actually feeling happy about it."

"Yeah, it's definitely a strange one," he agreed, sounding emotional and self-conscious. "Like I said in my note, I owe you big-time . . ."

She waved it away as Jasmine and Claudia came to shake his hand.

"I ought to be hating your guts," Jasmine informed him frankly, "we all should, and yet here we are feeling glad about your freedom."

He looked unsure of himself, and suddenly seemed so out of his depth that Dan put a steadying hand on his shoulder.

"You probably want to get home with your mum," he said, clearly reading the situation correctly given the relief that came into Archie's eyes. "There's a lot for you to take in, and there'll be plenty of time for us two to talk in the coming days. I'll call you in the morning, OK? I guess you don't have a mobile, so . . ."

"You can call me," Maria told him. "You 'ave my numbuh."

"Of course. Are you OK to get home? Do you need a lift?"

"'Ave mah cah," Maria told him proudly.

Surprising them all, Archie muttered under his breath, "So a death sentence then," and everyone, including his mother, had to laugh.

As they watched them walk away, Dan took Claudia's hand and said quietly to Andee, "We need to get them out of that estate or the next thing we know he'll be back dealing drugs and carrying knives."

"You're right," Andee agreed. "I'll make some calls," and wasting no time she began scrolling through her contacts.

Claudia said, "I've just had a text from Leanne. She and Tom have invited us to their place for a drink and food if we're up for it."

Marcy turned to Henry. "Are you?" she asked.

"If you are."

"Then count us in," Marcy said. She'd have time enough later to get over the loss she was already starting to feel of no more letters from Archie, in fact no more Archie at all. How very strange life was.

# CHAPTER FIFTY-THREE

*One Month Later*

I hear you've been inundated with requests for restorative justice since Archie's trial?" Richie prompted, looking and sounding very much, Claudia reflected not for the first time, as though he interviewed for a major TV company every day of the week.

Behind his glasses Dan's eyes shone in the amused, self-deprecating way that she loved. "It's true," he confirmed, "but there are a couple of points I need to make about that. First, there are RJ programs operating all over the country—our service only covers the Dean Valley region. So, if you want to know more about it, you need to get in touch with your local service. The second point is that some seem to be seeing it as an alternative to the justice system, and this is a big mistake."

Richie said, "And one that's being made as a result of Archie's verdict?"

"I'm afraid so." As the camera went in for a close-up on Archie, who looked as though he belonged in a boy band, Dan said, "I need to stress that Archie's and Marcy's case wasn't typical of how the process works—and no RJ case is an alternative to the judicial system. It's basically a mediation service that comes about usually at the request of the police or probation service, and each case goes through a rigorous assessment of its potential benefit to each participant before anyone is contacted."

"Meaning that not every case qualifies and will only do so if it's believed that the offender is genuinely remorseful?" Richie clarified.

"Exactly," Dan confirmed. "And, of course, we need to know that the victim is willing, although that comes later."

"Do any of the offenders ever try to fake it?"

"Yes, they do, and unfortunately it's been happening a lot since Archie's trial, but it doesn't take an experienced practitioner long to weed out those who are playing a fast one from those who are genuine."

"So what was it about Archie that convinced you both he and Marcy would benefit from restorative justice? Let's start with who referred his case to you."

With a glance at Archie, Dan said, "As I mentioned just now, this isn't a typical case. Marcy Kavanagh is a friend of mine and of another practitioner who works with me. When we saw how she was reacting to the effects of her injuries we decided that I should approach Archie to explore whether a restorative process might help her."

Turning to Archie, Richie said, "So what did you think when Dan first came to you with his proposal?"

Archie grimaced in a way that made Claudia reflect again on how much his confidence had grown since he'd been released from prison. A great deal had happened for him in the last month, and in spite of how he'd come into their lives, none of them, including her, could feel anything but pleased to see him turning his life around. "I kind of thought he was weird," Archie admitted, "you know, a bit Clark Kentish." Dan and Richie laughed, and Claudia smiled as the camera went in for a close-up of Dan and his superspecs. "I'd never heard of RJ before that," Archie went on, "so I didn't really get what he was going on about, but then he had this idea of me writing letters to Marcy telling her about myself and how I came to the point in my life where I committed the crime that badly injured her."

"And I'm correct in thinking that Marcy knew nothing about these letters for quite some time?"

"No, she didn't. Dan wanted to find out first what I had to say and if any of it might be beneficial to her."

To Dan Richie said, "And what did you think?"

Wryly, Dan replied, "Let's say there was a certain amount of editing necessary for the first few letters. Archie's language at that time was a little more colorful than Marcy would've been used to, or even able to understand."

With lively eyes, Archie said, "He didn't change the basics of what I was saying, or anything like that, he just got me to clean it up and make it more mainstream."

"So, in the course of Archie producing these letters," Richie said to Dan, "you decided that his remorse was convincing enough for you to take them to Marcy."

"Eventually, yes. Although Archie wasn't pouring out regrets and apologies in his letters, the essence of it was powerfully there, mostly in the way he was engaging with Marcy in spite of never having met her. He created a relationship, and an attachment, that meant a great deal to him long before he realized it himself."

"And what did she think when she read them?"

"I think initially she was quite resistant—not so much to reading them, but to engaging with them on any kind of emotional level, particularly one that involved forgiveness. In our conversations since, she's admitted that she wasn't anywhere near ready to forgive at that point, but after reading the letters she decided that there might be something to be gained, for them both, if they met."

"Was that a big deal for you, Archie? Meeting the woman you'd caused such serious injury to, and who you'd been writing to all this time?"

"It was major," he replied, "and I don't mind admitting how scared I was before it happened. Part of me wanted to pull out, I didn't want to see what I'd done to her, but then I told myself that if she was willing to face me, I had to do the same for her. I swear it wasn't about me trying to get off my sentence, like some of the papers have said, it was all about trying to do what she wanted me to do." He swallowed awkwardly. "I knew if Dan came back and said she wasn't interested in having anything to do with me I'd be totally gutted. I wouldn't have blamed her, obvs, but I knew it would floor me like nothing else if she'd told Dan to forget all about it."

"But she didn't, and you met and now we've got to where we are, with you having served eight months on remand before being found not guilty of recklessly endangering life. There's been a lot of criticism of that verdict, as I'm sure you know."

Taking over him, Dan said, "As with a lot of criticism of juries it's coming from quarters, mostly newspapers, who were not in court and so didn't have all the facts in front of them. The jury did."

"So, you object to headlines such as 'All You Have to Say Is Sorry' and 'Forgive Me But What Is Our Justice System Coming To'?"

"Actually, in a way I don't object to them, because it gets the conversation going about restorative justice. What I do have a problem with is their failure to point out how beneficial it can be for the victims of crime, even crimes of this severity. It isn't our aim to help anyone avoid whatever punishment a court decides they deserve—in most cases we don't get to see the offender until the trial has already happened, sentence served, and he or she is about to be released back into the community. In Marcy's and Archie's case we came in much earlier."

"And we could ask," Richie continued, "what's wrong with leniency when it's deserved? I think you'll agree, the judge was lenient?"

"Not everything has to follow the absolute letter of the law," Dan responded, "and sometimes justice and humanity are better served when it doesn't."

Nodding agreement with that, Richie said, "I know Marcy is reluctant to do interviews, but can you tell us how she is, and if she's still OK with the verdict—and suspended sentence?"

With a smile, Dan said, "She's doing very well, thank you, and she certainly hasn't changed her views on the way things ended in court."

"Do you ever see her now, Archie?"

"Sometimes," he replied.

"But no more letters?"

Wryly he said, "Not so far, anyway."

Richie laughed, turned a page in his notes, and moved them on. "So tell us what's happening in your life now. I hear that since your release you've received almost as much fan mail as Dan has RJ applications?"

While Dan appeared amused by this, Archie was noticeably less so. "That's just stuff," he responded, shrugging it off irritably. "It doesn't mean anything." Claudia was aware that he genuinely disliked the letters he received from girls—and women—offering to rehabilitate him, or give him opportunities like he'd never had before, or even to marry him, if he was interested. It took all sorts, and they were beginning to find out that there were many more sorts out there than they'd realized.

"OK. So, what are you actually doing with yourself?" Richie asked chattily, as if he didn't know.

With a quick glance at Dan, Archie said, "Apart from my community service, you know, cleaning parks, delivering meals to the elderly, that sort of thing, I'm about to start an apprenticeship with a landscaping company. If all goes to plan they could offer me a job and even sponsor me through agricultural college starting next year."

"Wow! That's a pretty amazing turnaround for someone who felt he didn't have much of a future only a few weeks ago."

"We're extremely grateful," Dan came in, sparing Archie's need to answer, "for the way some members of the local community have reached out to help him."

Feeling Dan's arms circle her waist, Claudia leaned back into him and smiled as he pressed a kiss to her neck.

"You're not watching that again," he groaned, "I thought you'd have had more than enough of it by now."

"Apparently not," she responded, although she did switch the recording off before turning into his embrace.

He kissed her fully and tenderly, bringing her more closely to him as he murmured, "Where is everyone?"

"Jasmine's at school, Mum and Henry are outside making plans to turn the old coach wash—aka the enormous sunken area between here and the Enclave—into a pond that's already sounding like a mini lake. And Archie's with them."

Dan's eyebrows rose as he regarded her carefully.

Claudia shrugged, clearly not altogether thrilled. "Mum thought it would be a good idea to consult him, given his budding interest in landscape gardening."

Dan nodded as he thought. "So, this is now the second time she's invited him here?"

"And I'm pretty sure it won't be the last."

"But you wish it would be?"

Sighing, she said, "I don't know what I wish, but don't you think it's odd that she wants to keep seeing him? I mean, he would be a perfectly nice lad, if you could put aside what he did. But how can we put it aside? You've only got to look at her to be reminded of it."

Dan said, "I admit it's unusual for a relationship to develop between a victim and offender after the RJ process is over, but it's not unheard of—and if it's what she wants . . ."

"I think we can assume that it is. She even told me she thinks she's looking better these days, and she's putting it down to how good it's making her feel to help him turn his life around. Honestly, it's like she's . . . I don't know, like she's *drunk* on forgiveness, or something, and can't stop herself proving how much she means it, or how good she is at it."

Brow furrowing, he said, "Whereas you are still having a problem with it?"

Her eyes flicked briefly to his. "Yes, but I have to admit that she *is* looking better lately. The scars are the same, obviously, but there's a brighter light in her eyes and a much healthier sort of aura about her. If I didn't know better I'd say she's undergoing some sort of religious experience."

He was suppressing a smile now. "From what I hear forgiveness can be quite . . . uplifting, but I don't think it's about that as much as what she says it is—she's getting a lot of pleasure out of helping someone who had a difficult start in life to find a new way in the world. Or, perhaps she just sees it as a way of turning a bad—a terrible situation—into something positive and good. Righting the wrongs of the fate that brought them together. Turning it on its head."

Claudia said, "I had a feeling you'd see it from her point of view."

"So tell me yours."

She shook her head. "I'm not sure what it is, only that I find it *odd* the way she's kind of bonding with him. Surreal, even."

"Have you told her this?"

"No. I don't want to upset her, especially when it really does seem to make her happy to see him."

"So you wouldn't want her to stop seeing him?"

"I want her to do, or to have, whatever works for her. I'm just finding it hard to get my head around the fact that . . . Well, that we're even having this conversation about my mother and a boy of nineteen who almost killed her."

"But it's not disturbing her, and that's probably because she knows where the real responsibility lies, as do you. There's no point going there though, at least not for the purposes of this conversation. Just tell me what Jasmine thinks of the . . . friendship."

With a helpless sort of grimace Claudia said, "At first, she wasn't any happier about it than I am, but she's her grandmother's granddaughter in so many ways, and now this turns out to be another of them. Or, to quote you, she knows where the real responsibility lies so what's to be gained from holding on to a grudge against Archie? If only life were so simple—I know, you're going to tell me it can be if I let it." She paused with a sigh, not sure what she wanted to say next, only knowing that Marcus was hovering like an evil specter at the edges of her mind, trying to force himself center stage, and she desperately wanted rid of him. In the end the words seemed to come of their own accord. "Jasmine recently found out that Archie has an 'amazing talent' for remembering lyrics and he's a 'totally awesome singer.' So, I think we can say that my daughter, along with her grandmother, has discovered a more highly developed sense of forgiveness than her mother is managing." She broke off at the sound of someone arriving outside and knew instantly who it was because no one else ever hooted their car horn like that.

"Now here's someone," she said dryly, "who I'm definitely growing more fond of."

Claudia went to the front door and opened it in time to see Maria tumbling out of the dilapidated VW campervan that someone on the estate had abandoned outside her house before she and Archie had moved out. Being Maria, she'd instantly claimed it, having already handed the old Astra over to Archie, and the local car mechanic had made it as roadworthy as he could, free of charge in return for the good publicity he'd got out of the trial. Since then, Maria and Claudia had attempted to turn the rust patches into arty daisies or smiley faces, while Archie had attached an old-fashioned air horn to the steering wheel. Maria loved it and never failed to use it to announce her arrival at someone's house, a road junction, or just because it delighted her so much to hoot it.

"'Ave come to clea'," she called out to Claudia, hauling her bag across the driver's seat and letting it drop to the ground while she shouldered the van door closed. "An' I braw sand'ches from garage in case ah I get 'ungry. You can 'ave one if you like. Is that Dan's car?"

"Yes, he's here. So is Archie."

"Saw the Astra. Scuze ma 'air," she grimaced, patting her head as she came into the house, "got pain' in it."

Seeing the yellow and lime green streaks threading through her small riot of curls, Claudia realized she must have been decorating the new (at least to them) second-floor flat that she and Archie had recently moved into on a smaller, less crime-infested estate behind Paradise Cove. Apparently, it had two bedrooms, a galley kitchen, and a large sitting room with a balcony that overlooked a municipal playing field. Since this was one of the public spaces Archie was taking care of as part of his community service, he'd gotten to know several people who used it, and had even joined a five-a-side football team.

"'ELLO!" Maria called out to Dan as she headed off in the other direction to fetch her cleaning kit. "Shall I star' in your craff room, Clau'ia?"

"That would be lovely, thank you," Claudia replied, and leaving her to it she went to join Dan at the Aga, where he was studying a recipe she'd downloaded onto her iPad.

"So today is a practice run?" he asked, needing to be clear.

Readily accepting the change of subject now that Maria was nearby, and actually glad to do so anyway, Claudia said, "It's to make sure we can do it, because apparently beef Wellington can be quite difficult."

"So *why* are we doing it? Oh, that's right, it's Richie's favorite. And we're sure he wants to celebrate his birthday with us?"

"Not just us, everyone's coming, and remember we decided to have this party before we knew it was his birthday. So this is to make sure it's acknowledged."

"There's a problem with cake?"

"Too predictable, apparently. Anyway, here's another lovely

surprise for you, Jasmine and Abby have hired a music system for the night."

His eyes narrowed curiously. "And that's a lovely surprise, because?"

"I don't know, I'm quoting them, but I'm told we'll know more soon. Oh, and they want the whole thing to be outside if possible, so they're borrowing heaters from Leanne and Tom. My job, apparently, is to decorate the house for Christmas . . ."

"Ah, so it's also a Christmas party?"

"Let's just call it a party. And we want to have one. Don't we?"

"We do, so let's get started on this Wellington that I'm guessing will be dinner tonight no matter how it turns out."

Assuring him he was right, she began opening cupboard doors and passing him the ingredients they were going to need.

It wasn't long before they were so engrossed in their task, along with listening to a play on Radio 4, that they didn't hear another car pulling up outside. They weren't even aware of Maria going to open the front door to let the visitor in. The first they knew of his arrival was when he said, "Well, this is cozy."

Recognizing the voice instantly, Claudia swung around, her heart already pounding as the blood drained from her flushed cheeks. "Marcus," she said faintly.

She'd known he was out of prison, and had struggled with the terror of him turning up here—and now here he was, all five foot eleven of him, with his boyish blond hair, large handsome face, and expensive clothes.

"Yes, it's me," he said, his smile managing to exude both disdain and charm in the way she remembered so well. "I can't believe you're surprised to see me. You surely must have known I'd come."

"Wh-what do you want?" she demanded, almost faint with remembered fear, with terror of what he might do now.

As Dan turned off the radio, Marcus regarded him with a baffled sort of condescension. "And who's this?" he asked, as if Dan were unable to speak for himself. Then, "Oh, yes, the restorative justice chap we've been seeing on the news." His smile crooked knowingly. "And here you are, cooking up something with my wife. We haven't heard about that in the press."

"What do you want?" Dan asked calmly.

Appearing astonished at the repeated question, then pleased, Marcus said, "Why don't we sit down?" And without waiting for an answer he unbuttoned his coat and pulled out one of the dining chairs to make himself comfortable. "Nice place," he commented, looking around. "I heard about the fire. Shame that. No sign of it now though."

Swallowing dryly as all her worst nightmares crowded in on her, Claudia said, "Why are you here?"

He frowned as if considering his reply, and planting his elbows on the table, he said, "You might be thinking that I've come to collect what's mine." His eyebrows arched invitingly, as though expecting her to spell it out for him. When she didn't, he said, "It was a lot of money, Rebecca. Oh sorry, I'm forgetting, it's Claudia now, isn't it?"

"It's not even a fraction of what you took from me," she reminded him, making herself sound stronger than she felt.

Dan said quietly, "Don't engage with him, just let him state his case."

Marcus laughed. "Good advice, Mr. Mediator. I'm not sure what she's told you about me, but we were very much in love, you know, and I have to say nothing's changed for me . . ."

"Marcus, stop it," she muttered.

"Sorry," he lamented. "I guess there are things you'd rather he didn't know. It's OK, I understand that, but—"

"Just come to the point of why you're here," Dan interrupted.

Marcus nodded, and seeing the old arrogance and self-confidence as assured as it had ever been, Claudia felt herself shrinking inside. Clearly prison hadn't changed him, he still had that same sense of entitlement, as if he were some superior being whose right to exist excelled any other.

"OK, I'll come clean," he said cheerily. "I want you to stop all the nonsense you're peddling around about me being behind the arson attack on this place."

Claudia's eyes widened slightly, but he put up a hand to let her know he hadn't finished.

"I get that it's only rumor at the moment, no one's actually gone to print with my name—I'd sue if they did—but the nonsense on social media is bringing me the kind of attention I'd rather not have as I try to get my life back on track."

"But you were behind it," she stated coldly.

He shook his head. "I know you're telling yourself that, but that's just your paranoia at work, and we both know how damaging *that* can be, don't we? We have a lot of experience of it, and if you remember it's usually yourself you end up hurting. But now it's affecting me. So, as it's a complete fabrication . . ."

"It's true," she snapped.

". . . and because I can see you've made yourself a new life here, I am prepared to disappear for good, even divorce you if that's what you want, in exchange for a cessation—or denial—of these malicious claims that are extremely annoying and unjustly blackening my name."

Claudia almost laughed; as if he hadn't done that all on his own.

Dan said, "She doesn't need to give you anything in order to get a divorce."

"And we know you ordered the fire," Claudia added. She connected with Dan's presence at last, realizing that she didn't need to be so afraid. "For all I know, there were a dozen or more people in the chain before it got to the boy who carried it out, but there's no doubt in my mind that it originated with you."

He appeared to find this amusing. "You credit me with far more influence than I have," he informed her, "but even if you were right—and you're not—you must know by now that you're never going to make a connection between me and that . . . *boy*. So, let's put all this behind us, shall we? You give me your word that there'll be no more attempts to tie me to your misfortune, and I will divorce you. In fact, I'll go one better than that, I'll even find it in my heart to forgive you for abandoning me in my time of need and never coming to visit me in prison." He looked at Dan. "How does that sound, Mr. Mediator?"

Before Dan could answer, the French doors opened and a chattering Marcy came in, banging her gloved hands together to ward off the cold and stomping her feet. "I think we could plant it up . . ." She broke off, seeming to sense something was wrong and as she saw who was at the table she paled with horror.

Marcus wrinkled his nose, looking from Marcy to Maria, who was hovering nearby, and back again. "Is this some kind of convention?" he asked in cruel amazement.

"Who let him in?" Marcy spat as Claudia fought the urge to stab him.

Before anyone could answer, Henry came in behind Marcy, followed by Archie.

Clearly realizing there was a problem Henry looked from Marcus to Dan and back again. "Are you who I think you are?" he asked carefully.

Marcus didn't answer. He was looking past Henry, with an expression of disbelief on his face. "Well, well," he declared smoothly, "I didn't expect to find you here, Archie boy."

Almost as soon as the words were out of his mouth he realized his mistake, and picking up on it, Claudia said, "So you two have met before?"

Archie's scowl was thunderous. "Yeah, we've met," he confirmed, "he's one of the PCs I used to deliver to."

"Which does not," Marcus informed the room, "in any way connect me to what he did here."

Dan said, "Given that you've just demonstrated, in front of witnesses, that you know Archie, I think much of your bargaining power has just evaporated. So I'm going to ask you to leave."

Marcus, white-faced with fury at his own stupidity, was already on his feet.

"Don't come here again," Dan told him, directing him to the door, "and don't try to make any other kind of contact with Claudia, her mother, Jasmine, or Archie."

"The fact I might know that boy," Marcus growled, "means nothing. I've never spoken to him or approached him in any way about anything to do with this place. If he says I did, he's lying."

"Is he?" Dan said. "Maybe we should put that to the police?"

Marcus glared at Archie. "I'll give it six months and the scum will rise back to the surface."

"Get out," Marcy shouted furiously. "Get out now."

Marcus walked to the door, tore it open and stalked outside. He didn't bother closing it, nor did he see Maria come out behind him, he only felt the clunk on the back of his head as it was struck by the can of furniture polish she hurled at him.

"An' don' come back," she shouted after him, and slamming the door she muttered, "effin' co'venshun," and even Marcy had to laugh.

ONCE SURE HE'D gone, Dan turned from the window and looked at Claudia. "Are you OK?" he asked.

She nodded, although she could feel herself shaking again, and didn't object when Henry encouraged her to sit down. "I can't believe he had the nerve to come here . . . What am I saying, of course he did, it's completely typical of him to think he can go anywhere at any time and intimidate people into doing exactly as he wants."

"Well, it didn't happen this time," Dan pointed out, "and it never will. Not here."

"What are you doing?" Claudia asked as he took out his phone.

Marcy said, "I hope he's about to inform DCI Gould of what's just happened?"

Dan nodded. "Most particularly about the admission, in front of witnesses, two of whom happen to be lawyers, to knowing Archie. I can just imagine how he's feeling about that now. It still doesn't tie him to the arson, but we'll let the police worry about that. All we need to concern ourselves with is making sure that an investigation gets underway—and that he doesn't come here again. Unless," he said before pressing dial, "we want to let him sweat it out, not knowing what we'll do, or when, which could end up saving you, Marcy, actually all of you, any more time in court."

Marcy didn't hesitate. "Let him suffer," she declared, "but if he does come near us, even with an email, you need to make that call and then let him know that you've made it."

Dan looked at Claudia. "Are you OK with that?" he asked.

"I think so," she replied. "Actually, yes I am." She looked at Archie, and felt a wavering sort of beat in her heart.

As he met her eyes he said, "I'm cool to play it however you want," and she realized from those few words that he knew exactly how she felt, understood her misgivings and was willing to do whatever it might take to win her trust.

# CHAPTER FIFTY-FOUR

I have a proposal to put to you," Marcy said, coming into Claudia's craft room and perching on one of the high stools next to the table.

Intrigued, Claudia abandoned the sketch she was halfway through and went to turn off her audiobook.

"First of all," Marcy said, "have you heard anything back from Marcus's lawyer since you filed for divorce?"

"No, I'd have told you if I had, but I'm not worried, honestly. It's still early days and it'll happen."

"Of course it will, I'm just asking. Anyway, it doesn't really affect what I'm about to suggest, and it's just some thoughts I've been having. I haven't even mentioned anything to Henry yet, and a lot of it will depend on him."

Trying to imagine what was coming, Claudia settled herself on another stool and waited for her mother to continue.

"What I've been thinking," Marcy said, rubbing her scarred hand as she often did unconsciously, "is that a time might be coming when I will want to move in with Henry, and if I did I wondered if you'd like Dan to buy out my share of this place?"

Claudia's eyes widened with surprise. She hadn't seen that coming, although perhaps she should have, certainly where her mother and Henry were concerned.

"Is it a good idea?" Marcy prompted.

Claudia said, cautiously, "I guess so, provided he wants to, but I don't think I can ask him."

"It's OK, I'm just putting it to you as a possible that we both might like to consider."

Unable to deny that it was something she was glad to think about, Claudia said, "Do you have any kind of time frame in mind?"

"No, not really, but with Jasmine off to uni next September I thought now would be a good time to start planning ahead."

That was just over nine months away, and Claudia was getting the impression that her mother would like these changes to happen sooner. "So, will you ask Henry?" she asked. "Or will you wait for him to ask you?"

"I'm not sure. What do you think I should do?"

Claudia pondered it.

"Actually, I think we ought to talk to Dan first, because if he doesn't want to buy into this place with you I won't want to leave you here on your own," Marcy declared.

"That's just silly," Claudia scolded, smarting at the fear of Dan turning her down. "If it comes to it and you're ready to move in with Henry, I'll use the money I took from Marcus—*my* money—to buy you out."

"But it would be better if Dan was here. Maybe you could talk it over with him, tell him I'll give him an excellent price . . ."

"Mum, I can't just . . ."

"Listen, I've seen you two together, so if you want my opinion he's not suggesting this himself because he wouldn't want me to think he's trying to crowd the nest, or push me out."

Accepting there was a chance that might be true, Claudia said, "OK, for the record, between us, I think it's a great idea, especially as you'll only be one thousand seven hundred and eight steps away if you do go."

Coming to hug her, Marcy said, "Talk to him and let me know what he says."

DAN BLINKED, ALMOST as though he might not have heard correctly. "Would you like to run that past me again?" he prompted.

Trying not to be annoyed that she was having to ask twice when once had already been awkward enough, Claudia was about to begin again when she caught the tease in his eyes and slanted him a menacing look.

"Come here," he said softly.

Going to him, she raised her face to his as he circled her in his arms. "Even if your mother asked for double the going rate," he said against her lips, "I'd want to do it."

Melting against him she gave herself to the deepening tenderness of his kiss, until it became the sort of kiss that wasn't going to allow them to stop there.

Because no one else was at home, they didn't.

An hour or so later, as they lay together on the bed that was now destined to become theirs, she said, "You know, I was thinking, if you do move in . . ."

"When," he corrected.

"When"—she smiled—"We could reconfigure things so that Mum's sitting room becomes your study, and maybe we could add a sunroom to the kitchen and build the deck out from there. That way we'd have a place for you to read and me to embroider while we listen to music, or just watch nature . . . Did I ever mention that I wouldn't mind building a small studio out there for a kiln?"

Rolling over to face her, he turned her to him and said, "Yes to everything, and now how about this? We could make one of the rooms into a nursery and see what we can do about filling it?"

"HERE WE ARE, two gin and tonics," Marcy declared, sitting down beside Henry on the comfy conservatory seat that overlooked his garden, the rooftops that staggered down to the sea, and the golden sunset a long way out on the horizon. "I've made yours extra strong because you might need it when I tell you what I have in mind."

Blithely he said, "Whatever it is, if it involves you I'm up for it. Oh, unless it's having to sing at this blasted karaoke night. I thought that went out in the eighties—and it was cheesy then."

Leaning over to plant a kiss on his cheek, she replied, "It's only you who's calling it karaoke, the rest of us are referring to it as a music event. Anyway, what's wrong with cheesy?"

He eyed her skeptically.

With a laugh, she said, "Jasmine has probably got something new she wants to play for us, and by the sound of it there'll be an entire orchestral backing. Should be wonderful."

"I won't disagree with that."

She sat quietly, thoughtfully, for a moment. "If we are expected to perform, and no one's said yet that we are, maybe we can do a duet. 'Don't Go Breaking My Heart'?"

"I couldn't if I tried," he responded dryly.

Laughing, she kissed him again and said, "No, it's not about the party that I want to talk to you, it's about whether or not you feel you could wake up to this awful face of mine every morning."

There was a moment before he seemed to catch on to what she might be suggesting. "Am I? Are you?"

She nodded.

Putting down his drink, he took her face in his hands and planted a loving kiss on the tragically scarred cheek. "I hope that's a good enough answer," he told her gruffly, "but if it isn't I can take off all your clothes and kiss every other part of you as well—and if that still doesn't convince you I'll just do it all over again."

# CHAPTER FIFTY-FIVE

It was just after six in the evening, with the sound of a brass band playing "Good King Wenceslas" drifting up from the street below, and the red glow of a brazier reflected in the window, as Dan prepared to leave his office. Everyone else had gone home, and he was in a hurry to get to the coach house to help with preparations for the early Christmas party. However, just as he was about to turn out the lights there was a knock on his door and to his surprise Archie came in, his face red from the cold, and his dark hair appearing even more mussed than usual as he tugged down his hood.

"Hello, son," Dan said warmly. "Wasn't I supposed to come and pick you guys up? Is your mum with you?"

"No, she's at home," Archie told him, not quite meeting his eyes. "I came because there's something I need to tell you."

Realizing it was something serious, Dan said, "OK. Shall we sit down?"

Archie nodded, but when Dan returned to his chair he remained standing.

What he had to say didn't take long, partly because he spoke quickly, but also because he'd obviously rehearsed it. When he'd finished he put a small package on the desk and shoved his hands back into his jacket pockets.

Dan regarded the package thoughtfully, taking in its meaning along with everything Archie had said. In the end, in spite of already knowing the answer, he asked, "Are you sure about this?"

Archie nodded. "It's how it's got to be, know what I mean?"

Not sure that he did know, Dan pointed to the empty chair and said, "Sit down, let's talk about it some more."

Archie stepped back toward the door. "No point," he said. "I just want you to pass those on, if you will."

"I will, but I don't think this is the way to do it."

Archie merely shrugged. "No right way, no wrong way." With the ghost of a smile he added, "Reckon it's your way though."

Catching the humor, Dan arched an eyebrow and looked at the package again before returning his steady gaze to Archie. "What about your mother?" he asked soberly.

Archie began jigging up and down nervously, impatiently, needing to be gone, but apparently not wanting to be rude. "She's cool. She's got me. That's what matters to her."

Knowing that to be true, Dan got up and walked around the desk to try and look more closely into the lad's evasive eyes. It was only possible for fleeting moments, not enough to reach him that way in an effort to make him open up further. He sighed inwardly, disappointed and frustrated. He could never be the father Archie needed, any more than Archie could be the son he desired, but there was a connection between them, a bond that was both important and meaningful. He knew Archie felt it too, that strange pull of emotion amid all the other conflicting feelings that came with the relationship they had.

Archie suddenly thrust out a hand to shake. "I could say it's been a blast," he said gruffly.

Dan continued to look at him, seeing only a shadow of the boy he'd first met so many months ago. Now, in spite of his restless, uneasy demeanor, he was a young man with a greater understanding of himself and the world around him, and a clear determination to do what he felt to be right. Though Dan might not agree with him over this, he decided not to argue. He simply drew him into an embrace, slapped his back a couple of times, and stood aside, freeing him to leave.

Archie's head dropped for a moment, then delivering a self-conscious fist bump, his kind of thank-you, he went.

Dan waited for the sound of footsteps to recede before taking out his phone to message Claudia, saying only that he was running late. Once it was sent he slipped the package into the inside pocket of his overcoat and followed Archie out into the night.

"SORRY WE'RE EARLY," Andee called out as she and Graeme came into the coach house kitchen carrying gift bags of wine and a flamboyant poinsettia, "but I have some news you'll want to hear before the others arrive."

Claudia and Marcy paused in the arrangement of canapés on festive platters, while Henry glanced up from tipping nuts and olives into bowls.

"Who else is here?" Andee asked, glancing out of the French doors to where much setting up of lights and sounds seemed to be underway.

"Jasmine, Abby, and Richie," Claudia replied, trying to gauge whether this was going to be good or bad news, and struggling not to come down on the wrong side. A quick glance at her mother told her that Marcy was also bracing herself, presumably with no idea of why either, while Henry seemed oblivious to the tension as he filled two tumblers with a highly aromatic glühwein, ready to pass to Andee and Graeme as soon as their coats were hung.

"OK, this is the best mulled wine ever," Andee swooned as she took a generous sip. "Did you make it?"

"Of course," Henry assured her with a wicked grin. "So, come on, don't keep us in suspense. What's the news?"

"Dan should be here," Andee insisted. "Where is he?"

"Running late," Claudia replied, "but he should be here soon."

"Well, he might know what I'm about to tell you anyway, so I'll carry on without him. Just before we left the house I had a call from my old boss, DCI Gould?"

Claudia nodded, remembering the name well, and feeling another flutter of unease.

Andee smiled and raised her glass. "Apparently Marcus Huxley-Browne was arrested yesterday and charged with conspiracy to commit arson. This morning he was remanded in custody."

Claudia's eyes widened with shock. This wasn't what she'd expected to hear, not even close.

Marcy said, "How? What happened?"

"All Gould could tell me was that Uncle BJ was persuaded to name the lawyer who 'commissioned' the arson—probably via BJ's gangland bosses, but no way was he going to give any of them up."

"In short," Graeme put in, "Huxley-Browne's brief shopped him, presumably in exchange for a shorter sentence. Who knows? The point is that pond life is once again off the streets and will almost certainly serve time for what happened here." To Marcy he added gently, "For what happened to you."

Marcy's eyes closed with a dizzying sense of relief as Claudia came to wrap her in her arms. It was taking a moment to connect with the fact that real justice was finally being served. They had no more to fear from Marcus, no need to try and persuade anyone that he'd been behind the fire; his lawyer—his crooked lawyer—had done it for them.

It wasn't until Henry put a drink into her hand and an arm around her shoulders that Claudia realized she was shaking. She looked at her mother again and wanted to weep for what had been done to her. No amount of justice was ever going to make up for it, nothing in the world could erase those scars from her face or change the fact that they were there because her daughter had married a monster.

As though reading her mind, Marcy planted her hands on her shoulders and regarded her fiercely. "We can move on now," she told her, "so let's forget about him. We don't want him at this party, and we especially don't want him in our heads."

She was right. Tonight, they were going to have fun—really crazy fun—and no way would Marcus Huxley-Browne spoil it. In fact, his arrest would make it an even bigger celebration, but for now only those here in this kitchen would know it.

A WHILE LATER Claudia was checking the clock as she and Richie helped Leanne and Wilkie off with their coats. *Where was Dan?* "OK, first things first," she declared as Tom came in with a hamper of seasonal goodies. "I know we promised beef Wellington for Richie's birthday, but I'm afraid it was beyond us, so we're having a barbecue instead."

"It's cool," Richie assured them. "Actually, watching Dad and Leanne ripping out 'Killer Queen' is what tonight's going to be all about for me."

"It's such a great idea, us all getting together like this," Leanne declared, hugging Claudia and blowing a kiss to Andee. "Tom and I have been practicing our number."

"Who are you performing with?" Andee asked Claudia as she helped pass around the mulled wine.

"Wilkie," Claudia replied, and slipped an arm around Leanne's mother's shoulders.

"We've had no time to rehearse," Wilkie informed Andee, "but I can tell you this, we're going to smash it."

Laughing, Claudia said, "Have you heard that Archie's been booked for a gig at the Mermaid on New Year's Eve?"

Everyone's eyes rounded, showing how impressed they were.

"He's been rehearsing with Jasmine since he got the call," Claudia continued, "so it's likely she'll play too. I've booked a table for us all, but don't worry if you can't make it . . ."

Speaking from the door Dan said, "Sorry I'm late. Has anyone even noticed?"

Laughing, Claudia went to help him out of his coat. "Where are Archie and Maria?" she asked. "I thought you were bringing them."

Taking the mulled wine Graeme was passing, Dan murmured, "They're not coming."

Overhearing, Marcy said, "What do you mean, they're not coming?"

"He came by the office half an hour ago," Dan explained, "and asked me to give you this." Removing the package from his pocket, he handed it to Claudia with a brief shrug, letting her know that this was none of his doing.

Aware of the others watching her, Claudia opened the package and took out two white envelopes. One was addressed to her, the other to Marcy, and there was no mistaking the handwriting they'd come to know so well.

"What's going on?" Jasmine asked as she and Abby came in from the garden. "Why's everyone so quiet?"

Slipping an arm around her shoulders, Marcy said to Claudia, "Why don't you read them out for us?"

Claudia glanced at Dan. "Do you know what they're about?" she asked.

"More or less."

Since he didn't caution her to stop, she slipped the single page from her own envelope and began reading aloud.

Dear Claudia,

I thought about coming to see you and telling you in person what I have to say, but I decided it would make us both feel too awkward so I'm doing it this way, or Dan's way, instead.

First up is the thanks I owe you for just about everything from not stopping your mum taking part in the RJ process right through to giving her your support when she stood up for me in court. I know you couldn't have wanted her to do it, you might even have tried to talk her out of it, but I guess she's her own person and that's why she means so much to you. (She means a lot to me too, by the way, but I get you're probably not interested in that.)

Next I want to say that I don't blame you for not wanting me around; I'd feel the same if I was you and someone had hurt my mother the way I hurt yours. Tbh, I wouldn't even let them in through the door, but I wouldn't have to because they wouldn't still be alive.

Lucky for me that you're nothing like me.

Anyways, it's really good of you to try and hide how you feel about me, but I don't think you should have to do that anymore. I totally get why you're not comfortable about me coming to see Marcy sometimes, or mixing with Jas and her friends. It's time I got out of your hair, made myself history, so that's what I'm going to do.

Thanks again for everything. You, Marcy, and Dan have put me and ma on a road we'd never have found without you.

All the best,
Archie

PS: I hope your b****** husband gets his comeuppance.

PPS: Please tell Jas I'm sorry to let her down for New Year's Eve, but I know she'll understand.

Claudia had barely finished reading when Jasmine said, "No I don't. I don't understand at all."

Marcy moved to take the other letter from Claudia, but before she could open it Claudia said determinedly, "No, it's not going to happen like this."

Marcy looked at her in puzzlement.

To Dan, Claudia said, "Will you drive me there?"

As he went for their coats Claudia told her mother, "Don't read it yet. Promise me—"

"OK, OK," Marcy interrupted, "just make sure . . ."

"Leave it to me," Claudia said, and putting on her coat she followed Dan out to the car.

Thirty minutes later Claudia and Dan were outside the front door of Maria and Archie's second-floor flat on the other side of town. As they waited for a response to Dan's knock, Claudia looked around the brutal concrete walls graffitied with mostly indecipherable hieroglyphs and lit by sluggish overhead lamps along with a few hardworking Christmas stars. There was little sign of anyone; a couple they'd passed on the stairs had muttered a polite "Merry Christmas" allowing her to believe that as insalubrious as this place might be, it was a whole world away from the estate Maria and Archie had come from.

"Someone's coming," Dan muttered, and a moment later the door opened to the width of a security chain, and Archie peered out at them.

Seeing his surprise, Claudia said, "Do you think we could . . . ?"

Maria shouted, "If iss carol singers, tell 'em sing ''Way in a Manger.'"

With a smile Dan waited for Archie to release the chain, and gestured for Claudia to go ahead of him.

The spicy scent of a Christmas diffuser mingled with fresh paint welcomed them as Claudia followed Archie along the newly carpeted hall to the sitting room. Maria was curled up on a sofa next to a faux log fire; the instant she saw Claudia her mouth fell open.

"Not carol singers," Dan joked cheerily.

Maria said, "Wha' . . . I don' . . . Ochie . . . ?"

"It's all right, Ma," he told her, "there's . . ."

"He din do nothing wrong," she declared.

"No, he didn't," Claudia agreed, "but there's something we need to put right." Turning to Archie, she looked him in the eyes as she said, "Dan gave me your letter and you're right, I have found it difficult accepting you in our lives. To be honest it still feels strange, but I need to tell you about something that happened yesterday because I'm already certain it's making a difference. Marcus was arrested, and I realized it wouldn't have happened if you hadn't told us about your uncle, or if you hadn't been at the coach house when he turned up that day. He connected himself to you in a way none of us could have foreseen or planned."

Archie's hesitant eyes held to hers as he said, "I heard they'd taken him in. It should have happened sooner . . . I'm guessing you haven't read the letter I wrote to Marcy."

"Not yet," she replied. "It's why I'm here. I'd like you to come with us because whatever you've written to her I think you should tell her yourself, face-to-face. You've got the courage for that, Archie, I know you have."

He didn't protest again, nor did he say he'd come.

"I think she deserves that much, don't you?" Claudia said gently.

BY THE TIME they got back to the coach house everyone was outside and it seemed they'd already eaten, thanks to Graeme and Tom manning the barbecue. The music was far too loud, but the instant Archie and Maria appeared in the doorway a cheer went up to drown all else.

"You came!" Jasmine cried, flinging her arms around them both. "I knew you would. Have you eaten? Don't worry if not, there's loads."

"I need your help with the sound system," Richie declared, coming to shake Archie's hand. "And are you still partnering me tonight?" he asked Maria.

Maria's eyes sparkled. "Coun' me in," she cried, taking a glass of glühwein from Andee.

"Who else is strutting their stuff?" Graeme wanted to know as he pushed a beer into Archie's hand.

"We all are," Claudia informed him, amazed by the way this was happening so seamlessly. It was as if there had been no interruption to the evening at all and she was losing a proper sense of herself. She saw her mother and Archie exchange a glance and they seemed, for a fleeting moment, to be communicating apart from the fray. They did share something, Claudia was aware of that, and though she didn't understand it she realized there was no point continuing to fight it.

"When do you want to do it?" she heard Dan asking Archie.

Archie looked at Claudia.

Understanding what they were talking about, Claudia was about to suggest they wait awhile when Archie said, "I guess now's as good a time as any."

Surprised and impressed, she accepted the wine Andee was passing her and went to retrieve the letter from her mother. Then, signaling to Jasmine, she explained what was about to happen.

Jasmine's eyes rounded with awe. "That is totally amazing," she murmured, glancing at Archie and giving him a smile. "Do you want me to do anything?"

"Just call everyone to attention and let him take it from there."

Minutes later Claudia was seated next to her mother at the table, with Dan on the other side of her while the others filled the rest of the places and Maria perched on the edge of the deck, proud gaze fixed on her only child. The chilly night was warmed by the overhead heaters and lit by the garlands of festive lights that Claudia and Marcy had strung all over the garden.

"OK," Archie began, speaking into the mic, and grimacing as his voice was carried off by feedback. Adjusting, he continued, "Jas has just told you what I'm going to do, so . . . Here goes, my last letter to Marcy . . . And I promise this time there's been no help from Dan . . ."

After a murmur of laughter, he began.

Dear Marcy,

You have taught me more than any college or university ever could—and definitely way more than any prison could. In different ways you and Dan have shown me how it's possible for people to come into our lives for the worst reasons and somehow make it better. I know you would definitely wish I'd never come into yours and no one could blame you for that, definitely not me. Tbh, I wish I hadn't come into it, because it would be a lot better if I hadn't, I mean for you, not me. Trouble is, we can't turn back the clock, and what's totally surreal to me is that no one seems to understand that better than you.

The other day you told me something in the way only you could, you said that if it weren't for me you wouldn't have known what truly special friends you have for the way they all stood by you, Claudia, and Jasmine during the terrible times you've been through. I don't know how you can give me the credit for that, but I do know that anyone who has YOU as a friend is the one who's blessed.

More than six weeks have gone by since the day you changed everything for me in court, and during that time you've carried on being kind to me and Ma in a way that one of us—me—could never deserve. You've set me on the road to a new career in landscaping by asking your friends to take me on, you've even continued to invite me into your home. I don't think there are many people who could do that; in my world no one ever would.

I heard today that your scum of a son-in-law has been arrested, and I want you to know that I've already told the police that I'll stand up in court to testify to make sure you don't have to. They said they'll get in touch with me when they know more. Whether anyone will come after me for it, I've got no idea, but I can't see he has any influence now, so I'm not bothered.

You might have guessed by now that this is a goodbye letter. I want you to know that I'll always remember you, and I'll do my best to live up to the opportunities you've given me, and to your belief in me. It's time now for me to free you up and make my own way with Ma. Just know that if there's ever anything you need and you think I can help, all you have to do is pick up the phone.

Knowing you has been far and away the best thing that's ever happened to me. Thank you again for all you've done; thanks, Marcy, for saving my life.

Yours,
Archie

As he finished reading, all eyes went to Marcy as she got up from the table and went to fold him in her arms. She held him tenderly as he hid his tears in her shoulder, knowing very well that he didn't want to say goodbye to her, but he thought it was the right thing to do. There were plenty of others who'd probably feel the same, but she was pretty certain that none of them were here in this garden. She realized that not even Claudia wanted him out of their lives now, or she wouldn't have gone to fetch him.

Whispering in his ear, she said, "Let me tell you something: if you don't stay and enjoy this party with us tonight, and you aren't there to perform with Jasmine on New Year's Eve, then we might have to take another look at this forgiveness deal."

# ACKNOWLEDGMENTS

Most books are not written in isolation, and this one is certainly no exception. I've long been intrigued by the concept, difficulty, even impossibility of forgiveness—so when I learned about restorative justice, I was more than ready to find out more.

Whether you as a reader could forgive the crimes committed within this book only you will know. I can't tell you whether or not I could, because I haven't been in the same situation. And that is what always resonates deeply with me, the assumption we'd know what we'd do in any given situation without ever having experienced it.

Most of all I would like to thank Dr. Marian Liebmann, OBE, for so much detailed and patient guidance through the process of RJ and the sharing of her expert knowledge. I have bent the rules for the purposes of the story and yet she continued to give support in the way she does for those who benefit so much from it.

I would also like to thank another extraordinary lady, Alex Raikes MBE, Director of SARI (Stand Against Racial Inequality). It was Alex who first introduced me to restorative justice and who paved the way to this book. I have yet to write the story that took me to her in the first place, but I am determined to do it one day.

Now I must express my deepest thanks to the burns surgeons who gave so generously of their time and knowledge to help me with the injuries inflicted at the heart of the book. First to Jeremy Yarrow, MBChb, BSc, FRCS (Plast.), of Morriston Hospital Burns Unit in Swansea. I will be forever indebted to you, Jeremy, for managing to condense so many years of training and experience into words and treatments that allowed me to bring feeling and authenticity to the story. (If there are any experts out there reading this and something is wrong, please know this will be entirely down to me.) Also a huge thank-you to Jonathon Pleat, BAPRAS, BBA (Plastic Surgery), based in Bristol, for setting the course, correcting my early drafts, and putting me in touch with Jeremy Yarrow.

Last but by no means least a truly joyous thank-you to my wonderful agent, Luigi Bonomi, for unfailing support and advice. And to the exceptionally talented and magnificent team at HarperCollins: Kimberley Young, Liz Stein, Sophie Burks, Elizabeth Dawson, Fleur Clarke, Rachel Quin, Kate Elton, Roger Cazalet, and every one of the unsung heroes behind the scenes who do so much to bring you the books. So many amazing accomplishments were achieved during the lockdown period, and so much fun was had too, albeit virtually, but no less enjoyable for that.

Susan Lewis
*November 2020*

## About the Author

**2** Meet Susan Lewis

## About the Book

**3** Reading Group Guide

## Read on

**6** An Excerpt from *One Minute Later*

Insights,
Interviews
& More . . .

# Meet Susan Lewis

Antony Thompson, www.thousandwordmedia.com

SUSAN LEWIS is the internationally bestselling author of more than forty books across the genres of family drama, thriller, suspense, and crime. She is also the author of *Just One More Day* and *One Day at a Time*, the moving memoirs of her childhood in Bristol during the 1960s. Following periods of living in Los Angeles and the South of France, she currently lives in Gloucestershire with her husband, James, and mischievous dogs, Coco and Lulu.

# Reading Group Guide

1. *Forgive Me* has letters from Archie dispersed throughout the book. Why do you think the author decided to include these? Additionally, how did it affect your opinions of Archie as a character?

2. What do you make of Archie and Dan's relationship? How does Archie's lack of a father figure ultimately affect his relationship with Dan? How is their relationship an example of redemption and how does that theme translate to Archie's relationship with other characters, including his mother and Marcy?

3. In what way did the death of Claudia's first husband influence her decisions throughout the book? As Claudia explores romantic interests, how do both of her previous marriages impact her relationship with Dan? Do you feel that Dan was respectful in his pursuing Claudia?

4. Did the reveal of the recipient of Archie's letters surprise you? In this scene, the narrative alternates between Archie's and ▶

the recipient's perspectives to provide context from both sides. What effect did this have on you?

5. While both Jasmine and Marcy were interested in learning more about the restorative justice program, Claudia had a negative reaction toward it. If you were in Marcy's position, would you want to participate in the program? And, how would you want your family members to respond?

6. What do you think *Forgive Me* is trying to say about restorative justice in general? What new perspective or insight did you gain on the criminal justice system?

7. Marcy experiences the most physical change out of all the characters. After seeing herself in a mirror for the first time, Claudia describes Marcy: "It was as if she hadn't heard, or had somehow transported herself to a place no one could reach her" (page 215). How did Marcy overcome this challenge and reconnect with her friends and family? How does her accident and subsequent recovery demonstrate resilience and personal growth?

8. Mother-daughter relationships are at the center of *Forgive Me*, between Marcy and Claudia and Claudia and Jasmine. How do each of these relationships shift and grow over the course of the book? In what ways do they grow stronger? Or weaker?

9. Maria, Archie's mom, is another important mother figure throughout the book. In the scene where Maria tells Fliss and Andee about Archie's crime, she is clearly emotional about the tumultuous relationship with her son. How does this scene demonstrate forgiveness and grace, especially between a mother and son?

10. How did Archie's final letter resonate with you? Focusing on the theme of your "chosen" family, how does his sentiment in the letter speak to that?

11. Almost all the characters give and receive forgiveness. Considering the uplifting ending, do you feel that the secrets and betrayals affecting the characters in the beginning were resolved and justice was served? ❧

# An Excerpt from
## *One Minute Later*

### CHAPTER ONE

# VIVIENNE

*Present Day*

The day started out so well.

It was sunny, warm—a welcome bonus for what had so far been a rainy April—with misty slats of sunlight streaming through the partially open plantation shutters. The delicious aroma of fresh coffee and buttery croissants floated up from Maxi's café next door, enticing her further into the day.

Vivienne Shager stretched luxuriously, her taut, lithe body unraveling its impressive length from the contours of sleep as her mind made a happy reconnect with the world and what it had in store on this glorious work-free day.

It was hard to believe that four full weeks had passed since she and the GaLs—Girls at Law—had run *and completed* an entire marathon to raise funds for the charity Heads Together. So much had happened in that time— mostly work related, but she'd also had an irritating bug that kept coming and going, trying to lay her low but never quite succeeding. However, she was feeling pretty good today, she soon realized. This was a huge relief, for she and the GaLs were planning some serious celebration of their fundraising efforts. The day was exclusively theirs; partners, spouses, offspring, parents, bosses, and colleagues had been given notice that they'd have to manage without the key women in their lives from midday until said women were ready to tip in the direction of home.

For Vivi, there was less of a problem on the family front, since she had no children and her partner, Greg, was going to Lord's for the day. Her mother fortunately didn't live anywhere close by. On the work front, her immediate boss, Trudy Mack-Silver, was one of the GaLs, so no difficulties there. This wasn't to say that Vivienne didn't have a mountain of work to get through; being a senior member of the in-house legal team at FAberlin Investments meant her desk and inbox were always crammed with issues needing urgent attention. Over time she'd learned how to prioritize the ceaseless flow of demands, though many of them saw her laboring late into the evenings and often over entire weekends. She didn't mind; she loved her job and even liked many of the giant corporation's upper-management team. They could be tough, bad-tempered, inconsiderate, and in some cases offensively sexist, but in times of crisis she watched closely, spoke confidently, and managed to learn a lot from those whose jobs she had in her sights.

"You give great kickback," Trudy often told her following an intense negotiation or fiery confrontation. "They respect you for it. It makes them listen, and provided you don't go wrong, you could be heading up the entire legal team by the time you're thirty." Trudy didn't have a problem with this, because she had no such ambitions for herself. She was happy to stay at the level she'd already attained, since it allowed her time to be an at-home-most-evenings wife to Bruno and available-for-school-runs mum to Nick and Dean. ▸

The other important thing about today was the fact that it was Vivi's twenty-seventh birthday, another reason the GaLs— all graduates of the London School of Economics law school— had decided that this should be the marathon reunion day. Combining occasions was something they often did; being so busy with their careers it was the only way to make sure nothing got overlooked.

Throwing back the pale blue striped duvet, Vivi stood as tall as her willowy five feet nine inches allowed, arched her long back, and gave a lazy side-to-side twist to stretch out her waist. Since ending her intense pre-marathon training, her body had softened slightly, making it, according to Greg, more feminine and curvier, and way sexier. He had a thing about large women, which made his attraction to her a bit of a mystery, given how slender she was. However, they'd been seeing each other for several months, nonexclusively, so their friends weren't living in daily expectation of some significant news. A baby. A wedding. Or perhaps something as simple as moving in together.

Despite their casual relationship, Vivi had to admit that he was a bit of a dreamboat in his way, sporty, witty, fiercely intelligent, and very well connected in the financial world, thanks to his gentrified family and their historic ties to the City. When he spoke, it was immediately evident that he came from privileged pastures; however, Vivienne strongly doubted that he gave a single thought to the relative ordinariness of her own. He wasn't a snob, or if he was, she'd never noticed. Nonetheless, she'd never taken him to meet her family, who still lived in the hopelessly unsophisticated coastal town that Vivi had called home for the first eighteen years of her life.

She'd moved on since uni, had redefined her focus, and was part of another world that could hardly be more different from the simplicity of her early years. Not that *she* had changed in character, for she was still the same upbeat and optimistic Vivi that her beloved grandpa used to call Vivi-vacious. This nickname came from her love of life and people, especially him and NanaBella, which was what she used to call her grandma on account of her name being Bella. Vivi also adored her younger brother, nineteen-year-old Mark, and there was no doubt that she loved her mother with all her heart and knew that her mother felt the same about her. However, their relationship was the most complicated and frustrating part of Vivienne's world, which was why she didn't often go home. She'd spent too many years trying to unlock the closed doors in her mother's heart and unravel the secrets Gina had never shared, and now all Vivienne wanted was to avoid the confusing and conflicting emotions she always came away with after spending time with her mother.

She wasn't giving any of this a single thought on this glorious spring morning, although she expected her mobile to ring at any minute, bringing a dutiful happy-birthday call from home. The postman would almost certainly deliver a card from her mother later, and a text would no doubt pop up at some point during the day, saying something like, **Hope you're having a fabulous day, but please don't have too much to drink.** There wouldn't be a present, because her mother had stopped buying them a few years ago, saying, "I always get it wrong, so there doesn't seem any point in wasting my money. If you want something, just ask."

That was Gina all over. In spite of being a glamorous and successful forty-six-year-old businesswoman with a good sense of humor and plenty of friends, she could be prosaically practical about things that called for frivolity or indulgence. (Although, Vivi reminded herself, their surprise trip to Venice when Vivi was a teenager had proved her mother could be both imaginative and impulsive when she wanted to be.) However, it was true to say that Gina was usually awkward with celebrations, and as for showy declarations of feeling, well, that wasn't her at all. Actually, she was nothing if not a maddening set of contradictions, because she could be a lot of fun when she wanted to be, and when it came to throwing a party, she didn't do things by half. Things had changed, however, since Gil, Vivi's stepfather and Mark's ▶

father, had left, just over nine years ago. Dear, wonderful Gil, who was still as much a part of their lives as if he'd never gone, except he didn't live with her mother anymore—and if anyone could work out the bizarreness of that relationship, they'd certainly have a better insight into Gina's mysterious psyche than Vivi had ever managed.

"Don't ask me," NanaBella had lamented at the time of the breakup. "I've never really understood your mother, you know that, and she could baffle the heck out of Grandpa when he was alive."

"But you always loved her and stood by her," Vivienne had pointed out, for it was true, her grandparents had always been there—for them all.

There was no NanaBella or Grandpa to stand by any of them now. Grandpa had succumbed to cancer when Vivi was six, and NanaBella had been the victim of a drunk driver four Easters ago while on her way into town.

That was another reason for Vivi to feel guilty about not going to see her mother more often. Gina had been devastated by the sudden loss of her beloved mother—they all had, including Gil. But trying to be supportive of Gina was like trying to hug a cactus. She couldn't accept love without becoming prickly and awkward; although she clearly wanted affection, she just didn't seem to know how to handle it.

What was that line about an enigma wrapped up in a mystery inside a riddle? Well, that was her mother, and even Gil, as besotted as he was with her, never tried to claim she was easy.

Reaching for her mobile as it rang, Vivi saw it was one of the GaLs and decided to let it go to voicemail. She simply had to go to the bathroom before speaking to anyone, and then she'd pop down to Maxi's for an Americano and pastry to fuel herself for the day. If her mother called and didn't get an answer, she'd assume Vivi was either out for a run, or at Greg's, or still asleep with the phone turned off. She wouldn't worry, because that was something Gina resolutely refused to do, in spite of the fact that the tight line between her beautiful eyes showed that she spent just about every moment of every day worrying about something.

Did she even realize that?

Vivi thought she probably did, but she guarded jealously whatever was causing her anxiety—and maybe it was many things—as though letting go of a single hint of an issue would snap the strings inside her and everything would fall catastrophically apart.

Standing in front of the twin-mirrored bathroom cabinet with its frame of snowball lights and inbuilt heat pad, Vivi pulled a face at herself and stretched out her jaw. She must have slept awkwardly because her neck seemed achy, and the stiffness in her limbs told her that she ought to get back to some proper exercise soon. Still, at least she was breathing more easily this morning, so the bug she'd no doubt picked up on one of several flights she'd made in the past three weeks might finally be clearing.

She was, by anyone's standards, a strikingly lovely young woman. With almond-shaped eyes, blue as a summer sky, and a full, sloppy mouth (her description), she was so entrancing that her friends swore she could hypnotize at a hundred paces. Her complexion was smooth and olive, her cheekbones high, and her light brown hair was a wayward riot of waves that fell about her face and neck in a style all its own.

Right now it was a tangled mess, and her still-sleepy eyes were shadowed by the residue of last night's mascara.

Last night?

Oh, that was right; she'd been at the office until almost midnight, after returning from New York on the red-eye in the morning. It had been a flying visit to the Big Apple, quite literally: one meeting, followed by a dull dinner at Bobby Van's Steakhouse and an overnight stay at the Beekman.

After dragging some sweats on over her pajama shorts and a T-shirt over her camisole, she slipped her feet into an old pair of flip-flops and texted Maxi with her order. Before leaving she quickly scanned her emails to be sure nothing earth-shattering ▶

had cropped up overnight, and finding that nothing had, she went through to the spacious open-plan kitchen-cum-sitting-room and gave a small sigh of pleasure to find it virtually drowning in sunlight.

She loved this apartment so much she could marry it. With its high, stuccoed ceilings, tall sash windows, and wonderfully airy rooms—all two of them, plus a full bathroom containing a utility area—she simply couldn't bear to think of living anywhere else. It was certainly one of the reasons why she and Greg hadn't considered moving in together. It wasn't big enough for two, and it would be crazy to make this their home when his riverfront duplex in Wapping was at least three times the size and, in real-estate terms, far more desirable. Plus, he owned his place outright, thanks to his father, while her first-floor, street-view section of a Georgian town house close to Hollywood Road in Chelsea was rented. It wasn't that she couldn't afford a mortgage; she was earning enough now to take on some hefty repayments, but the amount needed for a deposit in an area like this—in fact almost anywhere in London—was still out of her reach, largely thanks to her lavish lifestyle. Her friends had managed their down payments thanks to BoMaD—Bank of Mum and Dad—but her mother could never have found a near-six-figure sum without selling her own house or hairdressing salon, and even if she'd been prepared to do that (she wasn't), Vivi wouldn't have let her. However, her mother—refusing Gil's offer to step in—had practically emptied her savings account to help raise a deposit for the lease on this flat. Having viewed it with Vivi, she'd understood right away why her daughter had fallen in love with it, so she'd been keen to make it happen. Since that time, just over four years ago, Vivi had repaid almost two-thirds of the amount, and by the end of the year her mother's account, thanks to the interest Vivi had added to the loan, was likely to be healthier than it had ever been.

Still feeling slightly stiff, she performed a couple more stretches, then grabbed her phone and wallet and let herself out of the flat into the black-and-white-tiled front hall where her upstairs neighbors had parked a bicycle and stroller. There were also several paintings lining the walls, all done by the delightful and talented Maryanna, who paced about the large attic studio like a trapped cat in the grip of an artistic frenzy. Though her canvases were as indecipherable as they were confrontational (Maryanna's word), Vivienne had long ago decided that she loved them. She owned two but had left them in the hall for others in the building and their visitors to enjoy as they came and went.

The large black front door with its colorful stained-glass windows and shiny brass letter box was as grand as any Regency house could boast, as was the Doric columned portico with its ornamental box hedges in tall granite pots. Slender black railings edged the steps down to the pavement, where they turned at right angles to each side to provide a barrier between passersby and the void above the basement flats.

Maxi's was adjacent, with a handful of bistro tables spilling out of the wide-open bifold doors, its palm-strewn interior with plush leather banquets and slouchy sofas cooled by the gentle spring breeze. In spite of it not yet being nine on a weekend morning, the place was already buzzing.

After collecting her order—free for the birthday girl, Maxi insisted—and bowing her thanks to the Greek regulars whom Maxi encouraged to join in a chorus of *charoumena genethlia*, Vivi ran back up to the flat accompanied by the musical sound of many text messages arriving.

Five so far. As she read them, still catching her breath after the sprint, she sipped her coffee and blinked away a spell of dizziness. Remembering she hadn't eaten since yesterday lunchtime, she tucked into her Danish and turned on the radio. Though she probably wouldn't listen to the news, it was second nature to have it on in the background, and when she'd had enough of it she'd do her usual thing of planting her phone in the speakers and scrolling to some favorite tunes.

More texts piled in, mostly from the GaLs: Trudy, Shaz, ▶

Saavi, Sachi, and Becky, all saying
they couldn't wait to see her later.
In came a surprise message from
Michael (FAberlin's CEO), and then
up popped one from Greg.

> Have a great day. Can you do
> dinner with Carla and Seamus on
> Wednesday? Sushi?

She thought there might be a conflict,
so making a mental note to check before
getting back to him, she finished up her
Danish and began a quick sort of the
mail that had come through the door
while she was in New York.

Work hard, play hard, that was her
motto, and lately she'd been doing far
too much of the former. Boy, was she
ready to party today! ∽